"WHY DO YOU TREMBLE SO, MARI? HAVE YOU NEVER BEEN KISSED?"

"I have been given what passed for kisses, aye, sir," she whispered, unable to meet his gaze for fear of the unsettling sensations it stirred within her.

"And?"

" 'T'was my opinion that . . . that kissing is much over-rated," she blurted out.

"Your distaste is understandable. Until now, you have never been kissed by me."

With that, his hard, chiselled mouth crushed down over hers in a kiss that sent shockwaves through her.

His lips were teasing as he slanted them over hers, deliberately keeping something back even as he explored her mouth with a lazy, sensual thoroughness that left all her doubts in ashes. . . .

PENELOPE NERI

NO SWEETER PARADISE

ZEBRA BOOKS
KENSINGTON PUBLISHING CORP.

ZEBRA BOOKS

are published by

Kensington Publishing Corp.
475 Park Avenue South
New York, NY 10016

First Printing: January, 1993

Printed in the United States of America

Prologue

The Inner Temple, London. September, 1789

"Lawyer Kincaid! Tarry, sir. Do!"

The urchin plucked at the dark barrister's robes as Jonathan crossed the picturesque courtyard of the Inner Temple, headed for court at the Old Bailey nearby.

Turning on his heel, Jonathan saw an earnest scrap looking up at him from beneath a ragged thatch of hair. The grubby face seemed vaguely familiar. Remembering, he snapped his fingers. "'Tis young Pip, the George's boot-boy, is it not?"

"That's me, gov'na. I've come wiv a message from me master, I 'ave," Pip added importantly.

"From Roger?"

"None other, sir. Master Loring sez he must speak wi' ye this very day, on a 'matter o' great urgency,'" Pip said, obviously quoting his master. "He bids ye come t' the Royal George at eight o' the clock, wivout fail."

"Does he, now? Well, you may tell your master that you

delivered his message, and that I'll be there—'wivout fail,' young master Pip,'' Jonathan promised solemnly, though his green eyes twinkled. "Here. Take this for your trouble!" Jonathan fished a copper ha'penny from his pockets and flipped it to the lad.

Pip caught it on the fly, with a broad grin and a "Ta, gov'na—Gawd bless ye, sir!" before he took off at a run.

Knowing his friend, the inn-keeper, Roger Loring was rarely given to exaggeration, and had never been one to ask favors of even his closest friends, Jonathan was both mildly alarmed and deeply curious about what the even-tempered Roger's "matter of great urgency" might be. Had his fair Rose Wicks thrown him over after their marathon courtship of almost ten years? He strongly doubted it, for they'd finally set a wedding date for a fortnight hence. What, then, could be troubling his friend . . . ?

The case he presented in court that morning was a boring, complex matter of rightful inheritance and trusteeships, so the hours between the arrival of Pip and eight o' the clock dawdled by like a bawd on her way to Confession. But that same night, over tankards of bitter dark ale and roasted capon, Jonathan at last learned the reason for Roger's urgent summons.

It transpired that a group of men had made the private room at the George tavern their meeting place the Friday before. Roger's betrothed, little Rosie—the same serving wench Jonathan'd once been sweet on—had been abed with lung-ague that day, his friend explained. Through a crack in the floorboards of her bedchamber, Rosie had overheard these men discussing the assassination of His Royal Majesty.

"The King!" Jonathan exploded, splattering ale everywhere.

"God help us, aye," Roger confirmed gloomily. "D' ye see now why I sent for ye, Nathan? At first, I was minded t' turn the lot of 'em over t' the constables. But who'd believe a tavern-keeper's charges o' treason against such fine gents as the eight o' them? I didn't know what to do for the best. But

6

you . . . Well, you're another kettle o' fish, right? You're a respectable lawyer, a member of a fine influential family. The authorities'd listen to you.''

Deeply perturbed and utterly astonished by his friend's disclosure, Jonathan nodded. "You did the right thing, never fear, Roger. Only a fool would accuse others of treason without proof or witnesses to support his charge. Do you know when they plan the attempt? Where it is to take place?''

"Nah. But Rose sez they spoke of Epsom Downs . . . an' their leader called them the 'Octagon Club.' They mean t' meet in my private chamber again next Friday, so I doubt it'll be afore then. Will ye come Friday evenin' and see 'em for yerself? I'd feel the better for your opinion, Nate.''

"I will,'' he'd agreed.

Arriving somewhat earlier than the appointed hour, Jonathan saw his mount stabled by Jim Goodenough, the ostler, and took himself around to the rear of the coaching-inn. He entered by the back door he'd used in the old days, when he'd ostlered there himself.

A kettle of tasty mutton stew was simmering over the kitchen fire, tended by Roger's mother. Bidding her a hasty good evening, he inquired after her son's whereabouts.

"He do be above stairs, love,'' plump, red-faced Amy Loring told him with a disapproving frown. Energetically stirring her pots, she added, "He and that Rose Wicks are t' be wedded on Saturday next, and yet he's that taken with the wench, he must tumble her at all hours, day an' night!''

"Mistress Loring, I—''

"Why, 'tis unseemly, an unwed couple like them two spending so much time abed! Better he should give thought t' the running o' this inn and the care o' its patrons, than forever slinkin' off t' Mistress Rose's chamber!''

"If you'll—''

"Mark my words, those gents in the private room'll be takin'

7

their coin an' custom elsewhere, if their orders in't seen to right smartly!''

Jonathan's dark brows rose in alarm. 'Twould appear the conspirators had already gathered! That being the case, he had no time to waste!

"Serving wenches—pah! Idle trollops, every last one!'' Roger's mother grumbled, mopping the sweat from her brow with the corner of her apron. "They'd as soon dally with the lads as do an honest day's work for an honest penny. Now, in my day, we . . .''

Leaving her grumbling, Nathan took the back stairs two at a time. He made his way down the dark landing to Rosie's small chamber, where he'd once passed many a lusty night himself. A bar of candlelight showed beneath the door.

He knocked, but receiving no answer, he threatened, "Very well, you two love-birds! Decent or nay, I'm coming in!''

So saying, he lifted the latch and pushed the heavy door inwards.

His first thought was that he'd entered the wrong room, for Rosie's small chamber was crowded. Perhaps a half-dozen well-dressed and bewigged gentlemen looked up, aghast, as he stepped over the threshold. The bawdy greeting he'd planned froze upon his lips. *What nightmare was this?*

Beyond the men, he could see little Rose sprawled across the feather pallet, as still and twisted as a rag-doll. Her eyes were bulging from her swollen, mottled face as she stared up at the rafters above. Roger lay beside her, equally still. Blood matted his hair. More trickled down his cheek to soak the threadbare coverlet beneath him. His eyes and mouth were likewise open. . . .

"*Noooo!*'' he heard someone howl, not knowing it was his own anguished cry of denial. The knowledge that his dear friends were both dead—murdered!—slammed home like a boot to his belly. The shock drove all thoughts of self-preservation from him. "Why, dear God!'' he groaned. *"Why?"*

He reeled away, clawing blindly for the door-jamb for sup-

8

port. And, in the same moment, he dimly heard one of the men exclaim, "Don't let him run, you fools! That's Kincaid's son. He's seen our faces."

Through the fog of his grief, the words registered. He swung away, intending to bolt down the tavern stairs. But too late!

One man grabbed him by the elbow and swung him back around to meet a hefty punch to the jaw. Another raised a brass candlestick—still wet with blood—above his head. And, in the fleeting second before it crashed down against his skull, Nathan glimpsed a third horrified face.

He carried the image of that last man down into the hellish blackness into which he was flung.

When he came to, it was to the sounds of a woman sobbing.

"Owww, my darling boy! My poor, poor lad!" she wailed, her banshee howls going on and on.

The weeper was Mistress Loring, surely, Jonathan decided groggily. Struggling to sit up, he found his attempts forestalled. A booted foot was lodged heavily upon his chest.

"Get your damned boots off my—"

"Now, now, easy there, ye cutthroat swine!" a threatening, phlegmy voice growled. "Move a hair, an' I'll blow yer bleedin' brains out!"

Looking up, Nathan discovered the boot was attached to the leg of a hulking, red-nosed constable, who was scowling down at him. The black snout of a pistol was levelled at his brow.

"Murderer!" Amy Loring suddenly shrieked, flinging herself past the constable to get at him. She battered his head and chest with her fists, wild-eyed and strong as any Bedlamite. "Why'd ye have ter do it, why? You were like a second son t' me, you was! I fed ye like one o' me own, I fretted after yer health. An' now, this!"

"Enough, poor lady. There, there, mum, don't take on so. This rogue'll get his just rewards, make no mistake. Some Friday morn, ye'll be toastin' his hangin'!"

9

With that dire prediction, the constable gripped Nathan by his coat-collar and hauled him to a standing position. In that same move, he jerked his arms behind him and locked shackles about his wrists, then kicked him in the back of the knees to get him started for the door.

Still groggy from the blow to his head and from the shock he'd received, Nathan stumbled. With enormous difficulty, he pulled himself upright and demanded, "Where are you taking me?"

"Shut yer yap! When we want some lip outer you, we'll arsk fer it."

"Damn it, you can't do this. I demand to know on what charge you're arresting me."

"What charge, he says? He! That's a good 'un, in't it, lads?" the lout chortled and directed a snaggle-toothed grin at his two companions. "The charge is double murder, Kincaid—as well you know, seein' you're the one wot done 'em in!"

"Murder!"

"And as fer where we're takin' yer lawyership . . . why, where else but Newgate Gaol? Now, shift yer bloody carcass down them stairs, cock—an' not another bleedin' squeak, or it'll go the worse fer ye!"

Nathan felt the blood drain from his face. Christ! *Newgate*. 'Twas the gate-house to Hell!

The twelve weeks he spent in Newgate, awaiting trial, proved an eternity.

He breathed the gaol's foul vapors, ate its foul slops, suffered its stinking dampness and gloom, shared its mouldy straw with rats, spiders, and cockroaches. Moreover, there was no peace to be found there, for he was drawn against his will into countless vicious brawls and violent quarrels with the other felons over food, small items of clothing, or even a random "look" that had seemed overly bold and challenging to one of the convicts—especially the strutting Scot who'd coveted his

10

boots, and lost two teeth for his pains. He'd also fallen beneath the turnkeys' clubs too many times to count.

The coin in his pockets had mysteriously vanished between the George and the receiving room at the prison, while he lay half-dead in the prison-cart. Consequently, he hadn't the wherewithal to garnish the palms of his gaolers, or purchase favors and luxuries, as was the accepted custom. Moreover, instead of being allowed to summon friends and relatives to pay the few half-crowns that would have guaranteed him more comfortable lodgings, good victuals, and clean clothes in the Nobs' Common, he'd been flung headlong into the Common Felons' Ward. And there he'd languished.

As a result, it was a considerably changed Nathan who listened as the counsel for the prosecution brought forth witness after witness to testify against him that dreary December morn. And, one by one, that brilliant yet devious fellow managed to twist the nervous witnesses' testimony; to subtly word the questions that he set them so that their answers seemed to support the charges.

". . . That's right, sir. When I told Master Kincaid that Roger lay abed with Mistress Rose, his face turned proper queer, it did. Then, not a moment later, he were gone up them stairs as if the hound o' hell were after him!'' Amy Loring recounted tearfully from the witness box of the Old Bailey three months following his friends' murders.

"And you stated that the defendant had once courted your son's betrothed—er, Mistress Rose Wicks—himself?'' the prosecutor continued, peering impatiently over his gold-rimmed pince-nez at the sheaf of papers in his hands. Looking up, he glared at the frightened little woman in the witness box.

"Oh, aye, sir. Jonathan an' Rose was sweethearts, right enough—for a while, at least.''

"I see. And when was this, my good woman?''

"They was sweethearts right up until the day my boy an' the . . . the prisoner were impressed inter service aboard the *Resolution*. That'd be . . . what? Thirteen years ago? Twelve?

Aye, 'twas thirteen, for I recollect my Roger were but seventeen then, God rest his soul. As for her—well, that Rose Wicks couldn't ha' been more'n fourteen years at most, but already a flighty one, an' free wiv her favors! And yet . . ."

"And yet, both young men loved her. Was that not so, Mistress Loring?"

"Well, I suppose yer could say that at various times they—"

"Please answer the questions with a simple aye or nay, mistress," the prosecutor reminded her sternly. "Was Rose Wicks loved by both young men?"

"Well, then, me answer's yes, innit, sir?"

"Indeed, m'lud, respected gentlemen of the jury," the bewigged lawyer was hanging onto the fronts of his black gown as he turned to address both judge and jury, "one of those two young men had indeed loved Rose Wicks throughout those ten long years, saying nothing of his feelings to others, mark you, and displaying none of the insane jealousy that seethed in his heart towards your son, Mistress Loring. No, indeed, he did not." He paused for effect. "With great cunning, Jonathan Kincaid managed to keep his animal passions in check, until the fateful day Mistress Loring told the accused that her son and pretty Rose lay abed together at the inn. Then it was that Kincaid's jealousy was unleashed—and turned to murderous rage!"

"'Tis a foul lie!" Nathan exploded, springing to his feet, four years of apprenticeship at the Inns of Temple obliterated in his outrage.

"The prisoner will be seated!" Judge Poole, the magistrate, cautioned in a voice like thunder. "Counsel for the defense, you would be advised to caution your client to refrain from such outbursts or suffer the sternest consequences for his contempt!"

"Begging your pardon, m'lud. It will not happen again," Nathan's lawyer, Will Heatherton, apologized humbly.

Nathan was strong-armed back into his seat by both the bailiff and his lawyer. His green eyes were blazing, the flesh

12

about his mouth white with anger as he took his seat. Weak from a bout of prison-fever and from lack of food, he sat there, smoldering, scowling, the very picture of a brooding, filthy felon in his tattered garments; a sight to scare little children into being good.

But, far worse than the shame of his appearance was the knowledge that his father and older brother, Jeremy, were watching the proceedings from the public gallery. From where Nathan sat, he could see the sorrow and bewilderment in Simon Kincaid's eyes, and 'twas like a knife in his heart. Once again, he had disappointed his father; had brought shame and dishonor upon their family name. . . .

"As I described, a murderous rage overwhelmed the accused," the Prosecutor repeated with smug relish. "And so, after he had entered by the inn's back door—as the ostler, Jim Goodenough, testified this morning—and heard that the two lovers languished abed, he swore to kill the wench who'd scorned him, along with his rival, Roger Loring!"

With this, a sigh of lurid satisfaction rippled through the public gallery, like wind through a corn-field.

"Taking the stairs in haste, Kincaid hastened down the landing of the Royal George. He flung open the door to Mistress Rosie's candlelit chamber, and 'twould appear that he had timed his entrance well. The lovers were not expecting him!

"And so, with murder in his foul heart, the accused took up the heavy candlestick you see before you. Then, without compassion or pity, he bludgeoned to death poor, unsuspecting Roger, while his betrothed looked on in horror. And when he was certain his first victim was quite dead, the accused fastened his powerful hands about the throat of poor Rose Wicks, the woman he'd loved—and strangled her!"

The thundering silence in the wake of this impassioned delivery was more eloquent than words.

The trial unravelled inch by painful inch that morning, like the tangled skeins of a nightmare from which there is no awakening; half-truth and outright lie piling one upon the other, until the summations of the two opposing counsels seemed a poor climax to all that had been said before.

"M'lud, gentlemen of the jury, you have heard little to impress you about the accused's character in this courtroom. Jonathan Kincaid was an unruly, defiant youth. A lad of few morals with a fondness for brawling, strong spirits, wagering, and loose women. A prodigal son who scorned his worthy father's wishes that he become a commissioned officer in the King's Navy, and at sixteen years turned his back upon family and home to become, of all things, an *artist*." With a sneering smile, the Prosecutor managed to convey a world of contempt in that single word.

"He was an incorrigible youth, and has become the defiant and dangerous felon you see before you now. Moreover, he is so cunning, so diabolically clever, he has succeeded in hiding his true nature from the world for many years. Behind what did he hide it, you may well ask? Why, my good people, behind the robes of a barrister! Under the guise of practicing the ancient and esteemed profession of the very laws he has flouted! By so doing, he hopes to evade the might of justice and go free.

' I say to you, m' lud, good gentlemen of the jury, that you are wise and not so readily deceived by his ilk. Knowing this, I implore you, in your great wisdom, to see justice served and to find the defendant guilty, as charged!"

Judge Poole had then heard the defense's impassioned plea that all charges against his client be dismissed, on the grounds that the evidence against the accused was circumstantial. Had anyone witnessed the murders? Heatherton asked. Nay. Could even one witness testify that Jonathan had actually been seen to strike Roger with the candlestick? Nay. Heatherton had told the members of the jury once again of the eight gentlemen of the Octagon Club, and of the scurrilous purpose for which they had met at the inn. He had summed up by demanding that the jury find his client—an innocent scapegoat for two heinous murders committed by others—not guilty.

The jury foreman had requested a recess to confer with his fellows. With their departure, the afternoon had dragged by on feet of lead. When a wintry dusk fell at four o' the clock without the jury having come to a consensus, they had returned Nathan in chains to Newgate Gaol. The trial would resume the following morning.

His father and Jeremy had come to see him that evening, asking if there was anything they could do, anything he needed.

"Alas, what I want most, you are not at liberty to give me, Father," Nathan had said heavily, his fingers hooked about the grating like talons. His spirits had been at a dangerously low ebb, and he'd been unable to meet his father's eyes. Why, he wondered, could he not be more like Jeremy, the stalwart, reliable sort of son who made a father proud, instead of the devil-may-care womanizer and rake he knew himself to be— a son to give his father sleepless nights?

Whereas Jeremy had spent his youth learning to manage the Kincaid estates, Linden Hall, and the other family interests that he would someday inherit as his father's heir, Jonathan had passed those formative years in drinking and brawling with the village lads, and in tumbling his *maman*'s prettiest maids. In carousing and wagering and having fun. Life, he had determined at an early age, was far too short to be lived in the staid and somewhat stodgy fashion that brother Jeremy espoused.

"Hold strong, Jonathan," he heard his father say in a choked voice, and forced his thoughts back to the present. "I've not deserted you, my boy, nor given up your case as hopeless. I have friends of influence. Even now, they are making inquiries in the City. Alas, if only we had more time . . . !"

"'Twill make no difference, Father. They will find me guilty—I feel it in my bones," Jonathan admitted, voicing the premonition that had kept him wakeful this past week. He and his mother occasionally experienced such forebodings when

15

danger threatened them or those they loved, a legacy, Gabrielle Kincaid had laughingly claimed, passed on through the blood of her fey French ancestors.

"Then we shall appeal, of course."

"Thank you, Father," Nathan said, his throat constricting at the forced bravado in his father's voice. "I know I'm undeserving of your support. God knows, I've done little enough in my life to make you proud of me thus far! But I swear upon my honor that should I, by some miracle, go free, all that will change! I'll yet make you proud of me, sir."

"Nonsense, dear boy. I am already proud of you—more than words can say. And we *will* weather this storm. All is not yet lost. To all acounts, Judge Poole is counted a fair man and a fine magistrate. 'Tis said by all who know him that he is not easily deceived and cannot be bribed. If there is any doubt in Poole's mind that you are guilty, you will go free."

"Here. We brought you some clean clothing, Nate," Jeremy said in his too-deep voice when the weighty silence between words grew unbearable. He held up a hefty brown-paper parcel tied with string. "We thought you could wear these to court on the 'morrow. And there's a basket of victuals, too. Venison pie, a roasted chicken, fresh scones, and a bottle of Burgundy from *Maman*, with all her love."

"Splendid!" he approved, forgoing telling his well-meaning brother that his fellow inmates had killed men for far less than the contents of that parcel or the food in the basket. "Pass the victuals through the grating, would you? I'm starved, and if I'm not careful, the turnkeys will take the lion's share of them."

"Pah! Those poxy turnkeys are worse than useless!" Simon Kincaid declared. "They refused the coin I offered to have you lodged in the Nobs' Common, tho' I've yet to see them turn down any other man's gold! Why is that, do you suppose?"

"'Tis my belief that one of the Octagon's members has influence within these walls, Father," Nathan confided in a lower voice. "They fear I saw their faces, I believe. If I were

16

lodged amongst my peers, instead of this rabble, sooner or later someone might listen to my tale of treason.''

"Then why not murder you with the other two and be done with it?'' Jeremy asked.

"For that small mercy, I fancy I have Father to thank,'' Nathan said with a rueful grin. "He is a man of substance and has no little influence with great men at court. Too many questions would have been raised had I been found murdered in some alley. Instead, they made me the scapegoat for their crimes—and will let Justice do what they dare not.''

"In High Holborn, we heard them singing of you,'' Jeremy said bitterly, obviously distressed by the thought.

"Aye, I've heard their ditties, too.'' Nathan quoted:

> "Now, Lawyer Kincaid fell in love with a wench,
> And what was the lawyer to do?
> For the wench that he favored
> Had wandering eyes—
> And instead of just one swain, she'd two!
> 'Oh, Rosie, Oh, Rosie, Oh, Rosie, my sweet,
> You promised to me you'd be true!
> If I cannot wed you,
> Then nobody shall!'
> And he choked her until she turned blue.

> "Then Roger came in with a terrible grin.
> And he—''

"Sweet Jesu, enough!'' cried Jeremy with a shudder of horror. "Isn't it enough that you've disgraced our family name? That you're on trial for your life? Must you make sport about it, too? Dear God, how could you, Nate, 'when 'tis likely you'll be—'' He broke off and swallowed.

"—hanged?'' Nathan finished for him. "Go ahead. You can say it, brother. 'Tis no secret that murderers have their

17

necks stretched by old Jack Ketch, the hangman, is it now?" But his dark jest cut too close to the bone for his brother's liking.

"Turnkey!" Jeremy cried, ashen-faced. And then to the pair of them he stammered, "Forgive me, Nate, Father, but I cannot stay here another moment!" With that, he ran from the visiting cell.

"Forgive him." Simon Kincaid excused his oldest son. "He did not mean what he said. He is afraid for you, Jonathan. Afraid and helpless."

Nathan nodded. "I know. Go after him, Father."

Reluctantly, Simon agreed. "Very well. Until the 'morrow, then?"

"Aye."

"Be strong, my boy. And remember, you are in our thoughts and prayers. Your *maman* sends her fondest love. I leave you with mine. God bless you, my son."

He knew, as his father bade him a moist-eyed farewell, that Simon Kincaid harbored little hope he would be found innocent and freed. No more did he. Those who wanted him silenced would see to that.

His frantic legal counsel came early to Newgate Gaol the following morning. Heatherton's white half-wig was askew, his black robes wrinkled and untidy as he ducked and weaved his uneasy way between the jeering, jostling convicts who escorted him through the Common Felons' Ward.

"You're early," Nathan greeted him, drawing his partner into a quiet corner. "Trouble sleeping—or an unbridled eagerness to rejoin me in my elegant lodgings?"

Heatherton wetted his lips. "I have no heart for jests this morning, Nate. I bring grave news."

"Is there another kind, Will?" he asked gently, noting his friend's distress. "Come, then. Out with it."

Heatherton nodded, but would not meet his eyes. "Very

18

well. Last night, as Judge Poole and his lady wife rode home from Sadler's Wells through Islington, their coach was set upon by highwaymen. It overturned in a ditch. In his effort to thwart the thieves and bring them to justice, a pistol was discharged and . . ."

". . . Judge Poole was killed."

"I'm afraid so, aye. Another magistrate is to pass sentence upon you in his stead. H-how did you know?"

"'Twas written in the stars, my friend," Jonathan said softly, turning away. "Shall we to court?"

The bailiff bade everyone rise as the new judge entered from his chambers later that same morning. Beyond caring, Jonathan looked up into the man's face and was stunned as an icy chill of recognition swept through him.

Those bastards!

He'd seen the magistrate before, by God—in Rosie's chamber, the night she and Roger were killed!

'Twas the face he had carried down into blackness . . . and would never forget. 'Twas the face of the man who, following the jury's verdict of guilty, donned a black hood and sentenced him to be hanged on Newgate gibbet two Fridays hence.

Hanged by the neck, until dead . . .

"Wake up, lawyer," hissed a hoarse voice.

Wake? Ha! He had not slept a wink—nor would he on this night of nights! The seconds yet remaining to his life were slipping by like sand through an hour-glass, these last grains few and precious. He would not squander them in sleep.

"Who goes?" he answered from the blackness of the cell to which he'd been brought in readiness for his execution at dawn, as was the custom.

"'Tis Old Nick 'imself, matie, come t' ferry ye t' Hell!" the turnkey chortled, his laughter wheezing on the shadows.

"Then I regret I must decline your invitation, sir, for I have a prior engagement—in the opposite direction."

"Stow the jests an' stir yer bones!" the oaf growled. "Yer loving kin 'ave paid dear t' see ye gone from here. Either follow me now—an' look lively—or tarry 'til old Ketch comes, t' fit ye fer his rope."

"God's Teeth—am I to go free?" he whispered, afraid to hope.

"Not free, quite, nay . . . But as close t' free as I dares t' take ye," the turnkey added ambiguously. "What'll it be?"

"Lead on, sir," Nathan murmured.

By dawn's first light, a rambunctious crowd had gathered in the snowy streets of High Holborn to watch the lawyer be turned-off by old Jack Ketch. When the rumor that Kincaid had escaped during the night circulated among them, they were loud in their disappointment and in their clamoring for the second "event" of the day, their noise assaulting the ears of the tall, gaunt man who arrived at the goal in a rented hack.

With an affected shudder of distaste, this man stepped down to the cobbles, holding a scented 'kerchief to his nostrils. He deeply inhaled to drown out the odors of the stinking rabble and drew aside disdainfully to keep his satin sleeves from brushing up against the seamed and greasy elbows of the common folk of London, as he wove his way among the crowd thronging about the gibbet.

Those that noticed the man at all pegged him immediately as a fop. They rolled their eyes in amusement and disgust as he minced along.

The doxies were much in evidence that morning, painted and patched and decked out in their gaudiest finery, shivering in the cold as they propositioned the gents for a penny a tumble. The piemen, the pickpockets, the beggars, and the tract-sellers were all doing brisk trade, despite one "guest of honor"— Kincaid—having failed to put in an appearance for his execution. And between two fine, monogrammed black coaches with liveried footmen, their noble occupants having paused to watch

20

the high jinks of the hangings, the man spotted the judge, waiting just as he'd instructed him by messenger the evening before.

A handsome beaver hat sat squarely atop the judge's powdered half-wig, and his cloak was of heavy charcoal wool trimmed tastefully with rabbit. As he looked somewhat nervously about him, he tapped his gold-knobbed cane of ebony wood against the icy cobbles and pushed up the pince-nez that slid down his nose. Twice, he drew a gold watch and chain from an inner pocket and glanced at it with a worried tsk.

"I'd all but given you up for lost, sir!" the judge declared, darting the approaching man a worried, frightened glance.

"I'm sure you were hoping I had been," the man sneered. "Tell me, did my little note surprise you?"

Mutely, the man nodded. "You know it did. Enough of your games, sir! For God's sake, will there be no end to this? No limits to the price you would have us pay? Well, sir, we have decided we will permit no more of your blackmail. You pushed us to the wall with Hampton, sir. And then that other sorry business . . . !" The judge shuddered. "'Twas insane, what you asked of us! We—that is to say, Forbes and I—did only what we felt was best. For you, as well as for ourselves. You need help, sir. If you won't believe it, then devil take you!"

"Brave words, Judge, but you *need* me! If not for our little secret, you'd never have risen to the law courts of the Old Bailey—and do you know why? Because you're a born bungler. Weak. Spineless! Kincaid vanished from his cell last night. He was to be hanged this morning."

"'Tis not my fault he escaped! I did as you asked. If you want to blame someone, then blame the turnkeys! As for me and my family, I have had enough! I'm done with you, sir!" He swung about, as if to go.

Just then, they brought a second convicted murderer up the thirteen steps to the gallows, a notorious pirate named Captain English whom the common people had baptized Billy Blue-Blood.

As the crowd of ghoulish spectators surged forward for a better look at the buccaneer's last jig, they shoved the ashen-faced judge headlong into the other man's arms.

Quick as a flash, he slipped the bodkin from his sleeve and thrust it deep into the judge's heart before shoving him away.

On the contrary, my dear judge, he thought smugly, *'tis I who am done with* you, *fiddle-de-dee*.

"A trifle early to be in one's cups, is it not, sir?" he commented loudly. Then, raising the scented 'kerchief that concealed his face, he melted into the crowd, humming happily.

Andrew Hampton was next. He giggled. Ah, yes. He had something special planned for Andrew, *and* His Royal Majesty. Something *very* special . . .

"Two . . . four . . . six . . . eight—just like cherries on a plate!"

Chapter One

July, 1790

By six bells, the cowardly Harkabout knew his ship was doomed. Deaf to the choir of desperate screams that rose from the hatches, blind to the plight of his terrified crew, he filled a duffel bag with provisions and sneaked aboard one of the four small longboats, abandoning his ship and her convict cargo to save his worthless hide.

A handful of wild-eyed officers slunk after the captain. Still other desperate fellows saw what they were about and tried to follow them, scrambling over the bodies of the fallen. Three of the boats were quickly filled, but a fourth lay buried under fallen sail. Ruthlessly, Harkabout and his chosen few fought off the latecomers with club and dagger, stabbing and thwacking at the desperate fingers of the enlisted men who clawed at the longboat's sides and tried to board her. Slashing the lines, they lowered the tiny craft into the pitching blackness.

Eerie green lightning known as St. Elmo's fire flickered and danced about the *Hester*'s yardarms, shimmied down her masts and roiled across her decks in a spreading emerald fog. The sailors shivered and crossed themselves against the supernatural forces that were surely contained in the glowing wildfire! The rattle and boom of the thunder sounded like cannon as bolt after bolt hailed down upon the transport's pitching decks. There, one hardy, Christian soul still battled the elements single-handed, trying to wring order out of chaos, to snatch salvation from the jaws of despair.

Formerly the ship's carpenter, Jack Warner was now the *Hester*'s true master in all but name, barking orders at the top of his lungs as if born to the skipper's task. He chivvied the terrified convicts up from the stinking blackness of the watery hold, bellowing for the remaining crewmembers to make haste and rid the poor devils of their shackles. Time was fast running out!

"Look lively an' strike their irons, lads!" he roared over the howling wind, fighting against the slope of the deck to stand upright as he barked the command. "Free them! Let the poor sods die wi' some dignity!"

The handful of convicts he'd already freed with his own two hands shivered and wept, clinging to each other like children for comfort. Former city-sparrows, all but one shaggy-headed, powerfully structured felon seemed frozen in place by fear. This man took up mallet and chisel, and struck the irons from a fellow convict's ankles, them moved quickly on to the next and the next, laboring tirelessly to free his fellows.

"Damn yer black souls, help him!" Jack barked at the rest. "You, there—Kincaid, is it?—show these scurvy swabs 'ow it's done, or let 'em drown in their pretty bracelets!"

Shocked into action by Jack's threats, the convicts forced panic-numbed fingers to lift mallet and chisel, and did as ordered.

Far above, lanterns danced madly on the yardarms as the ship writhed in her death throes. Their sulphurous pricks of light were abruptly doused as a towering wash swamped over

24

them. A terrible groan rose from the *Hester*'s swollen timbers and her grinding hull. Moans, shrieks, and prayers from those trapped in the orlop decks below rose to mingle with the screams of the free men above, now slithering and sliding about on the streaming decks. The moans were abruptly silenced as monstrous waves flooded the decks yet again, sending frothy black water rushing through the open ports, swirling across the decks, and pouring through the hatch-covers to fill the stinking holds.

The force of the sea-water freed an untied cannon. It careened across the sloping deck to crush one poor devil against the bulkhead, pinning him there in a spray of blood that the wind and the rain whirled into pinkish mist. His dying shrieks rose shrilly; then cannon and man vanished as the *Hester* heaved once again and hurled them into the foaming sea.

Stephens, the pilot, was dead, Jack saw, still gamely lashed to his wheel. His neck had been broken by a falling spar, and his head lolled drunkenly. Crossing himself, Jack headed at a run for the gangway, fighting the bucking, slippery deck, the heaving stairwell, the screaming wind and the rain to reach the tiny cabin below.

With the pilot dead and Harkabout gone, there was precious little hope left for them now, he knew. The *Hester* was dying—had been doomed, if truth were told, since three days ago when young Tim had spotted the albatross. A bad omen, if ever there was one. In minutes, the ship'd go down, but before then, he must try to save the wenches. If he could get them into the last longboat, they'd have a chance, albeit a slim one.

The two young women were sobbing, clinging frantically to each other, when Jack reached their door. Their faces were pale ovals of terror in the darkness. He thought of his own five daughters at home, and his heart squeezed with pity.

"Hold hands, me lovelies," he crooned. "Aye, that's the way. Now, little miss, take this here paw and come along wi' Jack!"

Poor trusting lambs, in their terror they took his hands and followed him blindly. The younger girl was whimpering as they clambered up onto the *Hester*'s nightmarish upper deck, poor mite. The older girl was outwardly calm, keeping up a brave front, bless 'er, but little less terrified. Her turquoise eyes betrayed her terror as she looked wildly about her, as did the shaky rasp of her breathing. Jack could hear her praying under her breath as they inched towards the longboats, battled their way across flooded planking that would not keep still but tilted every which way.

Far above, the *Hester*'s tattered shrouds snapped and flapped like whips, caught in the teeth of the howling gale that had battered the vessel for two long days and two longer nights. Thunderbolts exploded overhead again, great, clattering peals more deafening than cannon fire. Lightning sizzled and smoked about the mizzen-mast, where the *Hester*'s once-proud pennants now hung in sorry tatters.

Harkabout did this, Jack thought, a burst of bitterness and hatred filling him. *Harkabout, that cowardly, blasphemous dog of a captain, doomed us all!*

Scoffing at superstition, Harkabout had taken the cat-o'-nine-tails to a crewman who had the crucified Christ tattooed upon his back. Jack had warned the captain of the folly of it—aye, he'd risked a flogging himself for daring to speak his mind, but he'd told Harkabout ill-fortune would follow the flogging, and follow it had, as surely as day followed night. First, the Holy Cross defiled and scourged. Then the albatross had been sighted. And finally, out of nowhere, had come that howling wind and rain.

"Make it stop! For the love of God, someone make it *stop*!" the younger girl sobbed, clapping her hands over her ears.

"Up inter the boat wi' ye, missie!" Jack ordered gruffly. "Look smartly, now! Your turn next, m'lady—and make haste! We've no time t'—*Damn ye, naaayy! Jesu, deliver us*!"

But even as Jack cried out, the monstrous wave looming over the *Hester* broke, spewing over the decks, swamping her holds.

The rush of black water swept everything—and everyone—over the rails as if all were broken matchwood.

"Hanged by the neck . . . Hanged by the neck . . . Hanged by—

"God's teeth!"

He came to with a groan. There was no part of himself that didn't hurt. Pushing up onto his elbows, he raised swollen eyelids to squint against the blinding purity of the light and looked about him.

There was brilliant blue sky above him; wet and unyielding sand beneath his battered bones. A large crab was perched squarely upon his chest, brandishing a monstrous claw a hairs-breadth from his face. Its eyes, like black beads attached to muscular stalks, were darting about to take his measure! More-over, its feelers waved to and fro beneath his blistered nose like a tickly feather duster.

He sneezed, cursing a blue streak as the reflex response fired lightning bolts through his skull. And yet, the pain was almost welcome. If naught else, it proved beyond all doubt that he was alive.

Alive! Good God, he'd survived!

The lingering fog in his head evaporated. With a wild whoop, he sprang to his feet, flung out his arms, and whirled full circle, sending the giant crab scrabbling sideways across the sand. It was true, he thought incredulously, looking about him with wondering eyes, he'd made it!

A calm turquoise ocean lapped at his bare feet. Bubbles of sea-foam broke over his toes. At his heels lay an unbroken crescent of white-gold, the sandy jewel of a cove backed by a dense grove of coconut palms. The grove extended westwards in a graceful curve, while beyond it loomed a knobbly spine of hazy blue mountains. The mountains ran the length of the island from north to south. Fluffy white clouds had gathered about many of the highest summits, while a smaller, cone-shaped volcanic peak lazily emitted puffs of dark gray smoke. The lower slopes were cloaked in dense green jungle.

The beach about him was littered with sea-weed necklaces, rocks, shells, and driftwood, as well as the man-made flotsam and jetsam cast ashore by the wreck of the *Hester*; lengths of rope, shattered timbers, canvas, and so on. The cloudless sky was fresh-laundered, as vivid blue as the satin lining of a cloak, with the sun worn like a golden brooch at its zenith. He could feel its heat frying his head and shoulders.

Aye, by God—*aye*! Against all odds, he'd survived! Neither a brutal miscarriage of British justice that would have stretched his neck on a gallows, nor the disease-ridden, rotting Hulks in the Thames—not even the ferocity of a two-day tempest—had been able to lay him low. He, Jonathan Kincaid, had bested them all!

Grinning like a drunkard, he suddenly looked down at his person. Now that his survival was assured, the next order of business was to ascertain his condition. Almost delirious with his good fortune, he chuckled. Everything seemed much the same and in fair working order. In fact, nothing had changed— but that he was free!

He had a year's growth of bushy black beard that reached to his chest, and wild, shoulder-length black hair. Both were courtesy of Newgate Gaol and the Second Fleet's deplorable lack of grooming facilities! Be damnèd if he wasn't covered with bruises, too, a legacy of the battering he'd taken on the coral reef's jagged teeth as the wild breakers had cast him over it and onto this shore.

As for clothing, all that remained of his filthy shirt was its long, pointed collar, fastened by a single bone button, and both full, deeply cuffed sleeves! The ragged parts were held together by a single thread. His back, chest, and abdomen were bare, save for a mat of dark hair. His brine-soaked leather jerkin had, by some miracle, survived intact, though it had dried stiff as a board, while his breeches—buttons lost and already torn

28

about the knees on the day the transport ship had set sail for Botany Bay—had simply grown more ragged from the storm's buffetting. As for what had become of his hose and boots, he hadn't a whit!

He wiggled his bare toes in the powdery white sand. It felt warm, yielding, as soft as a willing wench. Tears of self-pity welled, unmanly tears that he dashed angrily away with his fist. God knew he was no mewling babe, but he'd felt nothing as warm and soft as the sand for so blasted long! The walls of his cell had been hard, cold stone with a slippery finish of mildew and damp. His bed had been a slab of timber; his coverlets, moldy straw.

God's Teeth! Enough of these maudlin thoughts! All that was in the past. He'd been granted a second chance at life, and he meant to live it!

Resolutely, he flicked his head to dispel doom and gloom. Casting off the tatters of his shirt, he again donned his vest. 'Twould serve to keep his bare back from burning, if for naught else. And, thus rigged out, he was quite adequately suited for a castaway's solitary existence.

Solitary?

His grin faded. It became a dark, brooding scowl that made his handsome features stern indeed beneath the beard upon which he tugged thoughtfully. Laughing green eyes narrowed as he pondered the word "solitary" and the state it represented.

Was it possible that he alone had survived the *Hester*'s sinking? Aye, he admitted, 'twas possible—but unlikely, alas. If a sinner such as himself had survived drowning, then the odds were favorable that other, worthier souls had also gained these shores. Foreboding squeezed his vitals. If survivors there were, would they belong to the *Hester*'s stalwart Royal Navy crew of over eighty souls and thus be a threat to his newly won freedom? Or had some of the over two hundred male and thirty female convicts survived. Those wretched creatures who, like himself, had been chained in the transport's foul holds for seven hellish months. He shrugged. Neither prospect pleased him, but if he wanted an answer to his question, there was but one way to find it.

Not one to delay when action was called for, Nathan strode off down the beach in search of other survivors. His passage left a trail of footprints in the smooth sand behind him.

His explorations over the next hour or two proved more encouraging than he'd dared to hope. He found a fish-eaten body or two, bobbing in the shallows, but not another living soul. He also concluded that his chances for survival here were better than good. They were excellent. Indeed, not only did he feel certain he could survive, but he fancied he might do so in lavish style!

The coconut grove that fringed the sandy bay was home to colonies of chattering monkeys, to cockatoos and squawking parrots with rainbow plumage. As if they were fishmongers hawking their wares at Billingsgate Market on a Lenten Friday morn, their raucous din filled the air, providing ample proof of their great numbers. Their cacophony was sweet music to Nathan's ears. When hunger gripped him, as it must sooner or later, he would dine on succulent monkey meat, or upon the plump carcass of a freshly plucked parrot or two, he promised himself. Moreover, so numerous were the creatures' numbers, he wagered it would take no great skill at rock-throwing to bring down several of them—at least until they grew wary of the human hunter in their midst. And by then, the Lord willing, he would have discovered other, more subtle methods to put meat in his belly.

Between the lofty palms, he discovered numerous, tall banana plants many heavy with green bundles of fruit, as well as fruit trees—mangoes, papayas?—and others whose names he could not guess. All were similarly laden. In the dense shade of the rocks at water's edge, crabs were in abundant supply, as were eels, winkles, and numerous varieties of fish of impossibly bright colors. The latter were every bit as plump and gaudy as the parrots in the trees. Fins and tails flashing in the crystal shallows in tempting fashion, they showed no fear of him at all.

His mouth watered. He was fond of fresh fish, cooked to a turn. Why, if he closed his eyes, he could almost smell those little lovelies cooking, skewered over a red-hot fire just as he and James Cook's crew had prepared them in the Sandwich Isles. He was nigh drooling as he let his imagination stray a step further, envisioning the succulent fish reduced to mere skeletons of their former, tender selves, and himself reclining in the shade with a sated smile and a full belly. Blast it, he was starving *now*! Given a bit of twine and something for a hook, he just knew he could land a feast fit for a king! Surely the debris littering the beach would yield something suitable.

Shading his eyes, he gazed to left, then to right. The staves of a fractured barrel jutted up from the sand a few yards distant, for all the world like the rib-bones of a small beached whale. A goodly-sized length of sailcloth was caught between them. He made a mental note to salvage both items, for possible use later, on his way back to this spot, then continued on, scanning the sand and toeing aside heaps of both red and green sea-weed as he went, in search of an iron nail or something similar he could fashion into a serviceable fishhook.

Eyes narrowing, he came to a sudden halt.

What?

A pale foot jutted from between some rocks up ahead.

Surely it must be a mirage, an illusion created by the shimmering curtain of heat rising from the sand? But as he drew closer, he saw that the dainty pink-toed foot was not only real, but was joined to a long, shapely limb that could only be female.

Breaking into a jog that pained his battered ribs, he reached the scattered formation of rocks. There, he again came to an abrupt halt, brought to his knees by the vision that lay before him.

31

Caught between several large rocks—all that had prevented the outgoing tide from returning her to King Neptune's jealous bosom—sprawled a young woman.

Her arms were outflung as if to embrace the craggy sentinels where she lay, half in and half out of a shallow tide-pool. The ends of her long, red-gold hair were furling and dancing on the turquoise water like delicately fronded sea-anemones. Her eyes were closed, their luxuriant dark brown lashes curved like delicate fans upon cheeks the same coral-tinted, creamy hue as the tiny sea-shells netted by her tresses. Her face was slender and oval in shape, her nose small and narrow, her chin dainty but determined, her full lips almost colorless. Her lovely throat flowed into a delightfully curved figure that kindled an appreciative gleam in Nathan's eyes, for the swell of her ripe bosom and hips rounded out the tattered remnants of her clothing most delightfully.

Quite simply put, she was a beauty, Nathan decided, rocking back on his heels to contemplate how her discovery might affect his plans. Then he amended soberly that perhaps *had* been beautiful might be a more fitting description. So still did the wench lay, so horribly pale were her cheeks, dare he hope against hope she yet lived?

Chapter Two

Dropping onto one knee at her side, Nathan pressed an ear to her bosom. His dread vanished as quickly as it had been born. Merciful God, she was breathing! He could feel the warmth of her breath fanning his cheek, the gentle rise and fall of her chest beneath his head. Why, then, did she not waken?

Gently, he took her chin between his thumb and forefinger and turned her head to one side. Ah! The reason was plain to see, for a dark bruise about the size of a florin marred her temple. The tiny gash at its center had been cleansed of blood by the sea. His cursory examination revealed no other visible injuries. He was no surgeon, but if her innards had escaped damage, he had high hopes that she would shortly come to. And, God willing, would do so with no reminder of her ordeal but for a pounding head.

"Mistress Eve, may I present myself? Master Adam, at your service! Welcome to Eden!" he murmured, flourishing an imaginary tricorn. "And, if Dame Fortune smiles upon me, her lusty servant, to the delights that could be ours to share!"

Grinning, he leaned down, took up her bare, limp right arm and flung it over his shoulder. He did likewise with her left, then wrapped his arms around her waist and heaved. Staggering to his feet, he held her upright before him and started towards the coconut grove. Her legs dangled awkwardly between his feet, her toes plowed a furrow in the sand as he went. Blast! This wouldn't do at all!

He tried to heft her up a little higher, but . . . By all that was holy, slender she might well appear upon the sand, but in his weakened state, the wench weighed as doughtily as a farm lass!

Shifting her body so that her torso dangled over his shoulder and down his back like a Smithfield carcass, he took one ponderous step after the other, staggering up the beach through deep sand on legs that bent more and more at the knee with every step he took. God's Teeth! It was akin to wading through deep snow against a blustering wind, he thought, red-faced and cursing. Within but a few yards, his back was screaming, his bruised arms were begging for mercy, his legs were trembling, and his sagging knees clamored for respite. Devil take the spot he'd picked for a camp, he decided, sinking down and rolling the wench off his shoulder with a relieved groan. 'Twas too damned far!

He stretched out beside the girl so that their faces were but inches apart, her lovely pale one patterned by the shadows of the dancing palm-fronds far above them. Time enough for m'lady to change lodgings when she'd regained her feet. She could then transport *herself* elsewhere, he determined, now utterly drained.

Meanwhile, this spot would serve.

He awoke abruptly some while later to the screaming of a soul in torment. On and on it went, splitting his eardrums, sending sleep scattering like rats before a cur.

His belly churned. Bile stung the back of his throat. Dread wound crampy tentacles about his vitals. Hands clamped over his ears, he tried to muffle the sound, for in his semi-conscious state he'd quite forgotten where he was, and thought himself back in the bowels of the gaol. Surely the screams belonged to some poor devil put to the torturer's test, he told himself drowsily. But, as he did so, a small but punishing fist came out of nowhere and smacked him hard upon the nose. The well-aimed blow brought tears to his eyes.

"*Who are you?*" a harpy's voice screeched at him. Its tone was only a mite less ear-splitting than the screams that had gone before. "*And what are you? Where is this place? And why, in God's name, have you brought me here?*"

Nathan's watering eyes flew open, to find another pair of eyes—these as vivid turquoise as the ocean—scant inches away; wide-open turquoise eyes that were wildly staring, and were made abnormally brightened by the luster of terror. His "Eve" had come to, he realized belatedly, and his fatigue vanished. Reason returned.

"For the love of God, cease your caterwauling, wench, 'fore you deafen me!" he growled. Glimpsing a pale flash to his left, he managed to trap her wrist in the very moment she would have planted yet another blow upon his nose. "The *Hester*, wench," he gritted out, struggling to sit up while yet keeping a firm grasp upon her wrists. "She sank in the storm. God's Blood, do you remember nothing? Her captain—that callous swine, Harkabout, God rot him!—gave orders for all hands to abandon ship. He would have let us convicts drown with her but for the carpenter. Soon after, the ship foundered and then—"

"Thanks be to God, aye! Now I remember. The ship! And that awful gale!" the girl cut in, her voice husky. She shuddered as she did so, and the tension drained from her. "I recall Jack, God bless him. He came to our cabin and bade us make haste."

35

"Cabin, eh?" Nathan grinned. He liked a wench with a sense of humor, and this girl clearly possessed one, to call the *Hester*'s foul holds a 'cabin'! "A good jest, mistress!"

". . . He was kind to us," she continued as if he hadn't spoken, "tho' 'twas clear the skipper cared nothing for our safety. While he and his crew saw to saving their own skins, Jack helped us into a boat and began to lower it. Moments later, a giant wave washed over the ship, and we . . . we . . . !"

Her free hand, trembling violently, strayed to the bruise at her temple. She rubbed at the spot, wincing with pain as she tried to remember, then shrugging slender shoulders when she could not. "Alas, I remember nothing more until waking moments ago." She bowed her head. "Forgive me for striking you, sir, but I do not recall you from the *Hester*'s crew. In the shadows and my confusion, I mistook you for—"

"—a dashing sea-captain, about to steal a kiss? Or perchance a handsome pirate, bent on your seduction?" Nathan teased in a consoling tone, winking one green eye and grinning wickedly.

"Alas, neither one, sir," she denied pertly. "Rather, I mistook you for a . . . a . . . *demon*, sir! A hideous demon or a hairy satyr!" Seeing his crestfallen expression, she added defensively, "Fie, good sir, can you blame me? 'Tis your eyes that misled me! I' faith, never have I seen a pair so bright a green. Nor any man with hair as black—or indeed, so very *much* of it."

Nathan scowled, his vanity tweaked by her unflattering description of him. Women had always found him a handsome fellow. Why must this pert chit think otherwise?

"'Twas this green-eyed 'demon,' this black-haired devil, who nigh broke his back to carry you beyond the high-tide mark, ungrateful wench," he grumbled, sitting up and leaning against the palm trunk, his arms folded across his bare chest. He wore a salty expression on his handsome face now that even the wild black beard could not mask.

"Then I thank you, sir, with all my heart—and entreat your pardon for my error," she apologized prettily.

She seemed, he was pleased to note, a little embarrassed now by her mistake. He fancied the coral tinge to her cheeks had deepened to an apricot blush in the shadows.

"Was . . . was it also your kind self who plucked me from the sea?" she inquired in a more hesitant tone.

"Nay. I fancy 'twas the storm that cast us both upon this same deserted isle, mistress," he grudgingly admitted, wishing he could claim that noble deed as his own—or he had thought to lie.

"Ah. 'Tis a deserted isle, you say? Not New South Wales or any part of Australasia, then?"

"Far from it, I fancy. A small island is more likely. There are many such in these waters. Thousands, 'tis said."

"Then you'd sailed these seas before this voyage?"

"I sailed with Cook many years ago, as a young lad. Doubtless you've heard of Captain James Cook, the explorer?" She nodded that she had. "I was with his crew when he discovered Botany Bay. And, while no sea-captain, I yet have some conning of these parts, I fancy."

"Then tell me truly, sir. Are . . . are we stranded here?"

"Alas, mistress, we are. And, unless some passing Dutchman from Batavia happens upon us, stranded we'll remain."

"I see. And there are no . . . there are no other survivors?" she queried, her voice, already husky, dropping to a whisper that quavered with dread.

"I fear not. Or at least, none that I've encountered."

"God, no! Oh, poor, poor little Caroline . . . !" Her lovely face crumpled. He could have sworn he caught the sudden sparkle of tears in her eyes before she drew a deep breath, composed her features, and continued tremulously, "And how long did I sleep?"

"Well, the storm was last night. When I found you 'twas

soon after midday—the sun was high above me at the time—so that would mean a—''

"—whole day has passed! And now the moon has risen once again," she observed, hugging her bare arms and shivering as a chill wind riffled through the coconut palms.

Above them, the fronds stirred, whispering like gossips at a hanging. A nightbird uttered a harsh cry that was abruptly cut off, deep in the grove behind them. The sudden, alien call raised the hackles on Nathan's neck, though the girl seemed not to have heard it.

"I must have struck my head," she continued slowly. "It hurts . . . here."

In the moonlight, her hair, now dried, shone red-gold, he observed as she rubbed her temple. Her gold-flecked turquoise eyes were huge and thickly fringed, luminous in the half-light as she gazed at him questioningly.

"Aye, mistress, you've a handsome bruise there. I don't wonder that it hurts. Have you pain elsewhere?"

She seemed to consider his question, then murmured, "Nay, none. I think I am unhurt, save for some stiffness here and there."

"Good. Then rest a while more. Sleep heals the body faster than anything else, 'tis said. I'll make a compress to lessen the swelling and ease your pain. Are you hungry?" He was ravenous, he realized. He could hear his empty belly growling, treacherous organ! It craved the wormy sea-biscuits, rancid salt-pork and foul, greasy slop the *Hester*'s galley had regularly provided, despite the weevils and mold that had riddled the sorry victuals. He clenched his jaw. Confound his stupidity! He should have stayed awake until he'd built them a fire against the chill night air—and to keep possible predators at bay. He should also have found them something to eat.

"Indeed, no. I couldn't eat a bite. The very thought of food upsets me. If you'd be so kind, sir, a sip of water is all I require. And perhaps a moistened cloth . . . ?" Suddenly, she swayed where she sat, overwhelmed by a dizzy spell.

Nathan caught her as she toppled and gently lowered her to the sand.

"Cold . . . so very cold . . ." she whispered; then her glorious eyes closed with a downward sweep of dark lashes. She sighed once, as if utterly exhausted, and was still.

The poor little wench was shivering in her sleep, he saw. Taking off his jerkin, he tucked it around her bare shoulders. Stiff as it was, he had naught else for a windbreak.

Satisfied she was as comfortable as possible, he left the palm grove and strode down to the beach.

As she had said, the moon had risen; a great, bone-white disc of a moon such as only the tropics could display. Fat stars were scattered across the underbelly of midnight-blue sky. The starry night reminded him of his voyage with Cook. Standing upon the moonlit decks of the *Resolution*, anchored off the island of Tahiti, the astronomer, Green, had shown him the passage of Venus.

Tonight, the magical combination of star-light and moon-light kissed the rolling breakers beyond the craggy reef with an ethereal silvery-blue phosphorescence that was echoed by the glow worms which studded the rocks here and there with diamond pin-points of light. The beach was lit bright as day; so bright, he could see tiny white sand-crabs, disturbed by his feet. They vanished into invisible sand tunnels that caved in as he trudged along, wearing a worried frown. He was certain he could find the tattered shirtsleeves he'd discarded that morning with little effort, and that the cloth would serve well for a compress. But fresh water for drinking? Food? God's teeth, that was another matter entirely!

First thing in the morning, he must see about finding them a spring, if they were to have any chance at surviving. Until then, mayhap he could find a fallen coconut with milk to quench the girl's thirst? There must be dozens of windfalls scattered about the grove in the wake of the storm.

Chapter Three

He awoke early the next morning to find a glorious rose-and-gold dawn flaring across the sky and the sun perched upon the rim of the horizon like a golden guinea.

Though he knew from the drained coconut halves he'd placed beside her that she'd woken to drink, the girl he'd christened Eve still slept deeply at his side. She was turned half onto her stomach, her petticoats twisted around her. Her thrashings had bared the upper curves of her bosom, her shapely arms, and her long, slender legs. Her cheek was cradled upon the hand tucked beneath her head, while her other arm was stretched out on the sand beside him, as if in her dreams, she'd reached out, wanting him to comfort her.

The notion that she would seek his consolation was decidedly encouraging, for as signs went, it boded will for Nathan's lustier fancies. God's Blood, she was a toothsome baggage, if ever he'd seen one! By the light of day, the little wench was even lovelier than he remembered from last night, as fair of face and form as any goddess. Aye, by God, all going well, she would naturally turn to him for consolation and protection, for she considered him her savior and hero. And then—he chuckled—well, who knew what more she might ask of him after that. . . ?

Her wealth of red-gold hair fell across her body in spiralling ringlets that seemed, to his admiring eyes, delightfully winsome and fairylike. Her delectable nape and the fine, pale-gold down upon it were exposed, her rounded shoulders bare. God's Teeth, but every inch of her invited a man's lusty kisses and caresses! She was made for love, for desire and passion!

Watching her as she slept on, vulnerable and infinitely feminine, Nathan felt a hot stab of lust pierce his groin. His breathing grew thick and raspy with mounting desire. To say he was sorely tempted to accept her mute invitation was an understatement. God's Bones, he was no monk, but a *man*! A man of normal hot-blooded appetites who'd not bedded a woman in almost a year; for, being more fastidious than his fellow convicts, he'd refused the tarnished favors of the eager—and probably raddled—bawds that Newgate's foul confines had offered.

"Were I less of a gentleman, my pretty doxie," he muttered ruefully, "we would even now be celebrating our survival in a lusty tumble!" He reached out and thoughtfully rubbed a skein of her red-gold hair between his fingers, finding it as silky as gossamer to his touch. A vision of those tousled ringlets cascading over his chest as she bestrode his flanks danced in his head. "And were I more of a rogue, I would not have delayed our celebration o'er long!" he added, gritting his teeth.

However, it went against his inherently honorable nature to tumble any woman—even a doxie—whilst she slept, or was still confused by her injury. Nor would he force himself upon a pretty trollop whose name he did not know. Sighing, he cast her a lingering farewell glance, murmured, "Anon, sweet Eve. Anon!" and left her sleeping in the shade of the palms.

Time enough later for dallying with the wench. For now, it's work for you, Kincaid! Hard, honest work that'll drive your thoughts from lust!

41

Gritting his teeth, he resumed the task he'd begun the night before—husking coconuts. And, little by little, his lust abated.

As he'd expected, fallen coconuts had been easily come by, even in the dark of night. But alas, without a blade of some sort to split the hard outer shells, freeing the smallish nut within was a hellish task.

He'd husked two coconuts by pounding them against a rock that had a pointed edge at one corner, but it'd been the very devil of a chore, and all his hard work had produced only a scant cupful of sweet coconut milk and a few mouthfuls of chewy white meat.

The bananas had proved disappointing, too. The first ones he'd picked had been unripe. Still green and hard both inside and out, they'd tasted bitter as aloes to the tongue.

When he'd husked enough coconuts to render a little liquid to quench their thirst, he'd explore the jungle beyond the grove in search of riper bananas and other fruits. God willing, perhaps there he'd find a spring or a freshwater stream. Aye, fresh water was the first order of business! Then he'd do his best to build them a fire and keep it lit both day and night, for he'd not forgotten the harsh cry he'd heard cut short the night before.

She was dreaming again. It was the same dream—nightmare—she'd had before.

Looking up, she saw again the towering wave, the wall of water that had loomed over the *Hester* before it crashed down and destroyed the transport vessel. She could hear the terrified screams, the pleas of the crew for God to deliver them. She relived the vessel's ominous pitching and rolling . . . the treacherous slope of her slippery decks . . . the unholy green flickers of lightning that had danced along her spars and yardarms . . . the snapping and cracking of the flapping canvas high above as the gale ripped at the shrouds, tore them to shreds as if it were a wild animal with sharp fangs. And, once again, she remembered herself screaming as Caroline and Jack were washed overboard, spilled from the capsized longboat like salt from a shaker; the lantern swinging towards her out of the sheeting rain, determinedly as a pendulum, before it struck her broadside across the head. When she'd next come to, she was in the water and brine filled her mouth and streamed from her nostrils, choking her. Screaming, she'd floundered helplessly, tossed over and over in the pounding black surf like a rag-doll, certain that she was going to die.

She came awake with a heart-pounding jolt, her fingers closing convulsively over handfuls of powdery sand as she frantically fought for some solid grip; for she was still in the throes of her nightmare. But, little by little, she realized she was no longer drowning, not even in the water. Nay. She lay upon her back, and there was soft sand beneath her and a warm, scented breeze fanning her cheek. When her heavy eyelids fluttered open, she could see tiny monkeys cavorting in the palm fronds above her, peering down at her with inquisitive, bright eyes, or chattering noisily as they groomed each other or swung from frond to frond.

The man!

Belatedly remembering, she sat up and looked about her, half-afraid she'd find him there, half-afraid she wouldn't—not entirely certain he hadn't been a part of her awful dream until she saw the leather waistcoat he'd tossed over her. Real, then. Well, perhaps, she supposed, puckering up her lips in thought, her outspokenness earlier had driven him away? If so, she was glad it had! Truth was, he frightened her. There was *something* about him that set off alarum bells of warning in her head, but what exactly that something had been, she couldn't quite put her finger upon. Could it be that he reminded her of a wicked pirate, with that wild black beard, that unruly mane of inky hair, and his bold ways? She grimaced. More likely than not. She fancied he was a handsome devil beneath those shaggy locks, an amorous rogue who'd enjoyed more than his share of female attention in the past. What was more, she suspected he'd already considered the likelihood of adding her favors to the notches in his bedpost. There'd been that . . . that *look* in his startling green eyes, a speculative, predatory, wolfish gleam she'd recognized immediately as lust; a look that, to her disgust, had in all truth stirred a tiny answering spark of response within herself. *For shame, Mariah, you wanton baggage!* she upbraided herself. To feel even a spark of desire for that shaggy brute was disgraceful, she knew. But having cheated Death made one deliriously eager to celebrate one's survival in some form or other!

She looked about, but to her relief the man was nowhere to be seen, neither striding the white sand beach like a castaway king patrolling his island domain, nor lurking among the trees. At her side, however, he'd left several coconut halves, filled with a milky liquid. Thirstily, she drained one, then another. Hmm, how delicious it tasted, sweet and warm. It cleansed her mouth of the vile taste of salt. Lecherous brute or nay, she had to admit she had him to thank for the coconut milk. Twinges of doubt stirred in her belly. What if she had her wish and he didn't come back? What if he really had taken offense at her sharp retorts and abandoned her for good? Dear God, how would she survive?

For a moment, panic fluttered madly in her breast, like a moth beating dark wings against the glass chimney of a lantern. But, with supreme willpower, she managed to squelch her mounting hysteria. *Nonsense, Mariah! You're resourceful and intelligent, with centuries of good Winslow blood in your veins and no little courage. Even alone, you'd manage to survive perfectly well. But . . . alone.*

Grief welled then, choking her, as the enormity of her loss, the desperation of her predicament, slammed home. Her eyes stung, burned. *Oh, Caroline! My poor, dear little cousin, Caroline! Did you suffer terribly before the end finally came? Did you call upon your beloved papa and your cousin Mariah to save you, and know your cries went unanswered as you looked foul Death in the eye?*

Tears flowed down Mariah's cheeks. Sobs lodged like

weighty stones in her breast. They hurt so, they made her throat ache unbearably with the pain of her loss. Overcome, she flung herself facedown on the sand and wept . . . and from weeping, drifted back, exhausted, into healing sleep.

Nathan's foraging that morning uncovered an abundant fresh-water supply, but he almost paid for it with his life!

Soon after he left the coconut grove behind him, he encountered dense jungle that closed around him like a steaming wet, green blanket, robbing him of all sense of direction. Standing very still, he cocked his head to one side and listened intently. To his delight, he could make out the shushing sound of running water above the squawks and chattering above him in the tree-tops. Lady Luck be praised! Its source sounded quite near.

Eagerly now, he breasted and fought his way through tangled vegetation, lifting aside vines and creepers as thick around as a man's finger, flattening tussocks of waist-high grasses, following, always following, the siren song of the burbling stream.

But it was not, he discovered moments later, a stream at all. Staggering from the undergrowth into a delightful little clearing, he saw that the source of the splashing sound was a waterfall, one that tumbled down from a shelf of rock thirty feet or more above a broad, clear pool. Several banana plants flourished in the damp circumference of its cascade, while mossy boulders of various shapes and sizes were scattered about its grassy banks. Between these rambled giant vines with split leaves that measured nigh two feet across, crimson-flowering lilies and lush, bright green ferns, as well as darker, leafy plants with heart-shaped leaves as big as serving platters. Enormous butterflies of every color and design danced on the steaming air, for all the world like wind-tossed giant blossoms. Gaudy parrots and white-winged cockatoos squawked in the tree-tops overhead.

Indeed, it was a place of exquisite beauty, a true Garden of

Eden, with every plant and creature larger and more colorful than life. He wanted to laugh out loud with sheer pleasure. But then he spied something that froze the laughter on his lips.

Jesu!

Several hideous baboons were cavorting among the rocks above him, their long, broad muzzles lending them more a look of dog than of monkey! Baboon babies nursed at their mothers' breasts, clinging to their hairy bellies, while other small family groups appeared intent on grooming each other. On the flat, grassy area at the farthest side of the pool, away from him, a few playful youngsters wrestled, while high above them all, Nathan spotted a huge, scarred orange male!

Muzzle lifted to the breeze, the baboon patriarch was unmoving, crouched silently upon the highest rocky outcropping; a tyrant king on his lofty dais, standing wary sentinel over his clan. His deep-set, sulphurous eyes fixed on Nathan, an evil gleam in them.

Sweat springing out on his brow, Nathan gingerly backed away, uttering a silent prayer that he could vanish before they came at him. But it was not to be. The male had spotted him, and the hairy old brute pounded his fists upon his balding chest with rage. Raising his muzzle, he bared his fangs and let out a horrendous roar of challenge and threat before dropping onto all fours. Leaving his lofty post, he began bounding over the rocks, springing down from craggy shelf to craggy shelf towards Nathan, bent on attack!

With his roar of outrage, other baboons began tumbling down after their leader. In but seconds, the huge, hairy pack was converging in Nathan's direction.

Damnation! The vicious brutes would tear him limb from limb! Having neither pistol nor cutlass, he had no way to preserve himself but by judicious retreat!

He bolted back the way he'd come, barging down the rough path he'd forged on the outward trek, arms windmilling and legs frantically pumping, cursing the dense creepers and vines that impeded a speedy flight. So loud were the roars of the baboon pack, so terrifyingly close did they sound as they crashed through the vegetation at his heels, he fully expected at any moment to feel their long, wickedly-powerful teeth rending his flesh, drawing blood!

He burst from the coconut grove onto the beach like a ball launched from a cannon, and at once began gathering up rocks to hurl at his pursuers. Ammunition readied, he whirled to face them.

"Come on, then, you scurvy dogs!" he challenged. "I'm ready for you now, by God!" he roared, hefting a rock at an innocent tree.

But not one of the baboons burst from the jungle in his wake!

Thank God! The brutes had given up, he realized after a few minutes with no sign of them. Sinking to his knees in the sand, he came close to blubbering again like an infant, so enormous was his relief. Indeed, his flight for his life—coming so hot on the heels of his joyful discovery of that beautiful clearing with all the fresh water they could ever need—had thoroughly shaken him. By God, he was trembling, sweating like a horse. Disgusted, he chided himself. *Coward! Yellow-bellied lout!* Before Newgate, he'd not been one to turn tail and run like a whipped cur—nay, not from anything!

It took some time before his chest had ceased heaving and his heart had slowed from an alarming gallop to a more normal trot. Once it had, he slowly retraced his path to the girl's side and flopped down on the sand beside her. She was, he soon realized, awake.

"You were gone for ages." Her husky, somewhat accusing voice, came to him as she sat up with her knees bent and her arms curled around them. There was color in her cheeks this morning, he saw, though her eyelids looked swollen and red, as if she'd been weeping while he was gone. "I was afraid you'd decided to leave me. In all honesty, I suppose I couldn't blame you if you had, sir. I'm sure I wasn't very . . . polite to you yesterday, was I? But my head hurt so, you see? And I was quite upset, you know, about everything." A shudder moved through her. "I'm heartily sorry if I offended you in any way."

"Apology accepted," Nathan said magnaminously. His narrow escape had left him in a forgiving, expansive mood. With a courtly air, he inclined his shaggy black head. "Speak no more of it."

"Thank you."

She ventured a wan smile that was like the sun coming out after a downpour, her lush coral lips parting entrancingly over twin rows of pretty white teeth. With the forbearance of a saint, Nathan resisted the urge to bite her neck, toss her to the sand, and bury his face between her breasts. Instead, he asked casually, "More coconut milk?"

"Hmm, please!"

He handed her one of the coconut halves he'd refilled earlier. She drank it in a single, greedy swallow, licking her lips like a kitten when she was done.

"Good?"

"Hmm, not just good—wonderful!" she exclaimed, and he basked in the sunlight of her praise. "Er, last night, you asked if I was hungry, do you recall? Well, I really wasn't then, but I confess, I find myself quite starved now." She paused, waiting expectantly for him to produce something to eat, much in the manner of a child waiting for a magician to whisk a rabbit from beneath his cloak, Nathan thought.

Watching the graceful way she flicked her lovely head to sweep tangled red-gold curls over her shoulder, he gulped. In truth, he almost choked. Christ! The ache was back in his loins, twice as pressing now. Aye. He had *something* he would dearly have loved to whisk out for m'lady's pleasure, right enough, but 'twas no blasted rabbit!

"I regret there's only some coconut meat," he managed to mutter through clenched jaws. "You can . . . er . . . scoop it out with that shell next to you—the one with the pointed edge. See it?"

"Why, yes, here it is." She took up the broken scallop shell and used it like a blade to pry small chunks of coconut meat from the woody bowl and pop them into her mouth. He caught a glimpse of pink tongue before her teeth closed around it, and grew dizzy imagining that same tongue buried wetly in his ear.

She munched with unladylike gusto, then swallowed. "Hmm. Good!" She dug with the edge of the shell a second time, but in her eagerness, the clumsy implement slipped, stabbing into her thumb. "Ouch!"

At once, Nathan scrambled over to her, positioning himself so that their thighs touched. "Let me see. Did you hurt yourself?"

"Nay, 'tis nothing . . . really. A little scratch, no more. Please, the fault is mine, sir," she protested, and hastily snatched her hand from his, for he was clearly intending to suck her injured thumb! She eyed him warily now, wondering if he might, in fact, be mad. Was that it? Was the dangerous *something* she'd sensed about him madness? "Um, everyone says I'm . . . clumsy."

His ebony head was so close to her fair one, the tendrils of red-gold that framed her brow and temples tickled his cheek. "Clumsy? You? Rubbish! You're nothing of the sort," he denied huskily, breathing deeply to inhale the warm, female scent that enveloped her like a subtle, provocative perfume. " 'Tis no task for a slip of a wench. Here. Let me show you how it's done."

Before she could protest, he'd slipped his right arm around her waist and smothered her small right hand with his own. He did likewise with their left hands, so that she was, to all intents and purposes, embraced by his arms, with his bare, hairy chest pressed against her spine.

Her closeness made him feel weak and dizzy—her adorable nape was so close to his lips—and oh, so blasted vulnerable! Pure lust overwhelmed him then. It drove out all notions of honor or noble denial. God's Teeth, was he an *animal*? Aye. And he wanted *her* to be an animal! Wanted the two of them to couple like rabbits on the sand! With a muffled groan, he surrendered to his desires, ducked his head, and pressed his lips to her downy nape, hoarsely entreating, "My sweet, darling Eve, surrender! Cease this game ye play with me ere I go mad from wanting you!"

Eve? Her name wasn't Eve. La, he really *was* insane! No sooner had the thought entered her head than she felt his mouth upon her throat. "What're you doing? Cease! Don't you dare slobber over me, you beast!" she cried. "Stop that licking—stop it at once!" So saying, she twisted violently from his arms and scrambled to her feet. Her turquoise eyes were flashing sparks of pure gold in her outrage as she whirled to face him, five feet and three inches or so of magnificent, furious womanhood, clothed gloriously in the tatters of her bodice and ragged red flannel petticoats. "What ails you, you lecherous rogue? Are you insane? A lunatic?"

"Aye, wench, I fear I am indeed quite mad—mad with wanting you!" Nathan growled. "Come, my sweet, let's be gloriously mad together!" He held out his arms in the faint, desperate hope that she might yet melt into them. But in answer, she lashed out with her foot, kicking sand in his face and eyes.

"*Wanting* me? What crawling gutter slop are you, to take such 'vantage of a helpless woman?"

" 'Helpless'? Egad, 'helpless' does you scant justice, mistress," Nathan observed dryly, spitting grit from his mouth. "Rather, you defend yourself most admirably with fists and feet."

"Hhrrumph! Lucky for me that I do, sir, 'else I would lie beneath you now, all virtue spent!" she countered, tossing her red-gold hair defiantly.

"Ah, yes. Indeed you shall . . . er . . . would," Nathan agreed in a wistful tone. "But enough bantering. Time is wasting, and I am not, alas, a patient man! Come, pretty doxie, let's talk business, hmm? Let's discuss fair trade and barter. Now, as well you know, due to our mutual misfortune, shall we say, I find myself lacking the coin so much beloved by your ancient profession. So, can we not fix a price on your favors in fish, say? Or fresh fruit?''

"Fix a . . . ? What! Surely I mistake your meaning, sir?'' she cried, indignant and scowling. Her eyes sparked dangerously. ''A price? For my favors, you say? Dear God, surely you do not—cannot!—mean to proposition me?''

He gritted his teeth. His jaw clamped tight with frustration and impatience. ''My meaning's clear enough, wench, 'less your wits be addled! Enough of these games! Give me a blasted tumble, and I'll pay in the coin of *this* realm.'' He grinned and would have fondled her nearest ankle, had she not abruptly stepped away. ''Some ripe bananas. A bowl of fresh coconut milk. Hell's Gates, I'll even throw in a fresh crab or two, if ye please me. Agreed?'' As he spoke, he rose to his feet, standing tall and threatening in his bare feet before he confidently took a stride towards her.

''Stay back! Not another step! How dare you proposition me as if I were a common harlot! Devil take your impudence, you scurvy rogue! I'd die first!'' she shrieked even as she whirled and fled him, dashing down the beach towards the idly lapping, turquoise water, swift as winking.

He started in pursuit, his heavier passage raising drifts of sand that slowed his pursuit.

So, the wench wanted to play games, did she? He grinned as he tore after her. The naughty little minx meant for him to pursue her if he would win her favors! Well, by God, she'd chosen the right fellow! When she finally surrendered, he'd show her what he was made of; the physical endowments that had made the ladies of London—married and single, high-born or humble—beg for his favors. When m'lady doxie lay in his arms, purring her pleasure, uttering cooing praises to his virility, she'd regret these wasted moments.

But to his dismay, his Eve did not flee along the wet sand at water's edge, leading him on the merry chase he'd anticipated. Rather, she plunged directly into the ocean, wading deeper and deeper into it. She made no attempt to swim, even when the

51

water reached her chin and threatened to close over her red-gold head. God's Teeth! Surely not? It looked for all the world as if she wanted to drown.

Drown, rather than yield to him?

"Foolish twit!". he roared, and sped down the beach into the water, after her. He leaped through the sparkling shallows, then struck out with long, powerful strokes the instant the lapping waves were waist deep.

He came alongside her in moments. Though her eyes were closed, she was making no effort to swim, but seemed, as he had feared, resigned to die. Determined, even.

With a foul oath, he wound his hand through her flowing hair and began towing her back to shore.

"Leave go, you brute! Let me drown! Let go of me!"

She struggled and tried to fight him off, threatening to sink them both. Hooking one arm under her chin, he swam with her that way, spluttering and blessedly silent.

Only moments later, he staggered up onto the beach with the wench dangling limply across his arms. She weighed no more than a goosedown quilt, now that he was rested, but with scant ceremony, he straightway dropped her to the sand in a tangle of shapely limbs.

"What the devil ails you, that you'd rather die than lay with me? 'Tis not as if you, a doxie wench, were untried, after all! Or are you?" he demanded suspiciously, sudden doubt filling his mind. Had he been wrong? Could she possibly be a virgin?

"Nnnooo!" she spluttered. "And if I was, what business is it of yours, anyway? Oh, go away, curse you, you bearded monster! Leave me be! Let me die in peace!"

Kneeling, he leaned across her, his palms planted on either side of her head so that she could not flee him.

"Die? Dear God, am I so ill-favored, you'd prefer drowning to my arms?" he asked in a wounded voice, reaching out to gently stroke her wet shoulder. Before she could answer, he ducked his head and licked beads of salt water from her satiny skin, like a cat lapping at a dish of cream. "Am I so very cruel,

52

you would kiss cold Death sooner than my warm lips?'' To his delight, she neither cringed away nor flinched in distaste but grew very still, seeming lost in sudden meditation. Emboldened, he nuzzled her adorable pink earlobe and murmured, "Well? What say you, my sweetmeat? Am I then so ugly? So cruel?''

"I . . . suppose not. Your face is overly hairy, mayhap, but perchance you are not completely repulsive beneath those whiskers. . . .'' *Humor the lunatic*, she told herself. *Tell him what he wants to hear. Play for time.* Perchance that way, she could yet escape him!

"Then why, pray, did you flee me, hmm?'' he demanded in a purry growl of a voice that made her shiver despite herself as he kissed the darling dimple at the corner of her mouth. "Why seek to drown yourself, when you've been granted a second chance at life, and all its many . . . pleasures?'' He cupped a ripe breast in his palm while she was distracted by his crooning voice, idly thumbing the dormant little nipple 'til it hardened beneath the thin stuff of her bodice.

"Because those I love are dead. Gone!'' she choked out. "What's left to live for, pray?''

"What? Why, this, dear heart! This! You must live for passion, if naught else. For passion—and for me.''

"Ha! 'Tis cold comfort you offer, sir!'' she hissed, recoiling from his touch. La! The arrogance of this hairy madman; the gall, to think *he* could make her want to live! In a shaky voice she added, "And I'm warning you, stop pawing and nuzzling me, you filthy lecher! Nay, you must not make so bold again—*no*! Stop it, you swine! Do not touch me so! I forbid you to—aagh!''

Nathan swallowed her protests with his kisses, stole her breath away as he claimed her coral lips with his own.

Oh, that mouth, that glorious mouth!

Now that she was in his arms, now that he'd fondled her breasts and tasted the sweetness of her soft lips and the velvet of her honeyed mouth, the ache in his loins was a raging monster. In truth, his manhood was vast: had grown to a lofty mast, a rearing shaft that prodded eagerly against m'lady's rounded hip.

"Ah, sweet! Ah, love . . . Ah, goddess mine, surrender. Let me worship you! Let my kisses be a balm to your grief."

"Never!" she spat out, tearing her mouth from his.

"Aye, vixen, they must—I shall!" he breathed raggedly, and kissed her again, boldly slipping his hand inside her fraying bodice. God's Teeth, the feel of her petal-soft flesh beneath his own rough touch! How he ached to tease the rosy, pebbled nubbins of her nipples, to suckle both raspberry gumdrops on his lips. To achieve his wicked end, he hooked an arm around her waist and rolled sideways. The maneuver brought her atop him, where—if she'd yet harbored any doubt—there could be no mistaking his arousal or his intentions.

"Damn you, you lecherous, whiskery rogue! Let gooo!" she yelled, her hair a tangle of wet strands about her face, spraying water everywhere as she struggled to escape him.

But Nathan had grown deaf. Blind. He heard naught now but the roaring crescendo of lust's melody in his ears. Saw nothing but her vivid, feminine beauty poised above him. Smelled nothing but the briny bouquet of her damp, silky flesh, a perfumed aphrodisiac that tortured his senses. Grasping the fronts of her bodice, he yanked it down an inch, then two.

'Twas then she saw the raised welts of callus about his wrists—the marks left by iron shackles—and knew what it was that had alarmed her about the man from the first. Her savior was a *convict*, no less—one of the *Hester*'s transportees!

"You *bastard*!" she shrieked, punching him in the head.

Nonetheless, her rosy breasts spilled from their lacy confines to jiggle but inches from his lips. Transported by the sight of those rosy mounds, each crested by a puckered raspberry, Nathan closed his eyes. His expression that of a communicant with the blessed Host melting upon his tongue, he opened his mouth to sample her forbidden fruits.

"Why, coz! Can it really be you?" squealed an incredulous voice. *"Oh, God be praised, it* is. *It truly, truly is!"*

Chapter Four

Racing down the beach towards them came a fair-haired girl wearing a tattered green gown she'd bunched up around her thighs. Bare-legged, she was skipping joyously over the white foam of the surf that raced up the beach, waving and halooing madly as she came on.

Plodding behind her was a short, wizened little fellow. His weathered complexion, rolling gait, and white canvas drawers marked him instantly as a sailor. To Nathan's surprise, his "Eve" let out a wild whoop of recognition on seeing the incongruous pair.

"Caroline! Jack!"

She rolled off him, sprang to her feet, shot him a venomous yet triumphant glare, then raced to meet the pair, all notions of suicide clearly abandoned.

In a muddle of arms and hair, the two young women exchanged fierce hugs, kissing and squealing like piglets to find each other safe.

Nathan dawdled along in the girl's wake with markedly less

enthusiasm, making a supreme effort to recover his composure and hoping fervently that the lusty state in which the wench had left him would not be noticed by the newcomers.

Meeting the eyes of the sailor over the giddy girls' heads, Nathan nodded in sober recognition. Hostility filled him momentarily as the older man's knowing blue eyes at once strayed to his wrists. The irons had left tell-tale scars and bands of thick callus upon them, so there'd be no hoodwinking this shrewd salt, should he have cared to try. Which he didn't.

"Jack, isn't it?" Nathan acknowledged quietly.

"Aye, lad. Jack Warner, ship's carpenter. And you'd be . . . Kincaid, was it?"

Nathan nodded. "Aye, Jonathan Kincaid. Nathan to my friends. I . . . er . . . believe I owe you my life, do I not? But for your timely release, I would have drowned like a rat in the *Hester*'s hold. My heartfelt thanks, sir," he added with feeling, extending his hand. Would Jack shake it? he wondered.

Jack would, and he did so firmly, though he shrugged and seemed embarrassed by Nathan's gratitude. "Give over, lad. I did wot any Christian oughta do when I unchained ye. Think no more o' it. Even convicts have a right t' die unfettered, I reckon. That bastard Harkabout would ha' left the lot o' ye sorry devils t' drown like rats! I couldn't let 'im do it." He turned his head and spat upon the sand to show his disgust. "As it was, better'n a hundred of 'em went down wi' the ship afore I could free 'em."

"Why, hello there!" the young girl exclaimed then, turning and apparently noticing Nathan for the first time. She pulled free of the older girl's arms and stared at Nathan with unabashed curiosity, even taking a step or two towards him. "My! You do have a most fearsome aspect, sir!" she declared, her sky-blue eyes dancing with mischief. "With those black whiskers, you're the very image of Captain Blackbeard, the pirate!"

"For the love of God, Caroline, hush, do!" his 'Eve'

56

scolded, but the younger girl ignored both the hand her companion raised to hush her and the alarm in her tone.

Nathan scowled, irritation filling him. Good God, what did the wench think? That he was such an ogre he might launch an attack on this babe-in-arms, simply because she spoke her mind?

"Alas, I'm not near as exciting as Captain Blackbeard," he apologized solemnly. "Just an unfortunate castaway, I'm afraid, stranded without knife nor razor, Mistress . . . ?"

"Caroline. Mistress Caroline Amberfield, of Amberfield Acres. I'd introduce you two, but I suppose you've already met my cousin, Lady Mariah Downing?"

"Oh, indeed, I have," Nathan said with a wry, pointed look for the older girl's benefit. "You might go so far as to say we're practically *intimates*, are we not, Mistress Mariah?" The salacious double entendre gave him malicious pleasure.

"How nice! And isn't Mariah simply wonderful?" Caroline declared, casting an adoring look at her cousin, whose furious expression following Nathan's barbed comment quite contorted her lovely features.

"Aye, indeed she is. 'Wonderful' hardly begins to describe that paragon of gentle womanhood, Mistress Caroline," Nathan agreed, a hint of mockery curling his upper lip.

"I know. I'm so very lucky to have her! You see, she's not only my cousin. She's also my dearest friend *and* my chaperone," Caroline bubbled, dimpling merrily as she added, "though I doubt I'll need a chaperone for quite some time, don't you?"

Nathan made another, deeper bow from the waist. "Your servant, Mistress Caroline Amberfield," he said cordially, flashing her an amused grin. With her saucy, outspoken manner, her creamy page-boy of blond hair, and her dimpled baby-face, pretty Mistress Caroline was a winning little baggage indeed. "As I also remain *your* servant, dear, wonderful Lady Mariah," he added. There was more than an edge of sarcasm to his tone now as he bowed deeply once again, this time in her cousin's direction.

As their gazes collided over Caroline's blond head, Mariah made no attempt to mask her dislike of him. Rather, it blazed from her turquoise eyes like rockets of golden fire!

"And if I might make so bold, sir, your name is . . . ?"

"Caroline, for shame!" her cousin admonished again.

"Nay, Lady Mariah. Don't scold the young lady. 'Tis Kincaid, Mistress Caroline. Jonathan Kincaid. My friends—among whom I trust you will soon number—call me Nathan."

"Master Kincaid," Caroline echoed, bobbing him a curtsey, "um, I mean, Nathan, 'tis an honor to meet you."

"The honor is mine, dear ladies. Well, now. Our introductions completed, shall we adjourn to the shade of the palms?" Nathan suggested, gesturing to the sorry little camp where he and Mariah—the paragon—had passed the night. It was as if they were at a ball in Kensington, rather than stranded on some South Seas island, he mused. "Ladies, if you'll follow me. . . ?"

Arms linked and chattering like parrots as they recounted their respective rescues, the two young women trailed after him and Jack to the coconut grove.

"*Lady* Mariah?" Nathan queried of Jack in a low, doubting tone. "Does the girl speak truly, or is the title false?" It was possible. He knew the madam of a bawdy house in London who called herself "Duchess"—and insisted she be treated as such.

"Aye, lad, that un's a real lady—in title *and* in manner." He shot Nathan a look that said he knew full well what he and the girl Caroline had interrupted and that he didn't approve.

Nathan felt surprisingly guilty beneath the little man's accusing blue gaze. Though the twinge lasted only a second or two, it did, however, serve to rid him of all notions of arousal.

"Lady Mariah was quite recently widowed, I do believe, the poor leddy," Jack explained. "Then her father passed on soon after. So it was that, findin' 'erself with neither family nor home, her ladyship accepted her uncle's invitation to run his household in Port Jackson, an' take charge o' his daughter, Mistress Caroline fer 'im. The little wench's father is Paul Amberfield—him what be Governor o' the convict colony, see?''

Nathan groaned. Egad! His "mermaid," his sultry Eve; was actually a respectable widow, was she? He grimaced. Bad enough he'd believed the girl a doxie and propositioned her as such; now 'twould seem she had highly-placed relatives, including a doting uncle who would probably see him flogged for his lecherous advances, were they ever rescued!

"Somefin' wrong, Kincaid?" Jack asked with a sly chuckle and a crafty grin. "Of a sudden, ye look like curdled cream, lad!''

"Nay, nothing of import," Nathan denied staunchly, scowling as the two young women flopped down beneath the coconut trees' shade. Studiously ignoring him, though Nathan fancied she was actually very much aware that he was still watching her, Mariah proceeded to introduce Caroline to the delights of coconut milk and its delicious "meat," while the two men drew aside to converse in low voices.

"So, tell me. Are we four the sole survivors of the *Hester*'s sinking?''

"Paggh! Would that we were!" Jack scoffed. "Nay, lad, we're not all by a long mark—tho' you and Lady Mariah seem t' be the only ones wot made it safely over the reef. There's a handful o' the *Hester*'s crew, such as meself, wot made it, tho' we washed ashore around the point aways. The lads'll be here shortly, along wi' a few old laggers wot were of a mind t' join us.''

"Convicts willing to cast their lot with the *Hester*'s crew?" Nathan's ebony brows rose in surprise. "Rare birds, surely?''

"Some might think so, aye. But from what I've seen of 'em, they be decent enough fellows at heart, rough an' ready, ordinary lads with honest natures. Them wot fell by the wayside an' had no place t' turn but thievery and cut-pursing. Most of 'em's only crime was t' steal victuals t' feed their nippers. I ask you, wot's England a-comin' to, eh, Kincaid, when a man's transported for tryin' t' feed his family best he can?''

"What, indeed. Or when an innocent man is found guilty and sentenced to hang.''

Jack's head jerked up at this. His blue eyes hardened. "All convicts deny their guilt, Kincaid,'' he observed softly.

"I know it. Nevertheless, I was—am—innocent of the crimes for which I was made scapegoat. They would have hanged me, had my father not paid a king's ransom to my goalers. By dark of night—less than six hours from my tryst with the gallows—I was spirited out of Newgate and taken aboard the Hulks in the Thames. Two days later, I was rowed out to the *Hester* and shackled in her hold. The rest you know.'' There was a grimness to his leaf-green eyes now, a deep and abiding sadness in their depths as they met Jack's without flinching.

After searching his face for what seemed an eternity, Jack nodded. He clamped his callused hand over Nathan's bare shoulder and squeezed. "You don't have t' convince me, lad. I'm no one of import.''

"On the contrary, you saved my life, Jack. That makes you of the utmost import, to my mind! I would have you, of all men, know 'twas a life *worthy* of saving, for I am truly innocent. And someday I mean to prove it and clear my name.''

"Be damned if I know why, but I believe you. And that being so, take a word of advice from a friend. Like it or not, stick with us lads from the *Hester*, Kincaid. If you're innocent, you'll want nothing to do with Ruskin's foul lot.''

Nathan's slash of ebony brows rose. Green eyes hardened in a face yet grey with prison pallor. "Ruskin? Not that towering bully of a Scot, Angus Ruskin?''

"Aye, that's 'im. 'Bloody' Ruskin, some call him. He's as nasty a piece of offal as ever lived, that 'un. He and his covey of cutthroats, thieves, and whores have set up camp back there, by the swamps around the point.'' Jack jerked his chin in the direction of a narrow spit of land to the west from which he and the girl had arrived.

"Swamps?"

"Aye, by God. Them stinking mangrove swamps're everywhere!"

"Any fresh water to be had?"

"Nay, 'tis brackish and foul t' boot, with swarms o' tiny flies that sting like the devil swarmin' over it. Worse yet," Jack lowered his voice to an unhappy rasp, "I seen a crocodile there—a great armored beast just a-sunning itself in the shallows. Proper ugly it were, an' all." Jack shuddered. "If there's one thing Jack Warner can't abide, it's crocodiles an' such!"

"Hmm. I find myself with a similar loathing for baboons," Nathan confessed with a grim smile. Briefly, he told Jack about his hair-raising experience earlier that day.

Jack whistled softly. "'Strewth! A lucky escape, by all accounts! But you found fresh water there, ye say?" he pressed eagerly.

"I did. As fresh and clear as any mountain pool."

"Then God be praised! Ruskin's sorry lot've found none back there—not that they've stirred themselves t' look very far! They helped themselves to a cask or two of the ship's grog rations to quench their thirst. God knows how they managed t' save it in that gale! Right now, they're after celebrating their deliverance as might be expected of that wicked sort." He grimaced and rolled his eyes.

"I can well imagine."

"'Twas on the young leddy's account that we came on ahead of the others. Ruskin's lot were rollin' drunk, t' the very last footpad an' bawd. I got five daughters of me own, Kincaid, an' of a certainty, such fornicatin' and wild goings-on are no sight for an innocent little lass like Mistress Caroline. Wot's more, I didn't care overmuch for the way Ruskin was startin' t' eye us lads from the *Hester*'s crew. He'd as soon be rid o' the lot o' us, I wager."

Nathan murmured understanding, not surprised that the convict seemed eager to rid himself and his cronies of the *Hester*'s crew, who represented law and justice. Unease filled him as he digested all that Jack had said. Crocodiles, eh? Mosquitoes, too, from the sound of it. And now, "Bloody" Angus Ruskin, of all men!

Ruskin's fiercesome reputation was one he'd earned, Nathan knew only too well. He'd come to blows with the Scot his very first night in Newgate by refusing to relinquish his boots to the strutting ox. They'd fought tooth and nail on the filthy stone floor of the Common Felons' Ward, egged on by the howls and curses of the other inmates, until the turnkeys had intervened and hauled them apart. Nathan had been brutally flogged for inciting a riot, while Ruskin had lost his two front teeth— and a fair measure of his cronies' respect.

The incident had left the Scot with a seething hatred for Kincaid—a hatred tempered with grudging respect that had ensured the huge lout gave him wide berth. However, though a prisoner himself, Ruskin had continued to all but run the gaol by virtue of his cruelty.

Nathan had been assigned to a solitary cell to await his hanging, following his trial and sentencing. He'd not come into contact with Ruskin since that night, though he'd heard tales of other incidents involving the man that'd made his blood run cold.

Ruskin was by nature a monster, a strutting bully who'd ruled his prison domain with such brutality even his foul gaolers, themselves little better than vicious animals, had feared him and jumped to his bidding!

The idea of being stranded on a deserted island with Ruskin and his ilk was not one Nathan cared for a whit. A sudden foreboding filled him. Sooner or later, Ruskin would prove the serpent in this Garden of Eden, he was sure.

"Well, lad, enough yarning! What say we set to an' make camp? Hunt about for some dry wood, an' I'll build us a fire," Jack offered. "Afore we know it, it'll be dark again, and I allow I'd sleep easier with a fire blazing. Here. This'll get things started.'' The ship's carpenter withdrew something from his jersey.

To Nathan's surprise, the parcel contained several beautifully oiled and cared-for carpenter's tools—chisels and such— and a tinderbox, all dry as a bone, wrapped in an oilskin covering. The tinderbox also contained a pair of whalebone fishhooks.

"Aye, Jack, I'll gather driftwood," Nathan offered, a gleam of anticipation in his green eyes now. "There're dry coconut husks under yon sailcoth that'll have your fire started in no time. And," he grinned, "while you tend to our hearth, sweet wife, I'll hook us the finest, freshest fish you've ever tasted."

" 'Sweet wife,' indeed!" Jack grinned at his cheekiness, liking the younger man more and more by the minute, convict or nay. "Good lad! My innards are fair chompin' on themselves, I'm that starved!"

"He's going somewhere," Caroline murmured, nudging her cousin in the ribs as she peeked beneath her dark blond lashes. "Look! There he goes now."

"I told you, coz, I don't give tuppence where the brute goes. And nor should you! Oh, stop staring at him, do! He'll see you."

"Why shouldn't I look? Shorn and shaved, I think he'd prove quite the handsomest man I've ever seen. And looking costs naught, after all," Caroline added saucily.

"Handsome? Him? Never! Now, you just listen to me. We'd be best served if you forgot all about watching that rogue and instead set your mind to more important matters. Our predicament, for one. We're stranded here, after all, Caroline. *Stranded!* Two helpless women, alone and at the mercy of God-knows-how-many men!"

"There're twenty-three, counting your Master Kincaid and Jack—tho' Jack's a dear, and no danger to our virtue at all."

"All right, twenty-three men, then. And he's not *my* Master

Kincaid,'' Mariah corrected in an angry tone, "but a lunatic! Dear God, we'll be lucky to survive a week with our virtue intact.''

"Oh, pooh! Your virtue was squandered ages ago," Caroline reminded her pointedly. "As for mine . . . well, I think I'd rather like to lose it. It's such a bore, being a sweet little virgin.''

"Caroline!''

"Well, it is. I'd far rather be known as a scarlet woman. Someone mysterious and scandalous, like one of Uncle Harry's mistresses.''

"Bite your tongue! 'Tis wickedness to speak ill of the dead!. You know very well that my father kept no mistresses—.''

"He did, too—up until the very day he died—and you know it, Mariah. Everyone did! In fact, I heard Cook telling Poppy at the funeral that she wouldn't wonder if Uncle Harry's 'over-indulgence' hadn't brought on his death. Come, coz! Surely you're not so naive? You couldn't really have believed those gaudy women at your papa's funeral were his distant cousins?'' Seeing Mariah's expression, Caroline crowed triumphantly, "Ah ha, I thought not! No one could be *that* gullible, not even you. And as for us being rescued, you know very well that my papa will come for us just as soon as may be. He'll find me somehow, I know he will, even should he have to sail the seven seas to do it!'' the girl declared with utmost confidence. "It's just a matter of waiting it out. In the meantime, you should try to unbend a little, coz. Make the most of things, and at least try to enjoy the novelty of it all. Imagine, the two of us surviving a shipwreck and being castaways on a deserted island What a lark! When we reach New Holland, I shall write an accounting of my adventures.''

"It's easy for you to put on a brave face. You're very young and have no sense of propriety. You forget, I'm but newly widowed and still in mourning.''

"Mourning, oh, fiddlesticks! I may be young, but I'm no hypocrite. You hardly knew Lord Downing before he sailed off to India. And what's more, I'm almost certain you couldn't possibly have loved him, even if you did marry him. For his title, was it? Or the immense fortune you thought he had, but he didn't? Either way, I'm glad he's dead and gone. You're far too good and sweet, and I thought Edward was simply horrid.''

With that breezy declaration, Caroline stuffed an enormous wedge of coconut meat into her mouth and munched upon it with undisguised relish. ''Hmm. Dis ids dewishus!'' she exclaimed with her mouth full, then swallowed. ''Much nicer than that awful slop from the *Hester*'s galley. Did he find you these?''

''By 'he' you mean Kincaid, I suppose?'' Caroline nodded. ''Yes, he did,'' Mariah admitted reluctantly, making a face. '''Twould seem, despite his obvious shortcomings, that your 'Captain Blackbeard' has some knowledge of these parts. He claims he sailed with the explorer, Captain James Cook.''

''He did?'' The younger girl sighed dreamily. ''How exciting!''

''*If* it were true. Alas, I fear the man's a liar, as well as a rogue,'' Mariah countered through gritted teeth.

''Surely not. He seems rather nice, and he's such a gentleman, for all that he's lost most of his clothes.'' Caroline giggled. ''Did you notice what a broad chest he has—and that forest of dark hair upon it? Oh, and those muscles! I swear, 'twas all I could do to keep from swooning when he smiled at me. And did you see how his blue eyes kindled and sort of sparkled, coz?''

''They're green.''

''What are?'' Caroline frowned.

''His eyes. They're not blue, they're green.''

''Oh. Well, whatever their color, they definitely sparkled.''

''Did they? I didn't notice,'' Mariah insisted, lying through her teeth. ''You see, *I* have more pressing matters with which to concern myself. Here I am with naught left me but my bodice and red flannel petticoats—and those little better than

65

rags. And, if what you tell me is true, large numbers of men will be arriving here at any moment.''

"You lucky thing. I wish I'd lost my gown," Caroline came back enviously. "This rag's so terribly hot with these long sleeves and this awful high neck. I'm sweating terribly just sitting here, doing nothing.''

"Horses sweat, my dear. Not ladies.''

Caroline rudely stuck out her tongue at this reproof. "I know, I'll take mine off, too! You won't feel nearly as uncomfortable if we're both in our under—''

"Caroline Elizabeth Amberfield, you'll do nothing of the sort!" Mariah exclaimed, horrified by the thought. "And, if you have any fondness for me at all, please try to contain your fascination for that dreadful man.''

"I shan't do anything of the sort. He's exciting. In fact, if you must know, I've decided to make a study of him until we're rescued. For my novel. A very lengthy study, I hope. He's just the sort of man I'd like to write about. A perfect model for my hero.''

"Your hero? Come, come. Surely you wouldn't choose a common criminal as a model for your novel's hero?" Mariah baited softly, for Kincaid had returned, carrying an enormous load of driftwood. "I wager that scoundrel would make a far better villain!''

"Nathan's a convict?" Caroline exclaimed, taken aback for once, much to Mariah's satisfaction. "Oh, surely you're mistaken. He can't be!''

"Look at his wrists, you little goose. Do you see?" she whispered, nodding her head towards Kincaid. The livid marks left by the shackles that had circled his wrists on the lengthy voyage were visible, even from some distance. "Do you believe me now? *That's* what I've been trying to tell you—the man's a rogue!''

"Upon my word, Widow Downing, I've never heard you sound so disparaging about anyone before," Caroline observed in a teasing tone. "Let me see . . . wasn't it you who told me

66

to always keep an open mind? To judge a person by their deeds rather than their reputation? To look for the good in my fellow man, rather than the bad?''

"I . . . well, yes, it was.''

"Well, *my* intuition tells me that you're wrong, and that Kincaid's good, convict or nay. You'll see, Mariah. The truth will come out. I'll wager the poor man was falsely accused. There's a tragic story there—and I mean to ferret it out.''

"No! I forbid you to go anywhere near him!''

"You do? Then tell me this: if Kincaid's so very bad, so terribly, awfully wicked, why were you kissing him when Jack and I happened along?''

In the ringing silence that followed her question, Mariah felt heat and color fill her cheeks. Even her earlobes seemed afire! So. As she'd feared, her cousin had seen them! Now she had no choice but to try to bluff her way out of this. "Because the man's a vicious animal! He gave me no choice in the matter!''

"He didn't? None at all?''

"None!''

"Truly?''

"On my oath, I swear it.''

"Oh, you ungrateful thing, you! You always have all the luck!'' Her blue eyes shone. "Tell me, coz, did you enjoy it? Were Nathan's kisses wonderful, exciting beyond your wildest dreams?'' Caroline demanded eagerly.

"They were loathsome. *He* was loathsome. The rascal deserves to be whipped for his boldness. What's more, his awful beard scratched dreadfully. Now, cease this nonsense at once. I swear, if you'll not stop badgering me, I'll box your ears!''

"You'd box my—why, coz, whatever's wrong? You've gone quite pink again of a sudden!''

"I have not.''

"You have, too.''

"'Tis the sun's heat, that's all.''

"But we're in the shade here. La, what can have caused such a flush?'' Caroline glanced surreptitiously over her shoulder and saw that Kincaid was standing perhaps twenty feet from where they sat.

The brute was leaning against the trunk of a coconut tree, sinewy brown arms folded across a bare chest. His legs were crossed at the ankles, and he appeared to be dozing upright, though Caroline observed that his half-closed, sensual green eyes were watching her flustered cousin like a hawk's, while the barest hint of a grin played about his lips!

"Hmm. You're quite certain 'tis just the *sun* that has you so flushed, dear coz?" she inquired sweetly.

"Quite," Mariah gritted, glowering.

"Good. Then if you're quite sure you're all right, I believe I'll go and ask Jack if he needs some help. Coming?"

With that, the minx scrambled to her feet and went to help Jack build the fire before Mariah could scold her further, flouncing off and leaving Kincaid, damn him, grinning at their antics with ill-concealed amusement.

It was for all the world as if he'd somehow guessed that he was the subject of their heated conversation, and the knowledge pleased him, Mariah thought, sneaking a peak at him herself now from beneath dark brown lashes.

To her mortification, he saw her watching him and saluted!

Mariah looked quickly down at her lap and muttered a curse under her breath. Pretending to be utterly absorbed in scooping chunks of coconut meat from the woody shell in her hand, she ate piece after piece, hardly knowing what her mouth and hands were doing. Drat Caroline, this was all her fault! Fond as she was of her young charge, there were times when she could cheerfully have strangled her.

Chapter Five

"Dear Lady Downing! May I say once again what a true joy it is to find you here, not only safe but looking quite as lovely as ever?"

"Really, you're too kind, Lieutenant Digby," Mariah thanked the young naval officer, feeling uncomfortable beneath the man's too-intense grey eyes, which seemed to harbor an unpleasant, predatory gleam.

Earlier, Digby had graciously loaned her his uniform jacket with which to cover herself, and to her regret, she'd been grateful to the point of gushing her thanks. The result was that now, the man seemed to think he had every right to monopolize her company. Well, the sooner he learned otherwise, the better it would be for both of them. "Lieutenant, if you'll excuse me, I believe I heard my cousin calling?"

"Really, dear lady, you simply must call me Warren."

Accepting the hand he reluctantly extended, Mariah flashed him an apologetic smile and stood. With a gracious incline of her head, she beat a hasty retreat towards one of the simple bamboo-pole and banana-leaf huts the men had erected for their shelter that afternoon.

Looking about her, Mariah found it hard to believe that so few had accomplished so much in such a short time. Their little camp looked positively civilized already, thanks to Kincaid's organizational skills, she admitted grudgingly.

There was a crackling fire-pit in the center of camp, the huge driftwood blaze contained by a circle of stones. The huts, rectangular in shape, with woven walls of banana leaves and supports of bamboo poles driven deep into the sand, were scattered in a wide circle about it, at a safe distance from wind-blown sparks. The savory smell of fish turning brown over red-hot logs hung on the sultry evening air now as the men filled their bellies and talked on into the deepening tropical twilight.

She and Caro had eaten first, at Jack Warner's insistence, wolfing down the tasty repast of tender, flaky fish and delicious ripe bananas with a gusto that was genuine, if far from ladylike! She felt remarkably well, all things considered. Her headache had long since vanished. Her belly was now comfortably full. It was a beautiful, balmy night, with hardly a breeze to stir the warm, flower-scented air, and the deep-blue sky was a-glitter with starry points of light and a glorious moon.

On such a night, she would have enjoyed sitting about the fire with the other survivors, listening to them talk of their mutual adventures and safe deliverance from the storm, or joining in on the making of plans and the men's conversation, just as she'd once derived pleasure from conversing with her father's friends. But alas, she had not been invited to join them, she thought, not a little put out. Nor had Digby's proprietary manner encouraged her to ask him to inquire if she might join the men's circle. Hence her pretense that Caroline had called her.

With a grumpy sigh, she turned away and ducked under the banana-thatched roof of the hut she was to share with her cousin.

Caroline was already sound asleep, she saw, flat on her back

70

and wearing an angelic smile. Not in the least sleepy herself, Mariah lay down anyway, shifting the sand beneath her until it was comfortably mounded beneath her body.

She closed her eyes and silently offered up a prayer of thanks that she and Caro had survived the *Hester*'s wreck, added a postscript for their continued deliverance, then expectantly waited for sleep to overwhelm her.

It did not. Instead, she lay wide awake, restlessly going over all that had happened that day, and the dreadful, stormy ones that had come before it, her thoughts finally returning to Caroline's saucy observations about Kincaid.

As her cousin had pointed out, if he were clean-shaven, his beard shorn and his ebony hair clubbed back in a queue, the shaggy brute would prove handsome indeed. Hot on the heels of imagining him thus shorn came the vivid memory of his hard, hot mouth upon hers; the dark emerald fires that had smoldered so fiercely in his eyes when he'd kissed and caressed her.

Warmth flowed to her cheeks in the darkness, for her memories were strangely enflaming. Curious, she touched a fingertip to her lips and slowly traced their softness, imagining as she did so 'twas his mouth that brushed them oh, so gently, then with increasing ardor and pressure.

Just thinking about the rogue acted like a spell upon her already awakened senses. Memories of the kisses he'd stolen so boldly that morning had unlocked the secret yearnings of her heart and body, rekindling fragile sensations and tender emotions she'd locked away, buried beneath the terror of that awful night when Edward had made her his bride, and had turned her girlish dreams of love and passion into nightmares. Now feathery pulses quickened and throbbed deep in her belly; delicate, tickling sensations fluttered in her loins, and her breathing was shallow and unsteady. Her cheeks burned as if aflame in the shadows. Dear Lord! Though no longer a virgin, she sensed her body's immediate and urgent reaction to her wanton thoughts of that . . . that man and was frightened.

71

She ran her hands down over her bosom and discovered that her breasts had grown taut within the confines of her bodice, her nipples now tight, rosy nubbins made tender by even the slightest friction. She felt tense, restless, as if her entire body were hungering, thirsting, wanting what it had never known but instinctively craved with every thrumming muscle, with every tingling nerve and aching fibre of her being.

She stifled a moan and rolled onto her side, her knuckles pressed to her mouth to prevent the voicing of her torment—and her terror. By all the saints, she *wanted* him! She lusted after that . . . that bold, woman-hungry rogue; desired a lowly convict, a felon who bore the marks of shackles about his bare wrists and the scars of a flogging upon his back; yet at the same time, she was terrified by the reckless yearning she felt for him.

How did she know that he would not be like Edward, her childhood playmate spiteful Edward, who'd played the charming gallant, the adoring suitor, until she wore his ring upon her finger? On their wedding night, her husband had taken her virginity with ruthless cruelty, and had relished her terror and pain each night that followed.

Damn! And damn Edward, may he rot in hell! Her body, awakened but never fulfilled, clamored to be tenderly loved. She yearned so to taste the breathless rapture that Mama had hinted was passion's prize, and which her own husband had so cruelly denied her. Who knew what Fate held in store for her on this isle? How many days yet remained to her life?

They would never be rescued, of that she was certain. She had pretended otherwise for her cousin's sake, to set Caro's mind at ease, but the odds were overwhelmingly against such a miracle. The *Hester* had been driven many hundreds of miles off course by the storm, leaving her sister ships and the supply vessel that had made up the sorry Second Fleet far behind. Moreover, Jack had told her there were countless small islands in this hemisphere—perhaps thousands. Far too many to make any search effective. Poor, poor Caroline! The child was crying for the moon if she truly believed her precious papa would ever find them. There were destined to pass the remainder of their days, weeks, months—perhaps even years—upon this isle.

Tears smarted behind Mariah's closed eyelids when she considered the hopelessness of their future. Damn it! She wasn't ready to give up on life, when hers had scarce begun! Before she died, she wanted to know what it was like to be gently loved by a man. To feel her body unfurl like the petals of a flower, opening and blossoming in the tender warmth of his passion. To lay to rest forever the horrid spectre of Edward looming over her in the dark of night, his amber eyes aflame like the eyes of a tiger, panting and rasping in the shadows like a wild, rutting beast as he lay cruel hands upon her and took his pleasure again and again.

Dizziness brought her close to swooning where she lay. Her limbs trembled with the horror of her memories. Was she brave enough to do it? Dare she grab hold of the destiny Fate had handed her and wrest what little snippets of happiness she could from it?

Aye! a small, insistent voice urged. *Aye, Mariah! You can do it. Edward is dead and gone, and you are free! Take the chance!*

Why not, indeed? she decided breathlessly. After all, there were no censuring eyes to condemn her behavior here. There was no one to impress with her virtue—or lack of it. She was her own mistress, and besides, what had she left to lose? Naught but her heart, came the answer, and surely it was too battered, too hardened, to ever be broken by a handsome convict with a pirate's swagger and a pair of twinkling green eyes.

"Kincaid, you've made me want you, damn your black heart!" she murmured tremulously on the shadows, fingering the beams of moonlight that slanted through the gaps in the banana thatch with shaking fingers. Now all that remained was to discover whether Kincaid yet wanted her—and if he did, whether she was truly brave enough to see his seduction through to its logical end.

* * *

While Mariah tossed upon her sandy bed, her sleep plagued by naughty thoughts of Nathan Kincaid, the object of her obsession had all but forgotten her!

Once the crew of the *Hester* had joined him and Jack at the cove, endless discussions had ensued about their plight. Solutions had been sought to the inevitable problems they would face in the struggle for survival. These had continued even as Jack gutted the pile of fish Nathan had caught, one of the newcomers then roasting them on a rack of green branches set over the fire-pit.

The others had been eager to do their share to contribute to the feast, and so, with warning about the dangers they might encounter, Nathan had sent several of the men into the jungle in search of ripe bananas. He'd set others to husking the huge mountain of fallen coconuts he'd gathered. The results of their combined efforts had been a satisfactory and surprisingly substantial meal for them all.

As they congregated about the fire with full bellies and restored hope that evening, the question of a fresh-water supply had been the first and most pressing one raised. Their relief was great when Nathan disclosed that he'd discovered a plentiful source, although the pool lay hidden deep in the jungle and was guarded by a band of vicious baboons.

"With your permission, gentlemen, I plan to lead a party of perhaps a half-dozen men to the waterfall. Between us, I know we could put the fear of God into those hairy apes and send them packing!" His green eyes gleamed in the firelight. "We have a brace of pistols, a few cutlasses, and a musket or two between us, do we not? These—along with a goodly supply of rocks—should prove sufficient weapons for the task. But," he cautioned, "once we've secured the area for ourselves, a guard or two must be posted there at all times, in order to keep the beasts from returning." He looked around the circle of ruddy-faced men enjoying the fire Jack and Caroline had built and

74

the armloads of fish he'd caught. "I say we rotate these guards, turn and turn about, so that in due course, we'll each stand watch. 'Tis the fairest way. What say you?"

"I'm all for it," concurred Carmichael, the *Hester*'s mate. "It's a sound plan, and I'll be happy to stand my turn at watch. But . . . what about that wild cat you heard?"

"I'm more concerned about the baboons, to be honest, sir. You see, great cats hunt by night and sleep during the heat of day. And 'tis common knowledge they have a great fear of fire. I've given it some thought, and I believe we should build a second fire at the clearing itself—perhaps even place torches about the spot that can be lit after dark. The night watch must carry torches for their protection, as should anyone else who would leave camp after dusk. Agreed?"

All heads nodded sagely.

"There are twenty-three of us, excluding the young ladies. Can we hope to provide food for that many indefinitely?" asked one man doubtfully.

"Aye, we can, if we plan carefully," Kincaid reassured him. "There are enough monkeys in the trees above us to keep us supplied with meat for some time, failing any other game. There are also parrots by the thousands. The fish in these waters have no fear of man and all but throw themselves onto a hook! Fruit trees of various kinds are everywhere, too. 'Tis my reckoning we'd be best served if we divide our labors—choose some men to gather firewood, fruits, and such, elect others to fish, still others to hunt, and so on. The various tasks could be rotated so that no man would have cause to feel his talents were being wasted. And, in due course, each man would eventually become proficient at each task."

"*Your* reckoning, Kincaid? 'Pon my word, I confess I place little store upon a convict's reckoning!" The young naval lieutenant who'd loaned Mariah his jacket let out a derisive laugh. "And who would delegate these tasks, pray? Yourself?"

"Stow it, Digby. Let 'im wot knows best choose who does wot!" jeered Old Peg, a one-legged, pot-bellied convict who'd thrown in his lot with the *Hester*'s crew rather than Ruskin's lot. He wore a blue neckerchief tied about his balding head, and the tarnished silver ring in his left earlobe made him look like a pirate as he hitched himself to standing. "Nowww, siddown, Digby, there's a good li'l' lad," Old Peg urged in a crooning voice, prodding the lieutenant hard in the belly with the point of his wooden peg-leg so that Digby abruptly sat down. "And while yer sittin' there, ye snot-nosed, lily-livered little weasel, shut yer bloomin' yap so's the other can talk!" A wheezing chuckle followed his words.

Muffled laughter rippled around the circle, for Digby was none too popular with his fellow marines or the crewmembers, though one senior marine did complain loudly, "Now see here, you old devil, leave Lieutenant Digby be. Show a little respect for your betters, why don't you!"

"Bugger givin' 'im respect, cock! I seen 'is lordship here climbin' over his own men t' be first in the boats when the *Hester* went down, I did! Let 'im *earn* our respect, like other blokes do!" snarled Peg, his good humor evaporating.

"It seems you've forgotten your place, my friend," Digby snarled, clearly beside himself with anger at Peg's accusations. "I'll be damned if I'll let a gimpy old lagger like you call me a coward! No, not a chance, sir! I demand satisfaction for your insults!"

"And who be you callin' a gimpy ole lagger, then?" demanded another convict, one whom everyone called Big Ben on account of his small stature—which in no way affected his ego. "You've no call t' talk t' poor Ole Peg that way! 'Twas just as he said—I seen yer meself!"

"You say so? Well, we'll see about that!"

As he spoke, Digby leaped to his feet and lunged across the circle. Spitting on his fists, Big Ben did likewise. Nathan saw the flash of the blade Digby now held and gained his feet in a heartbeat.

"Enough! We'll have none o' that here, my lads!" he snapped.

As others sprang to overpower Big Ben, Nathan's fingers clamped about Digby's wrist. "Drop the blade!" he ordered crisply, his tone that of a man accustomed to command—and equally accustomed to being obeyed.

"Damn you to hell, Kincaid!" Digby panted. "I'll not surrender my weapon to a bloody convict!"

"On the contrary, you will," Nathan ground out. He tightened his grip until the man's fingers relaxed, suddenly numb. The weapon fell harmlessly to the sand.

"All right. You've won. Now, unhand me, you bastard!" Digby hissed, his grey eyes spewing hatred.

"Your word you'll return to your place?" Nathan growled. "Your word you'll let this pass? Come on, man, speak up— and smartly—else I snap your damned wrist in two!"

"Aye, blast you, you have my word. Now, let go!" Digby agreed sullenly.

With a curt nod of satisfaction, Nathan released him. He watched with narrowed eyes until Digby had sulkily regained his seat between Carmichael and Surgeon Love, then returned to his own place in the circle.

"I reckon this 'ere little dispute brings us to another question, don't it, gentlemen?" Jack spoke up suddenly, to Nathan's surprise. The little man was not overly talkative by nature, he'd fancied until now, and was not one to push himself forward. "We need a leader, we do. A captain, if yer like. Someone who says wot's wot, and wot's not, an' has the authority to see his orders carried out."

"Jack's right. We should elect a leader," agreed the ship's surgeon, Martin Love. "Any volunteers?"

"I'd be honored to serve you all in that capacity," Digby declared pompously, standing again.

A chorus of groans greeted his offer.

"Gawd love us, lads, 'ark at 'im! Not a bleedin' moment ago, he was ready t' slit Ben's throat, an' now he's up on his feet like a bleedin' jack-in-a-box, an' wants ter be captain. Pipe down, you bloomin' arsehole, while we pick someone we

77

respects!'' Old Peg got a guffaw of laughter from his fellow ''laggers'' or convicts, of which there were four in all.

''Lieutenant Digby has as much right as anyone else here to volunteer, Peg. I'll thank you to pipe down yourself,'' Nathan snapped, fixing a steely eye on Peg.

To his surprise—and everyone else's—the garrulous old troublemaker had the grace to look ashamed of himself. He hung his head with a muttered, ''Right you are, Kincaid. Beg'n yer pardon, Leftenant.''

Nathan continued. ''The choice of a leader should be put to a vote, with a show of hands. Lieutenant Digby has offered his services. Does anyone else wish to stand? How about you, Mr. Carmichael?'' The master-mate, who'd been second in command aboard the *Hester*, was an obvious choice for the job.

''I'll stand, if you fellows insist. But I give you fair warning, I'm not the best man for the job, for I have little knowledge of these climes, nor do I know how best to go on in our straitened conditions.''

''Fair enough. 'Tis best to be honest about it. How about you, Doctor?''

''I'm afraid not, Kincaid. My talents lie in other directions. But what about yourself? You've done a damned fine job of running things so far. And 'twould appear you have the working knowledge of how best to survive on this island, which most of us lack.''

Nathan shook his head. ''You flatter me, Doctor. I have some small experience, true. But I doubt the other gentlemen would accept a convict as their leader.'' A ghost of a smile hovered about his lips.

''On the contrary,'' disagreed Matherson, a quiet, scholarly fellow who'd said nothing 'til now. A botanist by profession, and the only other civilian survivor from the *Hester* except for the two young women, the man had been commissioned by the Royal Geographical Society to draw, for scientific purposes, the exotic varieties of flora and fauna that abounded in the new colony.

"For myself," Matherson continued, "I have no such prejudices, Kincaid. Today, you have proven yourself an intelligent and resourceful fellow. 'Tis fair to say that every man here tonight owes you a debt of thanks for his full belly and for shelter from the elements! Furthermore, 'tis my firm belief that the *Hester*'s sinking was an act of God. We have been stranded here by Divine Providence, for what purpose only God knows. If we are meant to survive, we must do so together—in which case, we cannot afford to dissent or consider ourselves better or worse than our companions. Rather, we must be equals, with each man dependent on the other. 'Tis true that in England we were convict, sailor, or scholar. Here, however we must of necessity be equals."

"Well said, Mr. Matherson! I didn't think you had it in you!" approved Carmichael with a broad grin.

As the others, with the exception of Digby, uttered ayes of agreement, the mate clapped Matherson across the back. The shy botanist grinned and ducked his head in a mixture of embarrassment and pleasure.

"All right, gents, who's for Kincaid, then?" Jack demanded. "Let's see a show o' hands!"

To Nathan's amazement, the vote was almost unanimous.

He, a convict, had been voted master of Eden!

Chapter Six

After the others had sought the shelter of their huts for the night, or else fallen asleep where they sat in the circle of warmth given off by the fire, Nathan retrieved Digby's knife from the sand. He turned it over, testing its sharpness with the ball of his thumb and finally deciding the morrow would be soon enough to return the weapon to the hot-tempered fool. Tonight, he had a purpose for such a blade.

Thrusting the dagger into his belt, he cast a quick look about camp to ensure that all was well, nodded to Carmichael and a young cabin boy named Timmy Something-or-other who'd volunteered to stand the first watch, and strode off down the beach in search of solitude.

'Twas one of life's little ironies that he'd been chosen leader of these men, he considered, for once upon a time, many years ago, it had been his father's wish that he become an officer in the King's Navy and learn to lead men. He grinned, for the youth he'd been then had fought such a course like an unschooled colt fights its master's reins.

The year 1775 had found Nathan restless and rebellious, quarreling with his father at every turn—or so it had seemed to him. Their often senseless arguments had almost driven his mother to distraction, for she was a genteel, serene woman who abhorred discord in her home.

While he'd not wished for a moment to cause the dear lady any unhappiness, Nathan had been determined, as are most lads of that age, to make his own mark upon the world in his own way, with no help from his father. Consequently, he'd hotly rejected the career chosen for him by Simon Kincaid. He recalled that day with a rueful shake of his head.

He had been summoned to the library of Linden Hall, the family estate near Dover. His father had glanced up from behind his desk as he entered.

"Ah, there you are, Jonathan! Sit down, my boy. Sit down," Simon had said as he'd closed the account book before him with a decisive snap and returned his quill to the brass inkstand.

"Good morning, Father. *Ma mère* said you wanted to speak with me, sir."

"Indeed I do, Jonathan—and upon a matter of some import. But first, will you take some Canary against the chill?" It was obvious from Jonathan's warm yet casual attire that his youngest son had but recently returned from riding the headlands above the chalk cliffs. The wind that blew inland off the frigid North Sea had whipped ruddy color into his cheeks and given a fine brilliance to the striking green of his eyes. His handsome dark looks were a legacy of his mother's Breton side of the family, Simon mused, as was his romantic streak and the stubborn independence of his nature.

"Thank you, but no, sir." Jonathan whisked back the tails of his broadcloth coat to take a seat. He rubbed his hands together to warm his numbed fingers. For all that there was a blazing fire in the hearth, about which his father's gun-dogs huddled, the library was chilly. This morning, the fragrant smoke of crackling pine logs was mingled, not unpleasantly, with the musty smell of the fine books that lined the room's walls, the aromatic scent of the snuff his father used, and the familiar odor of wet hounds.

"Well, my boy, I believe felicitations are in order. Today is the sixteenth anniversary of your birth."

"Thank you, yes, it is, sir," Nathan confirmed.

"And how did you find the grey mare I scoured the length and breadth of England to find?" Simon had asked, and his eyes had twinkled. "Is she to your liking?"

Nathan's smile had been broad. "She's a damned fine little lady, sir, in every respect. Why, I've rarely seen such spirit or stamina! My thanks to you, sir. I'll take excellent care of her."

"I know you will, my boy. Sixteen years, eh? An exciting age! At sixteen, you're no longer a boy but a man, with the world at your feet and your mark yet to make upon it," Simon continued. "How I envy you! I was but sixteen myself when your grandfather passed on. The running of the Kincaid estate, the farms, and business fell to me from that day on, and it was no easy burden for a mere lad to shoulder. But, it built strong character within me, and so I have no regrets.

"Now. The matter I wish to speak to you about. Had it been left to me, I would have had this conversation with you two years ago, when you reached fourteen. As it was, I postponed it 'til now at your *maman*'s request. As you know, she's a tender-hearted woman, and I suppose she's reluctant to see the last of her chicks fly the nest. I hope—in my indulgence of her whims—I have not waited too long and done you grave disservice as a father."

"Disservice? I don't understand, sir?"

"Why, we must act, and act soon, Jonathan, if you're to make something of yourself in this world! And so to that end, I have this past month taken certain steps to assure your future."

"And what steps would they be, sir?" Jonathan had inquired, his guts clenching. Please God, the answer he dreaded would not be forthcoming. . . .

His father, a tall, striking man, who shunned wigs and instead wore his greying hair clubbed back into a queue tied with a ribbon at the nape, stood and strode to the window. Drawing aside a long velvet drapery, he surveyed the grounds of his estate without speaking for a moment or two. A sweeping vista of a woodland park with lofty fir trees and shy spotted deer opened up, then was gone as he released the hanging. "Steps to ensure you a challenging, adventurous career that I'm certain an intelligent, active young man such as yourself will heartily approve."

Without further ado, his father had gone on to inform him that he'd decided his future lay in a career with His Majesty's Royal Navy. He'd added that he'd purchased Jonathan a lieutenant's commission in that service, so that after a respectable interval at the Portsmouth Naval Academy, he might go to sea with the rank befitting a gentleman. By joining the Royal Navy, he added, Jonathan would see something of the vast world beyond England, gain in maturity and knowledge, learn to both accept and dispense discipline, and acquire all the skills needed to lead lesser men. Indeed, under the Navy's rigorous tutelage, he would in all ways "become the better man."

Here Simon Kincaid had paused, clearly anticipating that thanks would be forthcoming. Jeremy, his firstborn, would inherit the manor, the chandler's emporium, his three merchant vessels and the Linden estate, in due course, as well as the flourishing dairy and sheep farms that went with them. By Simon's reckoning, he had provided quite well for his second son's future, in a time when second sons often went begging or were jostled off to join the ranks of the clergy. Jonathan would inherit his mother's country home in the South of France in due course, but until then would pursue an exciting career Simon would have relished for himself, had his circumstances been otherwise. He was certain that Jonathan would applaud his decision.

But to his dismay, gratitude and applause had been far from Nathan's mind. Rather than thanking his father, his eyes had first flashed with anger, then grown stony with obstinacy. Let his older brother, he'd argued hotly, do their father's bidding as meekly as any mouse. For his part, he'd have none of it. Join the Navy, be damned! Rather, he planned to go to London and there apprentice himself to the popular portrait painter, Joshua Reynolds, if the artist would take him on as an assistant.

Simon had been thunderstruck by this revelation. "What's this? You'd sooner paint pretty pictures and fritter your life away like a fop than embrace a gentleman's calling?" his father had bellowed, enraged. "Damn my eyes, what are you, son? A simpering sodomite with a fondness for pretty boys?"

"You know damned well I'm nothing of the sort, Father." Young Nathan had been filled with indignation, for if anything, 'twas common knowledge at Linden Hall and in the outlying villages that he loved the wenches rather *too* well. Just a month earlier, his father had been forced to turn off one of the chambermaids with whom he'd been caught dallying. "Whatever you may say, there is nothing unmanly or amiss with an artist's life—or the men who choose it."

"Be that as it may, you are *my* son. You will forget this nonsense and prepare to leave for the Academy within the week!"

"Nay, sir, I shall not. Even should you forbid me, I will pursue no other course, I swear it! My tutors have told me that I possess considerable talent in drawing. If Master Reynolds will but instruct me in oils and in painting technique, I know I'll make a fine showing. When my apprenticeship has been served, my portrait commissions will provide me a handsome living."

How pompous he'd sounded, Nathan recalled with a grin. How puffed up with the cocky certainty that youth imparts!

"*When* that time comes? You mean 'if,' you young fool— and who'll support you 'til then, eh? And by 'Reynolds,' I presume you mean that wastrel, Joshua Reynolds? Pah! The man's an untalented hack! He paints flattering portraits of silly, vain women—women with more of their husbands' money to waste than good sense!'' his father had scoffed in an effort to force his will upon him.

But Simon's arguments had been wasted. Jonathan had calmly repeated that he would be his own man. Outraged and disappointed by his son's cool defiance, Simon had snatched up his riding crop and started across the room, intending to thrash the young man into obedience and submission.

Jonathan endured but one stinging stripe across the back before his own temper snapped. ''By God, sir, you will not do this! I'm a grown man, not a lad in skirts to be thrashed like a pup!'' he growled, growing white about the lips as he jumped to his feet. ''If we cannot agree, then let's discuss this like men.''

''Men, eh? Why, you young pup, real 'men' don't become painters, don't ye know? And what's more, we'll see who's grown or nay!'' Simon Kincaid had bellowed, lunging at him a second time.

Already only an inch or two shy of his adult six feet three inches, and broad of shoulder even then, Nathan had easily wrested the whip from his father's fists. It had snapped like matchwood in his powerful hands, then he'd flung the pieces into the fire.

''Leave Linden without my blessing and I'll disown you, boy—as God is my witness, I swear it!'' Kincaid had thundered, raising a trembling fist at the lad. ''And mark me well, Jonathan, should you pursue this foolish course, henceforth you'll be no son of mine. Nor will you again find welcome in this house!''

''I have prayed it would not come to this pass, Father, for I would sooner have your blessing than anything. But . . . if this is your final decision, then you leave me no choice. Goodbye,'' he'd said heavily as he quit the library.

After bidding farewell to his sobbing mother and to Jeremy, he left Linden Hall without once looking back.

Five days later he was to be found in London, both he and his dappled grey mare lodged at a plain but decent coaching-inn named the Royal George on the outskirts of the teeming city.

His strong back and strapping build had once again served him well there. The inn-keeper, Toby Loring, had said that Nathan could earn board and lodgings for himself and his mount by caring for the inn's teams, and by doing the heavier tasks that were needed about the tavern. Suffering from rheu-maticks of the back himself, the poor inn-keeper could no longer bring up the great barrels of ale, rum, Canary, and cider from the cellars, and his only son, Roger was hard put to do all the heavy labor alone. Furthermore, Loring had added, since it was evident that Nathan was an educated lad, if he could see his way to balancing the inn's accounting ledgers every few months and to writing what few letters might be needed, he would be paid a shilling a week for his troubles.

Nathan had readily agreed to Loring's generous offer, know-ing he was more than equal to the tasks. After a month's work, surely the penny or two he could save each week from his shilling would pay for painting instruction in the studios of Joshua Reynolds.

According, after only one month, with his mouth dry and his heart hammering, Nathan had presented himself at the studio of London's most popular portrait painter. He'd taken with him a leather satchel of his sketches, and there had met his hero face to face.

The words tripping over themselves in his excitement and nervousness, he'd told the man of his great love of drawing, and of his ambition to become as great a portrait painter as Reynolds himself.

"Very well. Show me what else you can do, Master Kin-caid," Reynolds had urged, setting the sketches aside.

Nathan's heart had sunk. "Alas, I have nothing else to show you, sir. Are these drawings not sufficient?"

"They are promising, indeed. But I would see *how* you

work, my boy. Here, Master Kincaid. Have a seat. Draw me, even as I sit before you."

And draw Nathan had, sketching Reynolds with hands that shook so violently and gripped so tightly, they'd snapped the slim charcoal sticks in two, while his palms had made damp smudges on the heavy white paper.

He'd been afraid his nervousness had cost him dear, but his worries proved groundless. The face of Joshua Reynolds, faithfully rendered and extraordinarily lifelike, had twinkled up at him from the grubby page when he was done.

"Well, well! 'Tis hardly a flattering likeness, dear boy. But then, 'twas no pretty face to begin with!" Reynolds had quipped.

To Nathan's relief—and joy—after this brief sampling of his work, the artist had praised his talents. He could become one of his assistants, if he would work gratis. In lieu of payment, Nathan would have the opportunity to absorb what instruction he may by virtue of keen observation and practice. Did such an arrangement suit? Reynolds had asked. *Suit?* Suit! Oh, foolish question! Canonization could not have pleased Nathan more!

For the next idyllic year, he had worked as he never had before. By day, he'd been one of Reynold's several assistants, fetching and carrying about the City and doing whatever he was called upon to do. By watching the others, he learned all there was to know about colors and hue, value and tone; how to mix oils and pigments, both in jars and upon the palette. He learned such practical matters as how to stretch canvases and to make the wooden stretcher frames; he acquired the techniques of using to good effect the sable brushes and palette knives so beloved by painters; and he mastered the difficult and exacting arts of perspective, line, and contour.

But most of all, he learned his art by going with Reynolds to the palatial homes of his patrons, and watching while the maestro painted, carefully observing how he captured the very texture of silky female flesh, the twinkle and liveliness to be found in a widow's naughty eye, or the dewy glow of a maiden's blush. Nathan marvelled at Reynolds' genius. Indeed, the man could effortlessly impart the very essence and spirit of a living subject to his canvas, so that the finished portrait seemed about to sigh and draw breath!

By evening, however, his world changed. Rather than studios reeking of turpentine and linseed oil, or the perfumed drawing-rooms and boudoirs of the wealthy, his milieu became the sawdust-sweat-and-ale world of taverns patronized by the rough and ready, working-class folk of London. Then Nathan put away his pad and charcoal temporarily, and hefted barrels and ostlered for Toby Loring at the George, changing teams, grooming the mounts, feeding and watering the horses, cleaning harness and mucking out the stables.

When he tumbled into his pallet in the Royal George's garret each night, no matter how much his head spun with artistic ideas, no matter how badly his youthful muscles protested their overwork, he was asleep the moment his head brushed the straw mattress—but more content than he'd ever been in his life.

His decision had been right for him, he knew it; his only regret was that in following his heart's desire, his father had seen fit to disown him. Stern as Simon Kincaid might be, Nathan loved him dearly. He'd not wished to sever his family ties, and the knowledge that he was an outcast had saddened him deeply. When he'd begun to make a name for himself, he would return to Linden Hall in triumph and attempt a reconciliation, he vowed.

But then, almost a year to the day after his arrival at the Royal George, Fate had stepped in to alter his life irrevocably.

He had passed a hard day, running errands all over the city in damp, bitterly cold weather for Master Reynolds, and was already weary upon his return to the tavern shortly before dusk.

As he'd ridden home, he'd crossed his fingers and hoped that the foul weather might have kept travelers off the roads and at home for the night. If so, a cozy evening spent idling by the George's blazing hearth lay ahead of him, followed—all going well—by a lusty night with his sweetheart Rosie's charms to warm his spartan garret. But no such luck!

With much apology, upon Nathan's return to the George Toby Loring had explained that his deliveries from the vintner's had arrived late that afternoon, delayed by bad weather from reaching the City in the morning, as was usual. As a result, two huge drays awaited unlading in the inn-yard. And their matched teams of massive Clydesdales wanted for a nose-bag apiece, and watering and grooming besides.

Nathan had groaned at the prospect, for snow was falling heavily now. But he'd promised Toby he'd see all the barrels stowed neatly in the cellars beneath the inn.

He and Roger Loring, the inn-keeper's son and his friend, had shrugged off their reluctance and tackled the job with a will. They were stowing the last of the kegs just as Mistress Loring, Roger's mother, called down to the cellar and bade them come upstairs for their suppers.

They'd done so, relishing the hearty meal of savory beefsteak pudding, creamed onions, and peas she set before them, which they'd washed down with swigs of dark ale. Young, healthy, and ravenous from their hard physical labor, they'd supped as if they'd eaten nothing in over a year!

The noisy clatter of many hooves upon cobbles had signaled the late arrival of a coach and team in the inn-yard. The sound had brought Roger promptly to his feet. Nathan tried to sop up the last smear of gravy with a heel of bread, before he made to follow Roger outside. The steaming apple pie and sweet custard would have to wait.

"Nay, Nate. Sit down an' finish yer supper, lad. I'll see to this 'un," Roger had insisted. Waving Nathan's protests aside, he'd left the warmth of the tavern, venturing outside into the frosty night and the bitter cold to change the weary team, and harness fresh horses in the traces, leaving Nathan to savor his pie.

His belly full, he'd leaned back contentedly and looked

around him, half-minded to draw out the sketch-pad and charcoal he always carried tucked in his shirt and sketch for a while. He enjoyed watching the ruddy-faced patrons huddled about the blazing hearth of the taproom each evening. One old scoundrel was mulling his tankard of ale with a red-hot poker drawn from the fire's crimson coals, while a pair of old salts puffed upon clay pipes and spun their tall sailor's yarns, bringing the blustering wind and the salt-spray tang of the ocean alive with their expressions and words.

Such a diversity of features could be found on their faces! And, while few among the gathering could be considered comely or handsome, their faces were filled with character, a blueprint of the circumstances that had shaped their lives. Each line and furrow was a clue to good humor or to bad, each crease a testament to ease or lack, joy or sorrow on down the years. He never tired of looking at the faces of London's diverse citizenry, taking as much pleasure in his perusal of a lowly St. Giles' whore with her frowsy mop of tangled hair and her rouged cheeks as he would from observing the giggling, empty visage of England's mad King George III himself.

His first inkling that this night would prove in any way different from those that had gone before came when Rose, one of the George's serving wenches and his current light o' love, had come flying through the tavern doors. Her pretty face had been ruddy with cold, her mobcap and cloak askew. She was breathing heavily as she slammed the door behind her on a gust of frigid air.

Her blue eyes wide with alarm, she'd sung out, "Look lively, lads! There's a press-gang abroad. 'Tis headed this way, right smartly."

The younger patrons had needed no second warning. To a man, they'd begun diving for the closest exit, for the press-gangs were men of His Majesty's Navy on the prowl for likely lads to "press," or force, into service at sea!

A sailor's life being one of great hardship, danger, deprivation, and lengthy separation from home and family, few men went to sea willingly in these times, with the result that ship's crews were often short-handed. The press-gangs contrived to fill this lack of able seamen by roaming the taverns and grog shops, where they "enlisted" new recruits with the stout end of a billy-club. The unfortunate fellows would then be taken, unconscious, aboard a vessel, and held there in irons until the ship put out to sea and escape was impossible.

On hearing Rosie's warning, Nathan had at once sprung to his feet and dived for the tavern's rear door, intending to warn Roger that they must lie low for an hour or two until the press-gang had passed by. By so doing, they had avoided being pressed more than once since he'd arrived in London.

But that night, he'd been tired, and slower than usual on account of it. He had but poked his head out into the cold night beyond the rear door when a blow to the back of his skull had filled his vision with stars.

He'd awoken some hours later with a pounding head, to find himself shackled to a foully cursing Roger in the holds of a ship. Loring had gloomily informed him that they'd been taken aboard a vessel named the *Resolution*. Come high tide, they'd be sailing for parts unknown.

"Parts unknown?" Nathan had echoed, cradling his sore head and scowling. 'Twas a strange voyage that had no known destination! "How so?"

"How so? Why, my young cock, because this 'ere's an *exploration* vessel we've drawn, of all the cursed luck! Her crew and supplies 'ave been bought an' paid fer by the Royal Geographical Society, no less. Her captain's James Cook— you'll 'ave heard o' 'im, no doubt, God rot 'im?"

Ebony brows quirked in surprise, Nathan had nodded. He'd heard a great deal about Cook from his father, who had admired him. It was almost with relief that he realized they could have fared far worse than to find themselves upon one of the worthy Cook's vessels, if being shanghaied was inevitable. Nathan had grimaced in the hold's damp shadows. What irony! He had defied his father, turned his back on the sea-faring life and the

91

officer's commission Simon Kincaid had chosen for him—only to end up being pressed into the very service he'd rejected.

Roger, far from amused, had scowled and eyed him askance. "By God, I wonder that you can find summat t' laugh about, Nate! 'Tis ill-fortune enough that we've been pressed at all, but on this, of all ships! Who knows where we be bound or 'ow long we may be wandering the world? Who can guess what dangers await us on this voyage? What pestilence or famine? Or what manner of wild animals or savage 'eathens will try to part us from our lives?" He'd shuddered and shaken his head morosely, almost choking as he'd added, "Me poor old mother an' father! What'll become o' them, eh? Better mayhap we'd been murdered by footpads than brought to this sorry pass, for 'tis certain we'll not see home for better'n two years. For meself, I wager we'll never see England again."

Roger had been wrong, on that score, at least. They had indeed returned safely to England and home, in due course. But alas, it had been over four years, not two, before they'd done so.

By then, Roger and Nathan numbered among the very first white men to make landfall upon the unknown continent of Australia, then called New South Wales or New Holland, and to have seen firsthand the wonders of that new and savage land.

Catching a movement from the corner of his eye, Nathan glanced up. Well, well! He was no longer alone, he saw. Mariah was standing some yards away down the beach, gazing out at the ghost-white breakers as they boomed against the reef. Although still wearing Digby's uniform jacket, she hugged herself as if chilled, while her long hair twisted and lifted on the breeze like a flag.

How had she slipped past the guard he'd placed, he wondered, thinking what a small, vulnerable creature she seemed, etched against the vast ocean and the wheeling, star-filled sky. But, the lovely picture she created notwithstanding, she had no business being out here at this hour all alone. 'Twas courting trouble.

He saw her turn to watch as he came towards her, and sensed that her eyes were wary as he drew nearer. Did she expect a tongue-lashing for evading his sentinels? Or worse, perhaps, to her thinking, yet another lusty overture on his part? Either way, he was curious to see if she would break and take flight back to camp or bravely stand her ground? He grinned. Stand her ground, he'd wager a guinea on it! She'd not struck him as a milk-toast miss, nor yet a cowardly one, for all her fragile appearance!

"Lady Downing," he greeted huskily, halting while yet some distance from her.

He won his wager with himself, for she inclined her head in pretty fashion and made no move to flee him.

"Master Kincaid," she acknowledged in the husky voice he fonnd so very alluring. "Sleep escapes us both, I see."

He nodded, wondering how best to warn her of the folly of wandering abroad at night, alone, without sounding overbearing in the process. "It does indeed, madam," he acknowledged. "But wandering about alone is no way to recapture it."

She laughed softly. The low, seductive sound raised prickling hairs down Nathan's neck and tightened his groin.

"Oh, come, come! Pray, do not look so fierce, dear sir! I know very well that I shouldn't be here, but I'd hoped the fresh sea air and a stroll might relax me. I'd not planned to be gone for more than a minute or two, my word on it. But then, 'tis such a glorious night, I quite forgot my good intentions." She pouted and looked imploringly at him. "I slipped past the guards when they had their backs turned. Please don't punish them, sir."

He grinned. "How could I, when you plead so prettily for their forgiveness?"

"Then I am in your debt, Master Kincaid. I wonder, would you care to escort me on my little promenade, sir?"

He hid his surprise at her unexpected invitation behind a

solemn nod. "'Twould be my pleasure, m'lady," he agreed, offering her his arm and wondering what had caused her sudden turnabout from outraged virago to flirtatious coquette.

Shyly, she slipped her hand through his arm, and he could feel the slight tremor that ran through her as she did so. Darting him a nervous smile, which he returned, she set off with him at a leisurely pace, heading towards the pale finger of the point that jutted into the ocean.

The sand was chill and wet beneath their bare feet without the sun to warm it. The ocean sang them a restless, shushing lullaby. The tropical night wove its balmy spell about them both as, arm in arm, they walked, her red flannel petticoats flapping about her legs in the breeze.

She was a tiny little thing, reaching only to his shoulder, he realized. It took two of her smaller steps to match each one of his long-legged strides, yet she seemed content with their pace and did not ask him to slow down.

"England seems a world away here, does it not?" she observed. "A place and time remembered like a dream."

"A good dream, mistress?" he asked, curious to hear something of her past.

"For the most part, aye. Besides, time and distance have a way of lending a softening patina to even one's harshest memories, do they not?"

He wondered at the bitter edge to her tone, but was reluctant to pry and ask its cause.

"And what of you, Master Kincaid?" she continued when he shrugged and gave no answer. "Do you yearn for merry England?"

"Far less than you, I warrant, m'lady," he answered, a trifle more sharply than he intended, for naught but Jack Ketch's noose awaited him there! "In truth, 'twould suit me well were I stranded here forever. You see, here I at least have my freedom."

She could have pinched herself for forgetting—even for an instant—that his exile was not of his choosing.

"La, forgive me, sir! Truly, I meant no harm by my thought-

94

less question. In my clumsy way, I'd hoped to encourage conversation on your part. Oh, in truth, I am no good at this!'' she muttered to herself.

''At what, mistress?''

''At making amends! When I saw you on the beach, alone, I followed you here. I'd hoped to—'' She broke off, appearing flustered.

''Aye?'' he encouraged. ''To what?''

''I'd hoped to beg your pardon for my waspishness this morning,'' she confessed, the words escaping her in a rush. ''You were very kind to me. You took care of me, but I was rude and ungrateful. And under the circumstances, 'tis hardly surprising you should mistake me for one of . . . of those women! I planned to tell you that tonight, in the hope that we could start over and be . . . friends. But now I've ruined everything, haven't I?''

So saying, she halted and turned to face him. They stood mere inches apart as she gazed up at him, but he had never been so achingly aware of any woman as he was of Mariah in that moment. Of the way her hair danced on the breeze like the ribbons about a Maypole, exposing her lovely profile; the dark sweep of thick lashes against the pale splendor of her complexion; the ivory elegance of her throat.

''You've ruined naught, believe me. Moreover, m'lady, I fear 'tis I who should ask your pardon,'' he began, wishing the cursed moon were less bright, his own expression less exposed to the scrutiny of her bewitching, gold-flecked turquoise eyes. ''Madam, I apologize if my boldness offended you. My only excuse is, as you so rightly said, that I mistook you for a . . . er . . . doxie. As a consequence, I misread your . . . reluctance . . . for some merry game.'' He grimaced. ''Hence my lamentable perseverance.''

To his surprise, her silvery laughter rose, merry as bells, on the night air. ''In faith, sir, you're a rogue of the first water— but of a certainty no hypocrite! You beg my pardon for your actions very prettily, yet you say nothing of regretting them!''

"Regret them? God's Teeth, I would indeed be a hypocrite—and a liar!—if I did that!" Nathan admitted, relieved by her easy response. He grinned wickedly, his eyes catching the starlight like shattered emeralds. "You're a beautiful woman, Lady Mariah. What man would not desire you for himself? Nay, madam, my only regret is that I frightened you—and that I failed to seduce you, *not* that I attempted to!"

"And my regret is that I assumed your scars tell all," she confessed gravely. "I saw the calluses about your wrists, and straightway cast you as a felon and a rogue. My cousin Caroline was right, it seems, for all her youth. She reminded me that I should not judge a man by looks alone. Nor trust to the label that society thrusts upon him. As a magistrate's daughter, I should know better than most that such labels ofttimes lie—or fall far short of truth."

"The label they hung upon me was that of 'murderer, twice-damned,' m'lady," he said softly, watching her face for a flicker of disgust, a shudder of fear. But if she was shocked or frightened by his disclosure, she hid it behind remarkable composure.

"Ah. And was that label deserved, for whatever reasons?" she asked in a level tone that revealed none of her anxiety. At heart, she harbored grave misgivings about the wisdom of attempting to seduce a convict, a man who might well be dangerous. She needed to hear from his own lips that he was the falsely accused innocent Caroline had claimed. He'd certainly done nothing thus far to confirm her fears. On the contrary, he'd been kindness itself, save for his lusty attempts to tumble her, though he'd had ample time when they'd been alone to ravish and murder her a hundred times over, in countless gruesome ways, then feed her body to the sharks.

"'Twas not deserved," he gritted out in answer to her question. "I swear, madam, upon my honor, I have taken no man's—or woman's—life."

The strong certainty of his tone, his steadfast, unflinching gaze, were immeasurably heartening. Call her a trusting fool, a naive twit, but she believed him. "Then . . . shall we walk on, sir?"

Unable to quite believe her calm acceptance of his word, nonetheless Nathan's grin spread from ear to ear as he took her arm again. They continued their stroll, far more at ease in each other's company now.

Pointing above them to the star-filled sky, he showed Mariah the constellations, the twinkling star-pictures that Green, the astronomer, had taught him so long ago upon the rolling decks of Cook's ship, the *Resolution*.

Continuing their stroll, they laughed companionably as tiny sand crabs scuttled from their path, scampering for the safety of their underground burrows. Together they marvelled at the shimmering phosphorescence upon the inky water, while Mariah clapped her hands and exclaimed in delight over the tiny glowworms that studded the rocks, fancifully declaring they must be miniature candles lit by native gods to show their path.

They'd gone much farther from camp than Nathan had ever intended when a sudden shrill scream, followed by other fainter, strangely disembodied cries, broke the hush.

"In God's name, what was that!" Mariah cried. Instinctively, she moved closer to him for protection; so close, their bodies touched in an electrical contact that drove the breath from Nathan in a shocked grunt. Steadying her with a hand upon each arm, he could feel her trembling uncontrollably. Moreover, the wild flutter of her poor, frightened heart against his rib-cage was only a fraction swifter, more erratic, than the thunder of his own. Moved that she had looked to him—a convict, a stranger—for protection, without so much as a second thought, he gathered her into his arms.

"Come, come, there's naught to fear, m'lady. 'Tis but the convicts' drunken revelry you hear. By night, even a distant cry can seem close at hand."

"Revelry?"

"Aye. Jack tells me they salvaged some caskets of grog from the *Hester*'s stores. They were reeling drunk when he left their camp this morn."

"Aaah." She gave a little shudder and hid her face against his chest. "I can well imagine! Oh, Jonathan, I have thanked God countless times that 'twas you who found me, and not them!"

She looked up at him, blinking back tears. And any reassurance, any consolation, he might have thought to offer was forgotten in that magical moment, for her turquoise eyes were shining with trust and admiration as she looked up at him; two lustrous jewels ablaze in the masterpiece that was her lovely face. Those eyes were framed by tear-spiked lashes, and furling ribbons of her wind-tossed, red-gold hair caught the moon's pale fire. And, like her eyes, the lush splendor of her lips held an invitation too potent to ignore. Was it but wishful thinking . . . or did she want him to kiss her? Was it his imagination, or did her body strain, ever so slightly, towards his?

With a muffled oath, he tightened his embrace and drew her closer, though with a different purpose this time. "Ah, Mariah, sweet, lovely Mariah!" he murmured as he crushed her to his chest.

She tensed momentarily, taken by a fleeting fit of the old panic; then he saw her eyes close in expectation as he gently cupped her chin and tilted her face up to his. Closing his own eyes, he bent his ebony head to hers. He'd parted his lips; indeed, he could feel her warm, sweet breath upon his own lips when the folly of his actions struck home.

A shudder moved through him as, summoning an iron will to gird himself for denial, he lamely patted her cheek, like a doting uncle might pat the cheek of a favorite niece, before setting her firmly from him.

Disappointment . . . relief? . . . rejection—all three flitted across her lovely, expressive face as she opened her eyes to stare at him.

"Why did you stop, sir? Have I done something wrong?" she whispered, bewildered. "Or . . . do I displease you in some way?"

"On the contrary," he came back heavily. "You please me too damned well, madam!"

"You wanted to . . . to kiss me, I know you did!" she exclaimed, her soft cry ending on a choked sob. "Since I made no protest, why, then, did you not continue?"

"In truth, madam, I wanted—want—to kiss you, more than anything," he admitted gruffly, trying to quell the violent response of his treacherous body to her closeness and to what had so very nearly transpired between them. "Alas, I cannot."

"Cannot? You mean, you are in some way disabled? Or perhaps, *un*able?"

"The Deuce I am!" he denied hotly, his manly pride pricked at the thought. "Rather, I should say, may not."

"*May* not kiss me! But, how so, sir? Who forbids you to do so?"

He scowled and would not meet her searching gaze. "Tonight, the men elected me to lead them, Mariah," he explained heavily, as if no more needed to be said.

"And? What is that to us?" she demanded, her smoky voice almost shrill.

"We are twenty-three men all told, madam. Twenty-three *lusty* men who, for the greater part, have spent nine long months at sea without female companionship. Men who now find themselves castaways with but one very beautiful, desirable woman, and a girl who is little more than a pretty child."

"And?"

"Come, Mariah. Think on it! Can you not see the danger? Were I to make you my mistress, my men's jealousy would breed murder and mayhem! Hell, 'twould breed chaos! That, my sweet, my lovely Mariah, is why, most reluctantly, I put you from me," he continued ruefully, tracing the curving, gentle line of her jaw down to her obstinate little chin and then grazing her moist lips with his knuckle. "And why, alas, I must continue to do so. God knows, sweet, I want you sorely! But can I have you? Damn it, nay!"

Frustration broiled through her. His strong embrace had fanned her earlier longings into flame, while his almost-kiss had unleashed a maelstrom of wild, delicious sensations she was hard put to control, for she had never felt this melting way in Edward's arms, had never yearned to give herself to him. Oh, lord, how very wanton—how very courageous—she'd grown since her brush with Death! And, now that she'd succeeded thus far in overcoming her fears, she was anxious to see it through, to throw herself into his arms, to beg him to take her right here upon the cool sand, to know, finally, all that Edward had denied her.

"Very well. If that is how it must be, then so be it," she acknowledged quietly. "But please, sir," she implored, womanly guile replacing her momentary boldness, "could you . . . that is, would it be so very improper for you to . . . to simply hold me again? Surely a Christian man might decently offer such small consolation to someone—a child, say?—who'd endured what I have endured this past two days, and find no wrong in it?"

Child? Her? God's Teeth! He almost snorted his amusement aloud as he eyed the soft swell of her breasts as they rose and fell against the thin stuff of her bodice with every breath she drew. Did she know what she was saying? How very far removed from an innocent child she appeared, standing there with the moonlight glistening on the moistened lips she raised to him in an almost seductive smile, her glorious eyes—half-closed, long-lashed, and heavy-lidded—almost sultry with desire?

He wondered vaguely, as he moved towards her like one in a dream and once again drew her to him, as his dark head dipped to possess her parted lips in a deep, claiming kiss, what had become of the lieutenant's jacket she'd worn earlier? When had she slipped it off?

But then her mouth parted under his as she rose on tiptoe to press her softness against him, filling his arms with the curving feminine softness he'd been denied these many celibate months, and the damned jacket was forgotten. The taste of her lips and the wild clover of her inner mouth were so very sweet, his lust returned full force. It rose through him in a swamping tide that threatened to sink his stern resolve once and for all. He held her fiercely to his own lean frame and deepened his kiss, stroking her tongue with his own, splaying his hands across the taut globes of her bottom to bring her fully against him.

As his manhood pressed, hard and heated, against her, Mariah uttered a tiny, satisfied moan deep in her throat. Her ruse had worked! He wanted her, despite his claims, she told herself gleefully as she wove her fingers through the thick black mane of his shaggy locks. Her body tingled as his arms tightened about her. Each pore, each nerve, thrummed with excitement, quivered with eager anticipation of what was to come! Dear God, what a tender, exciting man he promised to be, this Jonathan Kincaid! Surely as a lover he would prove as different from Edward as the moon was from a saucer of sour milk. And surely—oh, surely—she would melt under the fiery yet tender ardor of Nathan's love-making, and would forget the beast who'd used her so cruelly.

She grew limp with the thought, her weight supported only by his strong arms about her, for her knees would scarce hold her any longer. She felt lightheaded, as giddy as if she'd imbibed a hogshead of Canary single-handed! Another moment, and Edward would belong to the past.

"Damn it, enough!" Jonathan gritted out suddenly, breaking away and thrusting her from him so forcibly, she almost fell. He clenched his jaw, knotted his fists, and planted his feet firmly apart in the sand, needing badly to brace himself somehow. If not, he would drop to his knees, pole-axed in the wake of that electric kiss! "You have had your 'comforting embrace,' have you not, madam? Now we must go back."

A mixture of anger and wry amusement filled him as he realized how closely he'd come to reneging on his vow within but hours of its making. God in Heaven! That clever *vixen*, with her sly prattle of children and comforting embraces! Child be damned! She was no child but a siren, a bewitching temptress, a seductive sea-witch who was not to be trusted, for her potent song lured him onto the rocks of his own destruction. His entire body ached with the effort it had taken to set her from him twice that day, and deny the fulfillment of his desire.

Blinking, Mariah gaped at him in disbelief, uncertain at first if she'd heard him correctly, until he repeated what he'd said. Once he had, there was no denying it, no pretending any longer.

Oh, you trusting little goose! she chided silently. She'd taken the shreds of her courage in her two hands, and had all but thrown herself at the man, steeling herself to endure his closeness, to pretend she courted his touch, playacting until her pretense became reality, and she'd truly begun to enjoy his kisses and caresses and to forget her fear. And what had he done? Why, the unfeeling, heartless brute had rejected her, had cast her aside! His words were like melted snow poured over her, tolling a death knell to her plans even as it cooled her passions.

Smothering her heartache, quelling her disappointment, she muttered angrily, "Aye, Kincaid, we'll go back to camp, curse your black heart! But, mark me well before we leave here this night, sir! Should you think to dally with me at some later time, be forewarned, I'll have none of you! You have made your choice this night, and so must live with it. Damn you, sir, I am no easy sailor's lightskirt from the wharves—a trollop to be picked up and put down as you see fit. The Devil I am, you . . . you shaggy oaf!''

Of all the blasted ill-fortune, she thought as she flung herself about and fled from him, back to camp. As she did so, tears of mortification, of fury—and perhaps more than a twinge of relief—stung her eyes. She estimated there were close to fifty unscrupulous, amoral, and thoroughly degenerate convicts on that accursed island. Fifty lusty *willing* men, any one of whom would be all too eager to oblige her and lay her ghosts to rest—yet she singled out the only one with a conscience.

In a tangled heap like a litter of mangy hounds, two dozen of the *Hester*'s most hardened convicts, male and female, sprawled about the crackling fire singing bawdy sea-chanteys, oblivious to the showers of orange sparks thrown off to dance on the night breeze or to burn holes in their already ragged clothing.

Murderers and cutpurses, thieves, and whores, they were half-stupefied with liquor, for grog and coconut milk were their only source of liquid, and to the last man and woman, they drank grog. Through bleary red eyes, they watched Angus Ruskin, their self-appointed leader, stagger from his lean-to and throw back his shaggy red head.

Their songs died away as, with fists like hams planted on either side of his waist, his massive legs braced apart, he opened wide red lips that were slick with spit. More spittle hung in strings amidst his red beard as he roared, "Come on wi' ye, then, Kitty, ye lazy bitch. Serve your master his evenin' dram, 'fore he wallops yer arse!"

The comely wench who tumbled from the shelter after him swept back her snarled mane of black hair and went up on tiptoe. Full breasts jiggling, she tilted the wineskin and let the rum flow from its spout. She kept on pouring until the thin stream had filled Ruskin's mouth. It overflowed down his chin and jaws, soaking his tattered shirt.

"Enough!" he snarled at last, angrily knocking the wineskin aside. "Would ye drown me, then? Is that yer foul plan, lassie—t' be rid o' Angus Ruskin?"

The laughter died on Kitty's lips. Despite her apparently sotted state, she was in truth stone-cold sober, sharp-witted enough to sense the malevolence in his tone—and the jealous threat behind it. Paling, she swallowed and shook her head.

Ruskin was having one of his "queer spells," as she called them, in which he thought the whole bloody world was out t' do him in, and the Devil whispered in his ear t' get even. When he was so taken, he'd murdered men for less than he'd accused her of.

She forced a smile to rubbery lips gone stiff with fear as he roughly kneaded her plump breast. "Me? Want ter be quit o' you, lovie? Blimey, I want no such thing! You know your Kitty better'n that, surely, hmm?"

Desperate to convince him, she tried to wrap her arms around Ruskin's bull-neck and kiss his coarse cheek, but Angus would have none of her.

Knotting his fingers in her hair, he cursed foully, jerked her to him, and thrust his face full in hers. His reptilian eyes were as empty, as cold and pitiless as the Highland moors he'd once called home as he snarled, "Ah, but *do* I know it, lassie?" He tightened his grip so that she whimpered in pain. "For your wee sake, I hope t' God ye dinna lie—for ye willna cast me aside like last night's slops for any man, ye ken? I'll carve yer bonnie face t' ribbons wi' ma dirk, ye slut, should ye play me false!"

As he spoke, spittle sprayed over Kitty's ashen face. His cruel fingers had set her scalp afire, but though he hurt her and though her belly heaved with revulsion, she dared not show it. "I swear—on me mother's grave!—there in't no one but you, not for me," she whimpered, hating herself for her cowardice. Hating Ruskin for bringing her so low.

"Nay?" With a disbelieving grunt, he flung her from him, so forcefully she fell heavily to the sand. "Och, see ye keep it that way, slut!"

After he'd staggered off down the beach to join the other convicts, another woman, older, hurried to help Kitty to her feet. Her frowsy blond hair was matted, her face was raddled with old pox scars, but its coarse features were kindly, for all the signs of hard use and harder living in the stews of St. Giles.

"All right are ye, ducks?" Leah asked anxiously, dusting

the younger woman off. In all honesty, there was little that could be done to improve the sorry appearance of Kitty's ragged low-necked blouse and skirt. Neat and clean but already far from new even when the *Hester* had set sail, their condition had not been improved by the battering of storm and surf.

"As right as I'll ever be, Leah, so long as that bleedin' sod draws breath!" Kitty muttered, dashing the tears from her cheeks with a scarred wrist. As she rubbed her bruised buttocks, her grey eyes lost their cowed expression. They flashed with defiance and the remnants of pride. "I swear, Leah, given 'alf a chance, I'd murder the bastard and dance on 'is bleedin' corpse."

"Oww, 'ave yerself a drink, ducks, an' give over. There's naught ye can do t' change things, but a tot o' Caribee will take yer mind off Bloody Ruskin."

Kitty shook her head. "No, Leah. No more drink, not this time, anyway. I've 'ad enough rum. I'm done with it, I am. Being sotted day an' night changes nuffink, don't yer see? When ye leave off the grog, it's all as it was before, innit? We're still 'ere, on this God-forsaken island—and Ruskin's still breathin', God rot 'im!"

"Aye, but if it numbs ye for a bit, what 'arm can it do?" Leah wheedled. "Tomorrow we could all be dead, so come on . . . have some wi' me? Just a sip t' keep old Leah company, wont'cha?"

But Kitty shook her head and walked away, limping a little now from a bruised hip, thanks to Ruskin's tender mercies. Leah shook her head and, drawing her shawl about her shoulders, returned to her place by the roaring fire.

Kitty set off down the moonlit beach, her heart heavy, her mind a jumble of disturbing thoughts. She contemplated several bloodthirsty methods of ridding herself of Ruskin's cruel dominance. But did Ruskin matter anymore, really? Surely they couldn't survive much longer on a diet of nothing but coconuts, a few raw mussels, a bit o' fish now and then, and bloody little else. She sighed heavily. Except for a handful o' decent lads, the men were too sotted t' hunt. Besides, being city-sparrows who, for the greater part, hailed from the stews and wharves of London, they'd not know how! The women were no better. And, sotted to the gills as most of them were, they didn't feel the hungry squeezings of their bellies or know that they were slowly starving t' death.

In her anger and upset, Kitty had gone some distance from their crude camp when she heard a sudden shout. Turning about, she saw Ruskin and several of the other laggers run to meet someone, and her spirits revived a little. Why, it was Joe Hardy and the other six men who'd gone inland that morning in search of game and fresh water. Oh, please Gawd, let them have found both!

As Kitty started back towards the men, she saw a lone woman break away from the group by the fire. She hoisted up her skirts and ran along the beach to greet Joe and the others.

Now, who might that be? Kitty wondered jealously, then realized it was Annie Billings, an inn-keeper's daughter from Islington. Annie's sweetheart, a handsome rogue called Tom Thacker, had been a "gentleman of the road" back in England. Tom, she remembered now, had gone with Joe's party.

Kitty sighed ruefully as she retraced her footprints in the sand. Annie and her Tom—now, there was a tale of true love, she thought with envy. Unlike the rest of their sorry lot, Annie was no felon, but a decent lass from a respectable, hardworking family—which was why pretty Kitty, doxie and pickpocket, hardly knew her. Word was that Annie loved her Tom so dearly, she'd chosen to accompany him to Australia, as the wives, families, and sweethearts of transported convicts oft-times did. When they reached Botany Bay, the couple would be wed. Perhaps, Annie had said happily, Tom would seek a pardon from the Governor, and they'd be given good land to farm for themselves. It had been no empty dream. Encouraging convicts who'd served their time or been pardoned to settle the new land was common, one of the ways the British Government hoped to colonize New South Wales.

Annie's belly was round and hard with child, Kitty saw. Her burden made her run clumsily, like a duck, tripping once or twice in the deep sand as she went, then gamely struggling back to her feet before carrying on.

But as Kitty drew closer, Annie brought up short. She looked wildly about her and asked Joe something. Kitty could see the confusion in her expression as Joe answered in the negative and glumly shook his head. Annie dropped like a stone to her knees and began to scream and wail, beating the sand with her fists like a Bedlamite.

Dread filled Kitty. Judging by Annie's carrying-on, something bad was up.

Curious and afraid all at the same time, Kitty decided to find out for herself what was going on and ran the last few yards.

"What's happened? Why, her Tom's dead, he is, poor sod," Joe Hardy told Kitty bleakly. "'Arry Pearce, too, Gawd rest their souls."

Two of their few good men lost. "Gawd, no! Not Harry. But . . . how? What happened?"

Exhausted, Joe sank down onto a rock and buried his head in his hands. Tears leaked from between his fingers. Kitty's heart went out to him. Her fingers itched to smoothe his curly brown hair or to banish the deep lines of worry from his face. Truth was, she was awful sweet on Joe, but too terrified of Angus and of what he might do to them both in one of his jealous rages to ever let Joe know it.

"We found no fresh water spring," Joe began. "And a wild pig we chased got away from us. So, we lads were on our way back t' camp with these pigeons we snared in the mountains when Pearce—you recall Harry couldn't stomach coconut milk, nor drink grog, but for a sip or two t' wet 'is whistle?" She nodded. "Well, 'e was nigh crazy with thirst, said 'e couldn't stand it no more. Jesus, Kitty, we warned 'im not to, but 'e knelt down by a swamp to drink. Next thing, we 'eard a snappin' sound and Harry screamed—Jesus Christ, it were 'orrible! When we turned around, one of them crocs had 'im fast by the arm. Its tail were thrashing about, an' blood was spouting up from Harry's shoulder like a bloomin' fountain.''

"Blessed Jesus!" Kitty whispered, the color draining from her cheeks. "And . . . Tom?"

"Well, you know ole Tom, how he always 'ad more guts than common sense, that lad? He drew 'is knife and went t' help poor Harry.'' Joe glumly shook his head. "We told 'im 'tweren't no bleedin' use, that Harry was good as dead, but . . . he wouldn't listen, so we lorst 'em both. See t' 'is Annie, would ye, Kitty, lass? She's took it hard, she 'as, poor soul . . .''

Kitty nodded, tears falling as she knelt at the pregnant woman's side, for Annie's eyes held an emptiness she'd never forget, should she live to be a hundred. "Come along with me, Annie, love,'' she coaxed, taking the young woman by the upper arms. "Let's go an' find Leah, shall we?''

Annie blinked as if awakening from a dream. She laughed shrilly. Her blank gaze shifted hastily away from Kitty's pitying one. "No time for that,'' she declared briskly, "for I'm t' be wed within the hour! I must make haste t' dress afore the vicar comes. I'll be wearin' Tom's favorite—the blue one with the lace at the collar and cuffs—for the weddin'. Oh, he's a good man, my Tom. Even me dad says so. Just a bit on the wild side, poor love, but no real harm in him, bless him. He'll make a fine father, don't you think?''

The shock of Tom's death had unhinged her, Kitty realized, stroking Annie's shoulder. "Aye, love,'' she agreed in a soothing voice, "the very best. Come along, now, chick. Let's get ye back to the fire.''

Thus began a long and sorry night that Kitty would never forget.

Leah managed to coax Annie into swallowing some rum and together the two women settled the younger one close to the fire, their own shawls wrapped around her for warmth.

They'd slept for only a few hours when Annie's moans

awakened them. Scrambling to her side, Leah discovered that the shock of Tom's death had prematurely loosened her babe from the womb. Annie was in hard labor.

In no time, she gave birth to a baby girl. The child was perfect but tiny as a doll. The birth pangs seemed to return the young woman to her senses. Weeping now for her Tom, she held her babe, kissed its little cheeks fondly, then thrust the infant into Kitty's arms and turned her back on it.

"Life is naught but pain and sorrow," Annie said softly. "Better my little daughter join the angels in heaven than suffer as I have."

"Don't be daft, Annie. This little wench needs ye!" Leah pleaded.

But although Kitty and Nancy, another of the women, both pleaded with her to put the babe to her breast, Annie would not.

In the wee hours of the night, the puny wails of the baby woke Kitty. The poor little mite was so blessed hungry, she was suckling on Kitty's finger. *Well, you'll find no nourishment there, ye poor little sod!* Kitty thought. Then she had an idea. She'd put the babe to her mother's breast while Annie slept! Annie'd not waken, not after the rum they'd given her and the fast, hard birth of her daughter.

But, Kitty discovered, Annie's place by the fire was empty. And, in the ruddy light, she could see the tell-tale footprints that led straight down the beach to the water. There were none leading back up.

"Wake up, Nan! Leah! Oh, Gawd, Annie's gone!" she cried.

She, along with Leah and Nancy, found Annie's body lying in the sand, not far from where she must have entered the water.

"Aw, well. Per'aps 'twas for the best. Annie's with her Tom now," Nancy observed sadly, wiping away a tear with her fist.

"Aye," murmured Leah with a grimace. "And unless I'm mistook, the little 'un will join 'em, 'fore long."

"No!" protested Kitty, cuddling the baby, now wrapped in Nancy's shawl closer to her breast.

But Leah, who'd once been a midwife and knew such things, was right.

As night slipped into day and the charcoal sky turned to rose and saffron, the infant girl slipped effortlessly from life into death with only a sigh to mark the passage between one and the other.

Kitty, weeping as if the babe had been her own, carried it to the water's edge. She kissed the tiny blond head and perfect little lips, and with a murmured, "Farewell!" placed her in the crook of her mother's arm. Soon the tide would turn and carry the bodies away—and with them would go the very last of Kitty's illusions.

Death was ever near—no further away than one's shadow. And who knew whose name it would whisper next? Had Tom or Harry expected to die? Had Annie known that today would be her last on earth? *No!* And with but a random blow from Ruskin's fist, Kitty knew she could join them.

If she did nothing to help herself . . .

Chapter Seven

"Well, lookee here, me bullies!" Old Peg exclaimed, slapping his beefy thigh as Nathan, obviously returning from an early-morning swim, loped up the beach into camp the following morning. "Will yer take a gander at this fine young cock!"

Doffing an imaginary tricorn, Old Peg shifted his considerable weight onto his sound leg. He swept Nathan, who was shaking his body like a wet hound in lieu of drying off, a courtly bow. "A very good mornin t' ye, me fine sir! Might I make so bold as to inquire your lor'ship's name?"

"Stow it, you old rascal!" Nathan retorted with a grin. He thumped Peg heartily upon the shoulder as he passed him. "You know damn' well who I am. Good day, lads! How goes it?"

Water streaming from his lean, muscled torso and plastering his ragged breeches to his flanks, he made his way to the fire. The men congregated about it gaped, little less astonished than Peg by the changed figure he cut; so astonished, in fact, they failed to respond to his greeting.

At that moment, Caroline ducked out of her hut. As she straightened up, the first sight that met her eyes was Nathan. She blinked, flicked her blond head to clear it, rubbed her eyes, then stared again.

"Mariah! Oh, come quickly, coz!" she hissed into the opening. "Such a miracle you've never seen!"

"What is it now . . . ?" Mariah grumbled, yawning hugely as she stumbled from the shelter. She'd passed a long, wakeful night in its sweltering, mosquito-plagued confines—a night that had seemed endless in her restless condition—and she was tired and out of sorts.

When she saw Nathan, her mouth dropped open in disbelief. "Sweet Mary! Can it be him?" she breathed, her vexation with him forgotten for the moment.

Gone was the uncouth convict! With the aid of Digby's sharp knife, the hateful brute had undergone a miraculous transformation since she'd seen him last. His wild Gypsy locks had been neatly shorn, then clubbed back in a tidy black queue at his nape by means of a leather thong. Still wet, his hair molded to his fine head in inky commas, as sleek as a seal's pelt save for a half-dozen unruly curls about his brow and temples. His long beard was also gone, and cleanly-shaven, the swarthy, strong-jawed face revealed was every bit as handsome as Caro had promised. Perhaps even more so, Mariah allowed grudgingly.

From beneath the slashes of raven brows, Nathan's twinkling green eyes tossed a laughing challenge at the gawping gathering. As he swept them a gallant bow, his smile made the lighter sun-furrows winging out from the outer corners of his eyes deepen into creases. His chiselled lips quirked up in a wicked grin as, fists planted on hips, his faintly-golden chest still wet and glistening, he roared, "What the devil ails you all this morn? Have you never seen a man shorn before, that ye stare as if thunderstruck?"

His questions jolted the stunned men into action. All at once, they began gobbling like turkeys and moving in every direction, bumping into each other in their efforts to resume their busi-

112

ness—but casting incredulous looks over their shoulders at the new Nathan Kincaid as they did so.

Shaking his head in mock annoyance, Nathan returned Digby's dagger to him, then sought out Jack. He squatted down on his haunches alongside him, ruefully shaking his head.

At least the ship's carpenter appeared unimpressed. He continued whittling away at a long, sturdy length of timber with mallet and chisel, curly wood shavings littering the sand at his feet. When he finally paused to look up, his eyes narrowed; then he nodded approval at Nathan's changed appearance. "Well, well! I'll allow that's some 'andy barbering ye've done fer yerself, Kincaid."

"Aye. But had I known 'twould cause such a damned twitter, I'd have kept my beard and flowing locks! What are you up to?" Nathan asked, curious as he gestured at Jack's whittling.

"This here? Why, I'm after carvin' a new leg for Ole Peg, lad. His un' be split, see, an' 'tis paining his poor ole stump. Am I right, Peg?"

"Aye, sonny. Hurts summat wicked, it do."

Nathan nodded. "Stay here today and finish it, then, Jack. Meanwhile, Peg, you'll keep the cooking fire going—and get a signal-fire started farther down the beach."

"Aye, aye, sir. That I shall do. You can rely on Old Peg."

"Tom Swift, you'll help Peg," he instructed one of the sunken *Hester*'s cabin-boys, a fresh-faced, earnest youth of no more than sixteen years who reminded him poignantly of himself at that age. "Gather kindling and stack it where it'll keep dry. The rest of you men, gather round and listen up!"

When they'd formed a rough circle about him, he propped one foot upon a rock and, resting a forearm casually across his bent leg, began to speak. "As I said last night, careful planning and teamwork are the keys to our survival here." He looked slowly about the circle of intent faces, studying each in turn. They appeared worthy fellows, almost to a man, from the seasoned, leathery crewmembers of the *Hester* to the stubbly-cheeked marines of His Majesty's Merchant Navy, the downy-jawed cabin-boys, and the scholarly, beardless, and pale botanist, Matherson. He was proud he'd been chosen to lead such men. "We'll have victuals and drinking water aplenty, *if* we all pull together. To that end, I'm assigning work details. Some groups will fish or hunt, others will forage, and so on. Each detail will answer to the man I've chosen to lead it, and he to me, in turn. Any questions?"

A chorus of nays greeted this announcement.

"Very well. Let's get to work! Brown, McQuade, and Taverner, you fine Yarmouth sailors will catch fish for our supper. Brown, you're in charge. Keep a weather-eye out for salt-water crocodiles and sharks. The coral reef out there will be alive with the brutes. Any questions?"

"None, sir," Brown said with an uneasy glance at his companions. Their expressions reflcted his own thoughts; the cold Yarmouth waters of home had never been troubled by the likes of sharks or crocodiles. "But it won't easy!"

"You're good men. I know you'll do your best. Master Carmichael, you and your men will be our hunters today. We look to you to provide game for supper this even'. Second-Lieutenant Davidson, Able-Seaman Crook, you'll accompany Master-Mate Carmichael."

"Aye, aye, sir!"

"Master Matherson, you and your squad will undertake the gathering of coconuts and any other fruits or edible plants you might find. I believe your botanical studies should stand you in good stead for this task, but a word of warning: stay clear of the marshes. Jack spotted a crocodile in the swamps around the point yesterday."

"Didn't I just!" muttered Jack with a roll of his eyes.

"Where there's one, there'll be others," Nathan added.

A further murmur of disquiet greeted this revelation.

Ignoring the muttered protests, Nathan continued. "With you, Master Matherson, sir, will go Big Ben, marines Stiles and Lewis, Lieutenant Digby, Tim Bright, Babbington, Jackson, Tim Archer, and Doolan. The remaining ten men will follow me to the pool to secure our fresh water supply.

"As I told you last night, the baboon colony there is vicious. Guard against underestimating the brutes! Though smaller than us, they won't shrink from attacking a full-grown man, and their fangs are long and murderously sharp."

"And just how are we to defend ourselves, Kincaid?" Digby demanded with a sneer. "By lobbing rocks at the brutes like French peasants?"

Nathan's lips tightened into a thin hard line, for the lieutenant was blatantly mocking his own account of the baboon colony pursuing him through the jungle. The quelling look he shot the lieutenant spoke volumes. "You'll arm yourself with whatever weapon you can lay claim to, Lieutenant—and that goes for the rest of you. As my own experience proved, rocks will serve admirably as missiles in a pinch, if you can find naught else. A hefty tree-branch makes for a stout club. Anything's better than nothing, in a scuffle."

"I've a cutlass," Carmichael volunteered.

Nathan nodded approval. "If the rest of you lads have daggers or cutlasses, even better. Draw your metal—and keep it drawn. We're going into the jungle. Only the good Lord knows what dangers await us there!" With those ominous words, he looked about the circle of men. "Any questions?"

A ragged chorus of half-hearted nays was his answer. Though stalwart Englishmen, they had little enthusiasm for exploring a jungle's exotic environs!

"God's Blood! Are ye British lions or squeaking mice?" Nathan demanded in a voice like the crack of a whip. "I asked, have ye questions?"

"*Nay!*" they roared this time, sending the parrots into squawking chaos above them.

Nathan grinned. "Now I hear you! Then, if you're all set, let's—"

"By your leave, sir, I have a question."

115

All heads turned as Mariah padded across the sand. All eyes followed her gently swaying hips as she came to a halt before Nathan Kincaid. Despite her incongruous attire, a Navy lieutenant's jacket worn over red flannel petticoats, she still contrived to look beautiful. Nathan saw how Digby's eyes lingered lustfully upon her, and he was stunned by the sting of jealousy that rose up in his throat like bile.

"Lady Mariah, good morning," he ground out.

She sweetly returned his gruff greeting, inclining her head. "And to you, Master Kincaid, gentlemen." Turning, she flashed a glowing smile at the bedazzled company, who bobbed their heads like nestling owls in response. "Master Kincaid, I could not help but hear your assignments for the men. However, my cousin and I were wondering, sir—are we women to be given no duties?"

Kincaid was thrown by her question. He frowned. "The jungle is alive with predatory beasts, madam. There are snakes, poisonous insects—all manner of dangers, both known and unknown. Hunting and foraging will be hazardous undertakings quite unsuited to gentlewomen such as yourselves."

"Why, how so, sir?" she challenged, lips pursed, turquoise eyes tossing out a challenge. "Last evening, I overheard Master Matherson declare that so long as we remain stranded on this island, we are not convicts, sailors, or whatever but *equals*. And you, sir, *you* agreed with him. I heard you."

"Aye, I did, but—"

"That being the case, should not men and women also be counted equals? After all, we will share the victuals the men's labors provide, will we not?"

"Of course. That goes without saying. But—"

"A pox on your 'buts,' sir!" she flared, turquoise eyes fairly crackling now. Tossing her red-gold hair, she planted her fists on her hips and insisted, "My cousin and I are in robust health, yet young in years, sound in both wind and limb—and far from the helpless 'gentlewomen' you describe. If we would eat, then

116

'tis only fair that we should share the work, dangerous or otherwise.''

His jaw tightened. "There is no need, madam."

"Oh, indeed there is, sir. In fact, I *insist* that we be allowed to help, or we'll not touch a bite you set before us. Come, sir. Speak no more of our helplessness. What would you have us do? Starve or do our part?"

Nathan's glowering expression said that he knew she was still stung by his rejection. He suspected—and rightly so—that her demands were motivated by spite and a desire to cross him. However, short of challenging her true motives before his men, he had no choice but to take her demands at face value.

"Your eagerness to do your part is commendable, m'lady," he said, making her a mocking half-bow. "You and Mistress Caroline may join Master Matherson's foraging party—that is, if Master Matherson has no objections. Matherson?"

"Certainly not, Kincaid. I'd be delighted, dear ladies!"

"Thank you, sir." Mariah gave the botanist a smile and a curtsey.

Still scowling, Nathan set his jaw and nodded in dismissal. "There being no other questions—move out!"

"Ouch! I trod on a rock!"

"I'm not surprised. First, you mistook that vine for a snake. Then you mangled that poor little plant because you were *convinced* it was a poisonous spider. For pity's sake, Caroline, stop complaining, do!" Mariah snapped, thrashing a path through the waist-high vegetation that walled them in as she spoke.

Rather than brandishing a stout machete to break the trail, she was wielding the puny length of bamboo Jack had gallantly presented her with before they'd set off. Unfortunately, the beaten-down grass sprang up the moment they'd passed by. Vines and creepers closed behind them like the Red Sea behind the fleeing children of Israel!

117

"It's all very well for you, Mariah You practically begged Kincaid to let us go a-blundering through this wretched jungle. Never mind asking me if *I* wanted to go or nay! Oh, this infernal heat! I'm suffocating in this wretched dress, and why? Because you're in a bad temper—from what cause, I know not—and determined to cross everyone!"

"You ungrateful child! I thought you'd welcome any excuse for an adventure. But, perhaps I misjudged you. Perhaps you'd rather we sat in the shade and twiddled our thumbs, day in and day out," Mariah retorted scathingly, "considered useless simply because we're women."

"Of course I wouldn't," Caroline admitted sheepishly. Her shoulders sagged. "Oh, coz, I'm sorry. I'm just cross because I'm hot and sticky, and I want so badly to catch my breath, to have a cool English sea-breeze fanning my face and not a loathsome insect in sight. And I'd *so* love a goblet of ice-cold water! If I close my eyes, I can almost feel it sliding down my throat like melting snowflakes."

"Aye, some fresh water would be welcome," Mariah admitted with a sigh, her irritation melting like Caroline's imaginary snowflakes.

"I do hope they manage to rid the pool of those wretched apes by the time we return to camp, don't you?"

"Do I!"

"Just imagine, coz, drinking real water again, instead of coconut milk."

"Mmm, heaven!" Mariah agreed. That exotic, sickly-sweet delicacy had quickly palled.

"And perhaps Nathan would let us swim in the pool, too?" Caroline suggested wistfully, plucking the damp folds of her green gown away from her body. She swept her limp fair hair up and piled it atop her head. "Phew! It's so humid today, I'm soaked, and yet the sun's scarcely risen! I feel like the grubbiest street urchin in St. Giles! Not to mention reeking like one."

"*Lady Mariah! Mistress Caroline!* Oh! There you are!" exclaimed Tim Bright, the *Hester*'s second cabin boy, suddenly

118

appearing between the bushes on the path ahead. "I was . . .
I . . . um . . . that is, Master Matherson sent me back to find
you. We thought we'd lost you. I . . . he—we, that is—were
worried something might have happened to you."

"As you can see, nothing at all has happened to *either* of
us," Mariah reassured pointedly. There was a twinkle in her
eyes as she said either, for he looked only at her cousin. "We
stopped to catch our breath, but we'll be along straightaway."

"Your pardon, m'lady, but Master Matherson said it's dangerous for you to fall behind. He said you'd best come along
with me when I found you," Tim said doubtfully, his attractive
features scrunching up in a frown.

"Then of course we'll go with you at once, Master Bright,"
Caroline promised, lowering her lashes and positively simpering. "If you would be so kind as to offer your arm . . . ?"

"*Yes*! Er, I mean, yes, miss, I would be delighted . . . er
. . . that is, I'd be most honored, Mistress Amberfield!" Tim
stammered, blushing to the roots of his golden hair.

Caroline smiled, extending her hand. To her surprise, Tim
drew his fist from behind his back and thrust a spray of delicate,
frilly white blossoms with pale mauve throats into it. "Here,
miss. Master Matherson says these are orchids. They're quite
rare, he reckons. I . . . I picked them for . . . um . . ."

"For me? Oh, how sweet of you! They're simply lovely.
Thank you, Timothy!" Caroline exclaimed, her face glowing
as she tucked one of the dewy flowers behind her ear and buried
her nose in the rest. "Shall we join the others?"

With that, she took the lad's elbow and let him lead the way,
for all the world like a South Seas' princess, Mariah clearly
forgotten.

"That little minx!" Mariah shook her head ruefully. She
muttered to the bushes, "So much for her complaints and her
fascination with Kincaid. A gawky lad smiles at her, and she
forgets everything but him! La!" With that, she plunged after
the pair, reluctant to be left behind.

The jungle—or tropical rainforest, as Master Matherson had

said it should more properly be called—was at once both threatening and beautiful, filled with all manner of wild life, both visible and hidden. Parrots and cockatoos squawked and chattered in the dense crowns of the trees way above her, flashing brilliant scarlet, green, or white wings. Insects of every kind swarmed the tree-trunks or scurried underfoot, while the humid air hummed with their busy song—and with a thrumming, secret life all its own.

Shortly after entering the forest that morning, they'd spotted a beautiful male bird—a bird-of-paradise, Matherson had said it was called—as large as a crow. Performing a courtship dance for his prospective lady-love, he'd been bobbing his magnificent golden-plumed head, spreading his emerald collar, and flapping his maroon wings in a comical fashion, while his long, emerald-patterned tail swept the air beneath his perch.

Kingfishers with iridescent blue-green plumage flitted from branch to branch, while fruit-bats slept away the daylight hours hanging upside in huge numbers and looking like leather gauntlets. She'd also seen bright-winged butterflies as big as small birds, numerous lizards, large and small, and—oh, yes—several horrid snakes hanging from the trees, some masquerading as slim, coiling creepers, others as big around as her arm and as beautifully patterned as any silk shawl, though she wisely hadn't pointed them out to an already skittish Caroline, who was a . . .

Mariah stopped short, looking about her in sudden confusion. She'd thought she was following the same path Tim and Caroline had taken, but they were nowhere in sight, nor were there any sounds to guide her. Of a sudden, the parrots and the monkeys had fallen eerily silent. The insects had ceased their lazy droning. The very air seemed to be holding its breath, and waiting—though for what or for whom she was certain she didn't want to know. For the first time since they'd entered the jungle, she was frightened. Neither snakes nor the threat of being attacked by wild animals had been able to alarm her as strongly as this unnatural hush.

A trickle of perspiration slithered down her spine to join the sticky puddle at the small of her back. With a muttered curse, she yanked off the stifling Navy jacket and flung it to the grass. Thunderation! Which way should she go?

"Mariah?"

The voice breaking the unnerving silence startled her, sent her whirling about with one hand flying to her mouth.

"Oh, Lieutenant Digby! You startled me!"

"I did? Then, my apologies, dear lady. Frightening you was the farthest thing from my mind," Warren Digby apologized smoothly. Thumbs hooked under his suspenders, he wove his way between the lush grasses, ducking low-hanging branches and festoons of dangling creepers to reach her side.

Something in his tone—something repugnant in his grey eyes and in the curl of his lips—sent skitters of alarm through Mariah as he stood beside her, so close his white uniform breeches brushed her skirts. The liquid green-and-golden light dappled his face as she glanced up at him, and what she saw in his features made her blood run cold. Nay, it could not be! He was staring at her, staring as Edward had been wont to stare before he . . .

"Did Master Matherson send you back to find me?" she asked breathlessly, swallowing hard to stifle the panicky scream that threatened. Damn her foolish imagination, to see a threat where none existed. 'Twas only Warren Digby, after all, not Edward. 'Twould never, ever be Edward again. Edward was dead, buried somewhere in India. She upbraided herself, yet her heart was hammering uncontrollably.

"That fussy old weed-gatherer?" Digby snorted, his expression contemptuous. "Hardly! No, I took it upon myself to double back and let the others go on alone." Slyly, he cocked his fair head to one side and added, "I knew, you see."

"Knew what, sir?" Mariah asked, moving hastily aside as he took a step closer.

He sighed. "Knew that you'd hung back for a reason."

Not understanding, she shook her head. "Not so, sir. I lost the path, became separated from my—"

"Nonsense, Mariah," Digby cut in impatiently. "Come, now. Admit it! Admit you wanted to be alone with me, and be done with pretense, dear heart."

"Pretense?" she echoed, still too stunned to fully comprehend what he'd said.

"Aye! Surely you didn't think I'd forgotten all those evenings aboard ship, you on one side of the captain's table, myself on the other. Remember? Ah, Mariah, those naughty, flirtatious little smiles you cast my way! You cannot imagine the sleepless nights I passed on your account."

"Not mine, sir! I cast you no such coy looks!"

"And I knew last night 'twas more than gratitude I glimpsed in your eyes—you know, when I gave you my jacket? And so, I waited—impatiently, I confess," he added with a chuckle, "intending to join you in your hut after moonrise. But then I saw you leave camp. I followed you down to the beach, but what did I find? That bloody convict—Kincaid—was already there, prowling about, up to no good. I had no weapon, so I hid and watched."

"You spied upon me!" she flared, furious. "How dare you!"

"Nay, my intent was to ensure your safety, and 'twas fortunate I was there," Digby continued in his self-righteous tone, "for I saw Kincaid try to force himself upon you."

"You're wrong."

"Not so." His eyes had taken on a feverish glitter now. His expression was hard and closed, his long, lean features stony and implacable. "Don't deny it, and don't try to defend him. I saw him, and your tears as you fled cut me to the quick. By God, if that filthy swine hadn't taken my knife, I'd have killed him!"

"Lieutenant Digby," she cut in sharply.

"Warren, Mariah. You must call me Warren, darling, if we're to be lovers." He reached out to caress her cheek, but she jerked her head aside as if his fingertips were serpents.

"Lovers!" The word exploded from her like a curse.

"Surely the heat has addled your wits, sir, for I surely gave you no fuel for your fantasies, neither here nor aboard the *Hester*."

"Fantasies?" The sensual, heavy-lidded look fled his eyes. Anger replaced it.

"Aye!"

"Oh, come, come, Mariah, 'tis no fantasy. I am, after all, a man of the world. I acknowledge that a young, beautiful widow like yourself has certain needs. 'Tis nothing to be ashamed of that you look to me to supply those needs. Rather, I am flattered."

She snorted. "You really are mad if you think that I would *ever* look to—"

"Nay, my dove, not mad, merely candid. Your eyes, your smile, your very tone betray your feelings. Deny it, if you must for pride's sake, but you want me. As I want you."

"Never!"

"Aye, 'tis so! And, since we are far from all we hold dear, we must do whatever we can to make our lives more bearable. Come, dear heart, let me love you. You'll see. We shall find such comfort in each other's arms—"

"Comfort be damned, sir. You presume too much! Oh! Let go of me, damn you!"

There was true terror in her voice as he jerked her roughly towards him, gripping her upper arms with fingers that bruised like manacles. She struggled to break free, but then his fair head dipped and instead of Digby's grey eyes but inches from hers, in the green-and-golden light she saw the cruel amber tiger-eyes of her husband. She was close to swooning even as she finally found voice to scream.

'Twas the nightmare of her wedding night, all over again. . . .

Chapter Eight

The jungle had suddenly thinned out before them, and it was there that Matherson found what he had been searching for since leaving camp that morning.

Before him lay a shady glade where all manner of lush plants abounded in the mutable green-gold light that filtered down between the tree-tops. Creamy-blossomed frangipani trees scented the sultry air with their perfume. Flowering lianas spiralled up the trunks and cascaded from the branches of towering teak or sandalwood trees. Delicate sprays of tiny white, lavendar or yellow orchids bloomed in butterfly clouds from woody stems that had attached themselves to the trunks of other trees. But it was not the rare and lovely orchids that had caused Matherson's excitement. Rather, it was the discovery of hundreds of deep-green plants with heart-shaped leaves as big as serving platters atop stout stalks that made him exclaim with delight as he knelt in the marsh to examine them.

"'Pon my word, what fortune! If I'm not mistaken, these are the very plants that Cook's men brought back from the

Pacific. The natives of Polynesia call this *taro* or *karo*. 'Tis the mainstay of their diet, as bread is to our own.''

''Happen you may be right, sir. But as for eatin' 'em, well, I don't like the look of 'em at all, sir,'' Archer said doubtfully. ''Nah, not a bit! Like as not, they be poison t' us white men.''

''Nonsense, my good man,'' Matherson denied, chuckling. ''The leaves may be boiled and eaten like cabbage, and are most beneficial to the blood. And the root—see, it's here, buried deep in the mud—is very large and starchy. When boiled and with that thick skin removed, it tastes like our humble potato, I've heard. Oh, what a find! Come along now, men. You, Archer, pick as many of those leaves as you can fit into your hat. Babbington, you do the same. Big Ben, you, Lewis . . . and Doolan—try to pull up the roots. We shall—''

''Christ! Wot's that!'' exclaimed Ben, as Caroline and Tim burst, laughing, from the jungle behind them. ''I 'eard summat!''

''A wild animal, perhaps?'' Matherson suggested doubtfully, looking uneasily over his shoulder, for he'd also heard the uncannily human cry. Glancing across at Caroline and Tim Bright, who were preoccupied in making sheeps' eyes at each other, he frowned. ''Mistress Amberfield, where is Lady Mariah?''

''Mariah?'' Caroline looked about her, brows arched. ''Why, she was . . .'' Her smile vanished when she saw no sign of her cousin bringing up in the rear. ''Wherever can she have gone? She was right behind us, wasn't she, Tim?''

''Aye!'' Tim agreed. ''You stay here, Miss Caroline. I'll go back and look for her.''

''No, lad, stay. I'll go,'' Matherson said firmly. ''Ben, accompany me, if you'd be so kind. The rest of you, wait here. I think a brief rest is permissible, until our return.''

With that parting, Matherson left the party lounging gratefully in the shade. He plunged back into the rank vegetation, Ben slipping after him like a shadow.

There was little indication of the way they'd taken on their outward trek, save for an occasional bent branch or a clump of trodden-down grass that guided the botanist in retracing their footsteps. Too soon, even these gave out. Matherson was about to admit that he feared they were moving in circles when they both heard another piercing scream.

"C'mon. This way, gov'na!" Ben urged, shouldering between some bushes to their right. Matherson followed hard on his heels.

They both brought up short at the sight of Lieutenant Digby kneeling upon the grass before them. Mariah was draped across his arms, her own dangling limply. Her eyes were closed, and her hair had escaped its ribbon and swept the jungle-floor beneath her. At the sound of their approach, Digby turned his head. For a second, his wild expression was that of a stranger; then he composed his features.

"What happened here, man?" the botanist demanded sharply.

"Deuced if I know, Matherson. The poor chit thought herself abandoned, 'twould appear, and panicked," Digby volunteered with a careless shrug. "I was following Bright and the other girl, you see, when I heard her cry out. Naturally, I turned back, and arrived to catch her as she swooned. Perhaps she spied a snake. You know how silly women can be about such things."

"I'll warrant she saw a snake," Ben muttered darkly. "A slimy bloody serpent wot walks on *two* legs!"

"Enough, Ben," Matherson murmured. "She's coming to."

Tight-lipped, Digby stepped back as the botanist waved him aside. He knelt on the grass beside Mariah. Taking her limp, clammy hands in his own, Matherson chafed them to revive her. "Lady Mariah! Lady Mariah, come along, now!"

Her lashes fluttered like dusky fans against the pallor of her cheeks. She moaned once, then opened her eyes, their pupils widening and then darkening with alarm as she looked beyond Matherson to where Digby stood, arms crossed over his chest.

"What happened, Lady Downing?" Digby demanded before Matherson could put the question, fixing on Mariah with an intense, threatening look that Ben, watching the exchange, observed. "Did a snake frighten you, was that it?"

"Tell us, dear lady," Matherson urged. "There's no need to be afraid. You're among friends now. Was it a snake—or some other creature—that made you swoon?"

For a second, it seemed Mariah might deny it. But then she nodded faintly and tried to sit up. "Yes, it was a snake. A truly horrid creature, slithering through the grass on its belly." For a fleeting second, her eyes flicked to Digby, then moved as quickly away. "I'm quite recovered now, really. You mustn't worry. 'Twas childish of me to swoon."

With that, she scrambled to a standing position, brushing off her grass-stained petticoats as she accepted the botanist's assistance. There were dead leaves in her tangled hair, Matherson noted. Angry red weals, as if made by a man's rough beard, marred the soft, creamy skin about her mouth. The lieutenant's jacket she'd worn earlier lay in a forgotten heap upon the grass, while the ribbon strap of her bodice was torn. Matherson's jaw tightened. If it'd really been a snake that had frightened her, then he was a Dutchman! "Are you quite certain you're all right? There's nothing you wish to tell me?" Matherson pressed, convinced all was far from well, and that the poor young woman was afraid to speak.

As Mariah followed the direction of his gaze, color flooded her pale cheeks. With trembling fingers, she reached up and knotted the ragged ends of her strap together. "Nothing, sir. I'm quite all right. May we rejoin the others now?"

"Very well. If that is what you wish, then take my arm. That way, I believe, Ben. Lead us on, if you would."

"Right you are, gov'na," Ben said, casting Digby a murderous look. He hawked and spat pointedly into a bush, before taking the lead.

127

Within moments, they had returned to the others, who exclaimed with relief on seeing Mariah safe. On Matherson's instructions, Caroline led her cousin beneath a fragrant, flowering tree so she might recover in the shade while the botanist put his rested party to work again. Once all of the men had been given tasks to see to, Matherson turned with marked reluctance to Digby, who'd followed them, but had made no effort to help.

"As for you, Lieutenant Digby, perhaps you'd be good enough to—"

"On the contrary, I wouldn't be 'good enough' to do anything, damn you, Matherson. I'm not an old woman, like some, to be meekly put to work gathering vegetables." Digby snorted in contempt.

Matherson colored under his sallow scholar's complexion. He loosened his ragged white stock and cleared his throat, an angry pulse twitching in his narrow jaw. "Now see here, sir! Kincaid said—"

"Kincaid, Kincaid. Devil take Kincaid!" Digby spat. "I've had a bellyful of that strutting convict. I spit on his damned orders—and so should any other self-respecting man! Carry on with your blasted leaf-picking, if it pleases you, Matherson. I'll have none of it."

"If you would eat, Lieutenant, you'll pull your weight," Matherson cautioned, a quiet sternness to his tone that surprised Mariah. The bookish botanist was proving a man of hidden depths. He added, "'Else, go hungry."

"Pah! Then so be it. I'd sooner starve than eat your vile weeds, schoolteacher!" Digby jeered. "Or any morsel Kincaid's fawning lapdogs might provide. Let him have his blasted 'taro'—and his little whore!"

With a contemptuous glance at Mariah, he lashed out viciously at the nearest plants and thrust his way back into the jungle. The dense vegetation swallowed him up as if he'd never been.

"Hell's bloody bells, I smell a storm a-brewin'," Big Ben

muttered darkly. "And this un's got nothin' t' do wiv the bloomin' weather, neither!"

"Amen t' that!" Lewis agreed, shaking his red head.

Mariah exchanged glances with Master Matherson, and knew by the concern in his eyes that he'd guessed what had happened. Judging by his troubled expression, he agreed with Ben's ominous prediction—as did she.

She shivered, remembering Digby's foul lips on hers, the cruel, bruising fingers that had plucked and torn at her clothing and kneaded her breasts as he'd forced her to the grass. Nathan's "little whore," he'd called her, and the expression in his eyes had been frightening. They must warn Nathan to guard his back!

That same night, the castaways celebrated their victory over the baboons in the newly-won clearing by the pool, feasting on monkeys, parrots, and fish roasted in a pit of rocks under the fire, and drinking all the fresh water they could stomach.

The waterfall's constant shushing sound was a melody Mariah was certain she would never tire of hearing, for it symbolized an end to parched throats, furry tongues, and the craving for water that coconut milk had never quite managed to dispel. She sat on a flat rock at water's edge, flannel petticoats immodestly hitched above her knees, dipping her blistered feet in the cool water.

Once the baboon troop had been soundly routed, Nathan and the others had inspected the clearing and surrounding area with great care. By the time Matherson's party returned to camp to hear the good news from Jack Warner, the place had been declared safe.

Old Peg had carefully taken embers from their signal-fire on the beach to this new area, and a third fire had been built there. When everyone left at dusk for their camp beneath the palms, guards Nathan had selected would remain behind to make sure the baboons did not return.

Mariah shivered, for despite its beauty, the clearing was a disturbing place, one that reminded her too vividly of that morning. When the night creatures awoke to hunt and uttered their eerie calls, or when their red or amber eyes shone through the emerald darkness, the guards would welcome the fire's cheerful blaze. She did not envy them, spending the night in this spot, far from camp. The clearing and pool seemed carved from the pulsing heart of the jungle itself; alive with pagan vibrations.

In an effort to dispel her uneasiness, she looked about her. Caroline was petting the baby monkey cradled in her arms, an orphan the hunting detail had given her, but she was watching Tim Bright's animated face, an adoring expression on hers, as he recounted some amusing story or other she appeared to have quite forgotten Nathan Kincaid's existence—and her fascination with him!

Jack Warner and Old Peg, Big Ben and Archer were making sport with the new leg Jack had carved for Old Peg—ribald jests about the size of the wooden limb, judging by their bawdy guffaws. The marines were throwing the dice one man had discovered tucked in his pockets, wagering sea-shells in place of the rations of grog they'd gambled for aboard ship. Only Matherson, deep in conversation with Nathan, seemed in any way low-spirited this evening, and Mariah guessed the reason for his glum face.

The leaves and roots of the taro plants he'd discovered had to be boiled before being eaten, a necessity the botanist had forgotten until they'd returned to camp. If the leaves were not boiled, an itchy rash resulted from eating this delicacy, he'd glumly told them. But, alas, lacking a kettle, there was no means by which to cook his precious find!

Seeing Matherson with Nathan reminded Mariah of Digby. Though she'd heard from Jack and Peg that the lieutenant had returned to camp briefly following his disappearance that morning, no one had seen him since or knew his whereabouts now. Some of the men were of the opinion he'd joined the

130

convict camp around the point. "Bloody good riddance to 'im, too!" one had declared.

She stood and made her way to where the two men sat.

". . . I believe we may be fortunate in recovering a number of items," Kincaid was saying.

As her shadow fell across them, both men looked up.

"Why, Lady Mariah! Won't you join us, my dear? Nathan's just been telling me that all is not lost!" Matherson declared happily. "We may be able to boil the taro roots on the 'morrow. Then, I promise you, we shall all sleep like infants, with full bellies and glad hearts!"

"You've found a kettle," she guessed. The flotsam and jetsam washed ashore with the incoming tides that day had yielded a number of "treasures."

"Not exactly," Nathan said, his green eyes twinkling with the secret. "But . . . we know where one can be found."

"Really? And where's that?"

"Aboard the wreck of the *Hester*."

"The wreck!"

"Aye. And 'tis only by a stroke of good fortune we discovered her whereabouts! Our fishermen spotted her main mast jutting up above the water this morning. The ocean was calm as a mill-pond, they said, with no sign of sharks or sea-crocs in sight. So, one of the lads decided to risk it and swim out to her. She lies in shallow water about a mile from where I washed up. God willing, we may salvage any number of things that will make our lives here far more comfortable!"

"How marvellous! And does Lieutenant Digby know of this find?" Mariah asked suddenly, a twist of foreboding in her vitals.

"I believe he does, aye. 'Twas shortly before he returned to camp that the *Hester*'s mast was sighted." Nathan paused, then demanded, "Why do you ask?" The jealousy he'd felt that morning reared its ugly head again. Was she enamored of Digby? Was that why she'd asked after the lieutenant?

"Did you tell Master Kincaid what happened this morning, sir?" she asked Matherson. Nathan should be warned about

Digby's loathing for him, or he'd run the risk of being caught unawares.

"Only that we exchanged hard words—and that he should guard his back, my dear. I . . . um . . . I said nothing of the . . . er . . . other matter, since you insisted all was well." There was mild reproof in his tone.

"What 'other matter'?" Nathan demanded, glancing sharply from Matherson to Mariah, and her heart sank. "Well?"

Mariah looked down at her hands, clasped in her lap, reluctant to tell Nathan about the incident. He would react with anger and, like as not, would want to call the lieutenant to account. She wanted no bloodshed on her hands! "I'd intended to say nothing about it, but perhaps 'tis best you should know what manner of man Digby is," she said at length. "This morning, I foolishly became separated from our group. Digby, he . . . he surprised me alone, in the jungle. He accused me of encouraging his attentions while aboard the *Hester* and again last night. When I . . . when I denied it, he became quite . . . ardent to prove his point."

Her expression told him far more than her simple explanation.

"That bastard! Did he hurt you?" Nathan snarled, springing to his feet. His face was dark with fury. Although she shook her head, he clenched his fists and cords rippled in his powerful arms. "By God, I'll kill him!"

"Please, Nathan, don't!" she cried. "'Twas for this very reason I decided to keep my peace. Master Matherson arrived before he could do me any great harm, really. I was more frightened than anything."

"You're sure?"

"Aye, I am. And, since it seems Digby has left our camp, and 'tis unlikely he'll return, I'm in no danger he'll try again. Please, forget about him. Don't let him spoil our celebration. Everyone's worked so hard. We have good food, fresh water— and each other! What more could we ask for?" she coaxed.

Like a raging lion gentled by a lamb, Nathan relaxed and let the tension ebb from him. "Very well. If that's what you wish, then so be it, for now. However, if Digby returns, he'll account for his actions to me. Upon my honor, he'll answer for them!"

He'd not been guilty of murder before, but he felt capable of committing it right then. Aye, and with his two bare hands.

It was soon after daybreak next morning when Ruskin, summoned by the shouts of his men, stirred his bones to leave his lean-to.

Well, well! They'd taken a prisoner, he saw, his shaggy, sandy brows lifting. An evil smile split his filthy beard.

"Who's this, then?" he growled, scratching an armpit.

"Dunno, gov'na. Caught 'im snoopin' about in the trees, we did. 'E were spyin' on us!"

"Was he now?" Ruskin eyed the sorry-looking captive's attire. White blouse, but no braided jacket. White breeches with gold buttons to mid-thigh. White stockings. No shoes. His red lips parted in a lupine smile. "Well, well! A sailor-boy, eh? An officer of His Majesty's bleeding Navy, no less, 'else I'm blind. What do ye say, laddies? Do we hang the bastard from the nearest branch, flay his back t' ribbons—or use him as the pretty lass he looks t' be?"

Ruskin sauntered over to the captive, who hung by the arms between his two men. He gripped his chin and jerked his head up. "Good morrow, my bonnie love! Will ye give us a kiss, lassie?" he asked, puckering his lips and making rude, smacking noises.

The captive, already fair of complexion, paled still further. "For the love of God, Ruskin, order your men to free me! I'm no spy—I've come to join you!"

"Oh, have ye now?" Ruskin sneered. "And why, pray tell, would a pretty sailor-boy like yerself want ter join our select wee company, eh?"

The convicts sniggered.

Their prisoner swallowed. "If we're to survive on this island, we need a strong leader—one such as yourself, sir. I . . . I left the others because they follow a man I cannot countenance.'' Despite his battered and bruised condition, he yet managed to sound pompous as he added, "One Jonathan Kincaid—a convict and a murderer!'' Realizing the folly of his words, he added hastily, "Not that I'm a man to hold anyone's past sins against him, you understand? I simply . . . er . . . found myself quite unable to respect Kincaid, and so, I came here to offer you my services.''

So, his old enemy, "Lawyer'' Kincaid led the other band? Ruskin's pale eyes gleamed with spite. They had old scores left unsettled from Newgate Gaol, he and Kincaid. . . . Meanwhile, the pretty boy's lick-arse ways made him sick to his gut, but, since he enjoyed a bit o' sport with his victims before he finished them off, he said silkily, "Och, is that so, Mr. . . . ?''

"My name's Digby, sir. Lieutenant Warren Digby, formerly an officer of His Majesty's Navy and now—''

"And now Angus Ruskin's pretty pet,'' Ruskin purred, stroking the lieutenant's buttock with a beefy paw. "Tell me, laddie, is it true what they say about sailor-boys? That ye make do at sea wi' out any wenches t' serve yer needs?''

Lulled by Ruskin's congenial tone and manner, for the moment Digby stood quite still and seriously considered Ruskin's question. Then abject horror filled his eyes as he realized the convict had been making sport of him. And worse. Ruskin's hand was upon his backside! He bucked violently to escape the fondling and let out a squeal like a suckling pig's.

Digby's reactions drew guffaws of laughter from the coarse convicts that surrounded them now. The women—former beggars, thieves, and doxies—whooped and catcalled. The boldest wenches screeched filthy suggestions as to what uses the captive might be put to, while their men roared with laughter or gestured lewdly and whistled.

A dark flush seeped into Digby's cheeks. Sweat broke out

on his brow and palms and the urge to piss grew overwhelming. Dear Christ, his welcome had not been the one he'd hoped for! Indeed, he thought it likely they'd kill him, after they'd had their fun with him. And what form their sport might take, he dared not contemplate!

Angus joined in with the others' merriment, adding his insults to theirs, but he quickly wearied of the sport. "I've had enough. He's yours, lads," he said finally, grinning as his men cheered. "Do what ye will with him—then slit his blasted throat an' feed him t' the fish!" He turned back to the lean-to, bellowing for Kitty to follow him as he went.

"Wait! I . . . I didn't come empty-handed!" Digby pleaded.

Ruskin paused. His expression grew sly. "Nay?"

"No! I have valuable information to trade!"

"Information, is it? And pray, what 'information' could the likes o' you have that'd save your lily-white arse, laddie?"

"Release me, and I'll tell you."

Angus hesitated, minded to bid him go to hell, but then he nodded to his two men. Weak with relief, Digby reeled about on jellied legs, too frightened to speak.

"Well? Out with it!" Ruskin bellowed.

"Kincaid has found water—fresh water," he babbled, "more than sufficient for all our needs, *if* he were inclined to share it—which he isn't!"

Ruskin's eyes narrowed. "And?"

"And then there's the *Hester* herself—they've found her wreck! She settled in shallow waters off the reef. They mean to send divers down to bring up whatever may be salvaged!"

"When?" Ruskin barked.

"This morning."

"Ah. And where is fresh water to be found?" the big Scot asked slyly.

"'Tis a hidden place, deep in the jungle—the very devil to find unless ye know the way, as I do," Digby lied. "Kincaid's posted armed guards there, to boot." The information tumbled from his lips in a torrent, so desperate was he to purchase his life. "Let me join you, Ruskin. If you do, I swear I'll show you the waterfall . . . where the *Hester* lies . . . *everything*."

"Clever laddie," Angus praised softly. "Ye've saved yer arse by tellin' me this. Lads, leave off yer funnin' wi' our new friend, do. Nancy, lass, take care o' Mr. Digby. See him given a bite t' eat and a wee dram of grog—and after, a taste o' your bonnie charms wouldna go amiss, I'd wager. Come sun-up, ye'll lead us t' the *Hester*'s wreck, Digby, lad. First, we'll see what weapons can be salvaged from her stores. And then—"

"Then we go after the water, right, Rusk?" one of his men supplied with a wolfish grin.

"Aye," Ruskin agreed. "Soon."

Digby, weak with relief, grinned like a simpleton as pretty Nan led him away.

Chapter Nine

Despite Mariah's fears, Digby did not return to their camp. And, with every day that passed without sign of him, she began to relax her guard and give herself up to the rhythm of their new life on the island, a rhythm that was dictated by the need to find food, draw water, and repair or reinforce their shelters; or by the vagaries of the island climate, an adversary that quickly proved more lethal than any stalking enemy, for within hours of each other, two of their small number lay dead.

The first to lose his life on the isle was a shy fellow named Booker, a flaxen-haired marine with the height and girth of a giant who'd volunteered to dig the camp a latrine with his bare hands, lacking a spade for the task.

For two hours he'd labored like a great, tireless hound digging for a lost bone, scooping out a long deep trough. Handfuls of powdery dry sand became handfuls of golden mud as the pit he dug grew deeper and wider.

Marine Stiles, husking coconuts nearby and keeping up a lively, running monologue that Booker commented on with an occasional grunt of agreement or a burst of laughter, had been the first to notice something was amiss.

". . . Wish t' Gawd we'd been stranded wi' a comely doxie wench or two, don't you, Booker, me lad? Cor, wot I'd give fer a tumble wi' a willing, plump-arsed chit right now, one wiv tits as big as melons! Them bleedin' baboons is startin' t' look right fetchin', they is—and Gawd knows, I've tumbled uglier wenches!'' Rolling his eyes and rubbing his groin, he'd brayed with laughter, expecting some similar reaction to his crude comments from Booker. The blond giant was shy, but he was no prude.

Accordingly, when Booker made no response, Stiles turned around. His saw his friend was red-faced and staggering about like a drunkard, and at first thought the huge man was overcome by laughter before he realized it was nothing of the sort. ''Whoa! Wot's up, matey? Hey, Booker!'' he yelled in alarm, just as Booker collapsed face down in the trough he'd dug. He rolled over, then lay there, moaning hoarsely that he was afire.

''Jesus, I'm burning' up!'' he whimpered. ''Water! For pity's sake, water!'' Moments later, his great body began thrashing about, limbs jerking uncontrollably, jaws threatening to bite his tongue in two.

''Sweet Jesus Christ! *Babbingtoonn!* Hop to it, mate! Fetch the sawbones, an' sharpish! Booker's 'avin a fit!''

By the time the portly ship's surgeon arrived, Booker's convulsion had passed. Surgeon Love examined him and found his face deeply flushed, his skin hot and dry to the touch, his pulse galloping, although judging by Booker's grimy uniform blouse, which was dry, the man appeared to have lost little sweat, despite his exertions.

''Did he go into the jungle?'' the physician snapped, but Stiles said no. ''Then did ye see any cursed snakes about, man?'' Again, Stiles shook his head. ''What about a spider, then? Or a scorpion?'' But Stiles' answer was again negative.

Moments later, Booker had suffered yet another violent fit and had died in Love's arms.

Mortified by his inability to help, let alone ease the poor devil's last moments, Surgeon Love had gruffly ordered Booker buried in the pit he'd dug little knowing it would prove his grave. And, citing an unknown fever as the probable cause of the marine's death, before they silently returned to camp, he had sternly cautioned the men who'd been working with Booker to watch themselves for symptoms.

Able Seaman McTavish, a thin wiry Scot, was the second to go. Apparently in robust health that day, he had been enthusiastically hefting rocks to make a crude wall about their camp—a defense against wild beasts, he'd informed his amused fellows, who'd declined to help him. Some while later, he'd suddenly complained that his head was splitting with pain and that the "tropick victuals" must surely have "set his belly awry." Then, red-faced, he'd flung himself about and staggered down to the water. But before he reached it, he had also taken a fit and died before anyone could summon the sawbones.

It was a glum company that gathered around the cooking fire that night following the two deaths, for each one of the survivors wondered if he—or she—would be next to succumb.

But when no further deaths occurred the next day, or the one following, the ever-observant Matherson remarked that in hot countries it was customary for the natives to sleep away the hours just before noon and not resume their labors until the cooler hours of early evening. Could hard work in unaccustomed heat have killed the two men? he asked.

"Heat? Never!" Surgeon Love had scoffed at such an idea, citing "foul miasmas" from the mangrove swamps or some mysterious tropical malaise as the culprit. He'd wistfully bemoaned not having the leeches so vital to his vocation, grumbling that if he had, he would have been able to bleed the two men, and draw off the bad blood that had surely made their brains boil and thus caused the fits. Given leeches, he was certain he could have saved their lives. When Matherson, in a sincere effort to ease the man's conscience, had offered the opinion that bleeding would not have helped, Love had frostily suggested that Matherson stick to the science of botany, with which he was familiar, and leave the science of medicine to surgeons, such as himself, who knew what they were about.

Nathan, Master Carmichael, and Jack, however, had privately put their heads together and come to the conclusion that Matherson was nearer the mark: hard work in an unfamiliar, steaming climate had been the one factor common to both men's deaths. Consequently, Nathan had given orders that henceforth, everyone would rest during the hottest hours of the day.

The evenings they passed in lively fashion—once the shock of Booker and McTavish's deaths had worn off—conversing about the camp-fire, unless driven inside their huts by one of the fine, misty rain-showers that frequently fell after dusk and lasted until shortly before dawn. All of them heartily enjoyed the impromptu entertainments one or other of the men felt moved to perform for his fellows.

Tim Bright and Tom Swift surprised them all with a song one night—a hymn, to be exact—and the sweetness of their youthful harmony brought tears to everyone's eyes. Memories of cherubic choirboys, musty, dog-eared hymn-books, and Sunday services celebrated in village churches of grey stone and slate filled them all with the longing for home and a familiar hearth—or indeed, any hearth.

Aye, without Digby's dissenting voice to stir up bad feelings, tension in the camp had eased enormously. In its place, friendship and trust were growing rapidly out of their need to depend upon each other for survival. Even Old Peg had relaxed and now showed his true colors as their "court jester," bringing laughter to the camp with his raucous clowning.

The spry, irreverent cockney, Big Ben, could do wicked impersonations, they soon discovered. He had them all holding their sides and laughing helplessly with his imitations of that faithless reprobate Captain Harkabout "flogging a dead horse," the horse in this instance being Old Peg, who lay upon his back with both arms and legs straight up in the air, a "tail" of coconut fibres stuffed into the waist of his sailor's cotton drawers and his headscarf over his face, as dead a nag as any you might find; or else Ben imitated the bookish Master Matherson, squinting short-sightedly as he exclaimed over some new "find" or other.

"Why, lads, 'pon my soul, this specimen is a very rare variety of rock—Rocatus Solidus is it's Latin name, I do believe. You will notice that, loike our beloved Master Peg, Rocatus Solidus rarely stirs its bloomin' bum t' hard work, much less sez an intelligent word. . . !" and so it went.

Irreverent to the last, Ben even dared to imitate Nathan, aping his long, easy stride and the bold set of his broad shoulders with uncanny accuracy, while barking absurd orders at which even his victim could not help but smile.

As for Nathan, he'd quickly found the beat of his position as their leader, shouldering the responsibility as if to the manor born. And with each passing day he proved himself more worthy of the confidence the men had placed in him, grew more relaxed in his role and less inclined to demand perfection of himself.

The morning following the discovery of the *Hester*'s wreckage, he had determined to risk attack from both sharks and sea-crocodiles and had dived down to the broken vessel. Making dive after dive in the succeeding days, he'd brought up whatever he could salvage from the shattered timbers for their use. The results had been rewarding. Several daggers, some cutlasses, a hammer, a saw, an axe, kegs of iron nails, and a half-dozen pewter mugs had been added to their supply of weapons and tools, as well as some other things, one of them being the precious black kettle brought up with enormous difficulty from its watery grave in the sunken vessel's galley. Matherson now was able to boil his blessed taro, and the cooking detail could produce a savory monkey or fish stew, replete with island roots and herbs. These ingredients they scooped up with their fingers from coconut bowls.

Jack Warner, meanwhile, was trying to repair one of the *Hester*'s longboats that had washed ashore at high tide one evening, though he'd confided to Nathan that he doubted he could replace the shattered planking along its side, let alone render it sufficiently watertight to stay afloat for very long without pitch to caulk its seams.

Caroline and Tim Bright, who were both convinced that they would eventually be rescued—Tim because of his abiding faith in God and Caroline because of her trust in her beloved papa, Governor Amberfield—had been presented with Harkabout's brass spyglass. The pair used it hourly to scan the empty horizon for signs of a sail. They had been given the equally vital task of keeping the signal bonfire on the beach ablaze both day and night.

Tom Swift, the *Hester*'s second cabin-boy, a bolder, stockier youth than gentle Tim Bright, had also developed a *tendresse* for Caroline as the first week had become the second, then the third, Mariah had observed. She was amused by the airy indifference the little minx displayed as the pair of lads fell over themselves in their efforts to please her.

The situation caused a good deal of rivalry between the two lads which sometimes led to blows—cockfights that Nathan and Carmichael quickly broke up before either lad suffered more than a bloody nose or a black eye. Nathan's punishment for their fighting—no victuals for two days except bland-tasting taro roots and water—had been mild compared to Caroline's harsh discipline; she ignored both Tom and Tim completely for three days, and treated them coolly for another two.

Aye, life had settled into an harmonious routine, all things considered, Mariah thought grumpily, the only discordant note being her own disquieting feelings for Nathan Kincaid.

She could tell herself he was only a lowly convict, could remind herself frequently that he had cavalierly rejected her affections. She knew quite well that common sense dictated she give him wide berth, but alas, 'twas far easier said than done; for somehow, the rugged, devilish brute drew her like a lode-stone!

She told herself that her fascination with the man would eventually dwindle, that it was derived from the unusual circumstances of their being stranded—nay, thrown!—together on this island rather than genuine attraction, but her fascination diminished not a jot! Rather, it seemed to gather momentum, like a snowball rolling downhill, so that her time was either spent in thinking about him or in watching him as covetously as a dog watches a bone.

When he emerged from the sparkling sea each morn, rivulets of water streaming from his tanned, half-naked body, his ragged breeches were molded to him like a second skin. The sight of him in such virile, masculine glory made her heart all but stop beating in a mixture of fear and guilty enjoyment. Her mouth dried up. Her palms grew moist as she looked him up and down, noticing how very broad his chest appeared . . . how lean and narrow his waist was . . . how very intriguing his belly looked, with its hard ridges of smooth muscle and its light furring of crisp, curling black hair. His muscular thighs were clearly those of a born horseman, and his buttocks were revealed to be splendidly spare and firm, like a fencer's, as he bent to retrieve his leather vest. . . .

"Good day, m'lady. Would you care to join me in a dip?" he'd offer, sweeping a careless hand towards the sparkling blue water, his grin betraying that he was well aware of her lengthy inspection of him. "'Tis a good way to cool one's blood."

Frosty as a spinster with guilt, she'd redden and retort primly, "I think not, sir. I have no inclination to feed the sharks." Or sometimes she'd declare, "I have not your peculiar inclination to immerse myself in salt-water several times a day."

"Nay? Then what *do* you have an inclination for, hmm?" the rogue would wonder aloud, his green eyes kindling wickedly, his tone so very devilish, only a simpleton would not guess what he was implying. "To become a Peeping Tom?"

With an indignant snort, she'd jump to her feet and scuttle, crimson-faced, back to camp, vowing she'd not be there the following morning when he rose from the water like a young Neptune or some fairy-tale merman. But, she always was.

Another morning, he acknowledged her presence with an entirely different greeting.

"How now, Mariah, here again, eh? And after you swore just yesterday you would never return, too! Tell me, why do you come here each morning? Can you have changed your mind? Dare I hope—pray—that that is why?"

"Changed my mind about what, sir?" she gritted out, knowing *very* well what he meant.

"Why, about being my sweetheart, what else? Or was it my 'lightskirt,' you called it?" He considered, pursing his chiseled mouth as he tossed her own words back at her.

She cast him a sour, gargoyle look that quite distorted her lovely face. "I've forgotten nothing, sir. Have you? The way I recall our conversation that night, 'twas you who cast me aside! You who prattled on about your men and your duty to them, and about the 'mayhem' and undisciplined chaos that would arise, should we become . . . close," she reminded him waspishly.

"Aye, quite so. But perhaps I've reconsidered the risks, and now find them negligible. Perhaps my concerns have paled beside far more intriguing possibilities." Slowly, he winked a green eye.

"And h-have they?" A quivery weakness assailed her.

"Why? Would you like them to do so?" he challenged.

She snorted her disgust. "I really don't give a tinker's damn whether you've reconsidered or nay, sir. I swore you would not pick me up and put me down at will, like some lightskirt, and I meant every word."

"By jove, did you really?"

"Aye!"

"Little liar!" He grinned. "'Tis a rare woman who can stick to her guns."

"Rare, perhaps, among the sort of females *you* are undoubtedly familiar with. In my case, 'twas no lie."

"No? Then, why do your eyes roll around like marbles rattled in a jar?"

"Roll around? They do not!" she spluttered.

"Ah, but they do. Indeed, they always do that when you're lying! I've noticed it, more than once."

"You're absurd."

"And you, madam, are lovely beyond compare—even if you are a liar."

"Flattery will get you nowhere, sir," she retorted primly. "You're quite incorrigible! Good day."

"Madam, I'm supposed to be incorrigible—I'm a convict, remember?" he'd retorted. "A dastardly scoundrel, a villain quite beyond redemption. A dangerous felon who's a threat to all virtuous women—a man who corrupts beautiful widows."

With his mocking laughter ringing in her reddened ears, she'd bolted back to camp just as she had the day before, cursing him under her breath but delighted beyond all reason that he'd called her lovely, nay, beautiful, no matter what else he'd said. Rattling eyes, indeed, that scamp!

In the privacy of her hut that night, she'd wondered, not for the first time, why it was she tortured herself this way, why she felt compelled to play with fire and thus risk being burned. That earthy, lusty scoundrel Jonathan Kincaid was undoubtedly a former rake, a ladies' man who'd never be content with the sort of harmless, innocent flirtation she was brave enough to embark on. Nay. Should she be foolish enough to dally with Kincaid, she sensed instinctively that he'd demand everything of her; everything or nothing at all. And she was very much afraid that, should it ever come to the moment of truth, she would shatter into a thousand terrified pieces!

She tossed restlessly. She'd been foolish to even think of trying to change things, she could see that now. Digby's horrid assault had proven it was too soon to try, surely. He had but kissed her, thrust his hand into her bodice and pinched her breasts, and she'd been so paralyzed by fear, she'd screamed hysterically and swooned, fainting as much from the hateful memories his actions recalled as from her revulsion at his assault itself.

Tears leaked from beneath her closed eyelids. They trickled in hot furrows down her cheeks to drip off her chin onto her pallet of dried grasses. Damn Edward to Hell! He had ruined her, ruined her for all time! She was useless as a woman, useless as any man's wife; destined never to have the children she so dearly wanted. And why? A shuddering sob ran through her. Because should she live to be a hundred, she could never let Nathan or any other man make love to her and so beget a babe. She was frigid. Unnatural. A freak!

Her tears turned to bitter sobs. What man would want a woman who shrank from his touch as if he were contaminated? A woman who loathed the taste of his lips upon her own? A woman who feared the possession of her body as other women feared the thrust of a sword? No man. Nay, not even lusty Nathan.

Her feminine intuition that he would prove a gentle, tender lover, and that he adored, rather than despised, women, and would deal with them kindly, had surely been nothing but wishful thinking on her part? Should he ever change his mind— should she ever find the courage to approach him again—he would probably prove like other men; like dearest Edward, her husband, who used his greater strength and hard, male body as weapons to punish and degrade women.

She would not go to the beach in the morning, she told herself; she swore it upon the fingernail-moon she glimpsed between the banana thatch. And this time, she was true to her word . . . after a fashion. She went by night instead!

Dawn the next day broke over the ocean in glorious lemons, lavendars, and pinks, but when Nathan left his hut for his morning swim, she studiously ignored him. Instead of trotting after him, she helped the marines, Stiles and Babbington, with the morning meal.

Afterwards, she'd been scheduled to remain in camp and gather kindling for the fires, but she coaxed Tim Archer into taking her place, and instead went out to pick bananas and mangoes with Matherson's party. That afternoon, exhausted, she slept away the hottest hours of the day, awakening refreshed just as the sun was going down in a fiery purple and crimson-streaked sky. Here, in the tropics, where there was no dusk to speak of, it would be dark in a matter of minutes.

As she left her hut, she saw Nathan, bamboo-spear in one hand and a blazing brand taken from the fire in the other, padding down the beach towards the water.

"Fishin', m'lady," Jack supplied, watching her face and anticipating her next question. "He reckons 'e saw natives using torchlight t' call up the fish when he sailed these waters wi' Cook. 'E was of a mind t' try it for 'imself. You know how 'e is."

"I do, aye, but 'tis unsafe for him to go swimming alone. Did he not warn us that we should go in pairs?" she said, sounding quite the stern governess.

Jack grinned. " 'Aye, miss, but 'tis a rare man who follows 'is own council. Not to worry. He can take care o' himself, that 'un. Swims like an eel, 'e do."

"I expect you're right. But perhaps I should go down and stand watch, you know, just to make sure?" Good God, just listen to her! The feeble excuse even sounded flimsy to her own ears.

"Well, it can't hurt, can it, m'lady?" Jack gave her a knowing little grin. "And you'll find out fer yerself if the fish are drawn t' the light, right?"

"Hmm? Oh, yes, the fish! It should prove fascinating."

Nathan had obviously decided to try his experiment at some distance from their camp. Mariah set off after him, irritated beyond measure when Caroline called out and demanded to know where she was going.

"Just to watch Kincaid," she answered casually, without slowing or stopping.

"Oooh, you brazen hussy, you!" Caroline accused, scampering after her cousin, her pet monkey clinging to her shoulder. "Chasing him again, are you, coz? And to think you once forbade *me* to speak to the man!"

"What on earth do you mean, chasing him again?" Mariah retorted. She'd been certain her morning strolls had gone unremarked by the others. In fact, she had gone to ridiculous lengths to make them unobtrusive.

"Oh, nothing, really. It's just that, well, I've been wondering what Nathan must think—about having *two* shadows, I mean," the girl teased, impish laughter brimming in her naughty blue eyes. "His real one . . . and you, my proud coz!"

"Why, you little saucebox!" Mariah flared with indignation. "A fine one you are to talk about Nathan having two shadows. What do you call poor Tim and Tom, if not your shadows?"

Caroline had the grace to look abashed, though only for a second or two, for Mariah's furious expression cautioned her to change the subject, and quickly, 'less she wanted a tongue-lashing. "Oh, never mind Tim and Tom, tell me about Kincaid and why he's going fishing at night? Surely he won't be able to see well enough to catch anything?"

"If you must know, he intends to find out if the fish will swim towards the light so he can spear them," Mariah explained, tapping her toe in the sand in her impatience to get away.

"Really? How absolutely fascinating! I'd love to watch that. Tim! Tom! Halooo, there! Come, follow me!" she called over her shoulder, linking her arm through a suddenly rigid Mariah's. "Let's all go and watch him together."

"Where are you young people off to?" Carmichael, the *Hester*'s mate asked as the four of them—Caroline, Tim Bright, Tom Swift and Mariah, who was scowling horribly—trooped down the beach in Nathan's wake.

148

"To watch Master Kincaid spear-fishing. He plans to use a lighted brand to draw the fish," Caroline supplied. "You should accompany us, sir. It promises to be great fun!"

"For pity's sake, shut up!" Mariah hissed, but it was far too late for that. Carmichael liked the idea. He called to Surgeon Love and Matherson, who in turn called up others of their company. Within minutes, Mariah was striding angrily down the beach like the Pied Piper of Hamlin, followed by not one, not two, nor even three unwanted companions but by their entire company!

The spot Nathan had selected for his night-fishing was a pretty little cove about a mile down the beach from their camp. The water was shallow at that point for some distance offshore, reaching only to mid-thigh by the reef, and 'twas calm as a mill-pond beneath the moonlight.

Appearing unsurprised by the score of eager spectators who'd gathered on the sand to sit and watch him, Nathan waded into the sea, the flaring torch held aloft in his left hand, its light reflecting a rusty hue off the water and bathing his handsome, rugged face and upper torso with ruddy color. In his right fist, he held aloft his makeshift spear, a straight shaft of bamboo with a sharp triangle of shell lashed to its end for a blade.

As Nathan had promised, the fish swam to the pool of light in great numbers and were easily caught. Small greyish-lavendar squid also found their way onto the end of his makeshift spear. Indeed, although each downward plunge was anxiously watched, he brought the spear up with a wriggling sea-creature impaled upon its point almost every time, and then a great cheer would go up from his admiring audience.

Soon, the others grew eager to try his sport. One by one, Nathan patiently showed them how it was done, until each would-be fisherman had managed to spear at least one fish or squid, and Jack found himself with a pile of fresh fish to be gutted and cleaned for their breakfast the following morning.

After the moon had risen in a lop-sided, cream-cheese wedge, the night air seemed chill to the castaways, who'd already grown accustomed to the steamy heat of day. Noticing that Caroline was shivering and hugging herself, Tim and Tom built a small fire, and they all huddled around it.

"I know, let's 'ave us a sing-song!" Ben suggested, and the others agreed. Moments later, lusty sea-chanteys, sweet ballads, and even Christmas carols rose on the purple gloom in turn, the sound of their combined voices floating out over the silver-washed sea as all joined in with the rousing choruses.

"Come on, Mariah, give us a song!" Caroline urged when she'd finished her own reedy rendering of "Greensleeves." "She sings like a nightingale, all of you, truly she does!"

"Oh, really," Mariah protested. "I sound more like a crow!"

"Nonsense. You're just being modest. Go on, sing for us, please, Mariah? Sing that Scottish ballad, 'By Love Denied.' 'Tis my very favorite."

The others added their voices to her cousin's urging, and Mariah knew there'd be no refusing them. Resigned, she stood up, shook out her skirts, clasped her hands before her and began, unsteadily at first, her sweet, clear voice growing stronger as her confidence increased. Each note was poignant, each word as bitter-sweet as the story her ballad told, that of a Scottish country lass whose love was not returned by her hunter sweetheart.

> "I'll tramp the woods alone, my mon,
> If ye'll no' walk wi' me.
> But nae forest glen
> Nor heathery moor
> Can set my puir heart free,
> For . . ."

Mariah's eyes met Nathan's as she sang, and her voice and her heart swelled until it seemed she was singing only for him, drowning in his emerald gaze, not wanting to surface, ever, so powerful was the current that ran between them.

The Scottish lass had cast herself into the dark depths of a mountain loch, preferring death to a life of unrequited love. Legend had it that on the anniversary of her death, her spirit took the form of a snow-white swan, and that you could hear her calling mournfully for her lost love over the still waters. When Mariah's last note died away, so potent was the spell she'd woven, utter silence reigned, a hush broken only by the crack and snap of burning driftwood and by the shush of the waves as they kissed the sands. Only after what seemed endless seconds did Carmichael, tears streaming down his cheeks, exclaim, "Bravo!"

The spell was broken. The others joined in, applauding and cheering loudly, save for Nathan, who was still gazing at Mariah. With obvious difficulty, he managed to break free and return to the gathering, flicking his head to clear it.

"Come on, lads and lassies, let's get back to camp!" he ordered brusquely. "The hour grows late. The guards at the lagoon are waiting t' be relieved."

"Oh, must we leave already? Couldn't we just pass the night here, Master Kincaid?" Caroline implored, yawning hugely as she lifted the little monkey onto her shoulder. Round brown eyes wide and curious, it buried its wizened pink face in her hair and peeked shyly at Kincaid between the strands.

"I'm afraid not, sleepyhead. It's a pretty place, I agree, but the cursed jungle reaches almost to water's edge here. It could hide any one of a dozen dangers—dangers that would be upon us before we so much as suspected their presence. Our camp's safer, by far."

"But we could post a guard here, couldn't we?"

Nathan shook his head. "Nay, Mistress Amberfield. I regret that tonight you must once again retire to your stately banana-palace beneath the palm grove! Though humble, 'tis a fortress far more easily defended." Sweeping her a courtly bow meant to soften his refusal, he grinned ruefully.

"Master Kincaid's right, Caroline," Tim Bright agreed. "But, with Lady Mariah's permission, I'd be honored to escort you back to camp?"

"Mariah?" Caroline implored her cousin, her blue eyes beseeching.

Mariah hesitated, tempted to be petty and refuse the request, for she was still a trifle vexed with Caroline for turning her romantic moonlight "tryst" with Nathan into a public fishing exhibition! But, it was not her way to nurse a grudge overlong. "Oh, very well, then. Tim may accompany you, on one condition. Timothy Bright, may I depend on you to behave as a gentleman should?"

Tim appeared affronted that she would question his integrity, but as a parson's son, his innate good manners kept him from voicing his indignation rudely. Instead, he blurted out, "If I should behave in any other fashion, m'lady, I give you leave to . . . to cut off my right arm!"

Mariah's stern expression softened. "I'm quite certain such drastic measures will not prove necessary, Tim. Hurry along, now. I'll join you shortly, Caroline."

With that, Tim and Caroline set off, arm in arm, followed by the others in noisy groups that included a sour-faced, scowling Tom Swift, Tim's rival for Caroline's affections.

"Shall I escort ye back t' camp, m'lady?" Jack Warner inquired, pausing at Mariah's elbow. He, Old Peg, Nathan, and four others were the only ones left. They carried most of the fish, strung through the gills on lengths of line, and the half-dozen squid.

Before Mariah could speak, Nathan answered for her, "Nay, Jack, I'll accompany Lady Mariah. You lads go on back."

"Aye, aye sir."

Something had kindled in Mariah's turquoise eyes, Nathan saw, when the others had left and he turned to look down at her. Was it laughter . . . or the dawning of fear? Laughter, he decided. The corners of her delectable mouth were twitching, as if she fought to smother a peal of nervous laughter,

He raised dark brows in puzzlement. "And what, pray, is so very amusing?"

"Why, you, sir!" she came back shakily. "Just three weeks

ago, you were as leery of being caught alone in my company as a nun caught in dalliance with a trooper. But now . . . La! Now you send your chaperones away!''

"'Tis because, dearest Mariah, I have realized what a fool I've been,'' he confessed in a husky tone that made goose-bumps tingle down her arms. "And because, after what happened with Digby, I believe 'twould be safer if the men considered you my woman, whether 'tis fact or fiction.'' Placing a hand on either side of her waist, he drew her against him in one smooth move. "But most of all, 'tis because tonight, my sweet Mariah, I cannot deny that I want you, right or wrong, no matter what others might think or say.''

His bold admission all but took her breath away.

"You do?'' she breathed.

Green eyes held hers captive for what seemed an eternity. She could not free herself from their thrall! He said nothing, nor did he need to. Her answer was in the emerald fire, in the silent potency of his gaze that, like a scorching wind, almost stole her breath away. When she could move, could think again, she found her mouth had grown dry and her heart was skittering crazily about. Worse, she did not trust herself to speak!

"Aye,'' he said at last, reaching out to take her hand, the last string of fish forgotten in the sand. "God help me, but I want you, Mariah!''

"Then . . . what will you do, sir?'' she whispered, swaying ever so slightly where she stood. Her hand was lost in his larger one, her emotions in chaos. Her face felt hot, and she was suddenly quite certain its heat had nothing to do with the driftwood fire the lads had built.

A roguish grin was his only answer. Without another word, he drew her hand to his mouth and kissed her fingertips one by one, his lips as soft and fleeting as wings. "What I will do, my sweet, is pay court to you. And the first step in any courtship is a kiss. 'Tis the overture to the glorious opera that shall follow.''

153

"Oh!" she exclaimed, and a shiver ran through her, for the sensual timbre of his voice, his words, implied far, far more than innocent kisses.

"Why do you tremble so, Mari, my dove? Have you never been kissed?" he asked softly, his green eyes sensual and heavy-lidded in the flickering light as he idly caressed a loose ringlet of her fire-kissed hair.

"I have been given what passed for kisses, aye, sir," she whispered, unable to meet his lambent gaze, for fear of the unsettling sensations it stirred within her.

"And?"

"'Twas my opinion that . . . that kissing is much over-rated," she blurted out. Heart fluttering madly, she swayed just a little where she stood before him, torn by the conflict within her. Half of her wanted desperately to run from him now, before it was too late, but she could not move an inch. Her treacherous feet were rooted in the sand! The other half of her wanted to toss caution to the winds and stay; to discover if a kiss from Jonathan Kincaid in any way resembled the loathsome kisses that Edward—and, more recently, Digby—had inflicted upon her.

"Your distaste is understandable, Mari, my dove. Until now, you have never been kissed by me."

His boast, though casually spoken, made her giggle nervously. "Indeed I have, sir. On the beach that night."

"Those trifles?" He laughed, a deep, chuckling sound. "Nay, Mariah, they were but the peckings of a lusty rooster long denied his hens. You shall have better anon, madam!"

"So you say! And do you consider yourself an expert in such matters?" she countered, hardly able to believe she was standing there, flirting with him in the moonlight, with hardly a trace of fear.

"Indeed I do," he said gravely. "From the perfumed boudoirs of London's most beautiful courtesans to the shady hay-lofts of Britain's farthest barns, I was once hailed as Nathan Kincaid, King of Kissers. Why, once she had been kissed by

154

me, King Georgie's mistress retired her lips. She sought no other's kisses for fear she'd find them wanting.''

She laughed softly at his outrageous boast, for his teasing, silly claims, his playful tone, did wonders for her nerves. "You! La, I wager you're more braggart than king of anything, sir!''

"You think so, eh, minx? Then, judge for yourself the truth—or falsehood—of my claims."

With that, his hard, chiselled mouth crushed down over hers in a kiss so different, so much more stunning than his others had been, it sent shockwaves through her.

His lips were teasing as he slanted them over hers, deliberately withholding, deliberately keeping something back, even as he explored her mouth with a lazy, sensual thoroughness that left all doubts in ashes.

Long live the King! she thought deliriously as his hands left her waist. His warm fingers grazed her spine. They traced each delicate little knob down to the swells of her bottom, then drew her firmly against the lean hardness of his body; while the fingers of his other hand plunged deep into the silky mass of her red-gold hair, to cradle her head.

Slowly, oh, so damnably slowly, his lips moved against hers, opening so that the heat and sweetness of his breath mingled with her own. She burrowed inside the stiffened leather of his vest to caress his furred chest, amazed—and delighted—when his dark-rose nipples hardened at the brush of her fingertips. Emboldened by the success of her first, accidental caress, she responded to his kisses, clasping her arms about his neck, plunging her fingers into the coarse black silk of his hair as he had done with her locks and pressing herself to him in silent, eloquent need. Where was the fear, the loathing? she wondered dazedly. Gone—quite gone!

He drew a sharp breath as their bodies touched, the heat of him fiery and hard against her soft, warm curves. With his tongue, he traced the margin of her lips, gently demanding that they part, commanding her to grant him access to the silken

155

sweetness within, then plunging within her mouth when access was tremblingly granted in a way that shocked and thrilled her all at once.

As their tongues played gently together, he cupped her breast, caressing the soft mound through her bodice until her nipple ruched. She made a soft, kittenish sound against his lips; one of startled wonder and delight.

"What say you now, my little love?" he asked tenderly, breaking away to draw breath. "Am I king . . . or lying knave?"

"Your Most Royal Majesty, I am convinced!" she confessed shakily, her turquoise eyes huge and luminous in the fire's shifting light as she swept him a curtsey. "I am your obedient subject, sire!"

Grinning wickedly, he nodded, well aware of the effect his kisses had had upon her. Her tawny-gold hair was charmingly dishevelled. Her eyes were luminous as the stars above them. Her lips were reddened and slightly swollen from his ardent kisses, her features rosy and just a little blurred by desire. She looked, in fact, exactly as he'd planned she should look; like a woman who warmly desired a man—but one whose desire, now piqued, had yet to be slaked.

"Then, on that happy note, we shall retire," he declared. "May I escort you back to camp, m'lady?"

"You may indeed, sir king!" she acquiesced, accepting the arm he offered.

But her eager, if nervous, anticipation of what was surely to come in the privacy of her hut's bamboo walls evaporated when he halted at the opening. He gallantly kissed her hand, then took his leave with only a wink and a whispered, "Good night, goddess. Sweet dreams." by way of parting.

Confound the blasted man! If he'd set out to arouse her dormant senses one by one, he'd succeeded all too well, for throughout that long, sweltering night, she could not sleep for thinking of him; could not get comfortable for squirming with

156

the remembrance of his heated lips moving against hers, the feel of his hard, virile body, and his gentleness as he'd fondled her breast.

Dawn was pinkening the sky again before she fell into fitful sleep after counting hundreds of paling stars, but even then, her dreams were of him.

And her torment was far from ended. Rather, it began in earnest the following morning, as they broke the night's fast.

Nathan seated himself across the cooking fire. He proceeded to devour her with his eyes from this vantage point, while he consumed one of the roasted fish he'd speared the night before. He licked his lips and cleaned the juices from his fingers, one by one, with studied thoroughness. As he did so, his sensual gaze sent a sizzling message across the divide; one that left her so weak, her own morsel slipped uneaten to the sand from her slack fingers. And later, when she bent to pick up the cooking kettle, intending to carry it down to the water's edge for scouring, he was at once behind her. His body brushed against hers, his flanks nudged her buttocks, his breath rose hot, stirring the fine hairs upon her nape, as he murmured, "Come, let me take that for you, Mariah. 'Tis too weighty for one so slender."

Take it? Ha! Fine chance of that! She dropped the blasted kettle as if the iron handle were red-hot, for his breath on her neck had sent weakening waves of goose-bumps down her arms and spine!

He accompanied her to the water's edge and there, too, insisted on helping her, cupping handfuls of sand as did she. But, instead of scouring out the inside of the pot, the rogue chose to rub the rounded curves of the outside! Watching the way his tanned hands caressed the bulging belly of the vessel in a peculiarly erotic, massaging fashion brought high color to her cheeks. It also made her long for those large, tanned hands to caress her curves, just so. . . .

"Is something amiss, my sweet?" he murmured, watching her discomfort from beneath drooping eyelids, and clearly relishing every minute.

"Aye! You're supposed to be scouring the *inside* of the kettle, you dolt."

"But the soot, sweeting! 'Tis the soot I'm scouring, see? The . . . er . . . bottom is covered with grime." His green eyes were devilish as he cocked his head to one side and glanced speculatively at *her* bottom, his hands continuing their lazy, circling motions over the kettle, drawing her fascinated stare and making her throat constrict almost painfully.

"The devil it is," she accused, thoroughly disquieted. "Oh, for pity's sake, stop that, do. Give it here! I can finish this alone. Go. Go!"

With a shrug, he brushed off his hands and stood. "As you will, Mari, my dove," he agreed with an amiable smile; then he took her grimy hand in his and kissed it. "Until tonight, *adieu, ma chérie*. . . ."

With that, he sauntered back up the beach, leaving her staring after him.

That evening, when she and Caroline returned to the hut they shared, their mouths dropped open in astonishment, for it was filled with flowers! There were dewy white frangipani blossoms with canary-yellow throats: flamboyant crimson hibiscus; masses of delicate, frilly orchids, both lavender and white ones; and tiny brown-spotted orange lilies. Crude palm-frond baskets overflowing with island flowers were ranged all over the sandy floor, while sprays of still others had been woven into the grass- and palm-frond walls of their hut, so that their heady fragrance filled its confines.

"Good grief! Who on earth . . . ?" Mariah began, frowning so hard and looking so genuinely puzzled that Caroline burst out laughing.

"Who, indeed, Mistress Innocence! Well, we know it wasn't Tim, because he was with us all day. By my reckoning, that leaves but one other capable of doing such a thing."

"Not Jonathan."

"Of course it was Jonathan, you silly goose! Who else would it be?" Caroline exclaimed scathingly, disgusted with her. "Everyone knows he adores you. The poor man's been trying desperately to court you in a civilized fashion for two weeks, despite our somewhat *un*civilised conditions here. In fact, the men are growing quite short-tempered about it all. They mutter that you should accept his suit and be done with it, else choose one of them."

Astonished by this tid-bit, Mariah blinked. "They do?"

Caroline nodded, crossing her fingers behind her back so that the lie wouldn't count, for behind Mariah's back, Nathan had made it *very* plain that she was to be his woman. He had warned that any man who tried to press his unwanted attentions upon her would come to grief.

"They do indeed!" the young woman confirmed. "Why, my Tim says Kincaid but stares up at the stars through the thatch each night, unable to sleep for thinking of you, and . . . Oh, look at Monty! He has a flower in his ear, the silly pet!" Scooping up the tiny, chattering monkey and crooning to it, she left their hut, adding over her shoulder, "I'm starved! See you at supper!"

Mariah was smiling dreamily and, though she would never have admitted it, a trifle smugly as, with a last backward glance at the flower-filled hut, she trailed after her cousin.

Chapter Ten

Nathan was waiting for her when she returned to her hut that same evening. Her heart quickening at the sight of his tall, broad-shouldered silhouette, she ventured a shy smile of greeting.

"What are you doing here, sir? I thought you long abed, or else fishing by moonlight!"

He grinned, "Alas, neither one." Sighing theatrically he added, "Tonight, lovely lady, I am like Romeo, pining for his Juliet. I skulk in the shadows below your . . . er . . . casement, hungry for a glimpse of thee."

Her smile deepened. She blushed. "I'm flattered, but 'tis late, sir. Are you not weary? Most of the others are already abed, except for the guards and the *Hester*'s lads, that is." In her nervousness, she continued breathlessly, "Master Carmichael and John Stiles have the watch tonight. They're spinning yarns, and have Tim Bright and Tom Swift hanging on their every word."

"Sleep evades me, aye, but nay, I've no eagerness to hear

their sailors' tales tonight. What about you, Mari? Are you tired?''

Though his comments sounded innocent enough, the sensual, husky timbre in which he voiced them was not. A trickle of excitement moved through her, making her hug herself about the arms as if the night air were chill as it rustled the palm fronds, rather than perfumed and sultry.

"Not really, no," she admitted, knowing only another sleepless night spent wrestling her fears or reliving hateful memories awaited her. "I . . . Why do you ask?"

"Come, come, my clever Mari, surely you know why I ask?" he countered softly, smiling and holding out his hand in invitation. "I said I was going to court you, and so I am. After a stolen kiss or two, 'tis customary in a courtship for the lovesick sweethearts to stroll in the moonlight. Take my hand, and come with me."

"But where shall we go, sir?" she whispered, slipping her small hand trustingly inside his larger one. The strength and vitality of the man was palpable as his firm grip enfolded her fingers in tingling warmth. For just a second, she was tempted to pull free and bolt inside her hut. *Nay, Mariah, don't! 'Tis Nathan, he'll not harm you. Has he not always been gentleness itself? Go with him! Take the chance! And, if he wants you, trust him, and lay your nightmares to rest, once and for all!*

"Come, my dove," he murmured, leading her after him between the huts. "Our trysting place is not far from here."

He led her along the beach to a tiny valley between four sugary, sand hills. Despite his promise, the dunes lay some distance from their camp, she judged, for it'd seemed to take ages to reach them. Or, had it been her nervousness, mingled with jittery excitement, that had made it seem distant?

The waves sang a sibilant song as they kissed the shore, a lullaby that was muted; while floating above them, the rising moon, escorted by a solitary bright star, sliced a slim, pearly

161

fingernail from the indigo sky. In its silvery beams, the white sandhills loomed like Egyptian pyramids from the shadows.

"Your bower, lovely Juliet," Nathan murmured, drawing her into his arms. Moon- and starlight cast his handsome features in mysterious ruddy tones and caught the flecks of gold in his emerald eyes as, sliding his fingers deep into the mass of her hair, he dipped his head to kiss her.

His mouth was hot and tender, salty-tasting as he branded the softness of her lips with an exquisite gentleness she'd only dreamed of. *You see, silly goose? He won't hurt you. You have naught to fear. Surrender to love!* Her fears diminished, she tilted her head back, twined her arms about his neck, and yielded to his kisses.

She felt so slender, yet so utterly feminine, that just touching her, kissing her, almost undid Nathan's control. He nuzzled her throat, raining feather-light kisses on her silken skin, then suckled gently upon her tiny earlobes, unable to believe the exquisite texture of her flesh.

Christ! It had been so damned long since a woman's softness had filled his aching arms. So many months since a woman's delicate fragrance had tantalized his nostrils, and the taste of her skin had set him afire with desire. *Too* long, by God— too long! And yet . . . there was a certain shyness in Mari's responses that warned he must woo her slowly and with the utmost tenderness, if he would win her.

Gently, he parted her lips with his own, sampling the clover sweetness of her inner mouth like a hummingbird sipping nectar from the throat of a lovely, delicate flower. With a tiny whimper, she moved her tongue against his, hesitantly matching its warrings. Her innocently sensual response drew a matching groan from Nathan. How his heart thundered! 'Twas torture to want her so and yet be forced to go slowly! The fever in his blood bade him make haste, urged him to lower her to the ground and throw himself upon her. And yet . . . he could not. Moreover, he *would* not. He was a man, by God, not some wild male beast in the rankness of its rut. And Mariah was a spirited, intelligent, lovely woman, a woman to be treasured and cherished, not some unfeeling vessel into which he might empty his lust.

His hands left her tumbling red-gold ringlets to caress her slender curves as he deepened his kiss. With infinite care, he stroked her ivory shoulders, then traced each delicate ridge of her spine down to her bottom. Sweat beaded his brow as he fondled her, for the weighty ache at his groin was nigh unbearable. Gritting his teeth, he wondered how much longer he could delay the inevitable. *God's Teeth!* Her nipples had puckered now, and the pebbled sensation of them against his bare chest through her threadbare bodice drove him to the brink!

Deftly spilling her breasts from her bodice's confines, he bent to suckle each perfect, rosy peak in turn, thunderstruck when she suddenly jerked back and thrust him from her with a shriek of protest.

His first, truly intimate caress had shattered her brittle resolve. *'Tis no use!* she thought despairingly as, against her will, her slender body grew rigid with terror. *I cannot!*

"Mari . . . what . . . ?

"Stay back!" she spat out. Involuntarily, her fingers curled into talons as, with another scream, she raked his face, tore out hanks of his hair. He threw up his arms to block her fists, but, oblivious to his startled yelps, she rained a hail of blows upon his unsuspecting head. "Nooo, nooo!" she screamed all the while, struggling wildly to escape the restraining hands he fastened about her wrists. "For the love of God, don't!" she hissed.

"Don't touch me! Don't!"

Shocked, he fell back, stunned by the wildness in her turquoise eyes, the rank terror on her face, leeched of all color.

"Mari, don't! There's no need for this. If you're unwilling, you have but to say—"

"*Stay back!* Not another step! I give you warning!"

"As you will," he agreed softly. Shrugging, he stepped back a pace or two and simply stood there, his weight braced upon one foot, his fists planted on his hips as he watched her, wondering what the Deuce could be wrong as she cringed before him. Her breasts heaved with each panting breath she drew. Her knotted fists, held at her sides, shook with the fierceness of her emotions so that she resembled a frightened little animal run to ground and desperate.

"You must have loved him very much," he observed quietly after several moments had passed. In that time, the tension had ebbed from her as surely and swiftly as it had arisen.

"Him?" she echoed dully, opening her hands and seeming surprised that her nails had gouged bloody crescents from her palms.

"Your husband."

Ugly, harsh laughter broke from her lips. "Loved?" she whispered, and to his horror a slow torrent of tears coursed down her cheeks. "Loved?" she echoed again, the word a strangled sob. "I never loved him. I *loathed* him—hated him with every breath and fibre of my being!"

"Then Downing did this to you?" he asked, stunned. He'd wondered if Digby's attempt to ravish her had caused such fear of men. "Your own husband?"

"Aye, my own, dear husband! And each day, I give thanks to God that he is dead."

"And what of now? Is it only me you fear, or all men?" He had hardly dared to put the question, for fear she would answer, 'Tis but you!

"'Tis all men," she whispered bitterly. "But—oh, Nathan, please forgive me!—I was so certain it would be different with you. La! 'Twas not my intent to lead you on, truly it wasn't!"

He smiled, wanting to ruffle her hair and tell her not to be such a silly goose. "Madam, rest assured, when it comes to women—especially beautiful ones—I need little 'leading on'!"

"You see?" she exclaimed. "You're not like other men. From the very first, I sensed it, though I couldn't admit it, even to myself. You've tried so hard to be . . . to be kind. You've teased me. You've made me laugh! But most of all, you've made me feel again, really feel, when I thought I should never do so again. These past two weeks, you've courted me like a . . . a desirable woman, a person, rather than a . . . a *thing*!'' She swallowed and dashed the tears from her eyes with her knuckles. ''Oh, Nathan, I want so very badly to be like other women! And I . . . I was almost certain that with you, I could . . . could be . . . Oh!'' She couldn't go on, but instead buried her face in her hands and wept silently.

Not knowing how his comforting might be received, he took her gently in his arms, pulled her against him and stroked her hair. He kept his embrace loose, giving her the freedom to pull away, should she wish to do so. But instead of struggling, she wrapped her arms around his chest and burrowed closer.

''The fault is not in you, my poor little Mariah, but in the foul cur who hurt you. Weep, *chérie*,'' he urged, his own voice husky with tears. ''Cry it all out, once and for all, and have done with it. Or if it please you, tell me all. You have nothing to fear. I make no judgments. I have forced no woman to my bed, nor shall I force you. You may tell me as much or as little as you wish, or you may say naught. The choice is yours. Whatever you decide, 'twill go no further than my ears.''

His gentle promises and his offer of a sympathetic ear proved her undoing, all over again. She had told no one, not even her father, about Edward or how it had been between them, though she'd discovered that her father had known about Downing's debauchery, and his appetite for young, innocent women. Now, remembering, she wept as she'd never wept before, her scalding tears soaking the crisp whorls on Nathan's chest as she clung to him.

Once she'd begun, 'twas as if a floodgate had burst open, releasing all the ugliness, shame and degradation of that night as, stumbling and clawing for words, she began. ''In truth, I expected no such cruelty from Edward. We had once been playmates, running wild in the Middlesex countryside like Gypsy brats, before Papa moved his household to London. I remembered him as a shy, gentle lad of whom I'd been fond, in my girlish way. He'd preferred his mother's company and reading tales of magic, knights and wizards to the frogs and fisticuffs that other lads favored. A sweet boy who'd given me robins' eggs, and who chose kisses as his forfeits in our games of blind man's buff and hide-and-seek!

"But on our wedding night, Edward bore no resemblance to the boy I'd known!" she whispered. "He had changed beyond my recognition—become a frightening stranger whose moods changed as mercurially as the wind! One minute, he would be the teasing, charming scamp of my childhood, and in the next, his eyes would blaze and he'd become a monster, an ogre I soon learned to fear! At one moment, I'd be sitting beside him, laughing at some little jest Papa had made. Then, in a trice, he had wound his fingers in my hair, and was dragging me from my chair.

" 'You must forgive us for retiring so soon, gentlemen, but I am sure you will understand that I am most anxious to bed my bride!' he'd call over his shoulder.

"I saw the faces of his guests as he bore me from the hall, and I shall never forget them," Mariah continued, "for their expressions were the same. *To a man, they feared him. They had not come to our wedding feast by choice, but at his behest!* The last thing I saw before Edward carried me up that winding staircase was my father's face, awash with tears. And, in his eyes, the same fear!

"In my terror I called out to him—begged him to help me— but he turned his face away. My own father!"

" 'You're no mewling babe, to be calling on your father to help you,' " Edward growled. " 'I am both your husband and your master now, 'Riah! As my wife, you will obey me!' And then . . . and then he . . .''

Her voice broke and for a few moments, she was too distraught to carry on.

Nathan, wise to the oftimes cruel ways of a wicked world, suspected the outcome of her story. He dropped to his knees in the sand and drew her down onto his lap. Stroking her hair, cradling her in his arms, he gently urged her to continue.

His own lust, he realized, had abated. It had been replaced by cold fury and a contempt for the monstrous excuse for a man who'd hurt her, and with frustration that by dying, Downing—curse his black heart!—had passed beyond a reckoning for his sins, at least in this world. He could only pray that God was just, and that at this very moment the bastard was roasting in Hell for what he had done to Mariah.

An overwhelming tenderness filled him. With all his heart, he ached to soothe her hurt, to soften her memories or make her forget them utterly. More than proving his innocence, he wanted to convince her that it was over; that Edward could never hurt her again. But, only by reliving her horror could she ever hope to put the past behind her, where it belonged, and go on with her life.

There, on that moonlit beach, upon a deserted tropical island lost in the balmy South Seas, Mariah's story unfolded. And in the telling, Nathan was transported back to a different, harsher time and to a darker, more brutal place, ten thousand miles away.

She told how Edward had kicked open the door to his gloomy chamber that night, had borne her inside like some evil robber-baron. There, he had flung her down upon the crimson velvet poster-bed and had ripped the garments from her back, stripping away gown, petticoats, and underthings until she lay naked before him, her clothes in tatters.

"I tried to cover myself, to hide from his tiger eyes. Oh, God, how those eyes made my flesh crawl! Yet he would not grant me so small a mercy, not that first time nor in any that came after."

" 'I want you naked! Do not attempt to cover yourself, Mariah,' he told me. 'I would examine the goods I have bought and paid for. Open yourself. Show me the precious maidenhead your father bartered for his hide!' "

"I tried—dear God, I tried—to escape his eyes. But he held

167

me down and looked where he would. When he was done, he took still greater delight in describing what he would do next. I swore I would sooner die first—that I would never do such shameful, wicked things. I begged and pleaded for pity. I ranted and cursed him to hell. I even promised him I would be all he could ever ask for, a dutiful loving wife, if only he would not . . .'' Her shoulders slumped. ''In the end, 'twas all the same. He wanted a whore, not a wife. And, since he was the stronger, he won.''

Nathan felt the gorge rise up his throat. *That bastard!* Edward Downing had brutally ravished his virgin bride, had relished the agony she'd suffered as he drove again and again into her untried body. He'd also enjoyed the painful perversions he'd inflicted upon her later that same night, and the nights that had followed. When she'd screamed and cried out that he was hurting her, he'd stuffed a 'kerchief in her mouth to keep her silent. When she'd tried to fight him off, he had bound her. And, much later, when he'd at last risen from her, his twisted lusts sated for the while, he had scoffed as she'd crawled, hurt and weeping, to the door, crying brokenly for her papa.

''Go ahead and crawl, Mariah. You'd as well get used to it. I intend to have you on your knees many, many times, my darling, before your father's debts are cleared.''

''He owed you money?'' she'd whispered, aghast.

''Not money, no. After all, there are other forms of debt, are there not? Your father chose to sacrifice you, my dear, rather than shed his lofty principles. Think about that while I'm gone. 'Tis all his doing, that you are here now.''

''He kept me locked in that room draped in crimson, where sunlight and air scarce pierced through the gloom.'' She shuddered. ''Servants brought me food and water, but they were forbidden to speak to me. I spoke only to Edward, when he came to me each night, and I thought I should go mad!''

''Did you not think of escape?'' he wondered aloud, stroking her tousled curls.

"Of course! I tried everything, but there were iron bars upon the window, and the servants feared their lord. They were careful never to leave the key in the lock. 'Twas like a nightmare from which there was no awakening! After the first month became two, I began to lose hope. I feared I should die in that chamber! And then, one day, something happened. I heard angry voices—men's voices—from outside the room. Edward's and others', quarreling heatedly. Then there were the sounds of much coming and going, and finally, the door opened and my papa was standing there.

" 'You are to come home with me, Mariah,' " he told me. " 'Your hu—Edward has bought himself a commission in one of the King's regiments. He has gone out to India to fight, and it may be quite some time before he returns.' "

" 'Thank God, I am rid of him!' " I cried.

My father continued. " 'I am to close up the house and turn off the servants in Lord Downing's absence, unless . . . unless you wish to stay here. You are Lady Downing now, after all, my dear. It is your right.' "

"But of course, I was more than eager to leave, although my feelings for my father had changed. I still loved him—he was my papa, I couldn't help it—but I no longer trusted or looked up to him. I wanted to ask him why he had given me in marriage to a beast like Edward, what awful debt he had incurred. But I could not find the words. I . . . I was afraid, you see."

"Your father had known all along, but still had done nothing to help you?"

She nodded, grateful for his understanding. "Just so. In my deepest heart, I think I already knew that. Papa would not meet my eyes. 'Twas all the answer I needed." She sighed. "Anyway, a few months later, Papa came home from London in great excitement. He informed me that Edward had been taken by a fever in India, and was dead. I was free—a widow! I had scarce absorbed the glad news when he'd added that I should begin packing my trunks. We were ourselves leaving England, to make a good new life in the colonies of the New World!''

"Did this surprise you? Had he spoken of such an ambition before?''

"Never! In truth, I was stunned, but I'd been so unhappy since my marriage to Edward, I welcomed the promise of a new life.

"It transpired that my uncle, Paul Amberfield, had been sent out to Botany Bay to replace Governor Philips at the penal colony there for a year. Afterwards, Uncle Paul intended to remain there and settle some land. He was preparing to leave England within the fortnight, and had asked my father if I, newly widowed, might be willing to act as chaperone and lady's companion to his daughter, my younger cousin, Caroline, who was to follow him out on the Second Fleet early in the New Year. Papa had accepted for both of us, and we were to leave England in January. As you can imagine, the next three months were spent in a flurry of preparations. We had both Edward's townhouse and our own small estate, White Oaks, to sell, business affairs to settle, trunks to pack, and so on . . .''

Nathan nodded.

". . . And then, after Uncle Paul sailed just before Christmas, Caroline came to stay with us. Dear Caro! Her naughty, blithe spirit was the very tonic my sorry heart craved. I began to forget Edward and his cruelties, remembering them only in my nightmares, which came less and less as the days wore on. It seemed we should never finish everything, but, somehow, all was in readiness by the New Year. Our home in Sadler's Wells and everything in it had been sold or packed, the servants turned off or established in new positions, and so on. We found comfortable lodgings at an inn in London, and settled in to await sailing.

"But just a few evenings before the Second Fleet was scheduled to set sail, a man came to our rooms at the inn. He and

170

Papa were closeted together for quite some time, and when the man left, Papa seemed quite agitated and, I thought, distraught.

"The next morning, he told me he had pressing business to attend to in the City. And, for the first time since my wedding feast, he met my eyes. There were tears in his as he patted my shoulder. Then he said the strangest thing. 'Just once more, Mariah, and 'twill all be over. We'll be free of him forever!' "

"He offered no explanations?"

"Nay, none whatsoever. He simply left. Later that morning, a clerk from his chambers came to tell me that he was . . . was dead. It had happened on High Holborn Street, the clerk said, as Papa was hailing a hack to bring him back to the inn. There was to be a hanging that morning. The streets were crowded with spectators. A passing hawker said he'd clutched at his chest, then fallen to the cobbles. The physician they summoned said it was apoplexy." She shrugged. "Anyway, I buried him in some haste, and three days later, Caroline and I sailed aboard the *Hester*. The rest you know."

Chapter Eleven

When her sad tale was done, she wept softly again, but these were cleansing, healing tears, he fancied.

Still cradling her in his arms, he lowered her to the sand and stretched out beside her, her back pressed to his chest, her bottom lodged snugly against his upper thighs. Holding her that way, it was some time before he realized that from weeping, she'd drifted into deep, exhausted sleep, her head lolling heavily upon his arm.

Drawing her closer, he buried his face in her hair and followed suit. The night air was warm. The dunes sheltered them from any chilling breezes off the sea, and the sand beneath them yet held some trace of the heat of day. *'Tis as cozy a cot as any to be found on Eden's Isle*, he thought ruefully as he drifted off.

He awoke a short while later to find her sitting up. She was hugging her bent knees as she watched him sleeping.

"Forgive me. I woke you."

"Nay, I woke myself. Come here, minx," he murmured, opening his arms.

She came into them a little shyly and curled up beside him, his chest her pillow, her palm flat against his rib-cage. Beneath it, she could feel the even pulse of his heart, like the throb of a drum. It was, she decided, exactly like him; strong, steady, comforting. Indeed, now that she'd unburdened herself to him, she felt wonderful, lighter than goose-down, as if an unbearable load had been lifted from her shoulders. But . . . what must he think of her?

"I suppose you think I'm a foolish twit now," she observed hesitantly, her chin quivering.

"Because of what Downing did?"

Too choked to answer, she nodded.

"Then you suppose wrongly, you silly little goose. Rather, I have only admiration for you. Although what Downing did to you was monstrous, you've survived admirably. God's Teeth, that you're not in Bedlam Asylum speaks for itself, wench!"

"But . . ."

"Aye?"

"If I've survived only to fear all men, then 'tis a hollow victory I've won! H-how shall I have a husband—or a babe, some day—if I cannot . . . you know!"

He chuckled. And tweaked her cheek. "Mari, my dove, trust me. God willing, your fear will lessen with time, for time heals all things. You may never forget, but 'twill grow easier, by and by. And one day, when you are ready, you'll find a worthy man who'll love you dearly, and with whom you'll make babes."

Her expression was almost comically dubious. It was obvious she thought he was patronizing her—or that he was a glib-tongued liar.

"'Tis so, believe me," he insisted. "He will be gentle, patient—all that a true husband should be. A man who'll not only be your lover but your trusted friend. And, because he loves you and because you love him, little by little you'll discover there's naught to fear from making love. That it brings pleasure and joy, not pain or shame. When that day comes, the babes will follow, as surely as day follows night,'' he added with a grin.

"Pah. Pretty promises! And I might believe them, were we elsewhere. But I know I'll find no such paragon as you describe, not as long as we're stuck upon this poxy island!'' she grumbled, sitting up again and scowling down at him. "Here, there is only you.''

He winced. "My thanks! You flatter me too much, m'lady.''

"Oh, you know I didn't mean it that way, unless . . . Nathan?''

Her tone was coaxing rather than grumbling now, and alarum bells clashed a warning inside his head.

"Aye, minx?'' he asked warily.

"I know you . . . want me. Won't you help me overcome my fears?''

"My name is Kincaid, Mariah, Jonathan Kincaid. 'Tis not Paragon Kincaid, nor Virtue Kincaid, nor Saint Kincaid, nor even Tutor Kincaid! I'm a rutting, randy brute—a fellow who has little patience with innocent virgins, let alone a woman who needs gentle handling, as do you. God's Teeth, nay! Give me a lusty wench with a glad and roaming eye—one who's ripe for a tumble any time, that's more my style, love.''

She scowled at his breezy dismissal. "Lying toad! You claimed you were Kincaid, King of Kissers, do you recall?''

"I do. And I *am*!'' He tweaked her nose.

"Well, then? Is the giving and taking of kisses your 'majesty's' only talent?''

"Good God, no. And I would be a liar, were I to say it was, mistress,'' he came back smugly.

"Really? Hrrumph. Well, I don't believe you anymore. You're a braggart, 'tis all; I see that now. A rooster who crows rather well, but one who lets his hens go wanting. A noisy blowhard, full of wind and hot air but precious little else. If not, you would help me."

His brows rose. "What's this? Ho, ho, do you challenge the King, wench? I scent a rebellion here!" he teased.

"Aye, Kincaid, you do! Come, look at this problem my way. There's every reason to believe we'll all die here on this bloody island, if not from the heat, or from snake-bites or starvation or disease, then from old age. Nathan, I am but twenty years of age. I would sample all the pleasures of this life 'ere I leave it. 'And 'tis within your power to help me overcome my fears and sample *this* pleasure. You can teach me—oh, you must! You're my only hope, unless we're rescued."

"What's this? An uprising 'gainst the King? Have a care, pretty rebel, there is but one punishment for rebellion in my kingdom."

"Aye, I know, I know. You'll subdue the rebels with kisses," she scoffed, turquoise eyes twinkling. "Or feed them taro and water, and naught else!"

"On the contrary, minx—I shall *tickle* them!"

Even as he made a grab for her ribs, she rolled back on her heels, sprang to her feet and spun away, scrabbling up one of the dunes on her hands and knees like a giant crab.

With a roar, Nathan plunged after her, throwing up great drifts of sand as, growling and roaring like a bear, he pursued her to the top of the dune.

"I have you now, rebel!" he roared and leaped on her, tackling her about the hips and bringing her down. His arms locked around her, they rolled over and over down the far side of the dune, ending up in a giggling, growling heap at the bottom of it.

Braced upon his palms, Nathan leaned up and grinned down at her in triumph, but his smile quickly faded.

It had started as a game on his part, a means to divert her thoughts to other, safer matters, but damn it, he couldn't ignore the electric tremor that jolted through him as their eyes met.

Nor could he hide his manhood's instant response to the soft female form sprawled beneath it.

"I win, your majesty," she whispered huskily.

"The devil you do," he rasped, and ground his lips over hers.

As he kissed her hungrily, she returned his kisses with what she hoped passed for a matching hunger, reaching beneath his leather jerkin to caress his chest.

Trailing her fingers almost shyly down the T of crisp black whorls to his oak-hard belly, she found the ridge of his belt. After a moment's hesitation, she reached still lower to cover his manhood with her palm, gasping at the size and heat of him, which even his breeches did not diminish.

"My liege, you are so very . . . lusty," she whispered shakily, feeling a ticklish quivering in her loins even as she began to tremble.

"God's Blood, woman," he rasped in her ear, his hot breath making her shiver, "lusty's not the half of it. Have a care, lest you finish me."

She withdrew her hand as if scalded and looked up at him hopefully, her turquoise eyes so innocent, so blasted trusting, he knew in his heart that he was doomed, that he wanted her and could deny her naught.

"All right. You win! Sit up, minx," he urged, rolling off her.

"Why?"

"If you would have me teach you, sit up, I say," he repeated, furious at his weakness, his lack of resolve. 'Twas always the same. A prettily turned ankle, a shapely bosom, a certain look in a wench's eye, and he was undone, his treacherous body afire.

She sat up, and Nathan knelt beside her. "All right, for your first lesson, answer me this. Where does a woman feel passion?"

"Where? Why, here, of course," she said scathingly, touching her heart.

"Wrong, vixen."

"Wrong!"

"Aye. When a woman feels desire for a man, she feels it *everywhere*, not only in her heart or her lips or her breasts. But, most of all, more than anywhere else, she feels it . . . here."

Mariah blinked, amazed. "In her eyebrows?" she squeaked.

"Not her eyebrows—in her head, simpleton," he retorted, shaking his own noggin. "When a woman is attracted to a man, she first *thinks* about him all the time, even when they're apart. She murmurs his name. 'Oh, Justin . . . my only Justin!'"

Mariah giggled at his girlish tone.

Ignoring her mirth, he continued, "She considers how handsome he is, and how the sound of his voice makes her feel. Perhaps she even imagines herself abed with him upon sheets of silk, perhaps in a chamber filled with candlelight and scented with flowers. Smell them, Mari! Smell the roses. The freesias. The carnations!"

"Aye," she said, breathing deeply, beginning to understand what he was trying to tell her. "I smell them. Orchids. Frangipani. The scent of the sea."

"Perhaps she also imagines them kissing and caressing. Then, her body responds to her *thoughts*. It glows with warmth. It begins to tingle with the stirring of desire. Her limbs grow loose and heavy. Her breasts—"

"Yo've made your point, sir. I understand that much," she cut in cheekily, sticking her tongue out at him.

"All right. Close your eyes, and we'll begin."

Obediently, she closed them.

"Good! Now, tell me, Mari, do you find me pleasing to look upon?" he asked softly.

"Now that you're shorn, aye, somewhat." Stifling a nervous giggle, she straightaway conjured up the image of Nathan as he knelt before her, his handsome face lit mysteriously by moonlight, his green eyes darkened by desire, his hair resting

177

swathes and curls of ebony silk against his bronzed skin. "Aye, I do," she amended shyly. "For a braggart, I find you . . . most pleasing."

He grinned, his vanity restored. "And how does it feel when I kiss you, like so?" He angled his head and lightly pressed his lips to hers, then delicately flicked his tongue along their joining until, with a tremulous sigh, her lips parted.

"Quite pleasant . . ." she whispered, a trifle unsteadily. "Aye, it feels very pleasing, but . . . I've changed my mind. I think . . . I think I'll open my eyes now!" She'd decided she did not want his tutelage after all, for strange new feelings were uncurling deep in her belly; feathery, frightening feelings.

"Nay. Keep them closed and tell me, how does it feel when I touch you, like so? Remember, Mari, keep your eyes tightly shut, and see me in your mind's eye. See no one but your Nathan."

Your Nathan! She liked the sound of that. "All right."

"'Tis Nathan whose hand caresses you. Do you like it when I stroke your neck, just so . . . and your soft little cheek, here—and what about here, chérie, when I caress your lovely shoulders?"

"Aye," she breathed, rocking ever so slightly. "I . . . I like it very much. Your touch, 'tis so warm and s-soothing."

"And here, Mari. What do you feel when I touch you here?" So saying, he lightly outlined the curve of her bosom with his fingertip, tracing circles upon each swelling mound.

She gasped and her lashes quivered madly.

"Keep your eyes closed, Mari! And remember, 'tis me, Nathan, who caresses your breasts, no other. Come, my sweet, tell me what you feel."

She gasped again and tipped her head back as he gently stroked her breasts, cupping the soft weightiness of both mounds in his palms, then teasing both nipples to stand erect with the balls of his thumbs.

"Oh!" she breathed as her nipples became hard, sensitive buds. "Ohhh! 'Tis strange, and yet . . . 'tis pleasing indeed.

'Tis as if—as if you touched me in . . . in two places at once!''
She felt her cheeks grow hot and pink in the moonlight. How
strange it was, to feel his touch upon her breasts and, in the
same moment, that fluttering pulse between her thighs, as if
he'd also touched her there. The thought of him doing *that*
made the pulse throb even stronger.

With a knowing smile, he dipped his head and, gently cupping her breasts, kissed each one through her bodice, wetting
the fabric.

He half-expected her to panic and thrust him away, as she'd
done before, but to his relief, she did not. Rather, her breathing
grew more shallow and rapid—but 'twas from desire, not fear.

Drawing her down onto the still-warm sand, he caressed
her little pink feet, her slender calves. He kissed her knees,
whispering silly, wonderful endearments all the while, sometimes in English, sometimes in his mother's French tongue. He
called her his "kitten" and his "sweeting," his funny "little
cabbage" and his "flower." He soothed and gentled her fears
with the hypnotic, husky timbre of his voice and with the very
gentleness of his touch, envelopping her in a cocoon of warmth
and pleasant sensation.

Inch by inch, he caressed her lovely body, dropped kisses
upon her lips, her breasts, her legs, again and again, until the
firm silk of her thighs lay warm beneath his palm. As his lips
brushed that secret flesh, he felt her stiffen. When she began
to tremble, he halted, reminding her all over again that he was
Nathan; that he would never, ever hurt her; swearing upon his
soul that he would do nothing unless she wished it.

"Bid me stop, and stop I shall," he promised, the timbre of
his voice husky as he lazily stroked the swell of her hips. His
palm skimmed her flat belly, moving in sensual circles just as
it had on the kettle's sooty curves that day, and nigh driving
her to distraction. "Bid me be gone, and go I shall, vanished
into thin air, like smoke!"

"Rogue!" She laughed at the silly notion of one so tall, so
broad and solid, vanishing so effortlessly, yet there was an

unsteadiness, a breathless quality to her voice that he recognized and took heart from.

At first, it seemed but an accident when his fingertips brushed the fleecy curls of her mons, for straightaway, his hand swept up to caress her belly again. He repeated the fleeting caress again and again, and then he cupped her Venus mound and his hand grew still. The fiery warmth of his palm suffused her secret core.

Please don't hurt me! she begged silently.

She tossed her head from side to side on the sand, red-gold ringlets stirring like a sunset sea, her hands fluttering like moths to a flame and then swooping down to claw at his fingers, trying to drag them from her body as her courage shattered.

Not again . . . nooo, never again!

Oh, lord, she could scarcely breathe! A fleeting image of Edward's eyes, tigerish and gleaming, as he leered down at her, of his cruel mouth twisted in a taunting sneer, filled her vision, obliterating Nathan's tender emerald gaze. She stiffened. Her hands fluttered . . . panic rose up her throat in a scream . . . *ohnoohno*, it was starting . . . oh, yes, oh, yes oh surely it wa—

"Nay, Mariah, don't! Remember, 'tis *Nathan* who touches you. Listen to me, my dove. Listen to my voice! Open your eyes and look at me! 'Tis Nathan who loves you now," his deep voice reminded her firmly, though it seemed to come from a great distance.

His words were like a lifeline tossed to a drowning woman, for in her heart of hearts, she had begun to trust him, knew he would not let her drown. Firmly, he drew her thoughts back to the moment, forced the hated images away with the sheer gentleness of his being, made Edward and all he had done to her slink back into the shadows of her past like a cringing cat.

She opened her eyes. "Oh, God! Oh, Nathan!"

"Hush, sweeting, 'tis all right. 'Tis over and I'm here." He kept up a stream of low reassurances, murmuring over and over again as he stroked her that there was nothing to fear.

Little by little, she grew loose and relaxed beneath his hands. He could feel the tension draining from her like an outpouring tide. "Ah, Mari, my lovely Mari, how beautiful you are," he breathed. "Skin of satin. Hair of silk. Eyes that outshine the very stars. Someone so lovely should know only life's pleasures, never its pain."

Shifting his body, he knelt between her thighs. Before she guessed his intent, he ducked his ebony head and loved her tenderly with lips and tongue.

The touch of his fiery mouth upon that secret, vulnerable part of her was like the kiss of lightning. Catching her lower lip between her teeth, she bit down hard to stanch a cry of protest, willing herself to surrender, to yield to his glorious caresses. Nay, not surrender, not yield, but enjoy.

Undreamed of pleasure flooded through her in golden waves that robbed her of breath, left her dizzy with desire—were her reward. The sweet, fiery ache grew all but unbearable. Her pleasure mounted, soaring like a lark, becoming so piercing sweet, so very pressing, surely she would burst—shattered into a million sparkling shards, fragments of light! Oh! She could not bear it! With a sob, she laced her fingers through his ebony curls to draw his head from her thighs. "Please, no . . . you must not!"

"Aye, I must," he whispered huskily, his breath rising hot against her mound and the sensitive flesh of her inner thighs. Raising her hips, he again pressed his mouth to her silken wetness, caressing her again and again with his lips and tongue.

She could be silent no longer! Little gasps and joyous sobs broke from her lips as she felt a pulse begin, deep in her belly. The throbbing built, engulfed her. She could not move. She could not speak. She could only remain motionless, rigid, 'til the sensation had moved through her in a rippling wave that crested, paused, and was gone. But oh, what ecstasy lingered! What bone-deep contentment remained in its wake.

Tears rolled down her cheeks, leaving glistening tracks upon them. "Thank you," she whispered, framing his handsome face with her hands and drawing him up her body to plant a salty kiss upon his lips. "Oh, thank you!"

"Thanks? Why, 'twas but the start, my love," Nathan murmured as he unfastened his breeches and shucked them off. "Say now. Would you have me stop or go on?"

His voice was hoarse, almost ragged with desire. Oh, poor, poor Nathan! He was a lusty man. She knew his patience and forbearance must have cost him dear, and yet, he had been so very gentle, so very kind. She had trusted him thus far. Surely she could trust him in the rest? And if 'twas all she had feared, surely she could grit her teeth and bear it, just this once, just once more, to give him ease, and show him she was grateful for what he'd tried to do? "Aye, go on," she whispered tremulously.

"Say now if you would wait, my dove. There are ways a man may find his ease. It need not be upon you. There will be other nights."

"Nay. Go on, I say, sir."

"If you are certain . . . ?"

"I am."

His body was lean and virile in the moonlight as he mounted her, parting her thighs with his knees to guide the tip of his manhood to her honeyed sheath.

Her nails dug deep into his upper arms as she clung to him fiercely, half in passion, half in fear. But then his broad shoulders blocked out the midnight sky and the wheeling stars, and there was only Nathan. His manly scent filled her nostrils. His mouth captured hers in a deep and sensual kiss, and her world became Nathan, began and ended with the feel and scent and taste of him, everywhere. With a choked sob, she opened, took him deep, embracing his flanks with her thighs.

A cry that was almost a roar escaped him as he eased forward, sheathing himself in the tightness of her body, gritting his teeth to move slowly as she ran her fingernails over his shoulders and down his scarred back. He groaned as she delicately stroked the driving hardness of his buttocks, his muscles flexing with thrust after deep, powerful slow thrust.

He took her thoroughly, masterfully, yet never, ever cruelly. His arms cradled her. His lips, sweet as wine upon her mouth, were as delicate as pussy-willows upon her breasts. The pleasure he gave her was so sweet, she sobbed with delight. Instinctively, she began to arch her body, to move her hips to match his glorious plungings, wanting more and still more of him inside her as the pulse returned.

But with the undulation of her hips against him, Nathan was undone. It had been too long—too long by far. . . .

"Ah, Mariah—my beauty! My . . . lovely—minx!"

With a great roar, he spent himself inside her, gripping her waist with hands of steel as he shuddered and bucked, and at last fell sated, to her side.

When they awoke much later, locked in a blissful tangle of limbs, the sky was already deepest blue, the fingernail moon fully risen. A hundred thousand candles blazed in the velvet sky, and silence and shadows cloaked the sugar-like dunes.

Mariah's arms were wrapped tightly around Nathan, as if she feared he might try to escape her while she slept. Her head was pillowed upon his chest, her red-gold hair strewn across his belly and arms like a handful of bright fairy-rings. Drowsy with contentment, he idly caressed her curls. And, after some moments, she stirred. He felt the flutter of her long lashes against his skin as she opened her eyes, the moist blessing of her lips as she nuzzled his chest.

"Nathan?"

"Aye, goddess?"

She laughed softly in pleasure at his pet name for her. "Nothing, sir. I but wondered if you slept."

"I did. And 'twas sleep both sweet and profound. Yet when I woke, 'twas sweeter still, for I thought myself still dreaming."

"How so?"

"Because you, sweet goddess, are still here, in my arms."

"La! You have a pretty way with words, sir. I cannot help but wonder where you acquired your eloquence"—she blushed—"and your skill?"

"Jealous of old loves, goddess?" he teased. "Surely not!"

"Oh, but I am, sir. Now that you have shown me what I've been missing, I am green with jealousy," she confessed, snuggling closer to him. The air had grown chill while they slept. Idly, she drew circles on his rib-cage with her fingertip, admiring the virile mat of inky hair that ran like a shadow down his bronze middle to lose itself in the dark mystery at his groin, hidden again now by his breeches. How magnificent he was, everywhere! By comparison, Edward's body had been a joyless, unlovely creation, his flesh fish-belly white, his torso thin as a wraith's and all but hairless. He'd possessed none of the virile, lean hardness of her handsome Nathan.

She smiled against his warm chest, for 'twas the first time she'd been able to recall Edward and their marriage dispassionately, without her heart racing with terror. Did he compare her to his other women? she wondered. And if so, did he find her wanting? "Tell me about them," she urged capriciously.

"Of my 'old loves'?"

She nodded vigorously. He chuckled, thinking what an innocent she was, widow or nay. Only a fool would tell a woman about those who'd come before her! Diplomacy was the way here. "Nay, pet. I cannot."

"Cannot—or will not?"

"Cannot." Idly, he caressed her shoulders as he continued, "From the moment I first saw you—a lovely mermaid, cast up upon the beach—my past faded into nothingness. From that moment, 'twas as if there'd been but one woman in my life—and she a sea-witch, a saucy baggage named Mariah, with red-gold hair, and a virago's temper to match her locks!"

"Oh, what a liar! What a flattering rogue you are, sir. I

don't believe a word but—oh, Nathan, I *love* you for your lies! They are just what I needed to hear.''

Laughing, he drew her up his length, held her squirming body fast, and kissed her soundly. ''Believe me now, goddess?'' he demanded when he was done.

''Aye. But only because I want to.''

''Minx! Remove those tattered rags and I will prove whose beauty has laid hold of my senses,'' he threatened, catching her about the hips.

''Again?'' she asked, wide-eyed with surprise and suddenly made breathless all over again by the ardor in his tone. Why, she realized, the thought of making love with him again was rather appealing.

''Again . . . and again . . . and yet again . . . until I have proven, once and for all, that making love is an act of beauty. A pleasure to be shared by a man and a woman for as long as both shall will it.''

Smiling like a witless wench, she escaped his arms and knelt on the sand. He had given her so much this night! Now, she wanted to give him something in return, to please him as he had pleased her.

Unlacing the ribbons that fastened her bodice, she shyly bared her breasts to him. She stood then, and with another deft move, the ties of her petticoats were undone. With a twitch of her hips, the red flannel layers slithered down her body to pool about her ankles. Wanton, incredibly brazen in her newfound confidence, she stepped from them and kicked them aside, standing before him in the moonlight, nude and unashamed.

Edward had enjoyed seeing her naked. But when he had feasted his eyes upon her nudity, she had cringed. Her flesh had crawled with loathing. By contrast, Nathan's green eyes were warm and tender. When he looked upon her, she felt beautiful, adored, desirable. She twirled once, twice, her arms outstretched, her red-gold mane swirling about her, his to admire, his to kiss, to touch, to take. All his . . .

He swallowed, dazzled. Sweet Christ, never had he seen such loveliness! The moonlight washed her in its silvery light, so that her fair, flawless skin became the palest pink of Italian marble. The glory of her red-gold hair tumbled almost to her waist, its spiralling curls revealing maddening glimpses of her rosy-tipped breasts, her small, firm bottom, the fleecy vee of coppery curls at the pit of her belly which surmounted long, supple legs. Aye, all that lacked was a giant oyster-shell, and she would be Venus, rising from the sea-foam at her moment of birth.

"Come here," he commanded, his voice grown thick again.

"Why, Master Kincaid, whatever for?" she asked archly.

He grinned, thinking she was learning the flirtatious arts of her sex with far greater speed than he'd thought possible. "Never mind your teasing, wench. Come here, I say—'else suffer the consequences!"

"More tickling?" she asked innocently as she padded barefoot to his side, wearing only a smile. She dropped to her knees on the sand beside him, her lovely mouth pursed and ready to return his kisses even as he cupped her face and drew her down.

"Tickling be damned, goddess. I have a better way to pass the time." As he kissed her, he fondled her breasts, rolling each rosy nipple between his fingers until she whimpered against his mouth and pressed herself against him.

"Anon, I shall tell you of my infamous past," he promised, stroking her sleek, warm belly. "I want you to know the man you have lain with tonight, and the cruel fates that conspired to bring me to this isle. But for now, my sweet, that sorry tale can wait. . . ."

'Twas close to dawn, he judged by the sky, before they were sated. As they lay cuddled together in the sand, she reminded him of his promise to tell her of his past.

Drawing a deep breath, he began, briefly recounting how he

186

had left home at sixteen to become a portrait painter, but of being press-ganged to join the crew of the explorer James Cook's vessel, the *Resolution*, instead.

"'Twas five long years before we returned to England, and by that time, Master Reynolds had begun his Royal Academy of Art. I could have studied there, had I wanted to, but somewhere during my travels I'd lost the desire to paint, save for my own amusement. Aye, 'twas the Law that fascinated me then, and the workings of Justice. And so, I went home to Dover and Linden Hall, made amends with my father, and told him of my decision to become a lawyer. 'Twas a profession he heartily approved of, thank God, and I think he was as pleased as I to mend the rift between us! He and *ma mère* gave me their blessing, along with a letter of introduction to an old friend of my father's, a professor of law who lectured at the Inns of Court in London. To my great good fortune, I was accepted by the Temple Inn Society. And, after four hard years of study and many gruelling examinations, I passed the Bar and was allowed to present my cases in court."

"But the practice of law is a far cry from a prison cell and a convict transport!"

"Indeed it is. And I shall tell you shortly how one led to the other, minx," he promised, tweaking her nose. "You recall I spoke of my friend, Roger Loring?"

"Indeed I do. He was the son of the inn-keeper, Toby Loring, was he not?"

"Aye, he was. Poor Roger! I yet miss him sorely. You see, after coming home from the sea, we'd remained fast friends throughout my years of apprenticeship at the Inns. Then his father, Toby Loring, passed on, and the running of the Royal George fell to Roger, as his only son. We were yet friends, but my new profession occupied much of my time, as did his new responsibilities as a tavern-keeper. Consequently, we enjoyed less of each other's company than in former years. But then, one day, Roger sent me an urgent message by his boot-boy, young Pip. He wanted me to meet with him at the inn that very night. He said he had something of the utmost importance to discuss, and that I should be there without fail.''

"And did you go?" Mariah asked.

"I did," Nathan said heavily, sitting up and running his hands through his hair in a world-weary gesture. "Aye, I went—as you shall hear."

In a low, controlled voice, he told her of his meeting with Roger and of learning of the Octagon Club's conspiracy to assassinate the King; of how he'd gone to the inn the following Friday to hear the treasonous plotting for himself, but had instead found his two friends murdered.

His voice broke when he described the awful scene and her heart went out to him for his loss. Her expression mirroring his own, her eyes wet with tears, as were his, she clasped his hands beween her own and held them fiercely, wishing she could do something—anything—to ease his pain or to take some of the burden from his shoulders.

"I knew before the new judge pronounced my sentence what the verdict must be," he said bitterly, his green eyes shadowed with the harshness of that memory. "If I were allowed to live, the would-be assassins feared I would bring charges of treason against the Crown—a crime which carries the sentence of death, as well you know. On the other hand, dead men point fingers at no one! The irony is, they were quite wrong. I could tell little, for in my shock, I saw only *one* of their faces—that of the man who later sentenced me to hang!"

"And what was his name?" Mariah asked breathlessly, round-eyed at hearing his tale.

Grim-faced with memory in the dawning light, Nathan began, "It was—"

"Kincaid!" The shout rang out, cutting him off. "For the love of God, man, are you here?"

Chapter Twelve

"It's Tim Bright and Tom Swift, the cabin-boys, sir!" Carmichael explained as he, Babbington, Mariah, and Nathan hastily returned to the camp by the coconut grove. "Those young devils sneaked off to the wreck at first light!"

"But why would they do that?" Mariah asked as she tried to keep pace with the longer-legged men.

"Ole Peg, he shares their hut," Carmichael managed to tell them between wheezing breaths. "He overheard 'em talking last night about how Mistress Caroline had said she missed her comb more than any other possession. So, that besotted young fool Bright decided to play the hero and fetch 'er one up from the *Hester*'s cabins! Swift's apparently the better swimmer of the two, so he went with him."

"Sweet Christ!" Nathan muttered, breaking into a run. "The wreck's a feeding ground for sharks at this hour!"

By the time they reached the spot on the beach where the *Hester*'s mainmast jutted above the water, almost all of their party had already gathered there. They stood in anxious groups, looking out to where the wreck had settled. Among them, Mariah saw, was Tim Bright. Wet-haired and dressed only in his sodden breeches, he stared into space while Caroline clung, weeping, to his arm.

"But Tim, you silly goose, I was only wishing aloud, I didn't mean it! I wouldn't want you or Tom to risk your lives for a silly comb, not for the world!" the young girl was telling him tearfully.

"Where's Swift?" Nathan snapped as he reached them, peeling off his leather vest even as he spoke. "Jack, loan me your knife, man."

"He . . . he dove down to the wreck two or three times, sir," Tim Bright stammered, misery in his tone and expression. "Then the . . . the last time, he didn't come up again! I tried t' find him, Mr. Kincaid—I truly did! But . . . but I couldn't hold my breath long enough, so I ran for Mr. Carmichael. Tom, he could swim like a fish, he could! He laughed at me— said he could do better blindfolded, an' that he'd fetch Miss Caroline her comb. And so. . . ."

But his words were wasted. Nathan was gone.

The *Hester* lay on her side in thirty feet of crystalline turquoise water. Colorfully striped fish swam in and out of her wreckage, but Nathan could see no sign of the lad.

He dove down amongst the coral beds of pink, white, red, and black that were like an underwater garden, brushing aside sea-anemones and fronded clumps of kelp that danced to and fro with the pull of the current, to gain the *Hester*'s decks.

The huge wooden hatch that had once sealed the hold must have been knocked aside when the vessel had settled on her starboard side. And, as Nathan swam over the grating, he saw the pointed dorsal fin and leering smile of a white shark as it swam from the hold.

Grabbing onto the shattered taff-rail, Nathan forced himself

190

to remain very still. His free arm was pressed against his side, in it was the hilt of Jack's dagger, his legs were motionless.

God in Heaven!

His heart seemed huge. His lungs, afire, seemed about to burst from lack of air as the curious shark swam up to him. It swam close enough for him to mark the gills moving on either side of its head, to see the notches in its tail.

For moments that were a lifetime, the six-foot shark nosed his side, his back, as if trying to discover what kind of creature he was, before it finally turned tail and swam away. As it passed him, its rough shagreen skinned his chest like a rasp.

After the shark had gone, Nathan surfaced briefly to gulp down some badly needed air, then dived again. This time, he noticed something he'd not seen on his first descent. Tom Swift's blond hair, streaming out from beneath the hatch-grating. The young fool must have tried to remove it single-handed, and had become pinned beneath its weight instead. Swift's slight frame was almost hidden by the massive hatch-cover.

Heartsick, Nathan hefted the heavy grating off him. He flung it aside and, tenderly cradling the youth's lifeless body, swam with it to the surface.

Those on shore watched silently as Nathan reappeared with his burden, stunned into silence by shock and grief. Only Mariah uttered a low, "Thank God!" as Nathan's dark head crested the surface, for she had been afraid he would also drown.

He waded through the shallows and, grim-faced and un-speaking, strode up the wet sand with the cabin-boy's body dangling lifelessly in his arms. Sixteen, if he was a day—the same age Nathan had been when he'd run away from home, the age when the whole world awaited—yet Tom Swift was dead.

"Bury him!" he cracked, his voice like a whip, as he flopped down, his head bowed on his knees.

"But sir, we've no spade or shovel," the nearest man protested.

"I don't give a damn if you dig with your blasted teeth, Stiles. I want this boy given a decent burial," Nathan growled, casting the poor marine a murderous look. *"Now!"*

"Aye, aye, sir!" Stiles murmured.

Mariah dropped to her knees at Nathan's side. There were tears brimming in her eyes as she hesitantly reached out to comfort him, stroking his shoulder. Beneath her fingers, his body was tense. She could feel the anger that crackled about him.

"Nathan, please, you mustn't blame yourself!" she implored. "'Twas not your fault. You did all you could to save him."

With a muttered curse, he flung her hands away. "Did I?" he growled, fixing her with a searching look.

"Yes!"

He shook his head, his expression bitter. "Nay, goddess, I think not. Had I been in camp, instead of sporting in the dunes with you, I would have been here in time to save him."

"Not so! You being here would have changed nothing! You heard Master Carmichael. The lads slipped away while everyone was still sleeping."

Nathan's jaw tightened obstinately. "And where were the guards I posted? Answer me that. They were slacking, Mariah—slacking because they knew I was gone and couldn't call them to account! Damn it, the men chose me as their leader! 'Tis not something I take lightly. Tom Swift and the others chose me to lead them because they *trusted* me—but when they needed me most, I failed them."

With that, he sprang to his feet and started striding back towards the coconut grove.

"Kincaid, wait!" Jack urgently called after him.

Nathan halted. "Aye, what is it?" he demanded, without turning around.

"Big trouble, if yer ask me!" Jack answered, nodding towards the point. "Take a look fer yerself, lad!"

Slowly, Nathan turned to look and his gut clenched.

Ruskin and his convict band were but sixty yards away, close to a score of men armed to the teeth with cutlasses, daggers, and clubs. Ruskin's arm was slung companionably about the treacherous Digby's neck, and the pair were smiling like a brace of cats.

"Something wrong, Lawyer Kincaid?" sang out Ruskin in a loud, carrying voice. "Would that be a grave your laddies are after diggin'—or the grandmother of all sandcastles?"

Jack Warner saw a nerve pulse in Nathan's jaw, saw muscles bunch throughout his lean frame as warning lightning flickered in his green eyes.

"Nay, lad," he warned softly out of the corner of his mouth, just loud enough for Nathan to hear. "Don't let 'im get t' ye so easy! Stand yer ground—let 'im make the first move."

Nathan exhaled the breath he'd drawn and murmured, "Aye."

"Blimey, in't that Kincaid a pretty cock! I'd go belly-up for that 'un in a trice!" Nancy whispered, her blue eyes shining, her pretty face lively as she stared across the stretch of beach at Nathan Kincaid. "Aye, an' I'd give no thought t' the ha'penny for it, neither."

Kitty laughed softly, but the laughter never reached her eyes. The death of Annie's baby so soon after its mother's suicide had done something to her, she realized. Somehow, her terror of Ruskin, his hold on her, had slackened. She felt strangely calm, resigned to whatever fate Lady Luck had in store for her. And, with the calm and resignation had come the determination to do something to better her lot, else die in the attempt.

Perhaps Ruskin'd try to get her back. Maybe he'd succeed and kill her. But whatever the future might hold, she was leaving him today, joining Kincaid and the others—*if* they'd take her! She knotted her fists. Oh, they just had to! If not, she swore she'd take the same way out that Annie had chosen. Aye, better dead than Ruskin's whore . . .

"Oy! Oy! Look sharp, our Kit!" Nancy hissed, nudging her in the ribs. "It's startin'!"

"Somethin' wrong, Kincaid? Do your men fear my laddies, wi'out their irons?" Ruskin sneered, then grinned at his men.

"Fear you?" Nathan smile showed contempt. "Hardly, Ruskin! I'd back one of my men against two of yours any day! But if 'tis a fight you're after, 'twill be a fair one, or none at all. Your men are armed t' the teeth, while mine are not." Now that he had a tight grip on his anger, he was not about to sacrifice even one more of his men to satisfy Ruskin's whims.

"Bugger weapons, sir! Let me at 'em, the scurvy knaves!" Stiles hissed, his fists bunched. He was like a terrier, bristling for a fight.

A chorus of hearty ayes echoed the marine's sentiments.

"Make a move, and you will answer to me," Nathan growled, and the men quieted down, sulky but obedient.

"Armed? Us lads? Why, we've naught but a dull cutlass or two and a wee meat-dirk between us, Lawyer Kincaid," Ruskin sneered. "Surely you're not afraid?"

"I'm not," Nathan responded curtly. "Are you?"

"Och, I dinna fear aught in this world, lawyer—and damned little in the next!" the Scot boasted rashly.

"Very well. Fight me," Nathan suggested softly. "You and I, Ruskin, man to man, with only our bare knuckles. As we fought in Newgate, if you recall? Can you whistle, Ruskin?"

By the flicker in Ruskin's colorless eyes, Nathan knew the man remembered that fight all too well—and that Kincaid had bested him. He also guessed that the defeat had rankled ever since, and had become a gnawing hunger for Ruskin to avenge himself.

"Aye, I recall," the big Scot said heavily, not liking the turn the confrontation had taken one bit.

"Then ye'll also recall that I won that fight," Nathan continued in an amiable tone, one calculated to rile Ruskin still further. "Or mayhap that very memory is why ye need so many men at your back. To do what you couldn't do yourself."

Nathan smiled and let the insinuation hang in the air, and the men behind him chuckled their approval. Ruskin had no choice, not now, they knew. He either had to fight Kincaid single-handed or be branded a coward and lose face and authority before his men.

"Let me fight him," Digby said to Ruskin. "I boxed at the Naval Academy. I don't like to brag, but I did rather well for myself, too." Digby's grey eyes glittered. Here was the chance he'd been looking for! By fighting Kincaid—and winning— he could both ingratiate himself with Ruskin's men and demonstrate to the convicts that he had the qualities of leadership their oafish Ruskin lacked.

Ruskin grinned, secretly relieved. He was much the worse for grog and knew he'd make a poor showing that day against the cool, calm Kincaid in a man-to-man fight. Let Digby take a battering, if he was so blessed hot to fight! "What say you, Kincaid?" he asked, ignoring the indignant, disappointed groans of his men. "Will ye accept this braw lad as my second?"

"Aye," Nathan agreed without comment.

Digby stepped away from the others and crossed the stretch of sand that separated the two groups. About midway, he halted.

Tossing Jack the knife he'd borrowed, Nathan did likewise, stopping about four feet from Digby.

The two of them were well matched, almost the same height, though Nathan was slightly heavier in build.

After Digby'd removed his uniform blouse, both men spat and put up their fists. Digby began to circle warily, dancing like a boxer from foot to foot. Calmly, Nathan waited for him to make the first move, and when Digby jabbed, he sidestepped and landed a solid clip against the other man's jaw.

With the first blow, a roar rose from his men. "Do fer 'im, Kincaid!" "Shiver 'is timbers, Nate!" they urged.

Nathan grinned, beginning to enjoy himself as Digby cursed and spat blood. This fight was the very outlet his anger over Swift's senseless death needed . . . and the perfect opportunity to call this man to account for his assault on Mariah. The thought of that bastard's foul hands upon her made his blood boil.

Back and forth, they traded punches, and it was obvious after but a few moments that Digby's claims had been no idle boast. He was a fine boxer, light and fast on his feet, his blows powerful and telling, but Nathan, a veteran of village brawls and bouts of fisticuffs, gave as good as he got. The two of them raised drifts of sand as they fought like snarling curs, first standing, then rolling on the ground; first Digby on top, then Nathan as each man grappled for dominance. They were egged on by the whoops and cheers of the one side, the hisses, boos, and slurs on the other.

The sun grew stronger, its heat fiercer. Sweat streamed down their bodies now, mingling with their free-flowing blood, but neither man would give quarter to the other or concede defeat, though both had split lips and faces that were bruised and hugely swollen.

Nathan had one black eye, Digby two, but still they fought. The watchers grew silent as the battle continued. The only sounds now were the smack of fists against flesh; the sobbing gasps, groans, or curses of the combatants; and the raucous screams of the seabirds wheeling above them. Time seemed to stand still, to pause with heated, bated breath, awaiting the outcome.

Digby was tiring, Nathan could feel it. Under ordinary circumstances, he would have declared the fight a draw and shaken hands with his opponent after he'd called a halt to the fight. But this was no ordinary circumstance, and instead, he revelled in the knowledge that he was slowly but surely gaining the upper hand. God damn it, he wanted blood—wanted to taste it—wanted to hurt the man who'd dared to frighten Mari; to vent days of bottled-up anger and frustration on the sneering, turncoat lieutenant who'd traded sides, and make an example of him the men would never forget! When he was done, Ruskin's convicts would think twice before they challenged him or his men again. And his own group would have no cause to regret that they'd chosen him as leader.

As Digby staggered backwards, Nathan lunged after him, raining thwacking blow after blow upon the man's head, his chest, until Digby groaned and gave up. He raised his fists in front of his face as a shield to protect his split eyelid, his shattered, bleeding nose, his mouthful of loose teeth, making no effort to return Nathan's attack. Nonetheless, Nathan continued to pummel his battered opponent again and again, until, through the crimson haze, he heard someone calling his name, over and over. Flicking his head to clear it, he saw Jack beside him, felt the steely bite of the wiry little man's fingers clamped over his shoulders to hold him back.

"Enough, lad!" Jack rasped. "You've won, damn it. Leave be!"

As if wakening from a dream, Nathan realized that Digby had fallen at his feet. Christ! Had he killed him? Nay, he saw with relief. The man was yet moving, trying to crawl away.

His chest heaving, Nathan nodded, spraying sweat and blood about him. Arms dangling, his shoulders bowed with exhaustion, he took a step back, then turned and staggered down to the water's edge. Behind him, his men cheered wildly, but he felt no sense of triumph as some of Ruskin's fellows dragged Digby away by the heels. Only a yawning emptiness where pity and compassion had once lodged.

When he had washed himself off in the sea, he returned to his men.

"Mr. Carmichael, Mr. Matherson, we've wasted enough time here, I do believe. We've work to do, if we would eat tonight, have we not? Regroup your men and get to it!" he snapped.

"Aye, aye, sir," they responded quietly, confused—and cowed—by the cold fury they had sensed in him.

His body screaming from its pounding, Nathan set his jaw and watched stonily as Ruskin and company made a half-hearted retreat back to the point. Sensing eyes upon his back, Ruskin turned and shook his fist in Nathan's direction.

"You'll rue this day, God rot ye, ye bastard!" The Scot's rough threat carried on the breeze.

Nathan planted his fists on his hips and laughed. "Not so, Angus Ruskin! Next time, 'twill be you they drag home by the heels—and I'll rue naught but sparing your worthless life!"

As he spoke, a young, black-haired wench broke away from the convict band. She hoisted up her ragged skirts and began running towards them, ignoring Ruskin's curses, his furious bellows to come back.

When she reached them, she flung herself down at Jack Warner's feet, her pale, pretty face beseeching as she plucked at his legs.

"Please, sir, let me join ye?" Kitty implored him. "I beg ye, don't turn me off. See, I was Ruskin's wench. I'm good as done for, if I go back to 'im!"

"If ye'd join our number, 'tis Kincaid ye must ask, wench, not me," Jack said with a doubtful nod in Nathan's direction.

"Aye, let her stay," Nathan said curtly, turning away. "What's one more, with young Tom gone? Mariah?"

He offered Mariah his arm, but with a look in her turquoise eyes he could not fathom, she sadly shook her head and turned away.

Ruskin had halted to look back in their direction, silently broiling with hatred. As he did so, he saw the exchange between the pair.

His fury over Kitty's desertion mellowed as his colorless eyes narrowed and fixed upon Mariah. So. The Governor's bonnie niece and Kincaid . . . was that the way the wind blew, then? He snorted. 'Twas no more than he would have expected, that Kincaid would be tupping the best of the sluts. In Newgate, Kincaid had turned his nose up at the favors of the prison's willing bawds, but clearly he wasna averse t' having a clean, fresh piece like that high-born bitch beneath him.

As his men scuttled back to camp, like curs with their tails between their legs, Ruskin stood alone and watched the bonnie Mariah trail disconsolately after Kincaid's band.

Her red-gold hair made a fiery banner in the sunlight as the sultry wind lifted it. Her slender hips swung enticingly beneath her red flannel skirts. Ruskin scratched his groin. *Well, well, now. Mayhap he wasna averse t' a clean fresh piece himself.*

Chapter Thirteen

"You've been avoiding me," Mariah accused. She came to a standstill on the beach a few feet from where Nathan, water streaming from his body, was examining the treasures he'd brought up from the *Hester*'s wreck just moments before.

He made no comment, but remained kneeling in the sand, his broad, lash-scarred back to her. Being ignored infuriated her as nothing else. The cool, calm demeanor she'd sworn to maintain snapped.

"'Twill serve no purpose to pretend deafness, sir!" she exclaimed loudly. "Ever since the day Tom drowned, I've been trying to talk to you, but you never stay in one place long enough. Well, you shan't escape me today, for I won't let you!"

"I've had a great many things to do, m'lady," Nathan growled, his tanned hands working with a minimum of wasted effort to neatly coil a length of line he'd brought up from the *Hester*'s wreck. He bent to examine his next treasure without bothering to look up. "If it appears I've been avoiding you in the process, then so be it."

Mariah's lips pursed in anger. Devil take the man! He was as surly as a bear, and insolent to boot, and for two pins, she'd let him stew in his own broth, except . . . she just couldn't! She missed the old Nathan, the sensual, teasing devil-may-care King of Kissers, far too much for that! Their *affaire* had been short-lived, thanks to his damned scruples, but she longed with all her heart to rekindle those first, fragile sparks, and fan them into an enduring fire.

"Aye, so I've seen," she agreed pointedly, grimacing. "You work from dawn to dusk, as if driven by demons. All the men remark on it. They're up at first light, but, lo and behold, there you are already, diving down to that cursed wreck again and again. Blast you, Nathan! When will it end? You've risked your life countless times down there among the sharks, and for what? A few paltry blankets, a wrecked longboat, a cooking pot or what-have-you!"

She paced the sand, back and forth, hectic color filling her cheeks as she railed at him. Her eyes were a snapping turquoise that was electric in the light, sharply at odds with the dainty pink frangipani blossoms she'd woven through her braided hair.

"You made no protests when I salvaged your trunk, woman," he observed in a scornful tone. "Nor do you shun its contents!"

Flushing, she glowered at him. What could she say? He was right, on that score. She'd been grateful beyond imagining when he'd brought up one of the chests holding her and Caroline's belongings. Its recovery had meant she could finally discard her stifling red flannel petticoats and immodestly skimpy bodice in favor of cooler, more modest attire, such as the aqua morning gown she was wearing.

Opting to ignore his comment, she continued. "Night falls, and 'tis you who stands watch over our camp, asking no man to relieve you. When do you sleep, sir? When do you eat? And how long can you go on this way without falling ill of exhaustion? Behind your back, the men say you're going mad,

Kincaid. That the tropic clime has addled your wits. I agree with them." It was a challenge, a desperate attempt to force him to show some emotion—any emotion—but the cursed man refused to take the bait.

"'Tis likely you're right," he agreed tersely, using a knife-blade to force the lock of the small wooden coffer before him. " 'Mad-dog' Kincaid. It has a nice ring, don't you think?"

Mariah muttered a curse but she peered over his shoulder nonetheless, curious to see the chest's contents despite his sarcasm.

Standing in several inches of salt-water were rows of colored India-inks in tiny pots, their corks still intact; sticks of charcoal, grease-crayons, a slim box of water-colors and soggy goose-feather quills. There were also several beautiful leather-bound sketching pads with blank pages, now water-logged and swollen to several times their original thickness.

The chest belonged to the botanist, Matherson, Nathan knew. With any luck, the sketch books' pages could be dried in the sun and rendered serviceable again. Perhaps the botanist could record his finds here.

Belatedly remembering Mariah, he scowled, looked up at her with narrowed eyes and observed coldly, "Have *you* no work to do, mistress, that you have time to pester me at mine?"

"Nay, none at all."

"Could you find nothing to busy yourself? No palm-fronds to weave into baskets? No shells to string for necklaces, like your cousin? I recall you were most eager to do your share when first we came here," he reminded her, his tone caustic as he remembered that morning. "How so? Has the novelty of equality palled so soon?"

Mariah snorted her disgust. "People change. *You* were once eager to tumble me at every turn, as *I* recall, sir," she reminded him pointedly. "'Twas not enough that I refused you, remember? Nay! When I would have drowned myself, you made bold with your hands and pompously bade me 'live for passion and you,' if naught else!" She snorted again. "And then, that night

202

in the dunes, you made love to me as if . . . as if . . ." Her voice, now choked and husky, broke. She averted her face and tried to scrub her tears away with her knuckles before continuing. "But now? Now, sir, you shun me as if I were some dockside trull whose favors you'd bought for a night and want naught more to do with. You avoid me as if I were a pariah who carries a leper's bell and cries 'Unclean'! La! Do not talk to me of novelties that have palled, sir."

"God's Teeth, you've changed, woman. You're growing quite shrewish," he snapped. Her accusal had stirred a twinge of guilt, though he would never admit it.

"Aye, mayhap I am. But then, 'twould appear we've both changed, sir—though alas, only one of us for the better."

It was patently clear she was not referring to him. And, despite his resolve to remain aloof, her cutting remarks needled him.

"Did you forget so soon? Tom Swift would still be alive if I'd been in camp that night."

"You don't *know* that, you sanctimonious dolt! What happened that day was an accident, as unavoidable as our shipwreck. 'Twas the hand of Fate, Lady Luck—call it what you will—that killed young Tom, not the almighty and omnipotent Jonathan Kincaid. No one else blames you, so why must you chastise yourself? You're our leader, Nathan, not God Almighty. You're one of us, the man we voted for—not some brass idol that we worship and expect to do no wrong!"

"Idol!"

"Aye, idol. In faith, you flaunt your misplaced guilt like a martyr in a hair-shirt, for all to see. 'There goes Jonathan Kincaid, a more pious and penitent fellow you'll never meet!' Pah! A pox on your piety and penances!"

"You asked me to help you. I did. Will you now throw my kindness back in my face?" he thundered.

"Kindness? Ha! Hypocrite! 'Twas not 'kindness' that drove you—admit it! 'Twas lust, simple, honest lust! Tell me, does your pleasure that night require such a public penance? I suppose it must. Why else would you make yourself a whipping-boy!"

"Damn ye woman, is that what you think?" he demanded angrily, his green eyes crackling. "That 'tis only a show?"

"Aye!"

"Then you're wrong," he gritted through clenched jaws.

"Am I? Really? Then prove it, sir. Be the leader the men need, not some paragon they can never hope to please. Put Tom's death behind you, where it properly belongs. Cast off your halo, you wretched man, and come down off your blasted pedestal!"

A muscle twitched at his temple, and she knew her words had hit home.

"Can you say in all honesty you do not hold me accountable for the lad's death, m'lady?" he demanded bitterly. "I saw something in your eyes that day—nay, don't deny it! And when I offered you my arm, you refused it and turned from me."

"Aye, sir, I did," she admitted, biting her lip. Then her jaw came up obstinately. "But it had naught to do with Tom, or blaming you."

"Then why did you recoil?"

"'Twas fear you glimpsed in my eyes, not reproach."

"Fear?" His ebony brows rose. "How so?"

"I saw your face when Digby fell, and its savagery frightened me. There he was, bleeding and begging for mercy; yet you showed him no drop of compassion. In faith, were it not for Jack pulling you off him, I believe you'd have beaten him to death!

"'Twas a stranger who offered me his arm that morn, Nathan. A Newgate felon—not the lover who'd held me so tenderly, I thought myself falling in love with him. A violent man stood in your place. One who—God help him!—seemed quite capable of . . . of . . ." Her voice trailed away. Her gaze slid uncomfortably past his.

"Murder?" he finished for her in a voice as soft as the sensuous tropical trade-winds.

"Aye," she confessed, her turquoise eyes awash with pain.

"And you wondered if I'd lied to you," he stated flatly. "If I was not, as they claimed, a 'murderer twice-over'?"

"Can you blame me for a moment's doubt? Oh, Nathan, if you'd seen yourself as I saw you then, you, too, would wonder" she added with a shudder, remembering. His face and torso had been battered, bruised, and bloody, his knuckles torn and bleeding, yet he'd worn an unholy grin that was hardly human, and his green eyes had glittered with bloodlust.

"And now?"

"Now I've had time to think about what happened. I fancy I've come to understand it, if not accept it. 'Twas guilt that drove you then, even as it drives you now."

"Guilt? Never!"

"Aye, guilt. Misplaced guilt over Tom's death. And the need to prove yourself to your men. And, perhaps, aye, to yourself."

She reached out and tentatively ran her hand down his wet, corded arm in a gentle caress, relieved when he tensed but neither flinched nor removed her hand.

"Nathan, my love, you have nothing to prove here," she told him softly. "You are among friends, men—and women— who admire you more than you know. That we are all alive and well, with warm shelter, fresh water, and full bellies, is proof that you are truly a worthy leader. The men have heard Kitty talk about Ruskin's band. Of how they are close to starvation and madness and are at each other's throats. And in their prayers each night, they thank God for Jonathan Kincaid! Why, Carmichael, Matherson, and the others have made a pact to petition Governor Amberfield to pardon you, should we ever be rescued. Do you know that? Doesn't that prove anything, you obstinate brute?"

He raised his dark head and their eyes met. A thrill of relief, of joy, ran through her as she saw Nathan's expression change. His jaw softened, His lips lost their tight, thinned aspect, and his eyes darkened as he looked at her, all bitterness dwindling.

"Mariah . . ." he began huskily, but he couldn't go on. God, how he'd craved the comfort of her arms these past two lonely weeks of self-blame and recrimination; yearned for the absolution and oblivion to be found in them.

"Hush," she whispered. Leaning over, she pressed her lips sweetly to his as he knelt at her feet. Tentatively, she traced the margins of his mouth with her tongue's tip; then she nibbled gently upon his lower lip.

Dear God, how very handsome he was! The weeks beneath the fierce island sun had burnished his torso a rich, deep bronze which, contrasted against the blue-black of his hair and the mercurial green of his eyes, only served to make him even more devilishly attractive than before, now that his bruises had faded. And, remembering their glorious love-making among the dunes, her arms ached to hold him again. Her body flamed with memories as she leaned over him.

Looking up at her, his eyes sparkled like emeralds in the sunlight, set within a frame of ebony brows and thick, sooty lashes that any woman would envy. His nose was straight, slim, and proud, his lips stern yet pleasingly formed. Clad now in salvaged white canvas breeches with a rope drawstring at the waist, he had a bare, hard muscled chest. His breeches, stiffening with salt as they dried, clung snugly to his hard flanks, the fabric straining across his arousal.

Mariah dared a smile then, a naughty invitation in her eyes. The smile curved the corners of her delectable mouth, surprising the dimple in her cheek before it spread to her eyes and made them even brighter with mischief.

So, your majesty? What's it to be, sire? that teasing, sensual smile seemed to ask. Do you want me, as I want you? Will ye take what I'm offering—or must I look elsewhere?

To her delight—and relief—he returned her smile with a lazy, sensual grin that was a little sheepish. That look! There was no question that he wanted her still! Her fears had all been for naught! And just gazing at him, kissing him, had roused a ticklish quivering in her own loins.

"Oh, Nathan!" she murmured, dropping to her knees before him. Facing him now, she curled her arms about his neck, nuzzling his stubbled cheek with sweetly puckered lips, stroking the wet black curls at his nape; then dipped her red-gold head lower to kiss the soft ridge where throat met collarbone, inhaling deeply. Hmmm. His skin smelled of the briny sea. Indeed, he tasted so clean, so salty and male upon her lips, 'twas hard to keep from biting him. "Promise you won't turn from me again, that you will tell me if there's aught amiss? These weeks have been hell on earth! Oh, love, I've missed you so. . . ."

A shudder jarred him, and for one, painful moment, she feared he might yet draw away. But he only whispered, "I know, my love. God's Teeth, I know."

He wrapped his fist about her braided hair and used it as a tether to gently pull her closer. Untying the ragged ribbon, he separated the twisted strands, setting them free to dance about her shoulders in a halo of red-gold. He tucked the fragrant pink blossoms that had fallen from her hair behind her ear. Then, cupping her lovely face in both hands, he angled his dark head and kissed her with a hungry ardor that stunned her, robbed her of breath.

The stabbing stroke of his tongue within her mouth made her very bones dissolve, and when his hand swept down her body to caress her curves—'twas as if she'd been stroked by fire, his touch enflamed her so!

"I rue the day I salvaged your gowns, mistress," he murmured, his hot, moist breath tickling her ear as he fought the ties at her back, clumsy in his ardor.

"Why so, sir?" she came back breathlessly, laughter in her voice.

"You know very well why," he murmured huskily.

With a grunt of satisfaction, he felt the damned ties give at last. Her back was bared to his touch as the gown fell away. Turning her, he kissed its velvety flesh, pressing his lips to her shoulders, the insides of her elbows, before tracing the little bumps of her spine. With his mouth, he nudged the fabric lower and lower, to bare still more of her to his lips.

She shivered and arched back, her red-gold hair tumbling down her back in a glorious cascade of pale fire, her eyes closed as she caught her lower lip between her teeth in an effort to remain silent. 'Twas torture, for what she really wanted was to cry out in pleasure at his feathery kisses and caresses—devil take who heard her!

When his lips reached the base of her spine, he tugged the folds of her gown still lower and cupped her bottom, lustfully squeezing both firm bare globes as if they were melons before, with a parting swat, he took both her hands in his and raised her to standing.

The aqua gown fell in a puddle about her ankles as she rose. With a fierce, hot stab of desire, he saw she was quite naked beneath it. Modest in the sunlight, she crossed her hands demurely over her lovely rose-tipped breasts to hide them from his scorching eyes, lowering her gaze to the sand. Yet her breathing was ragged with excitement, and her eyes had darkened to sensual teal-blue, when she looked up again.

Truly, she is a vision, Nathan thought, the breath catching in his throat. *A regal beauty who could make a man feel a king.*

Holding her eyes captive with his own, a sensual half-smile playing about his lips, he slowly unknotted the drawstring at his waist and let the canvas trousers slide down his lean flanks to his ankles.

His hard, masculine body was fully aroused, his shaft erect, rising proudly from the dark nest at his groin. Striding towards her, as naked as she, he looked down at her—one long, smoldering look—then swept her up and carried her into the ocean.

He waded out until they were chest-deep, warm waves lapping idly about them. Surrounded by water of the same sparkling turquoise as her eyes, he caught her to him in a crushing embrace and kissed her hungrily, deeply. He showered kisses over her face, her ivory throat, then ducked his ebony head beneath the foamy surf to suckle upon her bobbing breasts while his free hand slipped between her thighs.

She responded to the stroking of his fingers as if she'd been struck by lightning, arching backwards and crying his name to the vault of blue above them. Her fingers clamped over his bronzed shoulders as her ardor mounted, fuelled by the tugging sensation of his mouth upon her nipples and by the deepening rhythm of his fingers as he plundered her secret treasures.

Warm, lapping water . . . mounting desire . . . fervent caresses—'twas exciting beyond belief. Adrift on a sea of sensation, she gasped, then cried out with longing, pleading with him to hurry, to be quick and take her—for the love of God—*now*!

Lifting her astride him, he wrapped her legs about his waist and entered her in one fluid thrust that made her gasp with delight. Cradling her upon his body, he waded back to shore with her astride him, her bright head nestled in the angle of his neck and shoulders.

At the edge of the sand, where the waves could yet ripple over them in their race up the shore, he lowered her, opened her, took her; riding her with a virile mastery that drove her dizzy with delight. His thrusts partnered the incoming surges of the sea, until she knew not where one ended and the other began. 'Twas as if, in some magical way, the sea were her lover, her lover the sea, both of them caressing her, both of them filling her with a surging rapture so exquisite 'twas unbearable!

Throatily, she pleaded for an end to her torment.

"Soon, sweet goddess," he promised. His green eyes were dark with passion as he moved deeply, strongly, within her. "Aye, soon!"

So saying, he planted a fiery kiss upon her lips, then raised her bottom to thrust deeper and deeper, flexing his hips, taking her with him, lifting her up, up to the very heights of passion as the waves rippled over them again and again and the surf, booming against the rocks, showered them with bursts of spindrift.

Oh, God!

"Nathaaan! My love!"

Her mind took flight as rapture claimed her. Her spirit fled her, too, wheeling and soaring with the screaming gulls carving arcs from the blue, blue heavens on blinding silver wings.

As she cried out, Nathan found his own release, his roar echoing her own cries.

But these sounds were swallowed up, lost in the booming thunder of the surf as they rocked in the wet sand, the seafoam breaking over their nude bodies in frothy necklaces of bubbles.

"Why, Mariah?" he asked later, when, fully-dressed, they lay side by side on the warm, powdery sand, basking in the sun and the lazy afterglow of their love-making.

"Why what?" she asked lazily, snuggling deeper into the crook of his arm and idly brushing away the sand that clung to his damp chest.

"Why did you choose me to help you overcome your fears that night? You'd refused me before, remember, when we were alone."

She shrugged, her face turning pink as she sat up and toyed with the lacy fichu of her gown. "I changed my mind. There's no mystery about it. 'Tis a lady's perogative to be fickle, is it not, sir?"

"Quite so. As it is a *man's* perogative to wonder why."

She sighed. "All right. If you must know, 'twas because . . . because I'd begun to think what being stranded forever on this island would mean. To realize just how very fragile life is?"

"And?"

"There were so many wonderful things I'd planned to do in

my lifetime! So many exciting things I'd wanted to experience! But I was certain our days were numbered, and that I'd never get to do or experience any of them. So, on that first night I . . . I vowed I would not die until I'd at least known the delights of . . . of passion!'' She was mumbling by the time she reached the end of this confession, and with a shame-faced grimace, she hid her face, embarrassed. "Go ahead. Laugh if you want. I know you're dying to.''

"Madam, I am not,'' he lied gallantly, but had she turned to look, she would have seen a merry grin tugging at his lips. He cleared his throat. "And . . . er . . . what, pray, made you choose me to demonstrate those delights? Why not Old Peg, say? Or even Ben? Or Carmichael?''

She shrugged, certain he was making fun of her, however serious he might sound. Well, she'd wipe that smug little smile off his face straightaway. "I suppose 'twas because you were the least repulsive to look upon, sir,'' she said innocently, wanting to laugh at the flicker of pricked vanity in his eyes. "And, since you had already applied for the position from the first, so to speak, I decided, who better?'' Although her tone was flippant, she could feel her cheeks growing hot.

He chuckled. "And was I a worthy teacher, goddess?'' he inquired, tweaking her rosy cheek. "Would you have gone to your Maker happily, after that night, had Armageddon come?''

"Aye, damn ye! But if 'tis further flattery you seek from me, sir, then you must fish in other waters!'' she retorted pertly, knowing for certain that he was teasing her now. She recognized that tone.

To be honest, she couldn't really blame him. Her childish fears that they would die seemed foolish in broad daylight, with the azure sky a vault of cloudless blue above them and the sea lapping lazily at their feet. And her vow to experience passion's delights before she died? Well, that had been a tad extreme, as last wishes went, not to mention incredibly selfish on her part. Faced with almost certain death, she should have embraced a noble last wish. To save mankind from suffering, for example, or to bring peace to the world. To end poverty, inequity, and disease. But nay, not her. She had prayed instead for a lusty tumble, one that would put Edward's spectre to rest.

"By your leave, my sweet, I'll be well content to . . . cast my rod in your waters alone," he returned, grinning at his bawdy double-meaning.

She pouted. "Under the circumstances, I'm hardly flattered, since your other options are so few!"

He hid a smile, for despite everything, despite her nightmare marriage and her widow's state, her beauty and her spirit, at heart she was like all her sex. Make love to 'em until you turned blue, and it proved nothing. Give them every penny you possessed, and 'twas a pittance. Words, that was what they wanted, all of 'em. Romance and candlelight—and three, dangerous little words that every footloose bachelor in the world choked on and shunned like the plague. And why, damn it? Because those three little words would never roll glibly off the tongue like others, such as "Alas, my lady wife, she does not understand me." Or, the old chestnut, "I will leave her, dearest heart, if ye'll be mine." Still, Nathan loved women. He knew them well, and he knew what their little hearts longed for in the utterance of those words. Reassurance. Reaassurance that they were loved.

Unearthing a huge pink conch-shell with a deep-rose throat, half-buried in the sand beside him, he brushed it off.

"If you doubt my fondness, then here, take this," he urged.

"A shell?" It was enormous, quite the biggest Mariah had ever seen. She took it gingerly, as if its innards were still alive.

"It's empty. It won't bite. Go on, put it to your ear. Tell me what song it sings?"

She lifted the huge shell to her ear. And, as she heard the song of the sea within it, a smile of entrancement lit her face. "It really does sing! 'Tis the sound of the waves trapped within it, over and over."

"Do you hear no words?"

"Should I?" she asked, listening intently again.

"What is a shell-song without words," he asked softly, reaching out to stroke a ringlet of red-gold that fell past her shoulder and to caress her cheek with his knuckles. "Listen! Listen with all that you are, and you shall hear, Mariah. It says, 'He loves me! He loves me!' "

Her hand was trembling as he drew it to his lips. She did not trust herself to speak, nor could she meet his eyes. Tilting her chin, he kissed her gently upon the lips—a sweet, lingering kiss that owed nothing to passion—then drew her against his chest and held her there, stroking her hair.

They remained that way, holding each other in comfortable silence, for quite some time, until Mariah broke the spell by suddenly unfolding Nathan's arms and sitting up.

"Look! Out there, past the point," she cried. She'd spotted a dark shape between the shore and the horizon. "Is it a small ship?"

Squinting against the light, Nathan looked where she'd pointed and shook his head. "Nay, 'tis no ship. 'Tis frolicking whales, Mariah. Or porpoises."

She sighed, then turned her head to hide the tears of disappointment that suddenly welled up.

"My poor Mari. Are you so anxious to see Botany Bay, then?" he asked.

Her voice was husky with emotion when she answered. "Not for myself, nay, but for Caroline. The poor child is so very certain her papa will send a ship to find her. She and Tim Bright tend that signal fire like mother hens tend their chicks! Is there any basis for such hope—any at all? Or should I warn her gently that their efforts are in vain?"

"In vain? Nay. Let the child have her dreams! If Captain Harkabout and his cronies were picked up by another vessel, 'tis possible he might send word to Governor Amberfield. And if he did so, the Governor would send a ship to search these waters for his daughter, would he not?"

Mariah's eyes widened. "What's this? Are you saying Harkabout didn't go down with the *Hester*?"

213

"Harkabout die nobly with his ship, without trying to save his own cursed hide? Never!" Nathan grimaced. "Mistress Kitty told Jack that a 'reliable witness'—probably her Joe Hardy—saw our unworthy captain and a chosen few of his officers lower a lifeboat. 'Twould seem they were able to get safely away before the *Hester* broke up. Our Lieutenant Digby was to have joined them. Alas for him, he was too slow to clamber over the fallen bodies of his own men to do so, as Peg had accused him on our first night here."

"But . . . surely they couldn't survive out there, in so small a boat?" she murmured, gazing doubtfully at the vastness of the ocean that stretched from her toes to the hazy horizon, seemingly without end.

"Stranger things have happened, goddess. A captain named William Bligh was the sailing-master on one of James Cook's voyages. 'Breadfruit' Bligh, we called him, though he hated the name!" Nathan recalled with a grin.

"Well, about a year ago, Breadfruit Bligh's men mutinied in the Pacific Ocean. The crew of his ship, the *Bounty*, cast their captain and eighteen others adrift in a small boat. Those men endured three hellish months in that little boat as it drifted across almost four thousand miles of water, but they reached a place called Timor and survived to tell the tale. They also pressed charges against the mutineers! I overheard two of the *Hester*'s crew talking about it when they brought our grub."

"Then I suppose the possibility that we might be rescued should excite me." She grimaced, screwing up her lovely features. "Alas, somehow, it does not," she confessed with a rueful sigh. "I rather enjoy being free of the constraints placed upon females in our 'civilized' society!"

"Amen to that," Nathan agreed with feeling, for he had reaped the benefits of her freedom. He grinned, stood, and presented her with the conch-shell again as formally as if it were a priceless jewel, one she gravely accepted and held to her bosom—and her heart.

"You're hard on the road to becoming a native, m'lady!

Damn my eyes, with those flowers in your hair and that shell for a sceptre, you're a castaway queen—and one of surpassing beauty!''

As he raised her to her feet, she bobbed him a teasing curtsey in thanks for his compliment, which he acknowledged with a gallant bow and a kiss dropped casually upon the tip of her nose.

Hefting the chest beneath his arm and slipping the coil of rope about his elbow, he fondly took her hand in his large one. ''Come, let's see this chest returned to Mr. Matherson, goddess. I wager he'll be happy to have it. And then . . .'' He paused and winked wickedly.

''And then *what*?''

His green eyes glinted with dancing gold flecks in the sunlight. ''And then there's a special place I'd like to show you. A place unlike any you've seen! 'Tis a perfect place to make love.''

Her lovely face lit up, though she tried to hide her eagerness. ''Really? Where?''

''Patience, goddess. You'll see anon,'' he promised mysteriously, tweaking her cheek.

Carrying the conch-shell tucked in her left arm, she slipped her free one about his waist and leaned her head against his shoulder. Together, arm in arm, the rift between them mended, they walked back to camp.

Later that afternoon, he took her hand, and casting aside her protests that she and Caroline must prepare supper that evening, he led her down the jungle path to the pool.

Promising the guards there he would spell them for a while, he bade them make themselves scarce. With knowing grins that made Mariah blush to her hair's roots, they did so. When she and Nathan were alone, he turned to her, smiling broadly. ''Well, this is it. The special place I told you about!''

''Here?'' She tried not to look disappointed, but it showed

in her face. The pool was lovely enough, bowered with pale green ferns and lush, flowering creepers. And 'twould indeed be a pleasure to make love with Nathan here, either upon its grassy banks or within its sensual cool depths, but from the expression in his eyes earlier, she'd anticipated a more exotic setting, a place that was unusual, special in some way.

"Disappointed, are ye?"

"Nay, not at all," she fibbed brightly.

"Bloody little liar!" he retorted. "There go those eyes again—like bloody marbles! But come, goddess, undress. And, when you've done so, I shall show you a bower worthy of a goddess and her mortal paramour."

"A bower?" Her nose wrinkled as she frowned.

"Aye, my love. A hidden bower, known only to me. A bower with walls of soft green-velvet moss, and hangings of gossamer rainbows! Instead of balmy zephyrs to cool your lovely face, you shall have water in fine, misty sprays, and the song of the falls will lull you into sleep."

She laughed in delight as she stepped from the folds of her gown. "La, sir! You speak with the gilded tongue of a poet, but say nothing of the crocodiles that will nibble on my toes!"

"Nay, madam, not the tongue of a poet, for I tell no pretty lies as do they! 'Twill be as I said—and the only teeth that will nibble on your toes will be mine!" he declared, standing before her naked and without shame.

The male perfection, the leashed power of his well-muscled, hairy, bronze body made the breath catch in her throat.

"Ready?" he demanded, his green eyes twinkling, his handsome face smiling. "Or, would you ogle me a while longer, wench?"

"Nay, I've seen my fill! Lead on, sir!" she riposted cheekily.

He plunged headfirst into the pool and struck out at once for the farthest side, where the plunging waterfall met the pool and frothed up ripples of white water and strings of bubbles.

Shrugging, she followed him, knowing a moment's anxiety

when he vanished beneath the fall's outermost edge, but following when he did not resurface.

To her surprise, she came up within a narrow cave, one that had an opening that boasted rocky ledges, like steps, by which to clamber out. Nathan was standing at the edge of the "stairs," his arms extended to assist her out onto the rocky shelf beside him.

The light within was as bright as day, as if the shallow cavern were lit by a thousand candleflames. As he'd promised, the misty light was rainbow-colored, bands of rose, lavender, and green refracted by the braided ropes of water cascading down over the cliff-edge above. The rainbows played and wavered over the cave walls and upon their naked bodies in fairy-tale, dreamlike fashion, transforming the ordinary to the extraordinary and magical.

"Well? Do you like my hidden cave?"

Her eyes shone. "'Tis breathtaking!" She looked up, into his eyes, and saw the desire blazing in their depths; felt an answering thrill of response twang like the plucked string of a mandolin deep in her own body. Suddenly breathless, she protested, "But I really should be getting back to cam— Oohmm!"

Her half-hearted protests ended on a gasp, then a groan of pleasure as Nathan thrust his hand into the cascading water and diverted its flow so that it splashed over her body in a deliciously stinging, cool spray. He followed each rivulet down her nude body with his palms, rubbing water into every inch of silky skin, until her flesh seemed oiled where it caught the rainbow-colored light.

"What did you say, goddess?" he breathed huskily, his hot breath filling her ear above the roar of the waterfall. "That you would flee my fairy bower?"

"I said, I should be getti . . . getti . . ." Her voice once again trailed away as he nuzzled her throat with hot, hungry lips, then nipped and sucked gently upon her little pink earlobes as if they were grapes. He clasped her so tightly to his hard,

217

bronzed body, his springy chest hair rasped deliciously against her spine, raising goose-bumps up and down her arms in tingly waves.

"Aye, goddess . . . ?" Nathan repeated, laughter in the husky timbre of his voice.

". . . getting . . . back to—oh, stop, Nathan, do!" she cried, for his caresses and kisses were stirring dangerously familiar sensations inside her she'd soon be helpless to deny. "You devil! Are you insatiable?"

"Would you ask that of a man starved for food this fortnight past?"

"Oh course not! I would feed him."

"Then feed me what I'm starved of, minx!" he urged roguishly.

"But what about our—their—supper? Supper, aye, that's it. I'm cook tonight, remember? I . . . ohh, yes! Oh, aye! Nay, don't stop! Don't! Ever."

As she spoke, he'd reached around her to cup her swelling breasts. Now, with one firm, rosy little mound filling each of his tanned hands, he whispered husky endearments in her ear, uttered scandalous promises and deliciously wicked threats while he gently pinched and tugged upon her nipples, rolling the buds between his fingers until they hardened.

Silver wildfire raced between her breasts and loins in sizzling spirals. Oh, lord, his very touch crumbled the cornerstones of her control; made her want him again so very badly, the mundane task of cooking supper was now the farthest thing from her mind! She quivered. She trembled. She ached for him! She could feel the hidden portals of her womanhood filling with feathery sensation, swelling, parting, growing dewy with desire.

Closing her eyes, she surrendered and leaned back against him, glorying in sensation as he caressed her, as one hand swept down over the flat plane of her abdomen and belly, circling her navel, massaging the sleek plateau of her stomach, before moving lower to tousle her triangle of golden curls.

His touch was electric. She gasped with pleasure and pressed back against him, bringing herself firmly against the fiery, hard ridge of his arousal. His shaft nudged the swells of her bottom as he delicately plied her with rhythmic strokes of his fingers. Oh, God! Her knees felt weak, about to give way. She could barely find the strength to stand.

"I want you," he murmured thickly in her ear. "Right now. Again. Here, in my secret cave. Ah, Mariah, open to me, beloved! Let me inside you. God's Teeth, woman! I want you so, I can scarcely speak."

And so, he let action speak instead, and smoothly turned her to face him.

Capturing her soft mouth beneath his own, he kissed her lingeringly as his hands swept down her sleek, slippery body to her derriere, squeezing and stroking. And then, still devouring her delectable mouth, swallowing her breathless sobs upon his own breath, he grasped her thighs and lifted her up, wrapped her legs about his flanks so that the velvet head of his swollen shaft was poised at the threshold of her womanhood. Moaning, she arched forwards, just as he pulled her onto him, planting himself deep between her thighs.

As the fiery hardness of him filled her, she tore her mouth from his and arched backwards, uttering a silvery, trilling cry that soared above the waterfall's roar like the song of a lark.

Her glorious eyes closed, dusky lashes making shadowy crescents upon the rosy blush of her cheeks. Her hands were linked behind his neck, her fingers tangled in his queue. Their chests were pressed—his hairy and rough, hers smooth and dewy as the petals of an orchid—fiercely to each other. Their lower bodies were even more perfectly joined, as if they'd become a single creature, one without beginning or end or separateness.

Her red-gold hair spilled down her back in a tangled cascade as she rose and fell, sensuously undulating her hips and rocking back and forth to ride the throbbing length of him in a way that tore the breath from his lips in fractured groans of delight.

In faith, 't have her was pleasure and torment, all at once! He gripped her waist, matched her rhythm with his own thrusts, each one faster, deeper, more piercingly sweet than the last. Panting hoarsely, they were carried by their frenzied movements across the cave to the mossy wall of rock that backed it, then to one side and the other, until—at last!—amidst a fever-pitch of motion and emotion, they reached passion's peak, bathed in the fine, misty spray thrown off by the roaring falls.

Mariah cried out as she felt Nathan shudder and grow very still, holding her fast upon his length with hands of steel as he found his release with an explosive groan. Holding her breath, she felt his manhood pulse and buck, and the silvery leap of his seed as he spent deep within her womb, experienced the earth-shattering tremors that rocked him for herself, more exquisitely and intensely than she had done before. So wondrous was the sensation, she cried out, and in the same moment, was lifted and flung headlong into the swirling velvet of her own rapture. Like his, her exultant cries were swallowed up by the rushing song of the falls that cascaded, dream-like, all about them.

For some moments, neither of them moved or spoke. Their hearts still raced. Their breathing was too shallow for speech. She clung to him like ivy to a wall, her head cradled heavily upon his broad shoulders, her arms limply locked around his chest. His face was buried in her tumbling, damp hair, while his clasped hands supported her weight.

"Mariah?" he murmured at length.

"Hmmm-hmm?"

"Supper."

"Supper? What about it, my love?" she asked drowsily, snuggling deeper against him.

"You must prepare it, m'lady. I find myself ravenous! In faith, minx, you have drained me utterly and must now pay the price. I am obliged to eat and regain my strength."

"Then go find yourself something to nibble on, Samson," she bade him pertly, sounding plaintive as a weary child. "Per-

220

haps a banana or a mango. But pray, don't disturb me while you're looking for one. Aaahmm," she yawned hugely. "'Tis a blessed miracle how you can even *think* of your belly right now. I'm far too sleepy to think of food. . . ." She pressed her cheek to the soft web of flesh between his throat and shoulder, and sighed heavily, leaning full-weight against him.

"Aye, vixen, I don't wonder you're sleepy. But 'tis *your* turn to cook this evening, remember? Yours and Caroline's?"

She groaned and mumbled, "Aye, I remember." She sighed. "Can't someone else see to it, for once?"

"Would that they could, my sweet," he sympathized ruefully. "However, we agreed at the outset that everyone would do their part, did we not? In fact, if you recall, *you* were most insistent about it? And so, alas, you are committed, my dove."

With that, he withdrew his arms from beneath her and unfastened her legs, which had been wrapped around him 'til that moment.

Robbed of all support, Mariah slithered bonelessly down his hard body. She landed upon her bottom on the cold cave floor, at his feet.

"Brute!" she hissed, glaring up into his grinning face as she rubbed her hurt. She pouted. "Slave-driver! Bully! Horrid beast! Is this any way to treat your 'goddess'?"

"Food, goddess. Supper!" the wretch bellowed unfeelingly, and turning, he dived back under the crystal falls, leaving Mariah little other option but to follow him.

But despite her grumblings, she was smiling as she did so. La! How could she not? She had mended the coldness between them, just as she'd planned that morn—and in ways and places she'd never dreamed of!

Chapter Fourteen

"Look, sir, more tracks. Are they what we thought?"

Nathan knelt down and examined the spoor cast in the soft mud alongside the stream. He grinned up at Bright. "Aye, by God! Look lively now, lad, and bring up the others. Lord willing, we'll have roast pork for supper this evening."

They'd followed the tracks of a small herd of wild pigs from the banks of the stream that fed into "their" waterfall and the jungle pool below. In doing so, they'd discovered a narrow trail that wound up through verdant foothills, green with forests of bamboo and banana plants, and thence into the mountains proper. The path was one that the animals clearly took to their watering hole with some regularity, for the brush and undergrowth had been worn down with their frequent passage, making a trail that was easy to follow. Fresh gouge marks upon several of the tree trunks indicated places where a wild boar had rubbed his tusks, or paused to scratch his bristled hide. The creatures' droppings were much in evidence, too.

There were six in Nathan's hunting party that day, including himself and young Tim Bright, all of whom had volunteered to go farther afield in search of fresh meat to give some variety to their diet of parrots, monkeys, or seafood. Nathan had fondly kissed Mariah farewell, and then the group had left the coconut grove behind them.

Soon after, they'd found themselves skirting mangrove swamps where sly-eyed crocodiles, looking for all the world like mossy logs, sunned themselves on marshy banks among exotic waterlilies. They'd travelled through flat grasslands irrigated by chocolate-colored, serpentine rivers, and over floodplains where wildflowers and huge, bright-winged butterflies abounded. They'd marveled at plunging ravines with cascading waterfalls of breath-taking beauty, veiled with mists that were rainbow-colored in the dazzling sunlight, had gaped at slow-moving creatures resembling small, flat-nosed brown bears. They'd never seen them before. Large or small lizards regarded them unblinkingly before ambling away, and as always, chattering monkeys swung from bough to bough far above the jungle floor, while parrots—large and small, gaudy and plain—were winging overhead and raucously squawking.

They followed a trail that climbed steadily to the less heavily-forested slopes of the mountain range which ran like a backbone from north to south on the island. At higher elevations, they discovered an amazing variety of trees flourished. With the botanist Matherson's studies in mind, Nathan tucked a twig from each into his breeches' pockets. Antarctic beeches, oaks, and pines were growing everywhere, and among their sombre boughs, wild poinsettias flamed like scarlet blossoms of fire.

Climbing steadily higher, they found that the air was noticeably cooler, the terrain less heavily overgrown, and they could view the island's beaches of white sand and crystal, turquoise ocean from another angle. Seeing the curving line of the coral reefs, the feathery green tops of the coconut palms from on high, to the last man they'd marveled that any land could be so lovely.

Looking down at the panorama spread before him, Nathan

thought that 'twas as if grimy London, with her dirty streets and smoking chimney pots, her teeming stews and tenements, her unemployed thousands and her idle, careless rich, existed on some distant planet . . . or were but a lingering bad dream.

Having seen the vivid colors of the tropics—the brilliant palette of blue ocean and verdant green mountains; the torrid crimson, burning orange, and vibrant saffron of the sunsets—he began to wonder how the artist that yet lived within him could ever again be satisfied with the pastel loveliness of an English spring or the murky greys and violets of his homeland's misty autumn evenings.

Aye, he had loved his family's estate, Linden Hall, but in the fond, abstract way of a second son who'd known from childhood that the Kincaid title, mansion, and surrounding land would never belong to him. He'd felt the same about England; restless and dissatisfied with his life there, despite his success as a barrister-at-law. There'd been something missing, some indefinable something he lacked but could never quite put his finger upon. Oftentimes, when a case had seemed to go on forever, and hours of dreary testimony had piled one upon the other, his thoughts had strayed back to the strange and beautiful lands and the exotic people he'd seen as a lad on his voyaging with Captain James Cook—and had never been able to forget. And he thought he knew what that something missing was: adventure, change, challenge.

Here, in the New World, I could be my own master, he thought, not for the first time. *With hard work and endeavor, I could own land like this, perhaps a farm or a plantation of some kind; a place where I would truly belong, and could find lasting happiness*.

Aye, he could picture himself living such a life in these climes. And lately, when he dreamed his dreams, he was no longer alone in them. His beautiful Mariah was by his side, her red-gold hair woven with frangipani blossoms, a faraway smile curving her lips as she cupped a sea-shell to her ear and listened to its siren song. In those dreams, she was his island

224

goddess, his castaway queen; his soul-mate in fortune or adversity, joy or sorrow.

With each passing day, he was coming to care for her more and more deeply—so very deeply, despair often accompanied his daydreams, snuffing out the joy of newfound love. They were castaways, damn it all! What sort of life could he hope to give her, with nothing but empty dreams and a future that was doubtful in every respect? For unless, by some miracle, they should chance to be picked up by a Dutch merchantman plying these waters en route to Java, they were doomed to remain stranded here for the rest of their lives.

An even less pleasing prospect, by Nathan's reckoning, was the possibility—however slim—of Governor Amberfield sending a ship into these waters in search of his daughter, Caroline, and actually finding this island among the thousands of islets in these waters. God's Teeth, should that happen, he and the other convicts'd be taken to the penal colony at Botany Bay, where the best he could hope for was to become yet another felon with a life-sentence to be served out; or, if his escape from the hangman in London had been discovered, a short and merry dance at the end of a noose. Should the former come to pass, Mariah would be as far removed from him as the moon from the earth below. As for the latter. . . .

Never! he told himself. *If a British ship comes here, I'll die before I board her willingly. They'll have to kill me first, by God.*

Less than two hours after they left camp, an unfamiliar print in the earth drew Bright's attention.

"Wild pig, d'ye reckon, sir?" the youth asked Nathan eagerly.

"I'll be damned! It looks like it!" Nathan's grin reflected Bright's. "Stiles! Babbington! Hey, Archer! Ben! Over here, lads! We must plan our attack."

Soon after, the snorts and squeals of the wild pigs on the

narrow trail up ahead alerted Nathan that their quarry was close by.

Sure enough, parting the stand of bamboo before him, he could see four bristly black sows, a half-dozen piglets, and a scarred old boar with evil tusks and deep-set amber eyes, all rooting about in the grass with their snuffling, hairy snouts. 'Twas one of the sows they should go for, 'else a brace of their young, Nathan urged his men in a low voice. Although far heavier, the old boar would be tough and strong-tasting.

Gesturing silently, he sent his men in various directions to surround the animals. Then, praying the wild pigs would not scent them too soon, that their makeshift weapons would serve, that all he'd said about the animals' viciousness would be remembered in the heat of attack, he let out a curdling whoop:

"Chaaarge!"

They plunged into the tiny clearing like wild Indians, yelling bloodthirstily and brandishing their makeshift weapons as they rushed to attack. Armed with his stout pole of bamboo, to which he'd lashed Jack's knife, Nathan found himself in the very heart of the fray.

The stench of fear given off by the wild pigs was rank in his nostrils as the creatures squealed in terror and tried to flee in all directions. And, as they ran about, they slammed into their human attackers, squirming between their legs and knocking them off their feet.

"Get 'em, lads! Stick 'em good, me hearties!" roared Big Ben as Nathan—to his shame—went flying onto his backside, knocked flat by a terrified sow. The small convict's expression was wild with glee as he danced about, brandishing a wicked-looking hammer that Nathan had salvaged. He was none too careful in whose direction he was swinging it, either.

"Look out, ye stupid bastard!" Stiles yelled, ducking and weaving like a boxer to escape both Big Ben's hammer and the boar's lethal tusks. "If ye don't brain me, ye sorry git, 'at bristly bastard'll 'ave me guts fer garters, he will!" Wildly, he slashed at one of the females with his cutlass as she thundered

226

past him, and a spray of blood fanned from the sow's wound to spatter Stiles' chest and breeches. Stiles whooped wildly, elated that he'd drawn first blood and made a kill. Or, so he thought.

Instead of falling, the wounded sow gave a squeal of outrage and pain and turned to charge the marine, deadly in her terror and confusion. The first rush of her massive, bristly body slammed Stiles onto his back. His weapon was knocked from his fists as he fell. Unarmed and helpless, he bellowed with terror as the sow turned and lowered her head to savage him.

Bright released the squealing piglet he'd caught by the hind leg and ran to Stiles' aid in the nick of time. With a bloodthirsty howl, he plunged his makeshift spear into the sow's neck, where it lodged, shuddering with the impact.

The blow, although mighty, was not mortal, for it had failed to reach the sow's heart or spine, but it did serve to distract the female. Driven mad now with pain, loss of blood, and fear, the sow wheeled to attack Bright in turn. The cabin-boy, unarmed now, wisely decided flight was his only recourse. With a yell, he took to his heels and plunged headlong into the bushes. As both youth and sow charged past them, Nathan, Archer and the others together plunged their spears into the wild pig's throat.

By some miracle, she ran on for several yards, not knowing she was dead, before crashing onto her side and finally laying still. The numerous bamboo spears jutted from the sow's throat and made the carcass look like some fantastic porcupine's.

"Yahooo!" Bright yelled when he returned to the others and saw the sow was dead. "We did it!"

The hunters grinned and congratulated each other with much backslapping and handshaking, oblivious to the pig-blood that smeared their face and bodies.

Nathan chuckled at their antics, proud of their courage. Wild pigs had a well-deserved reputation for savagery. They had killed far better equipped and seasoned hunters than this little band! Watching them, he could well imagine what stories the lads would tell about the campfire that night, and just how exaggerated their "fisherman's" tales of this first "kill" would be.

While Stiles, entrusted with the precious axe Nathan had salvaged, went to cut a sturdy straight pole on which to carry their kill home, Archer and Bright lashed the pig's fore and hind legs together with lengths of rope. Triumphant, the hunters headed back to camp with the pig slung by its feet from the pole, the ends carried across the shoulders of Bright and Archer.

As they moved single file along a narrow cliff-edge that overlooked a patch of dense jungle and the beach and ocean beyond, Archer suddenly halted.

"Wait up, lads. Look!" he whispered, his eyes starting from his head as if he could hardly believe what he saw.

Below, skimming the glassy blue waters of a lovely bay that lay not three miles south of their camp, they spied two long, narrow-prowed vessels. These twin-masted native canoes with curiously-shaped sails were approaching the island at speed.

"You men go on back to camp," Nathan ordered crisply, jerking his head towards the trail they'd taken on their outward journey. "I'd like a closer look at our visitors before I join you."

"I'll come with you if I may, sir?" Bright volunteered, yielding his end of the pole to Babbington. When Nathan nodded, he grinned at the others, ducked, and followed Kincaid down the steep slope, sliding down it on his rump in some places, scrambling through dense undergrowth in others.

Nathan and Tim headed steadily downhill, skirting the swamps and weaving their way towards the beach that fringed the bay. They could hear snatches of a strange, rhythmic music on the breeze as they went, and exchanged puzzled glances and shrugs, unable to identify it.

Where the vegetation thinned and gave way to coconut palms, they ducked down and peered between the sea-grape bushes.

The two long canoes, paddled by brown-skinned natives, had almost reached the shore. The sound they'd heard was the natives, chanting in time to a small drum and a bull-roarer. The drumbeats served to keep their stroke as they paddled, for there was little wind to belly the sails and bring them ashore.

Nathan and Tim held their breaths as, reaching the shallows, the natives lowered their sails, shipped their paddles, and leaped from their craft. They smartly formed lines on either side of each canoe with the precision of seasoned sailors.

As one man, they quickly hefted the canoes onto their shoulders, then carried them up the beach at a barefooted run, out of reach of the tide. They beached the narrow vessels in the sand less than twenty feet from the sea-grape bushes where Nathan and Bright were hiding; then, talking excitedly amongst themselves, they drew weapons and supplies from the canoes' depths; baskets of huge taros, swamp cabbages, and such.

Suddenly dry-mouthed, Tim swallowed, fear stirring in his gut as he watched them, for each of the young native warriors was armed to the teeth with a wickedly pointed spear and a bamboo knife or two. If that were not enough, on slings across their backs they carried small bows and quivers filled with short arrows of black palm, each one tipped with what looked like bone.

Naked but for narrow loincloths, they were terrifying in appearance. Each young savage had long, kinky black hair that stood out in fuzzy-dandelion fashion about his head, like a war-bonnet. The brown arms and legs of each native had been ritually scarred and tattooed into a pattern that resembled crocodile armor. Their flat-featured faces were painted with stripes of black across the cheekbones and yellow over their broad noses, white stripes of pigment separating the colors. Red paint ringed their eyesockets, while through their nostrils, long or short splinters of wood had been driven. These jutted out at varying angles and positions, perhaps according to each youths' notion of what was pleasing to the eye, Tim thought with a shudder of horror, for what he was seeing was a far cry from adornment in the Devonshire parsonage where he'd been raised.

An old man with a sagging pot belly and wrinkled arms and legs gave a ringing command, and the native youths obediently gathered around him.

As they listened attentively, the old one, who seemed to be their chieftain or priest, gave a shout:

"Puk-puk!"

He raised his fist and brandished something above him, as if rallying his followers to some goal. The young warriors roared their approval and gestured with their spears, blocking Nathan's view. But as their cries died away, the watchers saw what it was the old man had brandished; two hideously shrunken heads, whirled aloft by their own black hair.

"Sweet Jesus in Heaven—they're *head-hunters!*" Tim whispered hoarsely, ready to bolt. He felt acid rise in his throat as his belly tightened from disgust and horror.

"Run and they'll be after us in a twinkling, ye young fool," Nathan growled softly, clamping steely fingers over Tim's shoulder. His green eyes were narrowed, his lips thinned and stern. "Less you want that handsome head dangling from old blowhard's belt, hold your position and pipe down. We must find out if they mean t' stay here."

"Aye, aye, sir," Tim mumbled, gulping and wishing with all his heart he'd not elected to follow Nathan. But, ever since Tom's drowning, he'd felt awful bad that he'd been unable to save him. And, although Kincaid had put no blame on him, nor uttered a single word of condemnation, Tim still felt guilty. He was certain the man he so admired secretly considered him lily-livered, worse than an infant, for what had happened. He'd volunteered to go with Nathan to prove his courage—but was bitterly regretting it now!

Soon after, the natives left the beach, plunging single-file into the jungle. Jerking a trembling Tim to his feet, Nathan followed them, gingerly weaving a course parallel to the natives' through the vegetation.

After several moments, the savages came to a small clearing, where there was a large thatched hut made of bamboo poles and woven banana leaves. The dwelling appeared deserted, though that was little wonder, for the grinning skulls that hung from all four corners of its thatched roof would effectively deter any intruder from invading its murky interior! Before the hut's doorway stood an enormous stone, clearly of some sacred significance, judging by the respectful way the young men skirted it.

The youths, given their orders by the old man, set about building a fire and attending to other domestic tasks, unaware that they were being spied upon. 'Twas patently clear that, for this night at least, they were going nowhere.

After some time, Nathan tapped Tim on the shoulder and jerked his head, indicating it was time for them to leave. Tim needed no second telling.

On the way back to camp, once they were safely out of the natives' hearing, Tim asked Nathan what he'd made out of what they'd seen.

"I don't rightly know, lad—though I have an inkling or two," he admitted truthfully.

"Do those savages live here, do you think, sir?" Tim asked nervously, looking over his shoulder as if he expected a painted head-hunter to leap out at him from the creepers and tangled undergrowth all about them. "If so, why haven't we run across them before?"

Nathan answered his first question. "I'd say not. For one thing, they had no women, old ones, or children with them, as one might expect if this island was their home. And there was only the one hut—and that of somewhat ornate design—instead of a proper village. Did you notice, lad? Save for that old man, they were all young. That alone suggests but one thing to me."

"It does?" asked Tim, his puzzled expression indicating the observation suggested nothing whatsoever to him!

"Aye. I'd wager what we saw were boys about to be initiated into manhood, young Tim. This island must hold some sacred significance for their tribe. As, perhaps, does the crocodile," he added, thinking about the tattoos the native youths had sported. "'Tis possible they come here from a nearby island to perform their manhood rites in secret."

Tim's throat was dry again. His tongue seemed suddenly too big to fit into his mouth. "Manhood rites? Ah," he managed to choke out, "um, these rites, sir—what form might they take?"

Nathan shrugged. "Who knows? They could be something as simple as more tattooing. You saw their scale tattoos?" Tim nodded. "Combined with prayers and feasting or whatever. On the other hand. . . ."

"Wh-what?" Tim squeaked. He didn't really want to know, but for some perverse reason he didn't comprehend, he had to ask.

"It could be something more ominous. They . . . er . . . might have to prove their manhood in some way. Mayhap by wrestling a crocodile with their bare hands? Or worse, taking a human head."

Remembering the hideous shrunken heads the old man had whirled about by the hair like pomanders on a ribbon, Tim was certain Nathan's last guess came closest to the truth.

"Mr. Kincaid, are they . . . cannibals?" he whispered, his question so faint, Nathan had to strain to hear it.

"Aye, lad. I wouldn't wonder at it," Nathan admitted. "But, skinny as you are, Bamboo Bright, you've little to fear. 'Tis Ole Peg we must watch out for. Now, there's a week's vittles for any cannibal crew!"

His attempt to lighten Tim's mood fell miserably flat, for 'Bamboo' Bright was far too preoccupied to even think of laughing. "But, if what you say is true, we must make haste to warn the others straightaway, sir!"

"No! Say nothing of what we saw to the others as yet, lad. I'd prefer to ask Mr. Matherson's opinion, before we start a panic."

Tim nodded gloomily. He turned an ashen hue then, and

said not another word as they found their way back to the camp beneath the coconut trees.

The succulent smell of roasting pork wafted on the sultry air as they drew closer to home. Clearly Stiles, Big Ben and the others had wasted scant time in getting the pig butchered and spitted over hot coals! Side-eyeing the lad, Nathan declared that he was starving, but Tim only swallowed, saying nothing.

After what they'd seen, the savory aroma made Tim sick to his stomach, rather than making him drool with hunger; for it reminded him all too clearly of a night aboard the *Hester*, just off the coast of Capetown, Africa.

He and some of the other crewmembers had sat about on deck beneath a starry indigo sky. Some men had passed the time in whittling or fiddling with bits of scrimshaw, others by mending their clothes, or thumbing through a tattered Bible, dicing, or just plain enjoying a pipe of baccy with their weekly ration of grog.

"I heard tell there do be cannibals in New South Wales, young Bright," a rascally old sea-dog, now drowned, God rest his soul, had told Tim, as the lad half-heartedly downed his sea-rations—a slice of spoiled salt-pork and two weevily sea-biscuits.

The tar had clearly relished the sudden greenish tinge to the cabin-boy's face, for he'd continued breezily, "Aye, them heathens do love to gobble up a white man, they do—snot-nosed lads 'specially, for their young flesh be sweet and tender. Why, Fuller—'im over there what sailed with Cap'n Bligh, God rot him—he's seen 'em at their pagan doin's 'imself, right, Full?"

"Aye," Fuller, who'd also drowned in the storm, had confirmed gloomily, taking a long pull on the stem of his clay pipe, "I have that, right enough. Them bleedin' savages dig long pits in the ground—like graves, they be. They line the 'oles with red-hot rocks, an' leaves an' such. Then, inter them pits go the poor sods wot they've taken captive in battle. First, they slaughter 'em like hogs, cut orf their heads an' stick 'em on poles t' make their savage magic. Then, they lay the bodies in the pits an' cover 'em over wiv sand, all nice n' tidy, like. The hot rocks 'n the steam from the leaves cook 'em up a treat in a few hours. Jesus, if the wind's comin' from the right quarter, ye can smell them cannibals cooking their grub a mile or more off-shore. D' ye know what roasting human flesh smells like, laddie? *Pork*. It smells like roasting pork, it do.''

Guffaws of laughter had followed Tim as he bolted for the taff-rail and lost his victuals over the *Hester*'s side. He'd quickly forgiven the men their wicked teasing, for by and large, they'd treated him with rough affection, of which such ribald teasing was an inevitable part. But, forgiven or nay, he had never forgotten Fuller's words. Nor had he touched salt-pork again. He'd vowed he'd starve first.

That night as they sat about the campfire, full-bellied and content with the roasted pig the hunters had provided, and the yams, taro roots and swamp cabbages Matherson's detail had gathered, Nathan stood and raised his hand, asking for silence to speak.

''Some of you may have heard that two native canoes were spotted heading for shore today,'' he began.

A ragged chorus of anxious ayes confirmed that they had.

''War-parties, sir?'' Ben asked, voicing the fears of them all.

''I don't know, Ben—but I'm not ruling it out completely. However, Master Matherson and I have discussed the matter. And, because the canoes were filled with youths and but one old man, we feel 'tis more likely those young savages have come to the island to undergo their manhood rites, in company with their heathen priest.''

''Man'ood rites? Wot's that, then?'' asked Ben.

''Trials of courage the young lads of their tribe must endure, before they are considered men and allowed to take wives.''

"See! I just knowed there were pesky wenches at the bottom o' this somewheres!" Stiles declared, shaking his head.

But for once, nobody laughed at his jest.

"T-Tim said you told him these tests of courage might . . . might include head-hunting," Caroline piped up, obviously nervous. "And . . . and cannabalism!" A shocked murmur rippled round the circle. "Is that true, Nathan, or is he just trying to frighten me?" She shot Tim a doubting, withering look.

To the last man, they turned to look at Nathan, anxiously awaiting his answer.

He scanned the circle of faces, carefully choosing his words before speaking. If he put the fear of God into them, there was every chance they would panic and try to run—and perhaps would fall into the natives' hands. On the other hand, human nature being what it was, too casual a warning would be too soon forgotten, and so equally dangerous.

"I'm afraid Tim was speaking the truth, my friends," he said solemnly. "Some of the natives in these climes believe the taking of a human head gives them magical powers—or at the very least, the spirit-powers of the one they have killed. They may eat the flesh of their enemies for the same reason. That, we do not know. But if we are right—and unfortunately, we have no real knowledge of their behavior—the manhood rites are truly a test of survival. 'Tis only the fittest and the most deadly among them who'll survive to return to their own island. Those young savages will kill each other, failing to find other victims. Or, if we play into their hands, they will kill us." The silence in the wake of his words was so great, he could have heard a pin drop. "Now, I don't know about you, lads . . . er, and ladies . . . but I would much prefer that they kill each other!"

"Aye, aye, sir! Us, too. What must we do?" Archer demanded.

"For a start, every one of you must stay close to camp whenever possible, until we're certain they've left the island.

235

Foraging and hunting details, go west rather than east, and keep your forays as brief as you can. All of you, go nowhere alone, and go nowhere unarmed. And keep your eyes peeled! If you see anything suspicious—anything at all—say, an arrowhead in the sand or a footprint, get back to camp and spread the word.''

"But what about the pool?" Mariah asked. "You promised we could swim there, remember, and it's been so hot of late!" In response, she received an encouraging nod from Caro, an affirming smile from Kitty,—and a glare from Nathan—which she sweetly ignored.

"Alas, the jungle-pool is not to be visited until the danger has passed. The guards may go there, when 'tis their turn to relieve those who stand watch, and the water-boys, in their turns, to draw water each morning and eve, but no one else. And that order includes you, m'lady Mariah, ladies," Nathan added pointedly, receiving a trio of scowls for his pains. "Anyone who disobeys me—male *or* female—will be sternly disciplined. Any questions?"

There were none. And so, on that disquieting note, Nathan gave them leave to return to their separate pursuits.

The first few days following Nathan's warning passed without incident, unless the steadily growing heat and humidity could be considered an "incident."

The castaways followed Nathan's rules to the letter. Made skittish by the threat of danger, they became overzealous, and were continually fancying they saw feathered head-hunters lurking in the trees. Upon investigation these threats proved no more sinister than innocent parrots.

But when another week commenced with no hint of an attack from savages, or indeed, any sign of the savages themselves whatsoever, the castaways began to relax their guard. When Nathan was about, they remained close to camp, went nowhere alone, and shunned the pool. When he left camp and went pigeon-hunting, it was a different story. Then, all vigilance was relaxed, and everyone, including Jack, carried on as they had before his warning. It was too blasted hot for fretting about savages, who, for all they knew, might well have paddled back t' their own cursed isle.

As ten days became a fortnight, Mariah, Caro, and Kitty grew more and more disgruntled. The heat sapped their strength and made even the lightest task an effort. Their long skirts added to their discomfort. Big Ben's and Stiles' constant pounding on the drums they'd fashioned from hollow logs made Mariah's head throb in time with their beat.

"I swear, I'd give my right hand just for a swim in that pool!" she declared wistfully as she and the other women sat beneath the shade of a palm one morning, fanning themselves with huge taro leaves. Not that fanning helped. Their faces were still shiny with moisture, their clothing ringed with damp circles.

"Me, too," Caro agreed grumpily. "My neck is chafed raw. And the bends in my knees smart like blazes. If I could only soak in some cool water for just a very little while, I know 'twould go away."

"I'd wash my hair," Mariah daydreamed. "La! It feels as if I have at least a pound of sand in it. What would you like to do, Kitty?"

"Well, seein's I can't swim, I'd wade about a bit, I reckon. Oooh, it'd be luverly t' soak me poor old feet . . ."

". . . And dream of handsome Joe Hardy?" Caro teased.

"Wouldn't I just!" Kitty confessed, reddening. *Now, weren't that somefing, a doxie blushing!*

"Instead of just thinking about it, let's do it!" Mariah urged, springing to her feet, her turquoise eyes alive with mischief borne of boredom.

"Nathan will never give you permission, not in a hundred years."

"He'll 'ave your guts fer garters, luv!"

"No, he won't. And do you know why? Because Nathan went hunting this morning, my dears!" Mariah revealed with a naughty grin. "And I know who'll give me leave to do anything, *if* I just play my cards right. Anyone coming with me?"

Chapter Fifteen

"Are you sure it's safe to swim here?"

"Would Jack have said we could, if there was anything to fear? Oh, hurry up, do, Caro! If you don't make haste, Jack will send the guards back and we'll have wasted what little time we have." Mariah dipped her toes in the water. "See . . . it's heavenly! Come on, Kitty. Let's show her."

With that, Mariah dived into the pool from the rock on which she'd been seated, wearing only a thin chemise that the water rendered almost transparent. Her breasts showed through the filmy cloth as she turned to float on her back, blurred flesh-colored mounds surmounted by tiny, darker peaks. Her red-gold hair fanned out behind her as she trod water, luxuriating in its cool embrace and thanking God for Jack. Succumbing to Mariah's and Caroline's pretty entreaties in Nathan's absence, the ship's carpenter had weakened and agreed to spell the guards himself for a while. And the three young women knew that, with a decent man like Jack standing watch over them, they could enjoy bathing in the fresh water pool without fear of being spied upon by Peeping Toms!

At that very moment, Mariah mused, the dear little man was no doubt patrolling the jungle that fringed the clearing, his gaze studiously trained upon the path at his feet, the patches of sky between the tree-tops high above him—in any direction but that of *their* scantily-clad company.

Jack was, as Mariah had fondly imagined, patrolling the area surrounding the clearing and the pool, and doing so with the quiet diligence that was his nature.

He made his rounds just within the edges of the jungle, close enough to hear the young leddies squealing and splashing, but unable to see them by so much as a glimpse through the thick vegetation. Their girlish giggles and antics turned his thoughts to his own daughters, far off in distant Norfolk—a lifetime from this bloody island, by God.

His eyes misted over. Would he ever see them again? he wondered. Had they somehow heard by now that the *Hester*'d gone down? Did they think their old dad dead and gone? His girls, their husbands, and his fourteen grandbabies—fifteen by now, if his Sally had safely delivered her third—were all the family he had left, since his dear old Minnie had passed on two years ago.

Pride filled him as he remembered how hard his girls used to work at gutting fish on the stone quays of Great Yarmouth Harbor. On those rare occasions when he'd been home from the sea for brief periods, he'd loved to watch them. When the Scottish trawlers landed a big catch at the Norfolk fishing village, there'd be bushel upon bushel of silvery herring stacked up on every side, but nothing daunted his daughters. They took some beating when it came to gutting fish, did his girls. Fair put the Scottish lassies to shame. Nay, there wasn't a gutting-knife wielded faster, nor a hand that moved quicker than those of the Warner girls. Everyone in Yarmouth said so.

Two of them—Margaret and the youngest, little Rose—had married Scottish fisherman off the boats; aye, and done none the worse for taking up with "forruners," despite his misgivings. The other two had wed stout Norfolk lads, one a farmer's son, one the game-keeper for a Squire Somebody-or-other, while the last was the wife of a shipping-clerk in offices at Lowestoft. Small wonder that un'd set her cap for a pen-pusher, rather than a country boy or a fisherman! Pretty Gert, with her grannie's golden hair and her mother's bright blue eyes, had always had airs above her station, always fancied herself a cut above the others, she had. Still, they seemed happy as mudlarks, the pair of 'em.

He turned, hearing a sudden furtive rustling in the bushes behind him. Thinking it was one of the guards he'd sent packing with strict orders to "make themselves scarce for an hour," he shook his head and scowled. Those randy sods! They talked of nothing but doxies and trulls and the lusty tumbles they'd enjoyed in the past, while slyly eying Lady Mariah, Mistress Caroline, and now, Mistress Kitty, like hungry wolves, smacking their chops over three helpless little lambs they planned to devour. He wouldn't wonder that they'd doubled back, the young rogues, fixing t' spy on the young leddies at their bath.

Indignation filled Jack. Well, by God, they'd get a tongue lashing fer their pains, an' no mistake. Aye, and mebbe his foot in their rumps.

"Who goes there?" he demanded, eyes narrowing. He turned slowly in a circle, looking for tell-tale movement in the foliage surrounding him, but there was none. Wondering if he'd imagined that furtive rustling, he pursed his lips, shrugged, and continued his leisurely patrol.

Moments later, a hefty cudgel came out of the bushes. It slammed down across the back of Jack's skull. With a grunt, he folded to his knees and lay still.

"I'll finish 'im orf, shall I, gov'na?" whined a coarse, eager voice as two men exited their hiding place.

"Ye'll not, ye murderous swab. Leave be an' come on wi' ye, laddie," growled the other. "If not for Warner an' his Christian conscience, we'd be long dead. This good mon willna die at my bidding. But as fer the rest . . . Och! Ye'll have yer fill o' blood soon enough, young Foxy."

"Wot about the wenches, Rusk? You promised, remember? You swore it!" Ruskin's companion reminded him, scratching his groin and jerking his head in the direction of the pool.

"Button yer trews, laddie. The lassies are goin' nowhere. We'll see t' their menfolk first and then," he winked, his mouth parting in a slick, wet-lipped grin, "ye can take your pick o' the wee sluts—after I'm done teachin' ma treacherous wee Kit a lesson or two."

"The yeller-haired chit—I'll have 'er first," Foxy declared, wetting his lips. There was a dreamy expression on his sharp-featured face, for all that his breathing was raspy and shallow with lust. "Can't be more'n fifteen, that little 'un, but she's a grown woman's titties on 'er, and she smells jest as fresh an' ripe as they come. Christ Jesus! Me bleedin' cock's that big, I'm like t' spill jest thinkin' about 'er, Rusk!"

"Stow it, Foxy, ye randy whore-son. We've old scores t' settle first, by God! Go tell the others t' get ready. And laddie . . ."

"Aye, sir?"

"Keep an eye on our pretty Digby. I dinna trust 'im."

Grinning, Foxy nodded.

"I in't no great shakes at swimmin'," Kitty confessed doubtfully, looking down at the water with longing, nonetheless.

Wearing one of Caroline's salvaged bodices and a single petticoat, she was hardly recognizable as the same terrified young woman who'd fled Ruskin's band for their camp three weeks ago. Adequate food, fresh water, and freedom from fear had taken the tired, harried look from her. And, though she'd come from a far different walk of life than Mariah and Caroline, she had friends now, too, for the cousins had taken to her from the first. All in all, Kitty was happier than she'd been since running off to London at the tender age of thirteen. In fact, if Joe Hardy had fled Ruskin with her, she'd have been delirious with happiness.

Kitty was a decent sort, Mariah and Caroline had decided, a hard worker who did more than her share about camp, and with no complaints. What was more, she had a cheery, no-nonsense way about her that had quickly endeared her to them all. Kitty could gut a fish, pluck a parrot, or skin a monkey without turning green, and do so quick as winking—no small talent in their difficult circumstances, Caroline felt. She loathed such tasks herself.

"You don't have to know how to swim, Kit. Come, wade in after me. I'll hang onto you. You'll come to no harm in the shallows," Caroline promised generously.

Moments later, all three girls were frolicking in the pool. Their shrieks and giddy laughter as they splashed and cavorted incited the noisy parrots to even louder squawks in response, and the small clearing rang with the sounds.

"Over here," Mariah called, swimming gracefully towards one side of the rushing falls, "I want to show you something. Follow me!" So saying, she suddenly dived under the torrent at its gentlest point—and vanished.

Caro, leading Kitty on a shallow course about the fringes of the pool, where delicate ferns and reeds grew in abundance, grabbed the other girl's hand and followed suit.

The three young women found themselves standing within a little cave behind the falls; its rocky shelf about four feet deep and just over six feet in height. The waterfall had hollowed the hidden niche from the cliff face over the centuries.

Before them, the falls cascaded with an endless, rushing roar that was deafening—and wildly exhilarating! The light slanting through its torrents reflected all the pretty colors of the rainbow, while the water itself was like twisted ropes of diamonds. Caro laughed with delight as the fine spray dashed against her face, for it was wonderfully cool and refreshing.

"What a marvellous hiding place!" Caro exclaimed, shouting to make herself heard over the dull roar of the waterfall. "How on earth did you find it, coz?"

"I didn't—Nathan showed it to me," Mariah yelled back, dreamily remembering the first time he'd brought her to the cave, and how they'd made love here, behind the rainbow curtain of rushing water. "We came here to . . . um . . . swim a few days ago. Isn't it wonderful? You could hide here forever and no one would ever find you, 'less they knew where to look."

"Like a bloomin' eel that Kincaid is, in't he? Spends more time in the water than out o' it, he do!" Kitty observed loudly with a grin as she looked about her at the cave walls. They were slippery with damp green moss, adorned only by a huge conch-shell that some previous visitor—Mariah?—had left in a corner, along with a handful of withered blossoms. Gazing with wide-eyed wonder at the rainbow curtain of water before her, she exclaimed, "Cor, this place in't half a far cry from St. Giles!"

Pleased that the others approved of her secret place, Mariah laughed at Kitty's comment. "I'm sure it is. And, now that you've seen my rainbow cave, we'd best finish our toilette while we have fresh water. I swear, I shan't feel truly clean 'til I've washed every last grain of sand from my hair!"

The others murmured agreement and followed her to the far side of the hidden cave once again.

"Oh, by the way, girls, don't tell Nathan I've shown you this place, all right?" Mariah asked, turning back to them. She grimaced, seeming a trifle sheepish. "He . . . er . . . didn't say 'twas to be our secret, exactly, but the selfish brute did seem rather determined to keep its discovery to himself, and I did so want to show it to you."

"Mum's the word, then, ducks," Kitty promised cheerfully, pressing her lips together and winking at Caroline.

"Cross my heart, I'll not say a word, coz," Caroline promised, grinning at Kitty as she crossed her heart.

"Good. Now, let's teach Kitty how to swim, shall we?"

"Me? Swim? Oww, give over, Mistress Mariah! 'Tis a city-sparrow, I am, not a bleedin' country duck!" Kitty protested. "Don't waste yer time."

"It's plain 'Mariah,' not 'Mistress Mariah,'" Kitty was reminded. "And when Caro and I have done with you, sparrow or nay, you'll put country ducks to shame!" Mariah promised, squeezing Kitty's thin hand in her own.

"La! If Mariah has anything to do with it, you'll be swimming as if you had webbed feet!" Caro teased. "Or gills!"

"Aye, or a bleedin' anvil slung 'round me neck," Kitty came back doubtfully. "Six feet, I'll go, right enough—straight t' the bottom!"

After they'd given Kitty her first "lesson," one which resulted in lessening her fear of the water somewhat, but made no great strides towards actually getting her to take her feet off the bottom, they squeezed out their hair, changed into dry clothes, and spread their chemises to dry upon the rocks in the sun.

"Jack's taking his time," Mariah murmured, looking warily about her as she rubbed the back of her neck. All of a sudden, she'd had the unpleasant, prickling sensation that they were being watched. "I'd have expected him to sing out long before this, wouldn't you?"

"Oww, like as not poor Jack's a-feared o' catchin' us girls in the altogether!" Kitty suggested with an impish grin. "Bless 'im, I've never met a sailor t' equal Jack Warner fer modesty. It in't hardly natural in a man, I don't reckon."

"Jack told me he has several daughters of his own," Caroline supplied, squeezing out her hair. "I expect we just remind him of them, and that's why he keeps an eye out for us."

"Thank Gawd fer 'im, too!" Kitty declared. "If Jack hadn't seen the irons struck on some o' us wenches in the *Hester*'s hold, we'd be feedin' the bloomin' sharks right now, we would."

"Amen to that!" Mariah murmured absent agreement, her attention elsewhere. Truth was, she still felt uneasy, although she could see no one peering at them from the ferns or the bushes. "Well," she said brightly at length, "Jack or no Jack, we really should be getting back to camp, I think. Nathan will be vexed enough, when he hears we swam here with those savages still on the island! Caro, Kitty, gather up your things and let's go. Hurry, now!"

The anxious edge to her tone alerted Caroline. She eyed Mariah shrewdly. "Is something wrong, coz?"

Mariah shrugged. "Naught that I can put my finger upon, nay. But 'twas suddenly as if someone had walked over my grave!"

"Cripes! You do look awful pale of a sudden," Kitty observed, putting a comforting arm around Mariah's shoulders. "Sure you're all right, ducks?"

Mariah nodded shakily. "Aye. It's—oh, Kitty, I just have the strongest feeling someone is—was—watching us!"

"Reelly?" Kitty scowled, looking about. Tossing her mane of wet black hair over her shoulders, she glowered pugnaciously and planted a fist on both hips. "Well, if I catch some dirty bugger spyin' on us, I'll poke his soddin' eyes out, I will!" she declared loudly.

Forcing a smile at Kitty's bloodthirsty threat, Mariah tried to shrug off her uneasiness and quickly led the way back to camp.

They'd not gone far when Caroline suddenly stopped dead in her tracks.

"Mariah!" she whispered hoarsely, pointing to something half-hidden on the ground, beneath the bushes. "Oh, Mariah, look! It's Jack!"

Jack was not dead, as they'd feared, but unconscious. As Mariah swabbed his face with a corner of her damp chemise, he revived and sat up, fighting her hands.

"Your head is bleeding. Lie still. You mustn't get up yet," she remonstrated.

"'Tis naught, m'lady, let me up! I must warn our lads in camp!"

So saying, he lumbered to his feet, swayed groggily, then took off at such a speedy toddle through the bushes that the three women were hard pressed to keep up with him.

"Warn them about what?" Mariah panted as they crashed through the jungle, headed at a jog-trot for the camp beneath the coconut grove. "Oh, God! The natives, you mean? Jack, did they club you?" she demanded breathlessly.

"I doubt it. Them heathen savages would 'ave had me head fer their pains, not left me lyin' there! Nay, 'twas Ruskin's foul lot wot did it—I'd wager me life on it. And that they'll attack our camp, an' all!"

To Mariah's horror, Jack was right.

When they were still a short distance from the grove, the sounds of a fierce skirmish reached them. Their blood ran cold as they heard Ole Peg cry out like a wounded animal caught in a trap, the cry ominously cut short. Foul curses followed, and the unmistakeable clash of steel against steel; the thuds of fists soldily meeting flesh.

"Oh, no!" Mariah whispered, the blood draining from her face. "Nathan!" Thrusting past Jack, she started forwards, a terrible dread in her breast, her blood pounding in her ears. In that moment, all she could think of was Nathan, dead or terribly wounded at Ruskin's hands. She knew if she lost him she couldn't—wouldn't—want to go on living!

I love him! she realized, and swayed dizzily as the knowledge slammed home like a fist in her belly. Aye, somehow, she'd come to love him. And her life would have no meaning, no joy, without him. She must go to him!

"Get back here, mistress," Jack snapped, jerking her backwards by her skirts. "'Twill do Kincaid no good if he must watch his back and you, too. You leddies stay here. Get down, and *don't move.*"

"Nay, Jack, we won't hide. We must help them somehow!" Mariah cried, but her protests went unheard and unanswered as Jack drew his dagger and left.

"Please, Mariah, be sensible. Do as Jack says," Caro pleaded, looking pale, jittery, young, and very scared as she cowered in the long grasses. Mariah had an obstinate gleam in her eyes that filled Caro with foreboding, for with the bit between her teeth, being her father's daughter, there was no telling what risks her headstrong cousin might take.

"Nay!" Mariah whispered, confirming Caro's worst fears. Her turquoise eyes flashed, took on an obstinate glint her cousin knew well, as her chin came up defiantly "I'll not cower here like some lily-livered nitwit while our friends risk their lives! Come on, girls. Follow me! We may be women, but we're far from helpless!"

Ruskin was beside himself with rage as he stood apart from the fight and watched the goings-on.

For several days now his spies had been watching the other camp, observing its comings and goings. And, by that blasted Foxy's reckoning, Kincaid should have been in camp at this time; should have *been* among the first to die! He'd singled him out, he had; he, Angus Ruskin, had marked the bastard for death.

But, Kincaid was nowhere t' be seen, damn his cursed soul, and only the old pirate and a marine had been killed in the first rush. What was more, 'though their ambush had taken Kincaid's men, who'd been idly yarning about a huge signal fire when they'd attacked, completely by surprise, a half-dozen of the party had quickly rallied and were now fighting like demons, despite being outnumbered two to one and poorly armed!

"Stick 'em, me hearties!" the marine Stiles whooped, brandishing his trusty cutlass and lunging at the convict, Foxy, as if he were pig-hunting rather than fighting for his life. "Come on, Ben, me lad! Stand beside me! Back t' back, we'll send these buggers t' hell—where they belong!"

Stiles' rallying cries emboldened his fellows, sent the thrill of battle racing through their veins like a shot of rum! In that same moment, Jack exploded from the coconut grove with a blood-curdling yell, and all hell broke loose.

Empty-handed, Big Ben made a feint in the direction of the traitor, Digby. When the sneering fool fell for it and turned, he brought up his foot and kicked him in the groin. As Digby screamed and doubled over, Ben followed up with a kick to the jaw, which neatly felled him. "Whore-son, turncoat!" Ben snarled, spitting in the sand. "Who's next t' die!"

A stocky thief sprang to meet his challenge, thwacking a club of knotted wood against his palm.

"Why, now, if it in't ole Jared Lee from Cheapside!" Ben jeered, whistling through his teeth. "How's yer mother, sonny? Still openin' 'er legs fer a ha'penny a toss, is she? That raddled old whore—she'd toss a monkey fer a tot, she would."

"Bastard!" Lee lunged forward.

Ben's eyes danced as he escaped Lee's first swing with a nifty sidestep and a lithe twist, cracking his fist against Lee's skull as he spun. Lee flew backwards into the sand. Ben followed in a leap, straddling him. They fought furiously, rolling over and over, curses and grunts filling the sultry air.

Matthew Love, the ship's surgeon, was trying to repel a hard-jawed felon with a Gypsy cast to his looks. The man was armed with a wicked stiletto, while Love had only a flaming brand snatched up from the fire. The Gypsy was like a sly, cruel cat playing with a helpless mouse before moving in for the kill. He laughed mockingly and jeered in Love's face, dancing backwards on the balls of his bare feet, or nimbly ducking and rolling to left or to right, like a tumbler at a fair. Each time, he lithely evaded Love's desperate thrusts of the torch, and the elderly ship's surgeon was sweating buckets and growing short-winded in his efforts to keep his attacker at bay. One sign of flagging, and the Gypsy would lunge, Love knew, the stiletto slipping between his ribs as smooth as silk.

"Come and get me, sawbones!" the Gypsy scoffed. "Singe my pretty locks if ye dare, ye old wind-bag!"

Jack saw the surgeon's predicament, his desperate expression, and bracing a foot against the chest of the man he'd just run through with Ole Peg's cutlass, he withdrew his bloody weapon and sprang to help him.

Yet even as he did so, it crossed his mind that it was inevitable the convicts would win, unless reinforcements—in the form of Kincaid's hunting party—returned very soon. Ole Peg and Babbington were dead, he thought bleakly. There were only four of their number left standing, including himself, and one of them—Stiles—was injured, bleeding from a chest wound. God knew how much longer they could fight on!

And then, out of nowhere, Jack's prayers for help were answered! From north, south and west, three screaming Furies appeared—red-headed, blond, and brunette. Their skirts were weighted down with stones, and there was murder in their eyes.

At Mariah's signal, rocks flew from dainty female hands in a deadly hail-storm.

"Oy! Oy!" yelled Kitty triumphantly. "Gotcha, Fox, ye poxy swab!"

The missiles, fired with varying degrees of accuracy, rained down upon the heads and backs of Ruskin and his startled men, drawing blood and blackening eyes.

As diversions went, Mariah's was a huge success.

Kitty's second rock gashed the Gypsy's cheek. Blood gushed down his swarthy face. With a roar and a foul curse in his Romany tongue, he forgot Love and turned to see who'd dared to stone him. As he did so, Jack saw his chance. He brought his cutlass around in a sweeping arc, hacking into the Romany's side. The man was dead before he hit the sand.

"Huzzah!" whooped Mariah, lobbing stone after stone at Ruskin's crew. With her red-gold locks furling like a bright banner on the balmy breeze, her turquoise eyes afire, her legs braced apart, and her hiked-up skirts heavy with stones, she was an Amazon warrior; diminutive in size but magnificent in her courage; beautiful—but deadly. "Here's one for you, Ruskin, ye great, gap-toothed ox!" she taunted. Drawing back her fist, she aimed a bulky rock at Ruskin's head. And, more by chance than skill, the stone struck him full in the face.

Ruskin let out a bellow of rage, like a pain-maddened bull. He threw his bulk forward, lumbering after her with blood streaming down his face.

Mariah hurled rock after rock at him, trying desperately to keep him at a distance. Her bravado rapidly dwindled when, despite her rain of missiles, he kept on coming.

"Get back!" she hissed. "Not another step, you brute!" she warned, but her voice quavered as Ruskin kept advancing on her.

"Run!" Kitty screamed, horror-stricken as Mariah stood, frozen in place by panic, with Ruskin rapidly closing the distance between them. "For Gawd's sake, *run*!"

Kitty dropped her own skirts and let her rocks tumble to the ground as she ran after Ruskin, desperate to keep him from harming her friend.

As Mariah snapped to her senses, abandoned her rocks, and turned to flee, Kitty leaped onto Ruskin's back. She anchored her legs about his waist and hung on like a monkey. Tearing out his red hair by the fistfuls, she pummelled his head and his massive shoulders with her clenched fists.

"Kitty, nay!" Jack yelled. He would have run to her aid, had Foxy not stepped into his path and swung at him with a cudgel.

"Damn ye, ye meddlin' bitch! Get awa'," Ruskin snarled,

trying to fling Kitty off his back. Gamely, she clung like a limpet, gritting her teeth, yanking on his ears and broken nose and screaming curses at him. Enraged, Ruskin brought his fist around. He dashed Kitty aside with a blow so hard, so vicious, she flew into the air, knocked senseless before she tumbled to the sand.

Without a backwards glance, Ruskin barrelled down the beach after Mariah, his great, sturdy legs gobbling up the distance.

Hearing his heavy breathing, Mariah risked a glance over her shoulder. Oh, god, he was gaining on her! Her heart almost stopped beating from sheer terror, for great clods of wet sand flew up behind his rapid passage, and not even the raucous screams of the gulls could drown out the foul curses and threats he roared as he came on. Like a lash, they goaded her onward, faster and still faster.

The stitch in her side now was agonizing. Every breath hurt, was torn from her lungs. Somehow, she forced her aching legs to pump like pistons, made her bare feet defy the drag and suck of the wet sand and race on. To halt and face him meant certain death.

When Ruskin bolted, his men followed suit. One by one, they broke and ran, leaving their dead and dying behind to swarm after Ruskin and Mariah like a cloud of flies.

Chapter Sixteen

They cornered her on the headlands of the point, a craggy promontory where flows of molten lava left by an ancient volcanic eruption had formed rugged ebony cliffs. Far below the sea, the surf boomed and flung ruffles of white water into the air over jagged black rocks.

Flinging about, Mariah realized too late that she was trapped! Not only Ruskin, but a dozen of his convict band surrounded her now; ruthless felons who'd never let her slip between them. Cliffs littered with pointed rocks as sharp as blades dropped away behind her. Dear God! No matter which way she tried to run, they'd catch her in a trice, unless . . .

Bosom heaving, she turned and stood her ground, waiting, letting them make the first move. Blood still roared like an inferno in her ears, and her mouth tasted cottony with fear, but by gritting her teeth, she brought up her chin and put on a bold face, defiantly staring them down as the pack came closer, encircling her like the drooling jackals they were. Her haughty, beautiful face, her withering stare, her defiant stance with fists boldly planted on hips and head thrown back, betrayed none of her inner terror.

But the convicts knew full well they had her cornered. Wetting their lips, they halted and exchanged knowing grins. No need t' hurry, not now, those grins said. After all, where could the pretty trull run to, unless through their number? Accordingly, they fanned out, one of them taking up a stance in each direction, with only an arm's length left open between them. Their eyes, hot with lust, feasted upon the young woman, ogling the ripe swell of hips and buttocks that rounded out her skirts, relishing the rapid rise and fall of her bosom against the fabric of her bodice.

Their hungry, gloating expressions filled the pit of Mariah's belly with a cold lump of dread. *This is it, then*, she thought, blinking rapidly as she tightened her jaw to muffle a moan. This was what it had all come down to. She'd outlived marriage to a man she'd loathed, survived being shipwrecked and cast away on a deserted island, only to meet her fate here, on this God-forsaken point. Jesu! Her short young life was destined to end upon the jagged rocks below this cliff. In a few seconds— a minute, an hour, at most—she would die here, all alone, for what choice had she left? Aye, she'd sooner leap to her death on the rocks than endure the touch of even one of those foul, dirty animals.

She thought of Nathan, then, and of the tender, intimate nights they'd shared; nights of sweet, wild passion that had made her forget Edward's cold, selfish love-making. Of how—too late, ah, God, too late!—she'd come to realize that, convict or king, guilty or innocent, she loved him with all her heart. Tears smarted like salt behind her eyes. She'd never told him that, and now he'd never know. *Goodbye, my heart*! she bade him silently. *Goodbye, dearest Jonathan, my only love!*

Gingerly moving backwards, she scrambled over the rocks leading to the cliff edge, feeling behind her for purchase with her hands and bare toes, but never once taking her eyes from the circle of ragged, leering curs who circled her like dogs surrounding a bitch in heat.

"Oi! Oi! Don't ye run orf, now, wench! Here, pretty kitty!" cooed one man, making rude, juicy smacking noises with his lips and rubbing his fingers together as he took slow, measured steps in her direction.

"Never mind 'im, slut. Come on over here, t' me!" invited another.

Her gaze shifted from one to the other, her eyes turquoise pools of dread as she desperately searched their faces for some hint of kindness or compassion that might sway her from her course. Alas, she found not a morsel of pity in any of their faces, only the viciousness of the callous. Swallowing, she tried to moisten her parched lips on her tongue, but found she could not. Her mouth was too dry with fear.

"Here, li'l wench. I'm yer man!" offered a third lout. "I've summat fer ye, an' no mistake!" he promised crudely, winking and rubbing his swollen groin.

The others chortled as her hand fluttered to her breast to still the deafening thump of her heart. She swayed and almost fell, and knew a moment of panic when it seemed she'd be unable to right herself. *Soon*! she promised bitterly. *Very soon. But . . . not just yet, please, God? One blessed moment more?*

"Alf knows how t' pleasure a leddy, lovie. Come here t' ole Alf!"

"Nay, here, t' me!"

"Nay, here!"

"Bugger them, dearie—I'm the one fer ye!"

"Here, pretty kitty. Here!"

She covered her ears with her hands and turned her back on the men, trying to blot out their foul invitations by calm resolve. The rocks beckoned from below, promising an escape, of sorts, in their jagged arms. Feeling sick with dizziness, she teetered on the cliff-edge, mutely asking God for the courage to do what must be done.

It came in a moment of sublime calm that was utterly devoid

of terror and dread. Of course, she had nothing to fear by dying! Papa and Mama were already in Heaven, waiting to welcome her. A moment's pain, and it would all be over, surely. It was *living* she should fear now. Not death . . .

With that thought, she drew a deep, shaky breath, closed her eyes, and took a single step forward over the edge, into space.

But in that same instant, Foxy suddenly yelled and lunged forward. *"Naaay!"* With a maddened roar, he made a frantic grab for her skirts, caught her hems in his fists—and hung on!

The sudden backwards yank slammed Mariah against the cliff-face. She cried out, her momentary calm shattered. Her arms windmilled frantically for some handhold, clawing out in a desperate grab for life—precious life! Cloth shrieked as her skirts rent with her weight. Mariah shrieked, too, as she suddenly dropped three more feet, to dangle over the cliff-edge like a spider hanging by a thread, wondering desperately as she thudded heavily to and fro how long it would be before the last few inches of her skirts gave and she plunged to her death.

Below, far beneath her dangling feet, she could see a circle of pointed rocks, much like the razor-teeth of a shark set in foaming white jaws. Dizziness overwhelmed her. Dear God, 'twas as if a monstrous mouth waited to devour her! And, though she'd been fully prepared to take her own life but moments ago, now that she'd been given a second chance, she found she didn't want to die, after all. *Any* chance at living, however tenuous, however unpleasant the prospects might prove, was infinitely preferable to dying.

"Please, pull me up!" she implored hysterically. "Oh, God, pull me up!"

"Beg me!" Foxy taunted. He was breathing heavily, but managed a rubbery grin despite the strain of hanging on to her skirts. The muscles in his scrawny neck and bony shoulders were bulging like cables against his freckled, pasty skin. Sweat soaked his lanky hair and grimy shirt, and his teeth and jaws were clenched with the strain, but he wouldn't let her go. Nay,

255

not this pretty slut. Save her pretty neck, an' she'd be crawlin' all over him, eager to do anything he wanted, she would!

"Let the bitch go, Foxy," crooned Angus in his ear. "Let Kincaid's bonnie wee slut plunge t' her death!"

"Nay, Rusk. She's mine—or will be, arter this," Foxy whined, his pale blue eyes casting a defiant look in the direction of Ruskin, who squatted on his haunches alongside him.

"Never laddie. Not in a million years! This bonnie, high-born slut'll never belong t' the likes o' ye. And d' ye know why? Because you'll always be horse-dung t' a bitch like that. Dirt beneath her boot-heel, that's what she'll think o' ye—how she'll *always* think o' ye. She belongs t' Kincaid, don't ye see, laddie? Because she *chose* him. And unless she chooses ye, ye'll never own her. Save yersel' the heartache, Foxy laddie. Let 'er go," he wheedled.

"Nay!" Foxy snarled, his spittle flying. "I know what ye're up t', Rusk—and it won't bloody work, ye hear me? Ye want her dead so ye can repay Kincaid for kicking yer arse in New-gate, but she's mine! *Mine!* You in't havin' her! By God, I'll kill ye first!"

"Och, nay, I dinna want what's rightly yours, laddie. Whist, ye misjudge auld Rusk sorely t' think I do, an' that's the blessed truth. I . . . but meant that ye should understand the way o' things wi' high-born lassies. That ye shouldna be surprised if the wee bitch turns on ye, an' bites the hand that saved 'er. Come, laddie. If ye want her so blessed badly, I'll help ye t' pull her up, shall I no'?" Ruskin promised silkily, wiping spittle from his fleshy lips on the back of his meaty fist. He held out his hand. "Here. Move over, laddie. You an' me, we'll pull the wee slut up t'gether. Ye'll have her, Foxy. Yer auld Rusk will see to it. Digby!" he yelled. "Climb on down! Give Foxy's sweetheart a wee boost!"

"My thanks, Rusk." Grinning now with relief and no little gratitude that Rusk had come around, Foxy nodded as Digby gingerly peered over the cliff edge.

The former lieutenant gulped. It was a long drop down if he missed his footing. "Now, see here, Rusk, I'd ra—"

"Do it, Digby lad. Do it—'else I'll carve your treacherous heart from yer chest while it yet pumps!" snarled Ruskin, his amber eyes wolfish. There was nothing he enjoyed better than using fear to bend the weak to his will, unless it was inflicting pain.

"Aye, aye, sir," Digby muttered, still looking mutinous and green about the gills. But without further protest, he turned and began backing down the cliff, inching his way towards where Mariah hung, her back to the cliff, her arms spread-eagled.

Digby's climb dislodged showers of pebbles and grit that scattered down around her, stinging her arms and face as she clung desperately to the rocky face of the cliff. Bile burned her throat.

Oh, dear God, she didn't want to die—but she did not want to become a toy for the convicts' foul pleasure, either. Such a fate would surely be worse than death! *Oh, Nathan, help me, my love! Save me*! she cried silently. But her only answer was the mocking scream of a lone gull as it wheeled over the pounding surf on wide, white wings.

"D' ye have her, laddie?" Ruskin called, peering down to where the girl clung, her cheek pressed to the igneous rock, her scraped and bleeding fingers curved into talons.

Digby edged sideways, blindly seeking footholds in the cliff face. She could hear his heavy breathing as he labored to reach her; then, a moment later, she felt his arm clamp about her waist. She flinched away, but his grip tightened. "Aye, aye, sir. I have her!" Digby yelled. "Haul away!"

With Digby pushing from below, and Foxy and Ruskin hauling on her skirts, it took but seconds for Mariah to regain the cliff edge.

As she reappeared, grubby-faced and weeping now in reaction to her brush with death, Foxy at once put his hands upon her, claiming her for himself with that proprietary gesture. Casting a triumphant grin at his fellows, he ducked his head to steal a kiss, mortified by his companions' scornful laughter as she recoiled and jerked her head away with a shudder of distaste.

"Hoity-toity piece, in't she, Foxy lad?" one jeered. "She'll take some tamin', that 'un!"

"Throw 'er down. Spread 'er legs an' show 'er who's 'er master, Foxy—if'n yer man enough fer it!"

Gripping her chin in a brutal fist, Foxy forced Mariah's head around and planted a foul wet kiss hard on the side of her mouth. "Ye see, lads? She's mine!" he crowed, taking her slender wrist in a vicious grip and jerking her arm up behind her. "Gimme a day or two, she'll do whatever I tells her. Right, lovie?" When Mariah stonily refused to answer, he jerked back on her bent arm, forcing bone against bone so painfully, she yelped with pain. "Answer me, slut!" Foxy snarled.

"Aye!" she ground out. "I'll . . . I'll do . . . anything— oh, sweet Jesu, stop!"

"See, Rusk? You were wrong!" Foxy crowed.

He turned to grin triumphantly at Angus Ruskin, but in that same instant, Ruskin's hand flashed over his shoulder. With no greater compunction than if he were squashing a fly, Ruskin turned his dagger sideways and, still smiling, slashed Foxy's throat from ear to ear. A thin red line gaped instantly beneath the bulge of the convict's Adam's apple.

"Wrong, laddie?" Ruskin purred. "Nay! See, Angus Ruskin's never wrong. I said the lassie wouldna have ye for her mon, and she willna. Not now!" With that, he threw back his shaggy head and roared with laughter as Foxy's eyes dimmed with the sudden realization of his death. His hand jerked convulsively to stanch the scarlet fountain that suddenly spewed from his throat. He gurgled once, then his knees buckled as he fell dead at Ruskin's feet.

"Bring the lassie back t' camp, laddies!" Ruskin roared as he wiped his blade on his stained breeches. "And be quick about it! Kincaid'll be along shortly, I dinna doubt. We must have a fine, warm welcome awaitin' him when he comes, must we no'?'' With a fastidious air, he flicked a speck of Foxy's blood from his filthy shirt-front and stomped off towards the convict camp without a backwards glance, confident that his orders would be obeyed.

"Not so high and might now, are you, my dear?" Digby purred as he gripped Mariah's arm. His contemptuous tone jolted her from her shock. In answer, she turned her head and shot him a look of such icy contempt, it froze the triumphant leer on Digby's lips. "Go to hell, Digby!"

With a foul curse, he kneed her in the small of the back and growled, "Get going! We don't want to keep friend Ruskin waiting, do we now? Who knows, he might let us lads have you, before your precious Kincaid walks into his trap."

Digby's words sickened her, added to the knot of unbearable dread already lodged in her belly. She had seen first-hand what madness Ruskin was capable of, what bloody lengths he'd go to in order to even the score with those who'd crossed him, as Jonathan once had. Her beloved would try to rescue her, she knew. And when he did so, he'd be walking straight into Ruskin's murderous arms.

"We're takin' on water faster'n I can say 'Billy-O,' Kincaid," Jack whispered hoarsely. "Shall I ship oars an' bail 'er out?"

"Nay, Jack. Save your strength. She'll stay afloat long enough for our purposes. Besides, we're almost there, I fancy. Look to the shore, man, dead ahead! Do ye see what I see?"

Jack grunted that he did. The amber flicker of the convicts' camp-fire was easily spotted from off-shore. And on bright, moon-lit tropical nights, their own leaky longboat would have been equally visible as they bobbed along, following the coastline to the convicts' camp. On this night, however, rainclouds partially hid the moon, an unlooked-for blessing that had made Jonathan's clever plan to attack from the sea and use the element of surprise to free Mariah more feasible. Ruskin would have posted guards about his camp to warn him of an imminent rescue attempt, but Jack doubted he'd had the foresight to place sentries on the beach. In but a few moments, they'd find out for sure.

As the longboat drifted on, only the lazy lapping of the waves against her patched sides and the distant boom of the surf striking the rocks below the point broke the hush. Jack cast a sideways glance at Kincaid, wondering what thoughts were going through the man's head. No doubt his innards were all a-churn with anxiety for his lady-love, or else they were tied in knots, anticipating the fierce fight t' come, but ye'd never guess it, not t' look at him. Clad in only his battered leather waistcoat and ragged breeches, a strip of red cloth wound pirate-fashion about his head and a gleaming cutlass gripped in his fist, he knelt in the bow, ready to spring through the shallows to the beach when the time was right. His strong jaw was squared, his broad shoulders were thrown back. With the dark strands of his queue whipping about in the wind, he cut a striking silhouette against the night sky and the ebony sea beyond: one dangerous in its dark and brooding intensity. The murky light caught his hooded eyes, reflecting a cold emerald fire that made a shiver crawl down Jack's spine. He'd seen those eyes grow light and leafy with merriment and laughter, or muddy as a woodland pool with sorrow and self-doubt. But never had he seen them like this. God help Ruskin when Kincaid laid hands upon him! He could almost pity the sod. Almost . . .

"'Tis close enough here, I warrant, Jack. I'll take my leave of you now, sir," Kincaid's hoarse whisper cut into Jack's thoughts.

"Aye. An' I'll be right behind ye, as we planned, never fear, Kincaid," Jack vowed solemnly.

"Aye, my friend. I know you will. Adieu," Kincaid said softly as their eyes met; then he was over the side and wading through the shallows to the pale curve of beach, a lone man armed with only a cutlass, and his love.

260

Chapter Seventeen

Nathan swam ashore about a hundred yards beyond the convicts' camp, wading out of the shallows and onto the sand with hardly a splash. Head down, he sprinted up the beach, diving for cover in a dense tangle of lianas, trees, and bushes just as one of Ruskin's number left the blazing fire for the darkness beyond. He passed not three feet from Nathan's hiding place, jauntily whistling a sea-chantey.

Holding his breath, Nathan waited, smiling thinly as the unsuspecting fool took up a familiar stance with feet braced apart, and began unfastening his breeches. Gazing skyward, the man sighed, so loudly that Nathan could hear him, before noisily relieving himself.

Nathan's smile deepened. The man was Jimmy "The Weasel" Watts, a former pickpocket and one of his old Newgate "chums." And, judging by the fellow's lack of stealth, Ruskin must be anticipating no attack from this quarter. Naturally, the wily bastard expected them to launch their rescue attack from the most *unlikely* direction—the mangrove swamps. Surely the ambush, if ambush there was, must have been set up by now. By moonrise, Ruskin's louts would have been hidden among the tall grasses and reeds, armed to their eyeballs, never dreaming of the surprise they had coming to them very soon.

While the man was preoccupied with refastening his trousers, Nathan rose from the shadows and jumped him from behind, hooking an arm about his throat and cutting off his startled yelp with a forearm against his windpipe.

"Pipe down, Watts, 'else I'll run ye through" Nathan threatened in deadly earnest, jabbing the point of his cutlass against the man's ribs.

"'S that you, Kincaid?" the convict whispered nervously.

"Aye, Weasel. Can I trust ye t' hold yer tongue, or must I slit your throat?"

When the man nodded vigorously, Nathan released his choke-hold and shoved him roughly forward with a growled, "Walk!"

"One down, and a baker's dozen to go!" he muttered moments later as he crept up on Ruskin's camp, having left his cooperative captive buried up to his neck in loose sand, some distance away.

Crouched down between the bushes, he could see and hear clearly everything that was going on in the convicts' camp. Of Ruskin, there was no sign, though a good half of his men still appeared to be slumped around the fire in a drunken stupor, posing little threat. Their frowsy-haired doxies were sprawled across their laps in various stages of undress, also dead to the world.

He shook his head in disgust. Never had he seen a sorrier crew. Both men and women wore ragged garments, as was to be expected for castaways, and looked filthy besides, which was, to his mind, quite unnecessary, given the abundance of sea-water to be had for washing and keeping themselves clean. Moreover, the remains of countless meals—bones, ashes, fish-scales, feathers, and what-have-you—littered the sand about the camp. God's Teeth! The air of neglect and despair about the place was palpable, and said much about the form Ruskin's leadership took. Judging by the state of their camp, morale must be at rock-bottom . . . which suited his own purpose perfectly!

All thoughts of the unsanitary lot vanished as he suddenly spotted Mariah. Relief filled him. She appeared pale, but, thank God, unharmed, sitting cross-legged before a ramshackle lean-to that resembled the poorly constructed nest of a demented shore-bird! Her wrists and ankles had been tied, and two men—this pair more alert than the others—guarded her. By the proud uptilt of her head, he could tell that, although a prisoner, she was far from cowed, bless her. Indeed, the defiant words she screeched at one of Ruskin's louts proved as much.

"You can keep me here 'til Doomsday, you stinking offal, you cringing curs. No matter what you do with me, Kincaid'll never take the bait." She raised her voice. "You've bungled it, Ruskin! He'll not risk his neck or his men for a wench he cares nothing for!"

Nathan grinned, thinking what a game little baggage she was. He could almost believe her brave claims that she was unloved, *if* the gnawing ache in the pit of his belly didn't tell him otherwise. He cared for her, by God—and a deal more than he'd ever wanted to care! *Be patient but a while longer, sweetheart! I'll have ye free in a twinkling.*

Returning to camp and hearing she'd been taken by Ruskin and his cronies had been one of the worst moments of his life, akin to finding Rosie and Roger murdered, to being sentenced to hang. He intended to tell her of his love the very moment he freed her—God willing—and then do whatever was needed to make her believe it.

One day, some day, a Dutchman would surely sail these waters and they'd be home free. He'd take Mari to Java and make her his island queen, his jungle goddess. They'd not have much but each other at first, but with hard work and some sound trading on his part, someday they'd rule an exotic, verdant valley where fragrant blossoms wafted sweet perfume on the sultry air. In that place he would be free to love her always, far from the shadow of the hangman's noose. But first . . .

He flicked his head and tightened his jaw, and in the shadows his green eyes became the emerald-satin eyes of a devil as he clenched his fists. First, he must get her safely away. Damn Ruskin to Hell! If he'd harmed so much as a single hair on her head, he'd skin that maggot alive.

An enraged snarl riveted his attention to the lean-to. He saw Ruskin duck out of it and loom over Mari, a fist raised threateningly over her head.

"Ye'd best shut yer yap, ye loud-mouthed shrew. Ma puir noggin's pounding an' I've had enough o' yer squalling fer one night! Ye'll do as my men say—'else answer t' me!'' He made as if to strike her, but even as his meaty fist swung down, one of her guards lunged forward and caught his arm.

"Nah, Ruskin, there's no need fer that! She's but a slip of a wench, and a scared one, at that. She'll be quiet. Just leave her be, eh?"

"Lay hold o' me again, Joe Hardy, an' I'll shiver yer bleedin' timbers, see if I don't!" Ruskin threatened, spittle spraying through the gap in his blackened teeth as he turned on Hardy like a great, lumbering bear.

Hardy, far shorter and slighter of build than Ruskin, paled markedly under his thatch of dark-brown hair, but like a feisty terrier, he stood his ground. "I've gone along wi' ye 'til now, Rusk, but I don't 'old wi' beatin' wenches," he said, so softly that Nathan had to strain to catch his words.

At this, Ruskin threw back his sandy, matted mane and laughed. "Aye, Hardy, I know ye dinna. And do ye know why? 'Tis 'cause ye're but half a mon! A *real* mon knows how t' keep his woman in her place. He knows the lassies like t' be clouted every once in a while—whist, mon, how else can ye show ye care for the faithless wee sluts? Why, I warrant if ye'd fetched that bonnie Kitty a wallop or two, she'd have lifted her skirts for ye laddie, 'stead of fer me. By God, but she were a

264

prime piece o' goods, your Kitty! She—Why now, wherever are ye off to, Hardy? Was it somethin' I said, laddie?''

Nathan watched as Joe Hardy, grim-faced and silently seething, strode from the camp. Seeing the direction in which Hardy was headed, he circled around and cut him off.

"Hardy!" he hissed from the shadows. "Over here, man!"

"Blimey! Kincaid!" Hardy exclaimed, ducking down next to Nathan.

"Keep it down, for the love of God! Would you have Ruskin hear us?"

"Whoops! Not bloody likely!" Joe apologized in a lower voice, then grinned broadly as he squatted on his haunches. "Hell's bloody bells, I just knew you'd come for your wench."

Nathan nodded grimly. "Aye, but 'twas you who saved her from a beating. I owe you, Joe."

Joe dismissed the matter. "'Strewth, that debt's settled easy enough. I'll help you t' free your leddy. In return, you let me join your lot. Christ, I've had it with Ruskin and the rest o' em. They're naught but shiftless drunkards, t' the last man-jack, an' I'll be done fer, too, if I stay with them! Is it a deal, sir?"

Nathan grinned in the shadows. "Aye, Joe. A deal it is."

They clasped hands to seal the agreement.

"And how's Kitty? All right, is she?" the little man asked anxiously, his heart on his sleeve. "I over 'eard Ruskin boastin' that he'd walloped her good, the dirty swab! She in't . . . she in't dead, is she, sir?"

"Kitty? Not even close! She'll have a roaring skull-ache for a day or two, I shouldn't wonder, but she's far from dead, if the lady's colorful language was aught to go by when I left camp!"

"Thank Gawd! Now, what would ye have me do, gov'na?"

A strange expression crossed Nathan's face in the murky light. "Well, Joe, how d' ye feel about digging?"

"Digging?" Joe asked, blinking.

"That's what I said. . . ."

* * *

"Dinna fret, lassie. I'll be back in a wee while," Ruskin purred, caressing Mariah's cheek with a callused finger the size of a sausage. "Ye'll scarce have time t' miss me, chick."

Her flesh crawled with loathing at his touch and at the hungry, lust-filled glitter in the eyes that swept over her body, lingering on the curve of her breasts and on the glimpse of shapely ankle and calf revealed where her skirt had caught in her bonds. He ducked his shaggy head and planted a wet, fleshy kiss upon her cheek, braying with laughter when she flinched and jerked her head away so violently and with such a shudder of revulsion, she almost lost her balance.

"Like it or not, I'll have ye t'night, lass. An' I wager ye'll not be s' blessed brave wi' your skirts flung over yer head an' yer legs spread, eh?" He licked his chops like a wolf savoring its next meal. "'Tis a broad furrow auld Angus plows—aye, broad an' deep an' true! Think on that, ma bonnie. 'Twill keep yer warm 'til I return."

Mariah glowered at Ruskin, damning him to Hell with her eyes as, with an obscene gesture, he stomped past her, headed towards the swamps. The sorry brute was more animal than man, and she told him so—though she muttered the insults under her breath this time, rather than screaming them within earshot as she'd done so rashly just before. That, she realized, had been a decidedly stupid thing to do, if she valued her life. She thought of what he'd said, the vile threats he'd made, and came close to swooning with dread. *For the love of God, Nathan, help me! And for pity's sake, hurry!*

"How about some grub, love?" one of the doxies, a young woman called Nancy, asked when Ruskin was gone. She offered her an over-ripe banana that she'd peeled.

"No, thank you." Mariah averted her face and warily eyed the red-headed woman. She couldn't help wondering if Nancy meant to do her harm, for the other convict wenches had been loud and obscene and far more threatening than their men when

Digby had first dragged her back to the camp. Thank God, the rum had silenced them long since. "I'm not hungry."

"Ow, 'ave a bite, ducks. Ye really should eat t' keep up yer strength, a skinny li'l scrap like you, but . . . well, I can't say I blame you," Nancy said enviously, wrinkling her nose at the brown-spotted banana, then tossing it aside. "I bet you do a mite better for yerselves in Kincaid's camp than the monkey-victuals we eat, day in an' day out, eh?"

"We have caviar on Sundays, actually. And Kincaid rations the champagne. Just a coconutful a day!" Mariah shot back.

Nancy honked like a goose in raucous laughter. " 'Rations the champagne'—ooh, you are a one! You're all right, you are, yer ladyship, as far as quality folks go, which I allow in't usually that far." Nancy sniffed. "Did ye know I seen you once aboard the *Hester*, when we was brung up on decks fer air? I sez t' Leah, 'Gawd, Awlmighty, jest take a gander at M'lady Hoity-Toity, all decked out in her silks 'n' satins an' her bleedin' sunbonnet. I wager she reckons 'erself a cut or two above the loikes o' us.' But I was wrong." She sniffed. "You in't half-bad."

Mariah managed a grin. "Neither are you . . . as . . . as far as . . . er . . . convict folks go. In fact, I'd say, thanks to that gale, we're about even."

Nancy grinned too, liking her even more. The high-born woman might look as dainty as a bloomin' cobweb, but she had guts, she did, and a saucy mouth on her! Emboldened, Nancy asked a trifle enviously, "So, 'ow's our Kitty? All right wiv your lot, is she? All settled in?"

"She seems happy enough with us, aye, and I hope we've become friends. She was wonderful! When Ruskin tried to catch me, she jumped on his back to keep him from hurting me. But Ruskin hit her, just . . . just threw her into the air. Then they chased me and, well"—she shrugged—"here I am. I'm sorry. I really can't tell you whether Kitty's hurt badly or not."

With a sober nod, Nancy returned to her place by the fire,

next to an older, drunken bawd who was snoring loudly. Mariah guessed from Kitty's conversation that the woman must be Leah.

Sighing heavily, she looked around. Of the thirteen or so men she'd counted upon her arrival, only a half-dozen, sotted by grog, remained. Those of Ruskin's men who were sober and still able to function had gone somewhere. And, judging by the low tones in which Ruskin had given his orders and the sly look he'd worn when he'd sent them off, she fancied "somewhere" was the place in which Ruskin intended to ambush Nathan and his rescue party when it arrived . . . *if* rescue party there would be.

"Well, well, my dear Mariah! 'Twould seem we're alone at last, would it not?"

The blood drained from Mariah's face as she looked up into Digby's pale, grey eyes.

"Jesus! I don't like this 'ere set up! Where the devil's Rusk?"

"Quit yer bleedin' whinin'! He'll be along in his own sweet time. Ye know Ruskin."

"Aye—and 'tis my thinkin' 'tis Rusk's quarrel with Kincaid, not ours." another man, Daniel Cooper, grumbled. "Think on it, lads. Wot we got t' gain by ambushin' the lawyer? Not a bleedin' thing, that's wot! We've still got our bloody lives, an' I fer one ain't in no hurry t' lose mine! Fer two pins, I'd give it up an' join Peg an' Ben an' the others . . . if they'd take me in. Leastways we'd have good grub an' water wiv Kincaid's lot!"

"Ye'd sell out, would ye, ye snivellin' Judas! Ye yellow-belly! Where's ye damned loyalty t' yer own kind, eh, matie?"

"Bugger loyalty! Foxy was loyal t' Rusk—aye, more than any man—and look what good it done 'im. Bloomin' shark-vittles, that's wot he is."

A blood-curdling whoop rent the steamy air.

"Christ A'mighty, wot the Divil's that!" cried Finnegan. "A banshee?"

The other five exchanged frightened glances, their pasty faces grey in the sparse light. The smell of the mangrove swamps was rank on the air, and the oppressive darkness of the banks where they'd hidden enclosed them like a warm, wet womb. They could see little more than each other in their hiding place, for rain-clouds hid the moon and visibility was poor.

"Ye stupid Irish tater, 'twas but a nightbird, callin' fer 'is mate!" one man growled. "Banshees, my arse! Pipe down!"

"I've heard many a nightbird, but never the loikes o' that unholy screechin'!" Finnegan said with a shudder, crossing himself. "There's evil spirits abroad, I say!"

"Nah, Finnie. Ye ate spoiled mussels fer supper, 'tis all!" The man beside him snickered.

But even as they laughed uneasily, a sudden, low throbbing began. The rhythmic music gradually grew louder and more insistent as the moments passed, until the steamy darkness around them reverberated with the pulsing beat.

"Drums?" one man wondered aloud, voicing the unspoken fears of the others.

"Aye . . . *heathen* drums!" squeaked another, his throat suddenly dry.

"Sounds like it t' me, an' all!" the fellow beside him agreed, looking nervously over his shoulder as if he expected a feathered heathen to leap at him.

"Drums, my arse. Who'd be playing drums out 'ere?" Dan Cooper scoffed, but his tone lacked its customary conviction.

"'Oo indeed?" Tailor acknowledged in a doom-filled voice.

They moved a little closer to each other for comfort as a sudden chorus of animal shrieks and curdling whoops rose above the drumming.

"Make 'em stop, Dan. I can't stand it no more. Fer Gawd's sake, make 'em stop!" one man babbled.

The hackles rose on their necks and more than one man's bowels churned with fear. To the last of them, their palms were slick with sweat. There was something out there, all right—something they feared more than bloody Ruskin or his threats.

Chapter Eighteen

Mariah shrank into herself as Digby knelt before her and untied her feet. He reached beneath her skirts to paw her legs as he did so, his expression gloating and eager, his pewter eyes glassy with lust.

"Keep your filthy paws off me!" she hissed, flinching.

"Who's going to make me, my sweet? You? I think not. On your feet."

As the ropes fell away, feeling returned to her numbed extremities in painful prickles. But, heedless of her discomfort, Digby gripped her elbow and jerked her to a standing position.

"Make haste, dear heart," he gritted out, shoving her ahead of him. " 'Tis past time we were better acquainted."

The devil it was! Wincing, Mariah stumbled along, dragging her painful feet a little more than her condition warranted. Perhaps by slowing him down, she could buy a little time. Nathan might be here even now, watching the camp and waiting for his chance.

"My, my, Lieutenant, aren't you the big, brave one. 'Tis

child's play to make a woman with her hands tied do your bidding, but Angus Ruskin is another matter. Surely you don't think that ox will stand by and let you have me. Never! He wants me for himself, and he despises you—just as I do. When he finds me gone, he'll cut out your heart, Digby! Cut it out and eat it raw. Or slit your throat, like Foxy's."

A flicker of irritation crossed Digby's face. "Hardly, my dear. Much as I detest your precious convict, he's by far the better man in a fight. So you see, Ruskin's as good as dead, once Kincaid finds him." He smiled, cat-like. "Clever of me, wasn't it? And such a tidy way to end things, too. While Kincaid finishes off the Scot, I double back for you. I doubt I've even been missed, on a moon-dark night like this!"

"Aye, Jonathan'll take care of Ruskin," she admitted, "but what guarantee do you have that he won't come after you? None that I can see. You'd best think again, Digby. Your precious plan has as many holes as a sieve," she jeered.

Digby stopped dead in his tracks, then made a herculean effort to cover his blunder. "Kincaid? Well, naturally I . . . I shall . . ."

"Aye? Go on." 'Twas clear the fool had failed to consider this event! "You'll what?" she pressed, needling him.

"I shall use you to bring him to me!" Digby said with a triumphant chuckle. "Mariah, you'll be my sacrificial lamb. And I'll take care of Kincaid when he comes for you—as I know he will, should he survive."

A few minutes later, he jerked her to a halt beneath two sea-grape trees some distance from camp. "Here will do. I trust you approve of the spot I've chosen, mlady. . . ?"

"You ask my approval? How very touching!" Mariah mocked. "But what difference does it make, really? When one is forced to wallow with swine, one still reeks of the sty afterwards, does one not?" She turned to face him, giving him such a disdainful look from beneath her sable lashes that heated color mottled Digby's cheeks.

"Another baring of your sharp claws, my dear, and I'll skin that pretty back!" Without further ado, he forced her to her knees on the sand and roughly shoved her onto her back. In almost the same move, he fell across her, his weight slamming the breath from her, his knees forcing her legs apart, so that he was lodged between her thighs.

"Nooo!" she cried, pushing at his chest with all her strength.

"Just 'nooo.' Is that all you can say? No witty jibes, Mariah? But, how so, m'lady? Has the cat got your tongue?"

Winding his fist in a handful of her hair, he twisted her head around and ground his mouth over hers, so viciously his teeth drew blood.

Disgust and terror rose up her throat in a gagging flood. Dear God, she couldn't breathe with his weight crushing her, and his foul mouth was locked over hers—he was smothering her!

Her breath came in desperate gasps as she flailed at his hated head. Tearing out fistfuls of his pale hair, she screamed at him to stop; swore he would not do as Edward had done, leave her with a legacy of pain and shame, and a terror of all men. Jonathan had shown her how beautiful love could be between a man and a woman. Jonathan had set her free. . . .

"Never again! You won't sully this for me—not you, nor any man! I've come too far, gained too much to lose it all. I won't—I won't let you. Damn youuu!"

She tried to squirm aside, to slither from beneath him and escape, but her flimsy efforts seemed to amuse rather than deter him. He dragged his mouth from hers and laughed in her face.

"You should never have chosen Kincaid over me, Mariah. He's nothing—a convict, a lout unworthy of your beauty and your breeding—while I am both an officer and a gentleman."

"Gentleman? You?" she scoffed, contempt in every line of her face as she glared up at him. "You're a pompous, preening arse, Digby—and that's *all* you'll ever be!"

"You haughty bitch!" he snarled. "When you see how Ruskin's men look up to me after tonight, you'll learn your

273

folly. You'll regret squandering yourself on him, and you'll beg to be my woman.''

"Never! I'll never beg to belong to you. Why would I settle for a court-jester, when I can have the King of Kissers for my love?''

Livid, he grasped her wrists in one fist and forced them up, above her head. Breathing heavily, he held them there and, with his free hand, yanked her bodice from the band of her skirts. Sucking in a breath, he plunged his hand beneath it to knead the cool curves of her breasts and to pinch their soft pink buds, so sharply she yelped with pain.

"Scoff if you will, Mariah. But the 'jest' will be on you, before I'm done!'' he threatened, smiling thinly at his witty pun as he thrust up her skirts.

When she felt him grasp her thighs, the bruising pressure of his knee pushing between then, she almost swooned, Her bid for time had failed. Jonathan could not stop him now. . . .

The darkness of that Time-Before-Nathan beckoned; the familiar darkness that offered amnesia and peace, escape from fear and pain. Blackness began to crowd out the white-bright, sharp-angled edges of reality. Velvet oblivion replaced it, softer than moth-wings, lighter than gossamer. . . .

As if from far away, she heard Digby's grunt of triumph, but felt his prodding fingers only vaguely, as though this were happening to another. She sensed him shift his weight to free his member, but her limbs had grown flimsy as cobwebs; her resistance was smoke on the wind.

With the knowledge that he'd won, that she'd failed yet again, had come merciful withdrawal. Like the tissue-paper petals of a poppy-flower, she was gliding into a black void where the Edwards and the Digbys and their kind could not follow her; she was a fairy dust-mote caught in a beam of ebony light, drifting aimlessly, remote from her helpless shell, unmoved by its plight. Whatever happened next, the horror could not reach her, not there . . . not now, where she had fled; into the farthest reaches of her soul. . . .

"Now!" Digby snarled, brutally thrusting forward.

" 'Now' my arse!" hissed Nancy from behind him. She raised her dagger aloft and plunged the blade deep into his hunched back.

Frozen in mid-motion, Digby went rigid. He threw up his arms and skewed sideways, a bubble of scarlet froth escaping his lips and trickling down his chin. With a gurgling groan, he slumped across Mariah and lay still.

Nancy swore, disgusted with herself, for he was not dead, more was the pity. Nay. The randy sod was wheezin' like a bleedin' squeeze-box with a 'ole in it.

"Come on!" she urged when Mariah made no effort to slide from beneath the lieutenant's body. "We in't got all bleedin' night, yer know, ducks! Upsadaisy!"

But Mariah continued to stare up at the night sky, unaware that Digby lay across her, or that his blood stained them both.

Just then, the full moon floated free of its misty veil of rain-clouds for the first time that night. By its light, Nancy could see the ghastly pallor of Mariah's face, the emptiness of her turquoise eyes. Muttering, "'Strewth!" and shaking her head about lily-livered twits, she shoved Digby unceremoniously aside and smacked Mariah hard across the cheek, so hard the stinging slap made tears well instantly.

"Oh!" Mariah blinked and gasped in shock. "What . . . ?"

"Don't gimme 'wot'—I belted ye, that's wot! An' wot's more, ye needed it! Now, pull yerself together an' get up!" Nancy snapped. Knowing she must be stern to jolt Mariah from her shock, she grasped her wrists and hauled her upright. "Kincaid's come for ye."

"Nathan? He's here?" At the mention of his name, joy came to her face. Life and vitality returned to her eyes. "Really?"

"That's wot I said, innit? He an' Joe have bin lookin' all over for you, ducks—we all was. Now I've found yer, I reckon we'd best find the lads an' scarper. When that soddin' Rusk hears you 'n' Kincaid 'ave flown the coop, I don't want t' be here, thank ye kindly. Come on!''

"Damn ye, ye scurvy swabs! There's nae savages here! 'Tis a trick!'' Ruskin roared as his half-dozen loyal followers broke from cover and scattered to the four winds, almost flattening him as they barreled past. "Come back, blast yer eyes, 'else I'll. . . .''

But there was no one left to hear his threats. No one left to care what he would or would not do. He was quite alone. And, as he stood there, pondering his next move, the drumming that had unhinged his men began again.

A thin, mirthless smile split his fleshy lips. Lawyer Kincaid's wee tricks, 'else he was an Englishman!

Muttering a foul oath, Ruskin turned slowly about, scanning the mangrove swamps about him for some sign of the hidden drummer.

Lofty trees that grew down to water's edge blocked the moonlight. Their bulk plunged the reeds and grasses fringing the swamps into inky shadow, shadow that might hide the lantern-eyes and snapping jaws of a crocodile. . . .

Crocodile?

Ruskin stirred uneasily, shifting his bulky weight onto his other boot. He took a firmer grip on the handle of his cutlass as he again looked about him, his deep-set eyes narrowed.

Where the devil were they?

Salty runnels of sweat streamed down his face, stinging his eyes as he tried to distinguish a human form in the undergrowth all around him. He could not. Och, that blasted drumming! The sound had wormed its maggoty rhythm into his brain! He couldna think straight fer its poundin'.

"Here's what ye wanted all along, is it no', Kincaid?'' he called loudly. "You and me, man t' man, blade t' blade? Well, here I am, laddie. Come an' get me, if ye want yer bonnie whore!''

There was no answer, save the heartbeat of the drums, and Ruskin's bowels began to churn.

''I know you're there, ye scurvy swab! Come oot an' fight like a man, damn ye!'' he bellowed.

Something stirred. Aye, it did! He caught a flicker of movement out of the corner of his eye and spun in that direction.

From the branches of the trees at water's edge trailed liana vines, hundreds of them. Leafy mangrove crowns huddled above the surface of the swamp, like monstrous spiders in the moonlight, for every crown had grizzled, witchy roots that hung down beneath it, then vanished into the water like countless hairy legs. Standing where he was, upon on a small spit of land that jutted into the swamp, 'twas as if he were surrounded on three sides by the black bars of a crude, circular cell. Not a situation he cared for . . .

Och, have done wi' yer fancies, ye auld fool! Ye're startin t' sound like yer lily-livered crew! But . . .

. . . vines . . . or snakes? Mangrove roots . . . or giant spiders? How t' tell one from the other in this cursed gloom! And that flicker. . . ?

He jumped as the humid night-wind stirred, casting oily ripples across the swamp's stagnant surface so that the brackish water glinted like liquid black diamonds in the moon-light, and spread in ever-widening circles. . . .

. . . Was it but the wind stirring the water—or had something moved down there?

Ruskin wetted his lips and sucked in a nervous breath, air whistling through the gap in his front teeth as he did so; the gap, made by lawyer Kincaid's fist, had robbed him forever of his bonnie smile. Rage boiled up inside him. Bugger Kincaid! And bugger his cursed men! They were all gone now, and he doubted they'd be back. He was alone.

Well, so be it. Angus Ruskin had been alone before. He

wouldna turn tail wi' his skirts flappin' aboot his arse—nay, never! He had too much to lose.

The gent with the cats' eyes had offered him a fortune in London, he recalled, if he took the job and did it right. *Five hundred* gold sovereigns he'd dangled before his nose—och, how could a mon refuse?

Fifty sovereigns he'd taken that night, t' seal their bargain, a fat purse he'd diced away in Newgate Gaol before the Second Fleet had even set sail. The balance was awaiting him in New South Wales, at the settlement of Port Jackson. 'Twould all be his, once the gent had proof that Kincaid was dead. It wasna too late, not yet. There was still a chance they might be rescued. And if they were . . . an' if Kincaid were dead . . . och, then he could lay claim t' the gold he'd been promised and live like a laird in the New World.

"What's wrong, lawyer?" he called again. "Are ye afeared o' auld Angus—is that it. . . ?"

Finnegan ran past Ruskin as if the hounds of hell nipped at his heels, his heart flapping against his ribs, his legs pumping like pistons that kept time with the frenzied throbbing of the drums.

Blessed Mary, Mother of God, save me!

T' be sure, the banshees were abroad t'night! Or if not banshees, heathen cannibals—head-huntin' divils of darkness! Either way, he was not about to stay there and let them get him, no surr! He wanted to be out in the open, standing in the blessed light, far, far away from the cursed swamps and the jungle, where the darkness pressed all around him, rank, breathing, and alive; filled with menacing shadows and formless threats.

Finnegan burst from the undergrowth screaming. He exploded onto the moon-washed beach like a scrawny, ragged cannon-ball.

Dan and the others were not far behind him, and for all their bravado, they were little less panicked than he.

They pulled up short as Finnegan, several yards ahead of them, suddenly careened to a halt, white sand spewing from beneath his feet. He dropped to his knees as if pole-axed, and a low, keening moan escaped him, rising to an ululating howl of utter terror and despair:

"Nooooooo!"

"For the love o'Gawd, what's wiv 'im?" asked Dan.

"Look! Right there! Sweet Jesus Christ, do ye not see them?" the man beside him babbled, ashen and almost incoherent with shock.

Dan saw, and his bowels betrayed him.

Two heads lay upon the sand in the moonlight; one with the brown hair of the pickpocket, Jimmy The Weasel, the blond one that of the foppish lieutenant, Warren Digby. Two native spears, feathers about their tips, had been planted in the sand between the heads, their bamboo shafts crossed. In warning. . . ?

And then, even as they watched, all six of them glassy-eyed and open-mouthed in horror but frozen by shock, Jimmy's lips *moved*.

Dear Gawd, the severed head of their old mate was tryin' to *speak*!

"Run!" the head gibbered. *"Run!"*

Neither Finnegan nor the others needed second warning.

Chapter Nineteen

"*Yahoooo!*"

With a whoop of triumph, Joe Hardy shimmied down the rough palm trunk, so quickly his palms were burned. In his glee, he hardly noticed the sting.

"We did it!" he crowed, hopping about. "We sent 'em packin', eh, Nate? Weasel? Cor blimey, their faces! They was white as corpses, they was! If I live t' be a hundred, I won't ferget it!"

Nathan grinned as he rose from behind a scattering of boulders at the water's edge. He strode out onto the moonlit beach, leading Mariah behind him. Her hand was clasped tightly in his left one, while Carmichael's cutlass dangled from his right. Nancy followed them, beaming from ear to ear.

"Nor I!" Nathan chuckled in response to Joe's comment, catching Mari to him and planting a smacking kiss upon her lips, to her obvious delight. "Damn and blast it, Joe, the sight of their heels. . . !" Still laughing and shaking his head, he released Mariah's hand, directed a lingering smile at her, and squatted down. Using the cutlass' blade as a shovel, he began scraping sand from about Jimmy the Weasel's "severed" head, revealing the man's neck still miraculously connected to his shoulders! "And as for that voice, by God, Jimmy, 'twas inspired! If ye should ever reform, ye could be treading the boards on Drury Lane, Garrick reborn! Do it again, lad!"

"*Run! Run!*" The pickpocket obliged hoarsely, and chortled. His arms now free, he wriggled about a bit, then spryly jumped from the hole, brushing himself off. "It were worf the risk, just t' see the smile wiped orf Finnie's chops fer once— not t' mention gettin' the chance t' join yer camp, Kincaid."

"I'll second that," Nancy declared. "Water, good grub, and peace o' mind, that's wot we'll be gettin' hereon." She flung her arms about Jimmy's neck and kissed the little man's cheek by way of reward before ruffling his untidy thatch. "Yer done good, Weasel. Bloody good!"

"Ta, love!" Weasel grinned from ear to ear, clearly unaccustomed to such demonstrations of affection from the ladies. He was so puffed up with pride, he almost strutted.

"An' so did you, ducks!" Nancy declared, going up on tiptoe and planting another noisy kiss on Nathan's lips, ignoring Mariah's scowl as she did so.

Nathan kissed her back, plainly enjoying himself. He tweaked Nancy's cheek before declaring, "And now, my friends, if we're done preening, we must find the others and head back to camp." Jack Warner, Big Ben, Stiles and the others who'd posed as "native drummers" should be nearby.

Slipping his arm around Mari's waist, he ignored her scowl and pulled her close. Green eyes darkening, he added huskily, "'Tis almost dawn. And I, for one, am ready for . . . bed."

"Oh? Do you forget, sir? We were to have 'words'?" Mariah reminded him pertly. "There was a matter of some urgency you wished to discuss with me, was there not?"

"I've forgotten nothing, you minx!" he denied, clearly amused, though about what the confused onlookers were uncertain. "However, those 'words' can wait 'til morning. First things first, my sweet, hmm?"

"Oh, indeed, sir." With that comment and a naughty grin that quite banished her scowl, Mariah looked up at Kincaid, such love and desire in her radiant eyes, a lump came into Nancy's throat.

Gawd, t' feel like that about a man—and' t' have 'im feel the same! It fair gave her the collywobbles, it did! Clearing her throat, she asked, "I'm with you two, ducks, but wot about 'im? Do we leave 'im there fer the crabs?" Wrinkling her nose in distaste, the redhead nodded towards the lieutenant.

Nathan frowned. Digby was still buried up to his neck in the sand and, wounded as he was, 'twas unlikely he'd be able to free himself. When the tide turned, he'd drown, if they left him there. Nathan felt no shred of pity for the lieutenant, though to his thinking 'twas a cowardly way to be rid of the bastard. "We'll drag him above the high-tide mark and leave him. Let his Maker decide if he lives or dies of his—*God's Teeth*!"

They turned as one man, jaws dropping, eyes widening as they saw what Nathan had seen; Angus Ruskin, his wild eyes glowing, his sandy mane flying as he broke from the jungle. In his ragged blue coat and thigh-high boots, his rusty cutlass brandished above his head, he looked like a crazy old pirate as he thundered down the beach towards them. Behind him, snarling like a pack of rabid dogs, came his furious handful of ne'er-do-wells, armed to the teeth and howling with fury at those who'd made fools of them.

"Scatter!" Nathan roared. Sweeping Mari behind him, out of the way, he raised his cutlass and sprang to meet Ruskin head on. Steel rang against steel, clashing and clanging on the night air as they crossed blades.

Mariah hesitated only a second before doing as Nathan had ordered and fleeing for her life, dimly aware as she picked up her skirts and ran for the fringes of the jungle that Nancy and the other two men—both unarmed—had also scattered, pursued by Ruskin's henchmen.

Safely among the trees, she stopped and turned, pressing herself up against the trunk of a tree to watch the sword-fight. Fingers crossed, she prayed that Nathan would triumph over the lumbering Scot.

At first, Nathan was on the attack, driving Ruskin back with nimble lunges and thrusts, his weapon an extension of his arm; then the tide turned and he was on the defensive, ducking and weaving, parrying thrusts, or else hastily skipping backwards, out of reach of the wicked blade, as Ruskin cut great, whistling swathes from the air, almost cleaving Mariah's beloved in two.

The ferocity of the fight brought them to the water's edge, and to the scattering of boulders where they'd hidden just moments before. Nathan, again on the defensive, sprang up onto the rocks, then whirled and jabbed at Ruskin, nicking his shoulder with the point of his blade. Blood welled dark against the faded blue of the big Scot's coat.

"Damn yer eyes, Kincaid! That drop'll cost ye dear!" Ruskin promised, redoubling his vicious swipes. The air sang with his sweeping cross-cuts, any one of which could have hacked Nathan in two, had he not shivered away from the blade's murderous edge.

"Nay, whore-son—'tis you who'll pay!" Nathan swore, his green eyes crackling with emerald fire, his lips a thin, hard slash.

'Twas clear that Nathan was the better swordsman. Light on his feet, he danced rings about the bear-like Ruskin, and had a gentleman's experience at fencing and sword-play that Ruskin, raised in the stews of Edinburgh and on the wild Highland moors, lacked.

Nonetheless, Mariah cast about her in the patchy light for a hefty fallen bough or a weighty rock, by way of insurance should Nathan seem in need of her help. She did so deliberately, conveniently "forgetting" the tongue-lashing he'd come close to giving her earlier, when she and Nancy had found him and Joe Hardy.

"Oh, Nathan, thank God!" she'd cried, running to him, overjoyed that he'd come for her.

But he'd caught her by the upper arms and held her away from him, his relieved expression quickly masked by one that was stern indeed. " 'Thank God,' you should, madam!" he'd ground out. "And while you're at it, thank Him that I have no time for discipline at the moment, 'else I'd turn ye across my knees and wallop your pretty rump! But . . . we will have words and time anon, mistress, my word on it," he'd warned her in a lower voice that had been doubly threatening because of its deceptive softness. "I would know why you went to the pool, after I forbade you to go there with those cannibals about—"

"But—"

"—and why," he'd continued in fine spate, ignoring her, "you took it upon yourself to wage war on Ruskin, after Jack had ordered you to remain hidden?"

She'd bristled at that. "Well? What was I supposed to do? Should we women have stood by and done nothing? Watched and wrung our hands like ninnies as they slaughtered our friends!" She'd tossed her head. A small twinge of guilt and a good deal of indignation had lent a fine heat to her tone and had returned the fire to her pale cheeks. Placed on the defensive, it had seemed prudent to attack, instead! "How could I have looked you in the eye after, had we done nothing? Answer me that. As it was, we lost too many of our friends! Blast it, one would have been too many!" Remembering poor Old Peg, who'd never play the clown for them again, she'd dashed away tears with her knuckles.

But Nathan, curse him—bless him!—had seemed unmoved. Setting his jaw, he'd promised ominously, "Anon . . ." And had let her simmer in a broth of doubt until his comment about "bed" had revived her hopes that she would—eventually—be forgiven.

Stout branch in hand now, she turned back to watch the duelling pair, and saw Ruskin's knee suddenly give way. He slumped sideways, his massive body thrown off balance, and she sucked in a breath.

Nathan saw his chance. With two hands, he swung the cutlass over his head, and brought it down in a lethal curve that would have split the Scot's skull in two had it plunged home.

In the instant the blow would have connected, however, Ruskin rolled aside, and the blade struck solid rock, with an impact that sent a ringing, numbing jolt the length of Nathan's arm and shattered the blade in two. Handle and stump spilled from his fist to the rocks with a metallic *clink*.

A malevolent smile split Ruskin's fleshy lips as he realized that Nathan was now unarmed and defenseless. Certain of his victory now, he leered, showing the gap in his tiger's smile.

''Four hundred and fifty sovereigns, laddie, an' they'll all be mine someday, wi' ye dead!'' he taunted, drawing back his arm to deliver the death blow.

''Count them in hell, whore-son!'' Nathan rasped. Suddenly, he lashed out with his foot, sending a blinding drift of sand into Ruskin's eyes. While Ruskin roared and clawed at his face, Nathan sprinted for the jungle. 'Twas no time for false valor.

''Wait for me!'' Mariah cried as he plunged into the undergrowth alongside her.

He pulled up short, his green eyes widening in surprise, then disbelief, then fury. With a look that promised Hell to pay, he caught her hand and all but dragged her after him.

Chapter Twenty

"I'll send ye t' hell yet, lawyer!" Angus Ruskin snarled, clawing the sand from his streaming face. "Ye willna escape me this time!" With a moan of pain and outrage, he lumbered in pursuit.

His stinging eyes and the painful nick to his shoulder, which stung like the devil and was bleeding profusely, had refueled his fury. Men or no men, he'd find that cursed lawyer and lop off his blasted head! But first—a slow, evil grin wreathed his fleshy jowls—first, he'd make Kincaid watch, bound and helpless, while he put that bonnie Mariah through her paces. . . .

The prospect pleased him; anticipation sent a pleasant weight and heat to his groin. With a howl, he charged for the tree-line where he'd seen Kincaid and the wench disappear.

The light vanished the moment he left the beach behind. He plunged between towering trees and lush, leafy shrubs, dangling creepers, and feathery ferns—and could not negate the uneasy feeling as he did so that they'd swallowed him up like a living thing.

Here, 'twas as if someone had pinched out a giant candle, for the fading silver of the moonlight and the pearly-pink glow of the coming dawn could not penetrate the leafy tree-tops that all but met far above his head. From the ashy grey-white of the sand, from curving palm trunks bleached silver and platinum, from a bright, glassy sea stained the color of old gold, he was plunged into the moist, deep-green shadow of the slumbering jungle. He sniffed deeply. By God, the sharp, wet, fecund stench was like the reek of a young, ripe whore in his nostrils!

Stepping high through lush dew-sodden grass in his unwieldy sea-boots—stolen from a bloated, fish-nibbled corpse the same day he'd crawled ashore from the wreck—he thrashed about in search of the pair, swinging his cutlass to right and left, and cursing the gloom . . . cursing the lianas that brushed his cheeks like serpents' tongues . . . cursing the wily roots that tried t' trip him . . . cursing the tangled vegetation that plucked at his arms like greedy claws and made a thorough search impossible. *Jesu!* They could be hidin' but a foot or two away from him, mockin' him, and he wouldna know it in this maze! 'Twas akin t' lookin' for a needle in a haystack, hopeless enough t' make many a mon give up the chase. . . . *But not him!* He thought of them clinging to each other, their hearts thundering wi' fear, their palms wet with sweat as he came closer, closer; and he knew he'd never give up, not this time, not 'til he had them.

There was, moreover, over four hundred sovereigns waiting fer him if he killed the lawyer. That prospect alone did wonders for a mon's flagging spirits! He thought of the grog-shop he would build at Port Jackson once they were rescued; the comely lassies he'd buy t' please him, the fine victuals he'd sup—och, the power and pleasure so much gold could bring a man!

And so, with the blinkered perseverance of the dumb, bovine creature he resembled, he blundered on.

* * *

"Oh, God! I can hardly breathe! And I've a—ah—stitch in my side!"

"'Tis not much farther, love. Come, take my hand—you can do it! See?" Nathan pointed. "There's the top of the ridge, right there. The wild-boar track will lead us straight home, once we reach it. Just a few more yards, and ye can rest, darling. Make haste!"

She nodded mutely, too winded to say more as they clawed their way up the almost vertical walls of the steep ravine on hands and knees, using tussocks of sere grass or rocky outcroppings for handholds. Sometimes, she slithered downwards almost as many feet as she'd climbed when a shower of loose rocks or shale gave way beneath her, skinning her knees and elbows raw as she went, but there was no time to give way to tears, or even to draw breath. Consequently, she was grateful beyond words for the strong, comforting hand Nathan extended to haul her up the last few feet.

Once they'd crawled over the edge, she flopped down on her belly and lay against the sandy earth, her cheeks filled with heat, her heart thundering so hard, it felt as if it would explode from her rib-cage, her legs trembling uncontrollably.

Nathan, his own chest heaving, his nut-brown face dewed with beads of sweat, dropped onto his knees, then sprawled alongside her.

"By God, 'tis a damned sight easier sliding down this blasted slope than climbing up it!" he said with feeling, remembering the day of the pig-hunt, when he and Tim had slithered down the slope to watch the natives beach their canoes, then followed them to their village.

"I wager . . . it is. But . . . Nathan . . ." she panted, her tone urgent.

"Aye?" he rasped, still breathing heavily.

"There's something . . . I must tell you, . . . right now. It can't wait."

288

He rolled over onto his side and, leaning on his elbow, regarded her seriously.

In the light of the rising sun, he was so very handsome, so very dear to her, he almost took her breath away as, catching her hand and drawing it to his lips, he murmured, "And I have something t' tell you, too, goddess."

"Really?"

He nodded. "Mari . . ." he began, his voice husky with emotion, his green gaze tender as it rested on her flushed face.

"Nathan . . ." she began, her own voice smoky.

". . . I love you!"

They said it together, then laughed helplessly as they tumbled weakly into each other's arms, giddy with the wonder of having chosen precisely the same moment to utter those three, precious words, and with the joy of knowing they felt the same.

They kissed feverishly, their lips hungry for the taste of each other, needing the intimacy of kisses and embraces both to confirm that they were truly together again and to celebrate their joy of loving and being loved.

"Oh, God, Mari, my sweet, my heart! I feared I'd lost ye t' that blackguard." Nathan groaned, showering little kisses over her muddied cheeks, her nose, her throat, between endearments.

"And I! 'Twas why I promised myself I'd tell you how I felt the very moment you rescued me . . . if you rescued me," Mari confessed, tears of laughter sparkling in her eyes as he nuzzled her ear, then stabbed the very tip of his hot, moist tongue inside it so that she came instantly afire with longing.

He loved her, just as the shell's song had promised! Oh, How could she possibly contain the delicious, bubbly feeling his words had given her? She wanted to tell the whole wide world that he loved her, just as she loved him; to stand on the island's highest peak and scream it at the top of her lungs!

Situating herself on his lap, she cuddled up against his chest, loving the feel of the arms holding her tight; loving the strength of his broad chest beneath her cheek, the strong, comforting beat of his heart. His arms were her oaken fortress, her castle's sturdy walls; within them, she felt safe, protected. As long as he held her, loved her, nothing could ever harm her again. *Nothing—and no one!*

Sir Jonathan, her beloved, her valiant knight, was there to slay all dragons.

Looking down at her adorable face streaked with mud and dirt, Nathan was overwhelmed by tender feelings. How would he have gone on living if he'd lost her? How would he have endured the days to come, knowing he would never hold her in his arms again? And he could never have withstood the long, empty nights without her warmth and sweetness to dispel their gloom. From his lust and her need and fear, and from their loneliness, had grown beauty and love. And, now that he'd found her, he would never let her go.

Lowering her gently to the ground beside him, he cradled her in his arms as he kissed the shadowed hollows of her throat, then drew the ragged edges of her bodice down to bare her lovely breasts.

Her turquoise eyes as radiant as the paling stars with desire, she gasped and moaned softly as he took first one pink bud, then the other, between his lips, and then twined her hands in his ebony hair to press his head to her bosom, as if she feared he would cease his ardent caresses.

He suckled deeply upon each tender peak until it blossomed and swelled, sending sizzling streamers of fire from each sensitive nubbin to that secret blaze between her thighs.

"Take me . . . oh, take me, my love!" she whispered, opening herself, drawing him onto her. Her eyes were darker now and half-closed, filled with silent entreaty, her lips full and rosy, her face and body flushed with passion as she caressed him. She teased his flat male nipples with her fingertips until they hardened, became dark-rose buttons, then traced the ebony T of his chest hair down over his hard, tanned belly to the bulky knot of his breeches. Covering the firm ridge of his arousal with her palm, she added huskily, "I can wait no longer. Now, I beg you!"

Her fevered pleas aroused him as surely as the silken texture of her skin and the touch of her palm upon him. *Jesu, how she enflamed him!* From a shadow of a woman who'd feared and loathed all men, she'd become the passionate lover of his dreams, glorious and sensual as nature had intended. No longer afraid, she gave herself wholeheartedly to him with a sweet, wild, wanton abandon.

Shrugging from his breeches, he eased himself upon her, his virile hardness and heat covering her smaller feminine form as he gathered her into his arms. As his flesh met hers, he groaned like a soul in torment, for the sensation of firm, warm breasts crushed beneath his own hard and hairy chest was arousing beyond belief. It made the very breath catch in his throat.

"I love you, Mari," he growled as, raising her hips, he thrust forward, plunging deep into the heat of her.

She cried out as his hardness filled her, with a pleasure so exquisite it bordered on torment. But, mindful that Ruskin might even now be drawing closer, Nathan silenced her cries with his mouth, kissing her with sweet-savage lips as he thrust deeper and faster between her thighs, sending her passion soaring with his.

Little by little, it grew lighter. Birds woke in their roosts, their calls breaking the eerie hush as the sun came up in a burst of gold. Their hooting shrieks and loud, raucous whoops sounded like human laughter—aye, laughter straight from the bowels of Bedlam, Ruskin thought, and like nae real bird-song of which he had ken. Were they real bird-calls, he wondered uneasily, or but more o' lawyer Kincaid's wee tricks?

Ye'll not fool me as ye fooled ma foolish laddies! he vowed, setting his jaw.

The noise the monkeys were making as it grew lighter was

real enough, curse them. The little demons chittered and chattered in the crowns of the trees way above him, grimacing at him from between the leaves with their wizened little pink faces. To Ruskin, it seemed the little bastards were making fun of him. Well, by God, they wouldna!

"Come doon here, ye ugly wee brutes, an' I'll break my fast on a spoonful o' your brains!" he threatened. Picking up a stone, he hurled it into the trees above him.

The injured monkey let out a shriek of pain and fear as the stone struck it. Its cries sent the others of the colony leaping through the tree-tops in all directions, screeching as they fled.

Ruskin grinned, well pleased that he'd scared the beasts off, but his smile quickly faded. That tree—the one with the vines that looked as if they'd been plaited like a lassie's hair—wasna that the same blasted tree he'd passed not long since? he asked himself, swatting away the cloud of tiny flies that were feasting on his wound.

He didn't know.

Truth was, he was a creature of the cities; the stews of London and Edinburgh, with their dark, narrow alleys, twisting rabbit-warren streets and wharves, were his turf. Of a certainty, he was nae woodsman, and couldna find his way through this cursed jungle. He wetted his lips and frowned, wondering if he was not stumbling about in circles.

But then, just when he was close to despair, he saw daylight, dazzling blue sky and white-sand beaches, twinkling through the trees up ahead. Drawing closer, he could hardly believe his luck.

Blast his eyes, he wasna lost in this stinkin' jungle where one cursed tree looked the same as the last. Och, he knew where he was all right—in the jungle behind Kincaid's camp.

Aye, he could see it there, between the trees, a crackling fire in the center, wi' the cluster of sturdy huts built o' bamboo and woven grass scattered aboot it. There was no sign of Kincaid, nor of any of his men, and not a lassie t' be seen. Mayhap Kincaid and the Governor's niece were still lost—as he'd feared he was—desperately searching a way home before he overtook them. And mayhap the mate—Carmichael—and the rest of Kincaid's laddies were all off, looking for them.

The amusing picture that idea conjured up pleased him enormously. Bloody fools! While they frittered away their strength, he'd be waiting here, biding his time, and recovering his.

Hunkering down on his haunches, he ignored the unhappy sounds his belly was making and tried to focus his attention on the empty camp before him.

Strange . . . He didna remember seein' that big hut wi' the soaring roof that put him in mind o' a sailing ship before. Nor the massive rock almost as tall as he was, set before the opening like a pagan standing stone from the moors of his native Scotland. He blinked, then gaped, noticing for the first time the skulls that hung in clusters at each corner of the large hut, each dangling by a hank of hair. They looked like obscene bunches of ivory grapes. Whist, those death's-head grins fair gave him the creeps!

He shuddered and did something he'd never done before, he closed his eyes and almost said a prayer. Och, for a tot o' grog t' whet his whistle an' calm his nerves! There was something verra strange aboot this camp, something he couldna put his finger on, unless . . .

Kincaid must ha' gone mad! Aye, that was it—the only answer that made sense. He and his scurvy crew had labored too long and too hard in the cursed heat. They'd all gone crazy as rabid dogs.

He must have nodded off, for when he awoke he could hear drumming again, coming from somewhere close by.

Kincaid, will ye no give up, laddie? I'm on t' yer wee games! he thought drowsily, smiling.

Opening bloodshot, swollen eyes, he saw that the camp between the trees was no longer deserted. Several men in fantastic costumes cavorted about the fire, chanting in time to the hypnotic heartbeat of the drums and flutes, and bowing low as they passed the upright stone, as if it were an altar. They wore capes of brilliant feathers about their shoulders, feather head-dresses with dancing plumes, and naught else but narrow strips of leather for a loincloth. Their brown-skinned faces were frighteningly painted with horizontal stripes of white and yellow, while their eyes were ringed in blood-red. Through their flattened noses, long splinters of bamboo had been driven, according to each man's fancy. Every one of the dancers carried a long spear tipped with bone and a shield that he brandished in time to the music.

Ruskin rose groggily to his feet, thinking as he retrieved his cutlass that Kincaid's hoax was even more elaborate than he'd given him credit for. The mon wasna just mad—he'd gone native!

"Here I come, lawyer!" he roared loudly, barrelling forward from between the bushes, his cutlass raised.

Grinning, he tried to put names to the costumed men, who whirled to face him as the drums fell ominously silent. Why, surely that skinny lad was Tim Bright, the *Hester*'s cabin boy? And that strapping young cock over there—the stocky lout whirling Cooper and Finnie's heads about by the ruddy hair— that must be . . .

Heads? Oh, blimey, nay!

The blood drained from his face. He went cold all over, ice-cold, cold as Death, as he realized he'd made a fatal mistake. The natives were na' Kincaid's men. These were *real* head-hunters, the camp their own heathen village! His bulging eyes riveted to those whirling, bloody heads, he tried to back away. But of a sudden, his booted feet were frozen to the ground.

His mouth dropped open in a silent scream as the oldest head-hunter raised a hand and pointed to him, screaming "*Puk-puk! Puk-puk!*" like a madman.

As one, the native youths converged on Ruskin, their excited mumblings like the deafening drone of giant bees. At last— but far too late to save him—Ruskin's teacherous legs obeyed

294

his frantic commands. Tripping, stumbling, babbling like a lunatic, he started to run, blundering through the jungle and begging for his life as he fled, while a dozen youthful initiates of the crocodile manhood society pursued him for their admission requirement—his sandy head. . . .

Chapter Twenty-One

"I think we should be starting back."

"Can you see Ruskin?" she whispered, alarmed. She started to get up, for Nathan looked troubled.

"Nay, Mari, there's no sign of him down below, my love. Don't panic. It's just . . . well, let's just say I have a feeling in my bones that he won't give up. I could see it in his eyes, when we fought on the beach. Aye, he's out there, somewhere, and as long as we both draw breath, he'll be coming after me— and you. I'd feel a damned sight safer if we were well on our way back t' camp within the hour." He paused and frowned. "Damn Ruskin t' hell! Maybe I'm addlewitted, but I don't understand it."

"Understand what?"

"Why he's so blasted determined to see me dead."

"That's easy. You fought with him in Newgate, did you not?"

"Aye—and won," he admitted with a thin-lipped smile of bloodthirsty relish.

"There's your answer. His blind hatred of you is only natural, given the sort of beast he is," Mariah observed seriously.

She stood and brushed off her clothing. Then, without further ado, she reached down, between her legs, and drew the back hem of her skirts to the front, tucking the cloth securely into the waistband of her petticoats to form a voluminous but serviceable pair of pantaloons. It would be much easier to walk with her skirts hitched up, rather than fighting full, flapping petticoats every step of the way.

While she adjusted the hang of her makeshift garment for comfort, she continued, "Ruskin's an ignorant, brutish lout. And when someone like that holds a grudge, he's like a carthorse with blinkers, 'til he's avenged himself. In his blind rage, he stupidly sees but one course of action open to him—violence—and will not swerve from it, even when that course might kill him."

"I suppose you're right, love. What you say makes perfect sense. But," he sighed, shaking his head, "I have this . . . this plaguey, unreasonable doubt gnawing at my innards that has nothing to do with sense. Blast it, my gut, if you will, tells me there's more to it than that." He grinned ruefully and, she fancied, a little bashfully. "*Ma mère*—my mother—always claimed I'd inherited her sixth sense from the fey French branch of our family tree. Maybe that intuition is trying to tell me something—to warn me."

"I've heard stranger things. But warn you of what?"

He shrugged, at a loss to explain. "Lord knows! I've wondered sometimes if—but nay, 'tis too preposterous. Forget I said anything."

"Nay, tell me!" she insisted, her hand on his arm, her expression searching as she looked up into his darkly handsome, troubled face. "What did you wonder?" she pressed.

"If Ruskin's not somehow connected to that damnable Octagon conspiracy!" he admitted with obvious reluctance. He shot her a defiant scowl, as if he thought she might laugh at him. "Aye, aye, I know 'tis far-fetched, and that I must sound like a fearful spinster who sees robbers under her pallet each night—"

"Not so! Under the circumstances, 'tis nothing of the sort."

"—but look at it this way. Once the conspirators realized that I'd cheated the hangman that Friday morn, they must have been frantic to discover my whereabouts and silence me, right?"

She nodded. "Aye. Go on."

"Given that my father had successfully bribed my gaolers—had had me spirited out of Newgate and England at the eleventh hour—then t'would have been child's play for the Octagon—with eight powerful conspirators and countless resources at their disposal—to also bribe, or coerce, my turnkeys into telling them they'd smuggled me aboard the *Hester*."

"And then hire Ruskin to silence you," she finished for him.

"Aye," he said heavily, darting her a grateful look. Bless her, she hadn't so much as smiled, let alone laughed at him. In fact, judging by her deeply thoughtful expression, she actually seemed to think his wild fancies might have some merit. "Ruskin had been sentenced to transportation for life before I was arrested. And there was little likelihood of his being found out, not on that poxy voyage! He could have killed me a dozen times over and none been the wiser, had we been shackled in close quarters. Fortunately for me, we were not."

"None the wiser—how so?"

"If you recall, the First Fleet was well fitted out and efficiently supplied, thanks to Governor Philip's careful planning and his insistence on its being adequately prepared. As a result, the lives lost during that first voyage were relatively few.

"Our sorry Second Fleet was not nearly so fortunate. Rather than the worthy Philip's hand-picked skippers, our transport captains were greedy, unscrupulous merchants, like that bastard Harkabout, for the greater part. Men who cared nothing for the convicts placed in their care. God's Teeth, Mari, below-

298

decks, we were losing men, women, and little children—even babies—like flies, to disease, lack of vittles, and overcrowding—and these deaths came within days of our sailing from England.

"If my instinct is sound, I would have been but one more sorry corpse to be slipped over the *Hester*'s side in a shroud of sail-cloth! Nay, sweet, Ruskin had naught to lose by undertaking to murder me, escaped gallows-bait! And perhaps he had a great deal to gain."

"But if you're right, surely the shipwreck would have put an end to his ambitions?"

"You'd think so. Still, perhaps like Caroline, Tim Bright, and the others, Ruskin's hope of being rescued has simply refused to die. Aye, Mari, the more I think on it, the more convinced I am that I'm not far wrong. I'd wager my right hand that Ruskin believes he might yet stand to profit from my death."

She nodded agreement. "But what of your other reasons?"

"Other reasons for what?"

"For leaving here with all haste?"

"Ah. That." He pinched the bridge of his nose again. The dull throbbing behind his eyes had returned full-force. "I noticed the sky, my love. Look, over there, t' the east. Now that the sun's up, d' ye see how red and rosy it is? There's an old saying: 'Red sky at night, sailors' delight. Red sky in the morning—' "

" '—sailors warning,' " she finished for him. "Are we in for bad weather, then?"

"Before long, aye. And I'd feel easier if we were snugly battened down in our own camp, before it breaks." He did not say so, but he was also anxious to make sure his men had returned safely, from their sortie into the convicts' den. God willing, he'd lost no more of them! The news that Old Peg and the marine Babbington were dead, Stiles injured, had been hard enough to accept.

"Are you all right?" she asked.

"What, me?" He looked up and managed a wry grin. "Aye, love, as right as any man can be after he's battled his enemies half the night and made love to an insatiable wench for the other half!"

"La! If you're after sympathy, sir, you won't get any from me," she retorted cheekily, "I wouldn't have missed last night for the world!"

"No more would I, vixen. Let's go!"

As Nathan had feared, the sky grew steadily gloomier that morning, hiding the sun as they followed the wild-boar trail that wound down through the mountains.

The grass here had been worn away by animals heading for the pool in the jungle-valley far below each morning and evening to drink, or to find a cool mud-wallow. Their passage had left a path of rutted earth scattered with stones. In places, this track was four or more feet wide, while in others it measured little more than two feet. Sheer, almost vertical, walls dropped away on Mariah's left, while far below lay dense vegetation, grassy emerald meadows, and rushing rivers hidden within narrow, plunging ravines that were impenetrable, except by viewing from above.

After they'd followed the trail for about an hour, they came to one of these deep cuts, the precarious-looking native bridge of knotted vines strung across it like a hairy spider-web.

Mariah's heart rose into her mouth when she saw the bridge. She pulled up short, balking. Her grip upon Nathan's hand tightened convulsively. *Dear God, nay!* She'd already endured so much that morning, fearfully letting Nathan lead her along the terrifyingly narrow mountain track they'd been forced to follow. For, although she could take reptiles—both four-and two-legged—and countless other strange and unlovely creatures like poisonous insects in her stride, she'd always hated and feared high places. Indeed, just looking at that fragile bridge swaying gently to and fro in the blustery damp breeze that had suddenly arisen, and at the rushing river far below, made her belly heave.

Whimpering, she pressed her back to the mountain wall and pulled her hand free of Nathan's, refusing to take another step. One more, just one, and she would surely fall to her death.

"Nay, don't look down, sweet," Nathan cautioned softly when he turned to discover the reason she'd halted and broken his hold. Ashen-faced and trembling as she was, his game little Mari was obviously scared witless. She'd plastered herself against the cliff as if nailed to it, her arms and legs spread-eagled, her spine welded to the rocky face of the mountain.

"We don't have to cross it, do we?" she moaned, her eyes wild with fear. "For pity's sake, tell me we don't!"

"We don't," he reassured her firmly.

"Thank God!" she whispered, biting her lip. Swaying dizzily, she closed her eyes, trying to stanch the tears that threatened to spill from beneath her eyelids. She was utterly exhausted, drained, weak with hunger, too weary to even pretend to be brave a moment longer. And standing there, terrified and desperate, was painfully reminiscent of that awful moment the day before.

Then, surrounded by leering, hooting convicts, she'd stood alone upon the rocky edge of the point, looking down on craggy black rocks, like fangs waiting to devour her, and deciding to take her own life.

Thinking about those moments made a cold, clammy sweat break out on Mariah's brow and palms. How in the world had she dared to even think of such a thing, let alone do it! Nevertheless, she'd been fully prepared to embrace a quick, clean end by jumping to her death, rather than endure the awful fate that would befall her at the convicts' hands; reconciled, until that the last, awful moment when she'd stepped into space and realized—too late—that she wasn't ready to die, after all. . . .

"Mariah, look at me! I said, we don't have to cross the bridge," Nathan repeated sternly, grasping her chin and forcing her to look at him.

"A-aye," she stammered. "I-I heard you. But . . . but I can't go on! The path, it's too narrow—and I'm so frightened. Oh, God, I'll fall, I know I shall. We both will! Oh, please, oh, can't we stay here?"

She opened her eyes then, and the expression on Nathan's face made her heart founder. His answer was no.

With an apologetic expression, he tugged off the twisted scarlet neck kerchief he wore like a bandanna about his brow and shook it out, folding the square of cloth into a triangle. A blindfold? For her?

"Come, let's cover your eyes, and I'll lead you."

"Not on your life!" she protested, trying to shrink into the cliff. "Do you take me for a fool?"

"'Tis the best way, Mari. Trust me. If you can't see what's below, you'll be less fearful."

"Nothing could make me less fearful," she insisted vehemently, shaking her head.

"You don't know 'til you try. Won't you trust me and try it?" he coaxed in his deep, gentling voice. "Remember, I love you, Mariah—more than anything in this world. I'd never hurt you or put you at risk, you know that. Won't you be brave, my love? For me?"

The cunning rogue, to play upon her feelings for him! But, in all honesty, she knew she was only deluding herself. They had to go on, whether she wanted to or nay. They couldn't perch here, upon this narrow track, indefinitely. Drawing a deep, shuddering breath, she nodded shakily. "All right. You win. I'll . . . I'll do my b-best."

"That's my girl!"

He slipped the bandanna about her eyes and knotted it securely behind her head. Then, taking both of her hands in his, he began slowly leading her down the path. A blindfold oftimes calmed frightened horses, he recalled with a rueful smile.

Hopefully, it would do the trick for his skittish Thoroughbred, Mariah!

To his relief, foot by foot, they began to make progress. And, despite her initial misgivings, Mariah had to admit it was easier this way and far less frightening, just as Nathan had promised. Unable to see what fate awaited her down below should she fall, she was not quite so terrified, and her limbs were no longer paralyzed with fear.

"There's a deeper ledge with a cave along here," he said after some time. "Me and the lads passed it the day of the pighunt. We'll rest there."

"Just in time, I fancy," she said breathlessly, gingerly placing one foot before the other, her hands gripping his. "Do you feel that? It's starting to rain." Fat droplets wetted her cheeks and misted her hair.

"'Tis but a shower. Just a few more yards, and we can shelter from it. God willing, it won't last long, and we can go on afterwards."

Before they reached the cave and flung themselves inside, the spitting shower had became a downpour that soaked them to the skin. Mariah tore off her blindfold when she and Nathan finally huddled side by side in the cave-mouth, to stare out at the dismal terrain beyond.

Glimpsed through sheeting rain that was swirled by sudden fierce gusts of wind, which moaned and howled like Finnie's banshees, the island's lush green mountain ridges and plunging ravines were heavily shrouded by mist and clouds. The sky was dark and ominous-looking, low-hung and brooding, offering little hope that, as Nathan had so optimistically promised, the deluge would be short-lived.

Although it was only morning, it had grown as dark as in late evening. The air was oppressively humid and close. 'Twas as if the end of the world was nigh. Mariah shivered despondently in her wet bodice and skirts.

Glancing over at Nathan, she saw that he'd dozed off sitting upright, leaning against the entrance to the cave. How she envied him! Tenderness filled her as she reached out to caress his cheek. Poor Nathan. He must be exhausted. She sighed and stood up. Too fidgety and restless to sleep herself, she looked around.

The cave was broad at its mouth, forming a recess about ten feet across and fifteen feet deep, but then it narrowed into a pitch-dark tunnel. She stood there, at the opening, her head cocked to one side. She could hear leathery rustling sounds and faint squeaks deep in the bowels of the mountain, and knew what creatures made those sounds. She shuddered. *Bats!*

Drawing quickly away from the tunnel, she looked around the dank cavern instead, sniffing and wrinkling her nose at its rank odors. Small animal bones littered the cave floor, the remains of some hungry predator's meal. There was also a piece of timber that looked too evenly fashioned to have been a piece of tree that had broken off and found its way here by chance. Curious, she carried it to the cave-mouth and brushed years of grit from its surface. She was right! The shattered plank, obviously once part of a sailor's sea-chest, had been carved with a name, an initial that looked like an *A*. That was followed by the name Tasman. Deciding to show Nathan her find when he woke, she propped the plank against the cave's wall and returned to the cave-mouth to watch the rain.

Visibility had decreased markedly in just the few minutes she'd spent exploring. Now rain was falling so heavily, she could see only a few feet in front of her. Was this the beginning of the monsoon season Matherson had described? She believed so.

Resigned to a far longer wait than they'd anticipated—and in all honesty, in no great haste to continue their hazardous journey, blindfold or nay—Mariah moved closer to Nathan. Wrapping her arms about him, she rested her head in his lap. How warm he felt, she thought enviously, snuggling closer to him. Perhaps it was fear that made her so chilled, combined with fatigue and her soaking, but despite the island's steaming climate, she'd not felt warm since she, Caro, and Kitty had gone to the pool to bathe yesterday. *Yesterday!* Had it been only a day since then? With all that had happened, it seemed more like a lifetime ago.

When she awoke, the rain had stopped, although the air was still damp and steamy. There was a deep puddle before the cave. Streamers of mist drifted between the ravine walls, and thick grey rain-fleeces blanketed the mountain ridges, obscuring their peaks. The sky was the color of slate, the sun invisible. There was no way of knowing from its color how long she—they—had slept. It could be close to noonday . . . or early evening.

"Damn their eyes! Strike the bloody irons, I say! Can't . . . can't let the devils drown. . . ."

She all but jumped out of her skin. Nathan's sudden loud, outburst had been so unexpected in the broody silence.

"What did you say, love?" she asked softly. But turning, she realized he was still asleep, and dreaming. Tossing his head from side to side, his limbs twitching, he argued incoherently with people she could not see.

". . . never forget his face—nay. He was one of them, damn his soul! Someday . . . clear my name . . . you'll see, Father. Make you . . . make you proud of me . . . Oh, God, naaay! Roger! Roger, get up, man! Damn it, you're not dead! You can't be!"

But instead, 'twas Nathan who got up, suddenly springing to his feet with a wild shout and lunging across the cave to tackle the invisible demon who tormented him.

Mariah cried out and clutched at his elbow. "Wake up! 'Tis but a dream!" she told him, turning him by his rigid arm to face her. "Nathan! Do you hear me? Wake up, I say!"

Slowly, he turned his head to look at her, and she saw that his green eyes were glassy and distant in the gloom. Then he blinked and seemed to see her clearly for the first time. "What?" he demanded hoarsely. "What did you say?"

"You were dreaming, my love. A nightmare! Talking and fighting in your sleep."

"I didn't hurt you?"

She shook her head. "Of course not."

Muttering a curse, Nathan ran a hand through his black hair in an agitated gesture, then drew her into his arms and embraced her fiercely. "Sweet Christ, Mari! 'Twas so blasted real! I thought Roger . . . and then there was Ruskin. . . ." He shook his head, flicked it as if to clear the cobwebs of sleep away, and winced at the bodkins of pain that lanced through his skull. "Ah, well, never mind all that. How long was I asleep?"

"I don't know. I was asleep, too," she confessed.

"Look. The rain's stopped."

"Aye," she acknowledged miserably, knowing what would come next. She pulled free of his arms and crossed the cave, away from him.

"I'd say it's past noon, perhaps even later. Mari . . ."

"Aye, I know," she admitted angrily, biting her lip. They couldn't stay in the cave forever. Whether she wanted to or nay, they had to go on. What choice did they have?

If the going had been hazardous before, it was doubly treacherous following the heavy rain. The dirt track was now slick with mud, their footing in jeopardy. One false move, and they could easily slip over the edge of the ravine. Going even more slowly than they had before, they inched their way along the path like snails.

Mari found she was surprisingly glad of the blindfold. Now that death seemed even more likely, it was small comfort to know she'd never see the ground rushing up to meet her if she plunged over the edge. Instead of dwelling on that awful prospect, she instead concentrated all of her attention on the dry, burning warmth of Nathan's strong hands gripping her own, trusting him to keep her safe, loving him more and more with every faltering step she took. He would never let her down or desert her, as her father had done by marrying her off to Edward, a man he surely knew to be evil. She sighed heavily.

By rights, she knew she should have hated her father for his betrayal, his desertion of her, but . . . she could not. As a mother loves a wayward child and forgives him anything, she loved her father with all her heart, despite knowing he'd been a weak man, in many ways, and that his weakness had cost her dearly.

With a shriek, she pulled up short as she bumped heavily into Nathan, who'd suddenly halted on the track before her. Even with the blindfold on, she sensed something was terribly wrong. "What is it?" she asked, tearing the neckerchief from her eyes.

But she could see straightaway the reason Nathan had halted so abruptly. The track before him had washed completely away, leaving only a mudslide, some twenty feet across, in its place!

"We'll have to turn back," he told her heavily without turning to meet her eyes. 'Twas the coward's way, he knew, but he couldn't bear to voice her deepest fear while looking her in the face.

"And . . . and that bridge?" she asked, holding her breath and praying, praying he wouldn't say . . . She only stared at him, her turquoise eyes huge pools of dread.

Looking down, Nathan hesitated. He saw the tree-tops of the jungle clearly way below, the leafy crowns jostling each other for space; the colors of the red earth, the dark green of the trees, the grey of the dour sky blurred and ran together like watercolors. For a fleeting second, he swayed dizzily, caught himself, then blinked rapidly. When he opened his eyes again, to his relief, his vision had righted itself.

"We have no choice now. We'll have to cross it," he said, answering her unspoken question in the calmest voice he could muster.

Chapter Twenty-Two

Although it had taken them several hours to reach the mudslide, the return trek to the bridge seemed to last but hellish moments.

All too soon, it seemed to Mariah, they were standing before the narrow scaffolding of lashed vines that reached across the yawning chasm. Beads of perspiration sprang out upon her brow and upper lip as she stared at it in horrified fascination, for 'twas as if some pagan giant had been playing the children's game of cat's cradle with a piece of shaggy brown string, then had strung his efforts between the sheer sides of the ravine.

She swallowed. Dear God, the bridge was certainly no more substantial than that. The base of it was made of short lengths of bamboo lashed together—and some of the pieces were missing, leaving yawning gaps over thin air. The waist-high rails on either side were airy handholds of vine, with rather more air than handholds. Far below, the angry brown river roared and flung up furious sprays of white water as it rushed between confining walls, forced passage over numerous boulders, or spumed up against craggy ledges. *Nay.* She stubbornly set her jaw, more determined than she'd been in her life. *Come what may, no force on earth could compel her to cross this bridge!* No, not even her beloved Nathan with his coaxing voice and his gently hypnotic entreaties for her to trust him, his wounded looks that always made her weaken in an effort to please him.

"Kill me if you must," she said dully, gingerly sitting down with her back against the cliff, her arms hugging her chest. "Do whatever you want—but *I'm not crossing this bridge.* 'Tis certain death to try it!"

He sighed, looking almost grey beneath his tan—a result of fatigue and anxiety surely, she thought with a twinge of guilt, knowing she was making a dangerous situation even more difficult for him by balking, but unable to help herself.

"Mari, if we had a choice—" he began.

"But we do have a choice! We . . . we could go all the way back," she pleaded hopefully.

"Not so. Ruskin will be back there, searching for us. And the native village lies but a short distance below the ridge where we made love. Nay, Mariah, unless you wish to risk losing that pretty head of yours, I'd not wander in those parts by daylight!"

"What! Their village was so close? Why didn't you tell me! You never said a word."

"Because I saw no purpose in telling you last night. 'Twould only have frightened you. And besides, we both needed to rest. But now . . ." He shrugged. "Now we really don't have a choice."

"You're wrong, sir. I do. And I'm not crossing it!"

"You will," he exploded suddenly, gritting his teeth and casting her a murderous scowl as his patience snapped.

"No, I won't, sir!" she inisted vehemently. "And you can scowl and bellow all you want—you cannot make me."

"Blast ye, obstinate wench, I'm giving the orders here, and I say we're crossing this bridge! On your feet!" he growled, grasping her elbow and tugging. "Get up. On your feet!"

"I will not."

His scowl deepened. "I knew I should have beaten some obedience into you yesterday."

"Perhaps you should have, aye, but 'tis far too late to worry about that now. Besides, 'twould have changed nothing today. I'm not being defiant, nor am I deliberately disobedient, my love, believe me," she urged, her turquoise eyes huge and shiny with unshed tears. "I'm simply too frightened to cross the bridge—and that's that."

He straightened, looking thoughtfully down at her now, his head bowed. Then he declared softly, "Very well. If that's all there is to it, then stay here—alone. I'm going over—with *or* without you."

He was bluffing, of course he was . . . wasn't he? He wouldn't really leave her here!

But when she looked up to see Nathan stepping onto the first bamboo rung of the bridge, one hand gripping the vine "railing" on either side of him, her conviction dwindled. Without farther ado, he started across the bridge of vines, treading lightly, swiftly, over the bamboo rungs, to all intents and purposes quite unaware of how the fragile bridge bucked from side to side under his weight or swung violently back and forth in the wind, though her heart was in her mouth until he'd reached the opposite side without incident.

On the far wall of the ravine, Nathan turned to look back the way he'd come. Mari was huddled on the narrow ledge across the divide, a small, dejected figure tightly hugging her knees. Her bright red-gold head was bowed, and he knew she thought he'd deserted her and was crying.

His heart went out to her as he ruefully shook his head. *Silly little goose!* Surely she knew he'd die before he'd leave her like that, alone and afraid. She didn't think him so callous and uncaring in his love for her, did she? He'd crossed over simply to prove once and for all that there was nothing to fear, that it could be safely done. And, having done so, he'd go back now and lead her across, just as he'd led her down the narrow boar-trail—inch by inch and blindfolded, if need be! Or carry her on his back, if that's what it took. Damn it, he'd knock her out if that was the only way! God's Teeth, he'd do whatever needed doing, until they stood together, safe on the far side, and she laughed and confessed that it'd really been easy, after all.

"You see?" he yelled. "'Tis safe as London Bridge! If I can do it, you can . . . can . . ."

He swayed groggily as the dull throb behind his eyes suddenly exploded in a frisson of agony! With a low groan, he then dropped down onto one knee, his chin bowed on his chest. Kneeling there, he struggled to clear his head—his ears—of a strange rushing, roaring sound, like that of the river in full spate below. Jesu! His body felt afire with heat. *So thirsty!* He tried to moisten his parched lips with his tongue, but though he swallowed, his throat was so painfully dry, he could only gag. The bone-deep weariness that had been dogging him all day suddenly overwhelmed him He had fought it for hours, and now, when he needed his strength more than ever, he feared he could not go on. . . .

Give me a moment, Mari, my love . . . but a moment's respite, and I'll come back for ye, he promised silently, but then all went black as he pitched forward, slamming face-down into the sodden grass and mud at the edge of the ravine, toppling as if felled by a native club.

"Nathan?" Mariah called sharply, angrier with him than she'd ever been before as she saw him pitch forward. Why, that heartless, unfeeling brute! That callous beast! First, he'd called her bluff and left her behind. Now he was pretending he'd fallen, curse him, although he must know how very frightened she was, all alone on this blasted ridge. "Jonathan Kincaid, you get up right now! I know what you're up to—and it won't work. You're just wasting your time. I'm not crossing this bridge, whatever you do, Nathan. I mean it!"

She stared at his crumpled form, far on the other side of the ravine, searching for some tell-tale movement on his part. But no matter how intently she watched him, there was none.

Seconds became moments. . . .

Moments became agonizing minutes.

Get up! For the love of God, get up! she begged silently. She continued to stare at Nathan's still form until her eyes ached and her vision blurred with smarting, scalding tears. A hard, cold little knot of dread gathered in the pit of her belly. "Nathan, damn you, get up!" she screamed. "Please! Please get up! Come back!" she implored in a lower, beseeching voice.

But neither curses nor entreaties had any effect.

Well, if that was how he wanted it, then to Hades with him—two could play at that game!

Still convinced he was faking, she huddled against the cliff face in stony silence, waiting . . . waiting . . . praying for the moment when he jumped to his feet and told her she'd won, that it'd all been a cruel game, a hoax to make her swallow her fears and cross the bridge to "save" him. *Just a little test, Mariah—to discover if you truly love and trust me,* he'd say, and she'd be too relieved to know that he was all right to be angry with him.

But when minutes became an hour—at least that long, she was certain—and he'd still not moved in all that time, the tiny quiver in her belly became a huge, fluttering moth of anxiety. Could he really be ill?

Gnawing fretfully upon her lower lip, she remembered how dry and hot his hands had felt while clasping her own as they'd edged along the narrow boar-path, the odd habit he'd acquired of pinching the bridge of his nose. Had it been the start of a bad habit, or had his head been hurting him?

A deep, chilling dread swept through her then. *It was no game.* Nathan was not the unfeeling trickster, the consummate play-actor she'd accused him of being. Unless he was more spiteful—and far more patient—than she was prepared to believe possible, he was truly unconscious. But, she admitted heavily, there was only one way to find out for certain.

She must cross the bridge. Alone.

* * *

Gripped by the peculiar sensation that she was in a dream, that nothing was real, she rose to standing, her spine and her palms pressed flat against the rocky wall behind her.

It was worse, standing, for she could see straight across the fragile bridge; could see how very easily it shifted with the wind and how wild the river far below really was, as it plunged along on its narrow course. Her heart was in her mouth. *She couldn't do it!* Perhaps she should risk going back the way they'd come, take a chance on running afoul of Ruskin or the head-hunters to find her way back down to the beach. Surely anything was preferable to crossing this bridge. . . . But, sick at heart, she knew that was impossible. It would take several hours to retrace their path, still longer to find a way back up to reach Nathan from the opposite side, providing he could be reached at all. By then he might well be dead already. She must summon up what little courage she had—and all the love she carried in her heart for that wretched, impossible man— and pray it was enough to see her through this ordeal.

Swallowing, she inched forward, leaned over, and with each hand gripped one of the rough vine rails of the bridge. *So far, so good.* Now, that terrifying first step.

The bridge lurched as she planted her right foot on the first bamboo tread, and she withdrew it as if she'd been scalded. It took forever to pluck up the courage to try again. This time, she put one foot down, then quickly planted the second foot a little apart from the first, hoping by bracing her legs, her weight might stabilize the light-weight contraption. It worked! She was now standing on the first rung of the bridge, and it was hardly moving!

She started across, a step at a time, not looking down but gazing steadfastly at Nathan, only at Nathan, still slumped on the far side, unmoving. The wind whipped her hair about as she edged across, foot by painful, frightening foot, its gusts so

313

strong and blustery, she feared at any moment it would pluck her from her swaying perch. The ribbon she'd used to fasten her hair back tore free and whisked away. Involuntarily, her eyes followed its flight and she glimpsed the river far below through the yawning gaps between the bamboo treads up ahead—and almost swooned.

You can do it, Mari, I know you can! You survived that monster, Edward. You survived a shipwreck. You survived Digby and Ruskin—you can survive anything, darling! Just close your eyes and pretend that I'm beside you. Think of me, beloved . . . only of me. Forget the blasted bridge and the river . . . forget everything else. In your mind's eye, see only me, hear only my voice. . . . I love you, Mari! Let my love give you courage! Don't be afraid! Come to me, my sweet!

It seemed Nathan spoke to her in those dark moments, stilling her fears with his gentle encouragement, coaxing her to be brave and go just a little farther, one step at a time, as he'd done the first night they'd made love amongst the sugar-like sand dunes, when everything within her had quailed with terror at his touch.

I'm coming, my love! she promised silently, and drawing a deep breath, she hesitantly carried on, taking one long stride over the missing treads, then another, looking straight ahead as she did so and not looking down again.

She was sobbing and trembling uncontrollably when she finally stumbled off the bridge and onto the grassy ridge where Nathan lay. Dropping to her knees, she clung fiercely to him, babbling, "I did it, Nathan! Oh, thank God, I did it!" over and over again, until she'd recovered from her ordeal.

Common sense returned then, and with it, her concern for Nathan. Drawing a deep breath and dashing her tears away with her knuckles, she gently rolled him over, onto his back, and with trembling hands, felt at his neck for a pulse, then pressed a hand to his brow.

He was alive, but his pulse felt very rapid. He was also burning up with fever, she had discovered. Rocking back on her heels and frowning, she considered what to do. 'Twas already late afternoon. There was little chance he'd come to before nightfall, let alone feel strong enough to continue their trek back to camp, even if he did. She must resign herself to spending the night here with him, and doing what little she could for his fever with whatever was at hand.

She looked about her. Unlike the soaring, opposite wall of the ravine, this side was gently sloping and was forested with low bushes, twisted trees, and tall grasses. It would eventually lead back to the beach. A few yards away, three stunted trees grew close together, spreading their leafy branches low over the ground to form a dense natural shelter. Hefting one of Nathan's feet beneath each of her arms, she dragged him under these trees and settled him on the grass as comfortably as possible. Then, tearing a ruffle from her threadbare petticoats, she soaked it in the sodden grass until it was thoroughly dampened, thanking God for the heavy downpour earlier. Using her primitive compress, she bathed his face and throat, unable to believe the fierce heat rising from him. His raging fever dried up the moisture left by her ministrations almost as quickly as she could sponge him down! And then, even as she sat there, watching him, he began to shake, his entire body racked by violent chills that made his teeth chatter uncontrollably.

Having no blankets to heap upon him, nor anything else with which to warm him, she slipped her arm beneath his head and lay down beside him, drawing him close so that he would absorb her body heat. And, as she cradled him in her arms, stroking his damp dark hair, she stared up at the darkening sky between the trees and prayed that his sickness was not the same dread disease that had stricken the giant marine, Booker, and the Scottish seaman, Mac-Something-or-other, during their first days on the island. For, despite Surgeon Love having been summoned, in a matter of hours both men had suffered convulsions and died. . . .

Chapter Twenty-Three

That night was the longest Mariah had ever known; a night filled with frightening sounds, threatening shadows and, a bone-deep anxiety for Nathan that nothing could ease.

She lay beside him to keep him warm, hugging him to her when he was taken by shivering fits, dozing off only when exhaustion overwhelmed her. Between these times, she huddled cross-legged against one of the trees, listening with mounting jitters to the stealthy rustling of wild creatures in the bushes, the slithering through the grasses, or starting with every creak and sough of branches stirring in the nightwind.

During those long, lonely hours, each mass of leafy shadow held a nameless threat, an unspeakable menace. A bulky bush became a kneeling, bushy-haired head-hunter with grisly trophies hanging from his belt; another, a ferocious wild beast licking its chops, poised to spring out and devour her and Nathan.

It rained on and off, fine yet heavy showers that soaked her to the skin and left her hair a wet and tangled mane. Though she tried, there was no way she could keep Nathan from also being soaked through. She took advantage of a bad situation and used the moisture to dampen her makeshift compress and bathe his forehead, or to ease the dryness of her mouth, licking raindrops off the leaves like a wild beast, too thirsty to care about anything but survival.

Between showers, the moon reappeared, floating high and free between banks of rain-clouds as if playing hide-and-seek with them. Its light silvered every drop of moisture that dripped from the trees or clung to a blade of grass, until the steamy night shimmered in a cloak of black, spangled all over with beads of silver.

Nathan grew increasingly more restless as the seemingly endless night wore on to dawn. His fever climbed, despite her efforts to cool him down. Delirious, he tossed and turned, his limbs jerking and flailing violently in all directions as if he were battling invisible demons. He grunted, groaned, cursed, and yelled so loudly, she was terrified his cries would lead their enemies to their hiding place, and so, in desperation, she was sometimes forced to press a hand over his mouth to keep him silent.

"Get away, damn your eyes!" he roared, flinging off her hand. *"You'll not take me—never! Damn ye, I'm innocent, as God is my witness! Father, tell them! You know I'm no murderer!"*

"Hush, my love," she crooned, lifting his damp head and cradling it upon her lap. Stroking his clammy cheek, she murmured, "There's no one here, Jonathan, my love. You're quite safe. 'Tis but a dream, my dearest love. An awful dream that will vanish when you wake. There, there, sleep, now. Sleep, my love. . . ."

"He did it!" he roared, suddenly fighting free of her arms and sitting bolt-upright. Eyes starting and wild, he extended his arm, with a shaking finger pointing to someone only he could see. *"Look—over there!"* he babbled hoarsely, clutching her arm with a grip like a vise. *"Can you not see him there,*

in the corner of the room? 'Tis Winslow—he who condemned me!''

"Truly . . . I see no one."

"Oh, God, oh, God, how could ye not see him, lest you're blind! He carries the hangman's rope! He wears the black hood! Look, there!"

Winslow? It could not be! "Come, now. Rest a little longer," she murmured, so shaken by his words that her body was suddenly icy and trembling. "There's no one there, no one at all, I say. 'Tis but the fever that paints these tortured images in your head. They are not real, my love!"

Something in her tone must have reached him, even through the depths of his fever, for he turned his head and looked at her wonderingly. "Not real? Am I ill, then, Mariah?" he asked groggily, trying to focus his haunted eyes upon her face.

"Aye, my love. Very ill, I fear," she confirmed gently, the tears that had brimmed in her eyes spilling down her grubby cheeks.

"Aaah. And . . . shall I die?" he asked, no more anxiety in his voice than if he'd asked her about the weather.

"Nay, my love, you will not, for I shall not let you," she vowed with quiet conviction.

"Mariah . . ."

Her tone if not her words seemed to satisfy him, for uttering her name like a prayer, he slowly nodded and sank back into her arms, falling into a deep and far less tortured sleep, while Mariah stroked his burning head and stared blindly into the night, dry-eyed now, her thoughts in chaos. There was an ache in her heart that ran too deep for tears.

Big Ben and Jack Warner wriggled through the bushes on their bellies, cursing the rain-showers that had soaked the lush grass and turned the ground into a muddy morass beneath it.

Parting the bushes before him, Ben peered at the activity going on in the native village before him.

318

Young brown-skinned savages with huge bushy, black heads adorned with bobbing bird plumes, and frighteningly painted and decorated faces, cavorted before a huge phallic-shaped idol of stone in the misty moonlight, brandishing spears and shields above their heads. Native musicians accompanied the dancers' frenzied whirling on small drums and flutes, or they twirled bull-roarers above their heads; but it was not their savage dancing or the wild, humming, pagan heartbeat of the music that made Ben gag, not their ferocious appearance that made Jack retch and grow pale and weak at the knees. 'Twas the human *heads*, four in all—the lips crudely sewn together—that the natives had impaled on short stakes over several low, smoky fires. These made the gorge rise in the two men's throats, for they were the heads of men they'd known, at least by sight— the heads of four white men.

"Oww, Jesus Christ! Cooper's made 'is last boast," Ben groaned. "An' Finnie, too. The poor sod's heard his last ban-shee, an' no mistake!"

"Aye. And that one wi' the red hair, 'tis Angus Ruskin, I'm after thinkin'? What say you, lad?"

"Aye. With that thatch, who else's noggin could it be?" Ben agreed soberly, looking a mite green about the gills for all his disparaging tone. "Aye, Jack, me old mate, that whore-son dog's copped it, curse his black soul! I allus knew he'd come to a bad end."

"Who's the fourth one?"

"Dunno—but it in't Kincaid nor the lass, so's I reckon we'd best scarper an' look for 'em elsewheres. Dawn's a-comin' up fast. It'll be full daylight 'fore we know it, an' I'd as soon be well away from 'ere before it is."

"Amen t' that!" Jack agreed vehemently, wriggling back-wards as he spoke. He let out a terrified yelp as a small hand clamped over his shoulder, spinning with his dagger drawn and raised to attack.

"Jack, don't! It's me!"

"Bloody Hell! Jack rasped in a hoarse whisper, seeing a

very dishevelled Mariah standing behind him, rather than the head-hunting cannibal with filed-down, pointed teeth he'd anticipated! Ashen-faced, he dropped down onto one knee to regain his composure. "Blessed Christ, m'lady, I almost killed ye!" he moaned, burying his face in his hands.

"Never mind that. Where's Kincaid?" Ben demanded, looking about him.

"I had to leave him behind and come for help," Mariah whispered, wringing her hands. "Oh, Jack, I think he's dying! He got me away from Ruskin, you see, and we were following the wild-pig trail back to camp when . . . when he fell ill. He's burning up with fever!"

"Calm down, m'lady. We'll see t' him now. Surgeon Love'll fix him up right smartly, once we get him back t' camp. You just show us the way. And m'lady, 'tis better ye do it quietly, eh?" he added softly by way of warning, jerking his head towards the native village beyond the bushes and pressing a stubby finger across his lips.

Mariah nodded and swallowed, her fingers straying subconsciously to her throat. Dear God! She'd had no idea she'd come that close to the natives' encampment, for the wind had carried the sounds of pagan revelry in the opposite direction! If she hadn't had the good fortune to stumble upon Jack and Ben, in another moment she'd have blundered headlong into the midst of the head-hunters.

"It's this way—and please hurry!" she murmured, leading them back the way she'd come.

Chapter Twenty-Four

"How are the drawings going today, sir?"

"Quite well, thank you, Kincaid. Would you . . . er . . . care to look at them?" Matherson offered. Always a modest and unassuming fellow, he indicated a pile of neatly numbered sketches with an embarrassed smile.

Nathan nodded and lurched to standing, fighting the dizziness and nausea that still swept over him whenever he tried to stand or move about.

It had been two weeks since Ben, Jack, and Mariah had carried him back down to camp from that cursed mountain ridge. Though Stiles and the other wounded men had quickly recovered, for much of the time since that morning, he'd been too ill to know where he was, let alone care overmuch about what was going on. And when they buried Ole Peg, he'd been drifting in and out of fevered sleeps that were plagued with nightmarish delusions, or had been racked with bouts of shivering that had left him weak as a day-old kitten.

Surgeon Love had examined him and had diagnosed his

illness as the dreaded "shaking sickness"—malaria. During one of his few lucid moments, he'd explained to Nathan that the disease was caused by the bite of the bloodthirsty mosquitoes that infested the mangrove swamps on the island, but—lacking quinine—he'd been unable to treat him effectively. It had fallen to Mariah, bless her, to nurse Nathan day and night, and she had, jeopardizing her own health in order to restore his. *Ah, Mariah!* Her sweet love, more than anything, had made him fight to grow well again, to come this far. She'd given him the willpower he'd lacked in the darkest hours, alternately haranguing, bullying, or cajoling him to fight the sickness and get well, to return to her, forcing him to struggle back up from the sloughs of despair when the easiest thing in the world would have been to give up and let sickness and death triumph.

When he thought of all she'd gone through—of the courage and enormous love it must have taken for her to cast aside her terror and cross that fragile bridge to his side and to make the solitary trek down the mountain in the grey hours before dawn to bring help back to him, risking her own life at Ruskin or the natives' hands—the depths of her love for him amazed him.

This morning, after a restful night—one free of cold sweats and nightmares—he'd fancied he was finally on the road to recovery. But even now, the effort to move about cost him dearly as he gingerly made his way over to the huge, flat-topped rock Matherson was using as a drawing table, cursing the trembling that had begun in his legs the moment he'd hauled himself upright.

Trying to control his treacherous body, he leaned against a palm trunk and sifted through the sketches, nodding appreciatively.

"Nicely done, sir. Very nice. When—if—you return to civilization, these drawings should provide invaluable information about the flora and fauna here."

"I hope so, Kincaid. 'Twould be comforting to think that

our time here has not been entirely wasted, not without some scientific compensation, would it not? Oh, drat and botheration! Will you look at this? Another blot! No matter how I try, 'tis still not right, is it? Zounds, without my spectacles, I simply cannot record these specimens! My assistant, Wyman, was the one with the artistic talents. Alas, the poor lad was lost when the *Hester* went down.''

''May I try, sir?'' Nathan asked, holding out his hand for the botanist's pen.

''By all means,'' Matherson agreed, his wispy brows lifting in surprise as he handed over the quill.

Reaching across Matherson, Nathan eyed the specimen, dipped the quill in fresh India ink, and, with a few deft strokes, corrected the drawing Matherson had been working on, a detailed botanical drawing of a delicately-fronded variety of kelp.

''By jove, you've caught those fronds perfectly! You're quite the artist yourself, it would seem, Kincaid. My meagre talent's a poor thing, compared to yours,'' the botanist exclaimed admiringly. ''A natural talent, sir?''

''In part.'' Nathan grinned and shrugged. ''As a youth, I aspired to become a student at the Royal Academy of Art under Master Reynolds. Fortunately—for the world of art—my father and the hard school of Life disabused me of that grandiose plan. I passed the Bar and became a lawyer instead!''

''Fortunately? Nay, sir, not so. The Bar's gain was surely a loss to the world of art. Yes, certainly. But, have you lost all ambition to excel in that field?''

''I have, save for the enjoyment I find in sketching. There was a time, sir,'' he recalled with a distant look in his green eyes, ''when you would never have found me without charcoal and pad in hand, haunting taverns and markets to sketch the faces of London's poor. Doxies, sailors, fishwives, barrowboys—God's Teeth, I have drawn them all!''

''Why, then, you must have some of this fine parchment and charcoal for your own use. Here, take whatever you require. I can think of no better means to keep boredom at bay, lacking books as we do, until you recover your strength. Come, sir. Help yourself to what you need.''

Nathan hesitated only a moment. In all honesty, after watching Matherson's laborious, far-sighted scribblings day in and day out this past week or so, the artist in him had itched to be sketching. And, as Matherson had so rightly said, his cursed weakness precluded more strenuous pursuits, for the time being. What better way, indeed, to pass the endless hours?

"My thanks, sir," he murmured, helping himself to some sticks of charcoal, a handful of broken pastels, and a pad of the now thick and furry parchment sheets he'd recovered from the *Hester*'s hold and then dried in the sun. With a grateful grin for the botanist, he made his way back to his makeshift bed beneath the palm tree's shade.

There he sketched until fatigue overwhelmed him, drawing after drawing flowing from his grimy hands. And that same night, for the first time since he'd fallen ill, he slept deeply and dreamlessly, his nightmarish ravings stilled.

"Hmmm. Still at your sketching, I see, Master Kincaid? Fie, 'twould seem you hardly notice I'm gone each day, let alone miss me!''

Mariah's teasing complaint broke his concentration. Setting pad and charcoal aside, he looked up and grinned in welcome as, pouting, she came towards him, holding a peeled mango that had had a huge bite taken from it. Traces of orange juice and pulp still clung to her mouth, and her cheeks were as full as a squirrel's with the luscious fruit.

"On the contrary. I missed you sorely today, madam, as I do each day—and well you know it, minx! Without the sketching, I would grow mad with longing for you!''

"Probably," she agreed with pretended smugness. "I alone possess the magical touch to soothe your fevered brow and bring you ease. Isn't that why you miss me so?''

"Nay, minx. 'Tis because old Love is a poor replacement for my lovely nurse—and far less pleasing to my eye, besides."

His eyes caressed her. And, beneath their lambent gaze, she felt the sultry heat of passion rising through her like a fever. "Aha! Then you admit you find me comely? 'Tis a good sign. A week ago, you were so sick, I wager you'd have a found a sea-cow pleasing to the eye! Surely you must be recovering, sir?"

"Aye, surely I must. And besides, Love would prove somewhat whiskery when it came to kisses—"

"Popinjay!" she accused, laughing at the squeaky falsetto voice he'd affected for the latter comment.

"Popinjay? Come here and kiss me, wench. We'll see who you call 'popinjay' after that," he challenged.

Still chewing, she dropped to her knees beside him, leaned over and planted a sticky kiss full upon his lips.

"There. How did that taste? Whiskery?"

"Nay. 'Twas delicious, Mistress Mango-mouth," he murmured, licking his lips as he lazily reached out to cup her breasts. At his touch, her nipples hardened beneath the thin stuff of her bodice. Groaning, he cupped both breasts in his hands and pushed them up, then dipped his ebony head to tease the stiffened nipples with his tongue, dampening the cloth of her bodice as he did so.

"For shame, sir! 'Tis broad daylight—someone will see!"

"Then tell them I was delirious, my sweet," he suggested wickedly. "Insist that the fever made me forget myself, and that I laid hands on you against your will."

"You! They'd not believe me for a moment, you rogue. Ooh, Nathan . . ." Her merry laughter died away, became instead a sultry purr of pleasure deep in her throat as she arched against his caresses.

Eyes deepening to forest green, he wound a hand through her bright hair and, using it as a tether, drew her to him and kissed her again; deep kisses this time that slaked his hunger for her lips until she was breathless.

"My word, sir! Surely you've regained your . . . strength?" she teased shakily, her turquoise eyes dark and liquid as she rocked back on her heels to regard him.

"That which counts, aye," he agreed roguishly, drawing a tiny circle with his fingertip on her palm, which seemed suddenly to burn as if touched by an ember. "But . . . come to me tonight, goddess, if you yet have doubts. You may judge for yourself which 'strengths' I have regained, and which I have not."

"Lecherous devil," she accused, laughing in the husky way he loved. Without further ado, she took another healthy bite from the mango, groaning with delight as its juice spurted and trickled down her chin, aware as she did so that Nathan watched, fascinated and jealous, as a solitary droplet found its way down the ivory column of her throat, then trickled into the shadowy valley between her breasts. "Mmm. Heaven! 'Tis like eating an orange and a peach at the same time. I swear—mmm—nothing on earth tastes half as good as a ripe, juicy—mmm—mango," she declared between lusty mouthfuls, licking her lips and fingers with loud, rude smacking noises.

"Nothing?" he murmured huskily, watching the sensual enjoyment with which she attacked the luscious fruit . . . and feeling a stirring in his loins as he did so.

"Nothing!" she denied firmly, ignoring the wicked innuendo to his tone. Nevertheless, her eyes twinkled with such mischief, he knew she'd caught his meaning and that her unabashed enjoyment of the mango had really been far from innocent. "Will you have some?" she offered, lowering her lashes and side-eyeing him archly as she held out the half-eaten fruit.

His eyes holding hers captive, he ducked his head, tore off a huge bite, chewed it slowly, then swallowed. The bobbing of his Adam's apple in the fine tanned pillar of his throat fascinated her.

"Fine fruit, indeed, mistress," he acknowledged softly.

"But . . . you have other toothsome berries I find far more pleasing to my palate."

"And you shall sample them all, sir, my word on it . . . *later*. For now, slug-a-bed, show me what you've been doing all day, while I labored to pick fresh fruit for m'lord's supper."

"Do these prove that I missed you, minx?" he challenged, tossing several sheets of sketches into her lap.

She had to admit they did, for the drawings were almost all of her; in various poses, she saw. One in particular made her blush, for in it she was unclad, save for showers of exotic blossoms that cascaded about her. Why, he'd even captured the tiny mole upon her left hip, the rogue! "For shame, sir!" she scolded, clicking her teeth and eyeing him sternly. "Would you have every man on this island see me as nature intended?"

He shrugged. "Can I help it if I see you only as a goddess clad in diaphanous robes, surrounded by the beauties of nature?" he countered.

"Diaphanous robes, my foot. Sir, there *are* no robes, 'less I am blind. Look!"

He winked wickedly. "Tut-tut. You're quite right. I must have forgotten. Ah, well, no matter. I'll add a line or two on the morrow, if you insist."

"I do indeed, and—oh, Nathan—this little portrait, it's splendid! Who is she? One of your mistresses?" Mariah demanded, a hint of jealousy in her tone. She wrinkled her nose. "She's very beautiful. I think—yes, I hate her!"

He peered at the drawing she was admiring. "She is beautiful, aye, but that's a drawing of my mother! Or *ma mère*, as she prefers to be called. Gabrielle St. Avalon Kincaid."

"Then she's French?"

"To the very depths of her being, *chérie*—and proud of it, too. Not, I might add, a popular trait these days, given England's relationship with France. Her father—my grandfather—is Comte Jean-Louis de St. Avalon, a French nobleman."

"Indeed?" she observed, impressed. "Then this handsome gentleman beside her must be your father?"

"Aye. And standing next to him, Jeremy, my older brother."

"Aye. I guessed as much. There's a definite resemblance between the two of you—though you're more handsome by far!"

Mariah continued examining the sketches, commenting from time to time as Jonathan told her about his family and his fears for the safety of his French grandparents, aunts, uncles, and cousins, should the Revolution sweeping Paris have reached their château in the country provinces.

When the *Hester* sailed from England, Paris had been in an uproar, overrun by mobs of the over-taxed middle-class and poor who had revolted to challenge King Louis XVI's divine right to rule them as their king, and who now wanted revenge upon the nobles who'd bled them dry over the centuries. As a consequence, many of his mother's aristocratic relatives and friends had been in grave danger of losing their heads to the pitiless guillotine. Gabrielle Kincaid had been frantic to bring her loved ones to safety in England, while Nathan's father had been equally determined to keep her at home, out of harm's way.

". . . That is why, when I was imprisoned, my father refused her permission to come to London. He feared that, once in the City, she would hire mercenaries to wage a daring rescue of her family, and would want to lead them to France herself. By so doing, she would put her own life at risk. She is a spirited woman, *ma mère*, and one of no little courage! Instead, my father promised he'd do whatever could be done for the St. Avalons through his connections at court. Did I tell you that you remind me of *ma mère*, my sweet?" Receiving no answer, he glanced up and saw that she was staring at the only full-page sketch he had drawn, that of a middle-aged man whose once-handsome features had been coarsened by over-indulgence. Her face, so rosy but moments before, had grown pale.

328

"Mariah?"

"Yes?"

"What's wrong?"

"Nothing! Nothing at all," she denied quickly. "I was . . . oh, just wondering about this man. He . . . he looks . . . somehow familiar, that's all. Why did you—that is, what made you draw him? Is he someone you knew in England?"

"I, know him?" Nathan's lips curled with contempt. "That murdering whore-son? That treacherous old scoundrel? Aye, my love!" His hands tightened into fists. "You're looking at the face of the man responsible for my being here, my sweet. Judge Harry Winslow, respected magistrate," he scoffed. "Loyal member of the Octagon conspiracy that I told you of—traitor. Would-be assasin and cold-blooded killer, to boot!"

So saying, he pulled the parchment from her hand and rumpled it into a ball, which he tossed aside. "Enough of Winslow, damn his black heart! Once my thoughts turn to him and my past, I can think of nothing but revenge and clearing my name!" He scowled, then his hard expression softened and in a gentle, sensual tone he coaxed, "Tonight, there are more pleasing things I would put my mind to. Come, Mariah, my dove, my heart! Will you not slip away with me to my hut? We could wile away the time 'til supper in discovering if my 'strength' has yet returned."

"You tempt me sorely but . . . later, sir," she hedged, forcing a quick, uneasy smile without meeting his eyes as she stood up. "For now, I am promised to help Nancy with the cooking. And there will be no supper for anyone, if I delay much longer."

"Tonight then? After moonrise?" he pressed ardently.

"Aye. Tonight," she promised, and ran off towards the camp proper before he could find further words to delay her.

But she did not come to him that night, or on the ones that followed it.

Nathan had been aware that he was being watched for some time, but he made no comment. Sooner or later, his fidgety admirer would decide to speak, for he knew that silent contemplation was not Mistress Caroline's forte! Until then, he'd continue drawing.

He did so, quickly becoming absorbed in the sketch he was making of Jack Warner at his carving, forgetting the young girl who watched avidly over his shoulder as he drew.

A deft stroke with the charcoal stick here, and he'd caught the stubborn line of Jack's lips, set thin and tight in concentration. A squiggle or two there, captured perfectly the intensity of Jack's frown as he labored at the craft he loved.

"Oh, yes!" Caroline exclaimed. "That's Jack! You've caught him exactly, Nathan. I've seen him with just such an expression at least a hundred times since we've been on this island. I say, you're awfully clever, you know."

"My thanks, Mistress Caroline," Jonathan murmured. There was a twinkle in his green eyes as he gravely inclined his ebony head. Truth was, he enjoyed her company, especially since Mariah had been avoiding him for the past few days, though he had no idea why she should do so.

Uncertain whether he was teasing her or nay, Caroline smiled wistfully as she flopped down on the sand beside him in the shade, fanning herself vigorously with a palm frond.

The day was sultry, the air close and humid, as if a storm was in the offing. Master Matherson predicted still more rainy weather in the weeks to come, as the topsy-turvy climate of these parts changed from summer to winter.

Caroline continued. "I wanted so much to have Master Reynolds—the famous portrait painter—come out to Amberfield Acres to paint my portrait." She grimaced. "But Papa said I was much too young, and a 'vain little flibbertigibbet,' besides. He promised to commission Master Reynolds when I was older—providing, you understand, that I was still 'passing comely' to look upon, or at least, not so very ugly I'd scare the poor man!'' She giggled. ''He's such a tease, my papa.''

''So it would seem.''

She sighed. ''I doubt I'll ever see myself immortalized in oils now, don't you?'' she observed sadly, tossing aside her makeshift fan and hugging her bent knees.

'''Tis hard to say, poppet,'' Nathan countered, reluctant to rob her of all hope of rescue. ''However, if you'd look kindly upon the scratchings of a far less talented artist than the esteemed Maestro Reynolds, you might, perchance, find yourself already immortalized—albeit in humble charcoal.''

''Oh, Nathan, you didn't draw me, did you? Really? Oh, where is it—do let me see it!'' She squealed with delight, her blue eyes shining.

The little vixen had dropped enough hints this past week for such a show of surprise to hardly seem genuine. ''Over there, lost in that stack of sketches somewhere,'' Nathan directed casually with a wave of his grimy hand. ''Help yourself.''

Straightaway, Caroline scrambled to the heap of drawings he'd weighted down with a rock at the base of the shady palm. She began shuffling eagerly through them.

Exotic island blossoms leaped out at her from some of the pages; hibiscus and orchids, bird-of-paradise flowers, and poinsettias, all worked in lifelike pastels; drawings of birds and animals filled still others, the heavy white paper alive with them, each claw and feather and petal faithfully rendered. She paused as a familiar creature caught her attention, its button-bright dark eyes peering out from between some leaves, a banana gripped in its tiny dark fingers. Why, it was her own little monkey, Monty!

Mariah's face filled many of the following pages. Each sketch revealed a different facet of her personality—and betrayed the artist's innermost feelings as palpably as words. With an intuitiveness beyond her years, Caroline recognized the love the artist felt for his subject, and she envied it. What she'd give for Tim to someday feel like this about her—and to be able to express his love so eloquently, without need of a single word.

Nathan Kincaid's love for her cousin was in every line of his drawings of her. There was Mariah wearing a dreamy smile, holding a huge conch-shell up to her ear as she knelt upon the sand. There she was again, in profile, her long, curling hair twisting on the breeze, her eyes dreamy as she gazed at the distant horizon, where a tiny ship was silhouetted. And in the next sketch Mariah was lounging in some jungle-bower, arms above her head and quite naked, her nude loveliness framed only by exotic flowers as if she were some pagan goddess, her turquoise eyes half-closed and heavy-lidded. With . . . desire?

Heat filled Caroline's cheeks and a strange quivering stirred in the very pit of her belly. Indeed, so potent was the mood the artist had captured, she felt like a . . . like a . . . drat, what was it called? Ah, yes, a voyeur, that was it; someone who spied upon others at their sporting.

Feeling guilty and, if truth were told, a teeny bit aroused, she quickly turned the pages in search of less disquieting pictures, crowing with delight as she spotted her Tim, wearing a necker-chief, pirate-fashion, about his blond head. Nathan had whimsi-cally drawn him with a cutlass in his fist, swinging from the rope-ladder of a ship. And in the depiction, watching his bold antics in apparent awe and admiration from the taff-rail, was Caroline herself, a little older and thinner of face, and—she blushed to the roots of her creamy-blond hair—quite beautiful, besides.

"Why, you . . . you have flattered me, sir," she exclaimed wonderingly, stunned by Nathan's rendering of her.

"On the contrary, minx. I draw what I see. And what I see is a beautiful young girl, soon to blossom into a beautiful woman."

"La! You are far too generous with your praises, Master Kincaid," she denied. "Have a care, lest I believe them and grow quite vain!"

Embarrassed yet delighted, Caroline hastily turned another page and giggled. "Oh, it's that awful Digby! What a buffoon you've made of him!'' Nathan had drawn the pompous turncoat lieutenant with devastating cleverness, exagerrating his worst faults and making his somewhat elongated, aristocratic features even longer. He had a huge head with, of all things, flaring donkey ears, set atop a tiny body that bristled with Royal Navy epaulets, braid, and buttons. His snug white breeches had sprouted a donkey's tail and his hands and feet were neat little hooves.

She frowned as she withdrew the last parchment sheet, for it had obviously been crumpled and discarded, then smoothed out in an attempt to salvage it. Only one sketch filled this page, a portrait of a middle-aged man, shown full-face and worked in great detail. The portrait had been shaded and cross-hatched to suggest contour, angle, and flesh-tone so cleverly, it was instantly recognizable to her. ''Nathan?''

''Hmm, minx?'' Nathan responded absently over his shoulder, still absorbed in his sketch of Jack.

''How on earth did you make this sketch of Uncle Harry? And, if I might be so bold, why?''

''What's that?'' he murmured, setting pad and charcoal aside.

''This sketch, here.''

''What about it, minx?'' he queried, dusting off his hands.

''Well, it's of my Uncle Harry. I'd recognize him anywhere! Do you know him, then?''

Nathan turned to look. And, when he saw which sketch she was holding, he sprang to his feet. The breath knotted in his throat as he tore the paper from her fingers and gripped her wrist instead, squeezing it tightly. She winced, afraid he would snap the bone in two, but he did not slacken his grip.

''Who? Who did you say it was, wench?'' he demanded. His eyes were twin emerald glaciers as he glowered down at her from his great height.

''U-Uncle Harry,'' she repeated timidly, terrified by the crackling fury that surrounded him like an aura. ''J-Judge Harry Winslow, Mariah's f-father. Please, Nathan! My hand . . . you're hurting me!''

"Mariah's *what!*" The blood drained from about his lips as he released Caroline's wrist, almost flinging it from him. As he stood there, his handsome features revealing confusion and anger, his jaw working, 'twas as if he'd forgotten her very existence. "But the name . . . Damn it, nay! How could it be?" he muttered as he began to pace back and forth liked a caged panther. And then, he whirled about and, thrusting the sketch in Caroline's face, barked, "Mariah's father, you said?"

"Yes, s-sir," Caroline whispered, rubbing her sore wrist. She was half-afraid to answer for fear he'd explode again, but more afraid not to. "He—Harry Winslow—married my papa's sister, you see. My Aunt Alicia was Mariah's—"

"—mother," Nathan gritted out in an icy tone that sent chills crawling down Caroline's spine. So. This explained why Mariah had been avoiding him these past days, the peculiar expression on her face when he'd shown her his drawings, and her sudden preoccupation with the cooking of supper. It made sense now, damn it! Mariah's father had been one of the Octagon conspirators in Rose's room that fateful night; That same Harry Winslow who'd donned a black hood and sentenced him to hang. Sweet Christ, the father of the woman he loved had been one of the callous bastards who'd brutally murdered poor Roger and Rose!

"A-Aye," Caroline stammered, scrambling to her feet. "Mariah's mother. Now, by your leave, sir, I . . . er . . . I really must go and find Monty. Heaven knows what he's up to." With that, she fled in search of Mariah, the drawings scattering as she went.

When she dared a backwards glance, Nathan was still standing there, beneath the shade of the palm. The rumpled sketch of Judge Harry Winslow was gripped in his clenched fist, and there was a chilling cast to his darkly handsome, stern face; a deadly expression that made Caroline wonder if, after all, they'd been wrong about him. At that moment, Jonathan Kincaid looked more than capable of carrying out every one of the heinous crimes of which he'd been accused.

Chapter Twenty-Five

"Caroline? Is that you?"

The shadowy figure turned. And, for a fleeting second, a stern male profile was etched against the hut's square window, limned demonically in orange-red by the flames of the signal-fire blazing on the beach beyond. Mariah gasped and shrank back into the doorway, poised to flee, but then she realized she knew the intruder. *'Twas Jonathan sitting there, in the dark.*

Recognition did nothing to ease the turmoil of her emotions. If anything, it worsened! Her heart quickened painfully. She knew only too well why he'd left his sick-bed to seek her out, and the fluttery feeling of dread she'd carried in the pit of her belly ever since the afternoon she'd seen his sketches became a roaring monster of doom. She'd been avoiding him for days, hoping to postpone just such a confrontation. She could do so no longer.

"Frightened, my sweet? How so? 'Tis only me, your be-loved Nathan," he jeered in a hateful, coldly-mocking tone she'd never heard him use before. "At my request, your little cousin shares Kitty's hut tonight, dear heart. I wanted to talk to you, you see?''

His words, his tone, confirmed her deepest fears, tied knots around her innards. What, in God's name, could she say to him? *What!* That the magistrate who'd donned a black hood and condemned him to hang had been her father . . . but that it didn't matter, if they truly loved each other? Or should she claim ignorance, instead, and pretend she knew nothing when he accused her? Her shoulders sagged. A sob caught in her throat. The euphoria of loving Jonathan, of knowing he returned her love, had been shattered like crystal dropped on a stone floor from the moment she'd seen the drawing he'd made of her father. She was terribly afraid there was no way on earth the shards of that love could ever be pieced together again.

''Please, Nathan, another time. I am . . . unwell,'' she began tremulously. ''Besides, the hour is late. We will talk on the morrow.''

''For shame! Such a cold welcome for a man who quit his sick-bed to find you, Mariah? In truth, I would have expected a warmer welcome from my lady-love! But then, perhaps ice-water runs in your veins? Perhaps true warmth is beyond you.''

His caustic tone flayed nerve-endings already rubbed raw by days of fretting, endless hours in which she'd tried to find the courage to tell Nathan that the man he'd drawn was her father. Instead, she'd taken the coward's way out and decided to pray that he never learned the truth, but clearly, he had somehow guessed her secret . . . or been told the identity of the man in his sketch. Was that why Caroline had been looking for her earlier? Why she'd avoided Mariah at supper? Had she, in all innocence, told Jonathan who the man was? Mariah's jaw came up.

''Enough, Nathan. There is no need for ugly insinuations. Speak your mind, and do it plain. Caroline told you that the man you sketched was Judge Winslow, my father, did she not?''

336

" 'Out of the mouths of babes . . .' Aye, damn it! Just so," he flung back at her.

"Then . . . then I am deeply sorry you found out that way. Believe me, I would have told you myself, the very moment I saw the drawing, but for . . . for the look in your eyes when you spoke of him, when you told me what he'd done to you." Remembering his expression, she shivered and hugged herself. "I could not bring myself to speak, Nathan! I was far too frightened by your anger to tell you!"

"And so you took the coward's way," he jeered. "You said nothing, and you ran. You avoided me!" he accused contemptuously.

"Aye, I did. But . . . can you blame me? You believe you have just cause to hate my father. That being so, what could I, his daughter, have possibly said that would have changed your feelings? Would you have listened, if I'd said you were wrong about him? That for my part, I shall never believe my father capable of cold-blooded murder, or of betraying the profession he loved? Would it have been better to tell you that I loved him, Jonathan? That I always will?"

He snorted and flung up an angry hand to dismiss her protests. "*Love!* Pray, madam, do not speak to me of love and that whore-son Winslow in the same breath. How can you love a rogue who'd send an innocent man to the gallows, answer me that? Or defend someone who'd bludgeon two helpless lovers to death? And for what? Because they'd overheard a damning conversation between him and his fellows, and must be silenced! Tell me, Mariah, is the man I describe worthy of your love? *Is he?*"

In the meagre light, he lurched to standing. Now he loomed over her, a dark, threatening figure in the hut's close confines, his green eyes blazing down into her pale face and anger crackling about him.

Tentatively, she touched his forearm with her fingertips, hoping by the contact to reach some part of him as yet unsoured

337

and unhardened by vengeance and hatred. But she felt only the heat of the fever rising through him anew in the second before he flung off her hand, and her frail hopes withered and died.

"I can love him because I know in my heart that, somehow, you are wrong, Jonathan, and that my father was innocent," she said quietly, adding, "In the same way I knew in my heart that *you* were innocent, when first I fell in love with you."

But it was futile to plead with him. It was all unfolding exactly as she'd dreaded! Nathan heard nothing she said. He didn't *want* to hear. The anger, the thirst for revenge and exoneration that had kept him going, given him the courage to endure even in his darkest hours, refused to release its stranglehold on him now.

In the merciful shadows, she blinked back tears. Sorrow swelled in her breast, along with the first keen ache of grief. Through no fault of her own, she had lost him tonight, unless . . . Intuitively, she sensed there was but one way she could still get through to him; one means by which she could yet reclaim his love. By telling him what he wanted so desperately to hear. By denying her love for her father. By admitting that her papa had been a murderer and a scoundrel. In a word, by lying. Her shoulders sagged. Nay. She was no Peter the Fisherman, to deny her love for her father, her trust and belief in his goodness. That she could never do.

"Tell me, Nathan," she demanded suddenly, tears blurring her voice. "Did you not swear you loved me that night on the mountain ridge, when Ruskin hounded us?"

His jaw tightened. A muscle throbbed at his temple. "I did."

"And what about now? Do you love me still? Or am I suddenly unworthy of your love—not because of any wrong-doing of my own, mark you, but because I am my father's daughter?"

"If you truly loved me, Mariah, you would share my hatred," he rasped, sidestepping her question. "My enemies would be your enemies!"

"Not so!" she flared, pushed to her limits. "Whether you

love me or nay, my thoughts, my feelings are my own. Love does not give one the right to tell another who to love, sir, or who to hate. And my heart is ever loyal, even to those undeserving, mayhap, of my loyalty.''

Did she speak of her cursed father or himself? Jonathan wondered bitterly, livid at the unbending pride in her tone, at her refusal to see things his way. "Is that so? Then I pity you, m'lady Downing,'' he ground out, "You squander your admirable loyalty on a dead man. On a man who was, moreover, unworthy of it—and of you. A man who was a ruthless butcher, a party to treason! A traitor to his country and to the robes of his office!''

"That, sir, is your belief, not mine,'' she retorted, shaking all over with rage and upset. "Now that you have said your piece, I will ask you to leave my hut straightaway.''

"Never fear, madam. I go most willingly,'' he ground out, and lurched unsteadily past her, storming out into the sultry tropical night.

Shaking uncontrollably, Mariah flung herself down upon her makeshift bed. She wept and cursed until there were no tears left within her to shed, no word remaining that was vile enough to heap upon him.

Much later, feeling emptied and numbed by the weight of her grief, she pressed her palms to her flat belly. What, she wondered bleakly, would become of the new life unfolding within her . . . ?

The rains came in the wee hours of that night, teeming down upon the thatched roofs of the bamboo huts and puddling on the dirt floors as it pounded through gaps in the banana leaves. Mosquitoes, hiding from the rain within their walls, made attempts at sleep a nightmare with their whining and their painful bites. There was much grumbling and scratching at itchy welts as everyone congregated about the smoky fire for breakfast the following morning, bleary-eyed and yawning.

Mariah was awakened from a fitful doze by Jack Warner's cry of alarm. Hurrying outside, she found him some distance from her hut, kneeling beside Jonathan, who sprawled unconscious in the sand.

"What happened to him?" she asked quickly, dropping to her knees alongside Jack, her sadness forgotten in her concern.

"Don't rightly know, m'lady. I just found 'im a-lyin' here. My guess 'ud be 'e wandered away from 'is hut last night, then passed out where ye see 'im now. The rain didn't do 'im no good, neither. 'E's fair burning up again, 'e is."

Nathan's face was waxy pale, save for two bright spots of unhealthy ruddy color that rode high on his stubbled cheekbones. Her hand upon his brow confirmed Jack's suspicions. He was indeed burning up, and the ominous rattling to his breathing frightened her. "Quickly, Jack, find someone to help you carry him inside, out of the sun."

She was still at Nathan's side at dusk, bathing his fevered body, when a great shout rang out from the beach. In the ensuing hullabaloo, she was at a loss to know what was going on, and unable to leave her patient to find out for herself, when Caroline and Kitty, all a-twitter with excitement, poked their heads in the hut's doorway.

"Oh, coz! A ship's been sighted off-shore," Caroline exclaimed. "I just know we'll be rescued! Come on!"

"Aye, come down to the beach with us, won't ye, ducks?" Kitty urged, her pretty face equally flushed.

But Mariah reluctantly bade them go without her.

"I'd love to go with you, but I dare not leave Nathan. Unless I'm mistaken, he's deathly ill, and there's so very little I can do for him. Go on, the two of you. Find out what's happening; then come back and tell me all about it!"

Everyone ran down to the beach with Caroline and Kitty, to cheer and wave frantically at the sails Tim had glimpsed. Damp kindling was heaped onto the signal-fire and a great pall of smoke bellied up into the darkening sky. But despite their efforts, the vessel sailed blithely on, giving no sign that its master or crew had spotted their signals. And, after an hour or more had passed, those on the beach sank to their knees and stared glumly at the starlit sea.

They kept the signal-fire blazing all that night and throughout the next day, piling it high with driftwood until amber flames leaped three or more feet into the air. Orange embers danced on the sultry breeze, and a high column of smoke rose in a drifting column against the hazy blue sky, a beacon that should have been visible for some distance out to sea.

All eyes anxiously scanned the hazy lavender line of the horizon. Talk was scant, for everyone's thoughts were preoccupied. *So much hope!* They'd had so much hope when they'd glimpsed the vessel's ghostly sails glimmering through the dusk the evening before! But alas, she'd sailed on without seeing their signal-fire. Dare they hope she might yet come about and tack a course for their island, as the botanist Matherson had so optimistically declared? Or were they doomed, as dour Surgeon Love had predicted, destined never to be rescued, condemned to spend the remainder of their lives on this deserted isle, far from their loved ones, friends, and civilization? Long faces betrayed their fears while heavy, dark-ringed eyes betrayed the sleepless night they'd passed on the beach, gazing seawards and waiting; always waiting.

And so, after hours without sign of a sail that morning or early afternoon, they left the beach and trudged back to camp to tend to their individual duties. Though low in spirits and lower still in optimism, they had to eat. Game must be hunted, fish caught, and fruit gathered, despite their disappointment, they told themselves. But even chirpy, ever-cheerful Jack seemed to have lost his jaunty air, Mariah observed, glimpsing him through the hut's opening as he dawdled by, scuffing his feet in the sand.

341

"Nothing?" she called anxiously.

"Not a sign, m'lady," Jack confirmed gloomily, grimacing. "How is 'e?" he asked, nodded towards Nathan. "No better?"

She shook her head and set aside the pewter mug she'd been holding up to Nathan's lips. "I managed to get a sip or two of water into him just now, but more spilled down his chin than wetted his throat. I . . . I fear . . ." She swallowed, unable to go on as tears made her eyes smart and a burning, tight sensation clogged her throat.

"Aye, lass?"

"I fear he's—oh, Jack, I fear he's lost all will to . . . to . . ." No. She just couldn't bring herself to say it. To admit it would make it real.

"Live?" Jack supplied.

"Yes!" she acknowledged, misery in her tone. "Oh, Jack, what can we do? When he left me last night after our quarrel, he wasn't the same man we know. There . . . there was a desperation to him that frightened me!"

Jack nodded sympathetically. She'd tearfully told the ship's carpenter everything earlier that day. "Perhaps 'e weren't 'imself, but Kincaid give up? Not 'im, m'lady, never fear. 'E's tough as bloody nails, that 'un! 'E'll pull through an' surprise us all, ye'll see—if fer no other reason than t' take 'is vengeance an' clear 'is name. And m'lady . . . 'twill come right between the two o' ye, ye'll see. Time is wot it takes. 'E's a fair man, Kincaid—an' any fool can see 'e loves ye. When 'e's thought it through, 'e'll see 'e can't blame ye, and seek t' mend things."

"I hope so," Mariah whispered. She forced a wan smile of thanks for his kind attempts to encourage her. "Oh, Jack, I pray so, with all my heart!"

Chapter Twenty-Six

The sun was a golden ball high in the sky directly above their camp the following morning when Tim sang out excitedly from his lofty vantage point in a swaying coconut palm:

"Sail ho!"

An explosion could not have had greater effect on the castaways! Like lemmings, all dropped what they were doing, turned, and rushed down to the shore. They milled about there, gazing seawards, shading their eyes and scanning the sparkling turquoise water for some sign of the promised sail.

"Where away, lad?" Carmichael snapped impatiently, squinting against the brilliant tropical light. He could see nothing but endless, dazzling blue water in all directions, the white caps blinding in the sunshine.

"T' the west, sir! There! Look!" Tim had spotted a tiny speck against the distant horizon through the brass spyglass Nathan had salvaged weeks ago. Moments later, he lifted the glass to his eye once again and confirmed his sighting in a voice that squeaked with excitement. "Sail ho, due west, Mas-

343

ter-mate! A merchantman, I'd say—and carrying all the sail she can handle. Just look at her go, sir! Isn't she a sight!'' He tossed the spyglass down to the master-mate, who lifted the instrument to his eyes with trembling hands and adjusted the focus.

Moments later, he hoarsely confirmed Tim's findings, and the company cheered.

Sure enough, as the moments passed, they could all see the merchantman, her sails only a broad white wedge on the distant horizon at first; then they could make her out in finer detail as she steadily sailed closer to shore. Her billowing canvas was snow-white in the sunlight as her bows rose and fell, cutting a creamy trough through the turquoise water, while above her, her pennants streamed, snapping proudly in the breeze.

Within the hour, they could pick out her crew, nimbly swarming up the rat-lines, one sailor perched in the crow's nest. They could even discern her individual masts and the colors she flew; the red cross of St. George, surmounting the white cross of St. Andrew and Scotland—the Union Jack of Great Britain.

''Huzzah!'' yelled Carmichael, abandoning his normally serious demeanor to dance a merry jig on the sand, much as Caroline's pet monkey capered after a tot of rum. ''Praise God, we're saved! We're going home, my friends! *Huzzaaah!*''

The former crewmembers of the ill-fated *Hester* and the handful of merchant marines were ecstatic. They cheered and whooped, exchanging hugs and clapping each other across the back as the vessel sailed closer. There was no question now. She'd spotted their signal-fire, and was headed straight for the island, like a bird winging home to its nest.

Tears of joy were streaming down their faces when, at last, the ship dropped anchor beyond the coral reef, a half-mile offshore. The shouts of her hands as they worked the capstan, the orders her mate barked to her crew, floated clearly across the calm blue waters to the watchers on shore—music to their ears!

Surgeon Love read out the name painted in curling black-

and-gilt script upon her bows. "She's called *Lady Deliverance*, my friends!" he whooped. "And never," he added happily, "was a ship more aptly named!"

"I knew it!" Caroline crowed, her blue eyes dancing as she whirled about like a dervish, her skirts hitched up around her knees. "You see? I told you my papa'd come for us, didn't I, Tim? Didn't I?"

"Aye, sweetheart, you did!" Tim exclaimed gleefully. Grinning, he took her by the waist, twirled her around, and kissed her full on the lips, both of them so giddy with joy and relief, they didn't care who saw them. "Imagine, a respite from eating bananas, day in and day out! And no more head-hunting cannibals to watch out for! No pesky mosquitoes to plague our sleep."

"And no more bloody crocodiles an' snakes!" Jack contributed loudly for good measure, getting into the giddy mood of the moment.

The convicts were understandably far less enthused by the prospect of being rescued. With bleak faces, stony eyes, and heavy hearts, they watched as the *Lady Deliverance* lowered bumboats into the water, then as her captain, three of his ship's officers, and two squads of uniformed marines scrambled down the Jacob's ladder into them.

The marines took up oars and rowed briskly, bending their backs and matching their strokes to keep time with the boatswain's rousing chantey. In no time at all, they'd brought the two small crafts smartly to shore, where they were greeted with more cheers.

"Well, this is it, Kitty, my love," Joe Hardy murmured, catching Kitty about the waist and hugging her to him. "Looks like we're bound fer Botany Bay after all, like it or nay."

"Aye," Kitty murmured, squeezing Joe's hand and smiling up into his serious face. "It do, dunnit? But, don't ye fret, love. It'll all work out fer the best, ye'll see. We'll 'ave a good life there. We'll do our time, make no trouble, and before ye know it, we'll be free, reg'lar settlers in a fine new land."

345

"Aye, love."

"There's hope fer us there, Jack. A chance at a better life than we'd have had in Lunnon. The future's bright, an' it's waitin' fer both of us. I c'n feel it in me bones!"

"Waitin' fer the two of us, together, as man and *wife*," Joe reminded her firmly, moist-eyed. "And for any little 'uns we might be blessed with."

"Aye, love. We'll be together always," Kitty echoed softly, wrapping her arms about Joe's waist. He was a kind, decent man, and she loved him with all her heart. She'd be proud to bear his children, to spend the rest of her days as his woman, his wife.

Joe leaned down to plant a kiss on her lips. As she returned his caress, she spotted Mariah over his shoulder. The young woman had left Nathan in the hut when Tim had sung out that he'd spotted a sail, and was now standing apart from the others on the beach, her arms crossed over her chest as she hugged herself. She made a sad, lonely figure amidst the wildly exultant castaways, her bright hair twisting on the breeze, her eyes distant as they gazed at the swiftly approaching longboats. She looked so very alone, so very bereft, Kitty's gentle heart went out to her.

"Just a minute, all right, love?" Leaving Joe with a lingering hug and a meaningful nod in the other woman's direction, she went to Mariah's side.

"Cripes! What a day! Who'd have thought it, eh?" Kitty observed softly, nodding at the bumboats. "Us, being rescued, after all these weeks! I'd 'ave wagered me last farthing it'd never happen, I would—but I'd 'ave lost, wouldn't I?" She grinned.

"None of us really believed this day would come, I don't think. I suppose the *Lady Deliverance* being here means Harkabout must have survived," Mariah responded absently.

"Looks like it, dunnit? I'll bet that evil old bastard told Governor Amberfield a tall tale t' make 'imself look good, too!"

346

"Aye, no doubt he did."

Kitty clucked at the apathy in her tone. "Owww, ducks, come on, cheer up, do! I can't bear t' see yer like this. Let's 'ave a smile, just fer ole Kitty, hmm?" Kitty cajoled.

Mariah sighed heavily. There were tears brimming in her eyes. "I'm sorry, but I don't feel much like smiling right now, Kit. My heart . . . my heart weighs too heavy for smiles this morn'."

"Nathan's no better, then?"

Mariah shrugged. "I think not. Tho' Surgeon Love said he thought he detected some slight improvement, for my part, I'd have to disagree. Oh, Kitty, he grows weaker by the hour! His cough is no better, and he still has that raging fever that comes and goes. I' faith, 'tis a miracle he's hung on this many days!" She bit her lip, unable to continue for the moment. "Still, I suppose, considering Nathan's feelings about being rescued, 'tis for the best the ship's come now. Before . . . before our falling out, he swore he'd never be recaptured. That he'd sooner die than serve a life sentence for a crime he didn't commit. At least this way, by the time he recovers—if, God willing, he recovers at all—he'll be aboard the *Lady Deliverance* and bound for New South Wales, the choice taken from him."

Kitty's brows rose. "You really reckon he'd scarper, if 'e knew what was goin' on, then? Even if it meant stayin' on this bloody island forever?"

"Reckon?" Mariah laughed harshly. "I *know* it, Kitty! He told me he would—and Nathan always means what he says. Aye, he'd make a run for it, if he was himself."

They both turned to look as a wild cheer went up from the others. The onlookers surged down the beach, splashing through the shallows to welcome the captain of the *Lady Deliverance* and carry him ashore upon their shoulders like a returning hero. Moments later, the marines dragged the bumboats up onto the sand and formed ranks behind their captain, smartly shouldering their muskets.

A thin, angular man, the captain of the *Lady Deliverance*

347

cut an impressive figure as he stood before their expectant numbers, sporting a cockaded tricorn atop a snowy half-wig and a smart navy-and-white uniform. The latter boasted a spotless white stock at the throat and lace frothed from the cuffs, while the shoulders and collar of its coat were adorned with lashings of gold braid.

Addressing them all, the captain introduced himself as Thaddeus Burroughs, a skipper of the East India Company. He had, he told them, sailed from Portsmouth, England, eleven months ago, as master of the *Lady Deliverance*, carrying supplies and fifty convicts, as well as a number of free settlers going out to colonize the new land of Australasia.

Upon his return voyage, he was to have taken on cargoes of spices in Java and India before sailing home. However, he told them with a smile, before leaving the penal colony, he'd been persuaded by the acting Governor of New South Wales, Paul Amberfield, to postpone his return for a few months. Amberfield had instead prevailed upon him to search these waters for any survivors of the *Hester*'s sinking—in particular, the governor's beloved young daughter, Caroline, and his dear niece, Lady Mariah Downing.

"By the grace of God, dare I hope these young ladies number among the survivors?" Burroughs inquired doubtfully, looking about the ragged gathering.

"Indeed they do, Captain," Carmichael declared, beaming. "Mistress Amberfield, Lady Mariah, please come forward."

Caroline did so eagerly, almost dancing from foot to foot and hardly able to keep still in her excitement, while Mariah left Kitty and joined her cousin at a more sedate pace.

"Your servant, Captain Burroughs," Caroline said prettily, making the captain a dainty curtsey and smiling her dimpling smile, both gestures sharply at odds with her ragged attire and her bare, sandy feet. "Really, I cannot begin to tell you how overjoyed we are to see you and your vessel here, sir—nor how very eagerly and *anxiously* we've awaited this happy day! Is that not so, coz?"

"Quite so, Caroline. Captain, 'tis indeed an honor," Mariah murmured with markedly less enthusiasm, also making a curtsey and offering him her hand, which he took. "My cousin has said it all for both of us. We are indeed grateful beyond words, sir."

"There, there, don't mention it, dear lady," the captain, obviously bedazzled by Mariah's radiant beauty, murmured, patting her hand consolingly. "Suffice it to say that I'm honored to take part in reuniting two such delightful young ladies with their loving guardian. Governor Amberfield was beside himself when he heard of the mutiny and the *Hester*'s sinking from Captain Harkabout. Needless to say, he will be joyous beyond words to hear of your safe deliverance."

He bowed deeply, straightened, and cleared his throat. "And now, my good people, I have with me a list of the *Hester*'s company, and of her . . . er . . . transportees. If you would be kind enough to answer when your names are called, we will attempt to ascertain who has survived the *Hester*'s sinking, and who, lamentably, did not."

The roll-call—consisting of the *Hester*'s over eighty crewmembers and marines combined, and the over two-hundred convicts who had filled her holds—took some time to complete. And, although the *Hester*'s few remaining officers and marines sang out readily enough when their names were called, the convicts answered with understandable reluctance and in sullen tones when Captain Burroughs got to them, for after every one, he added the crime for which they'd been convicted and deported.

". . . James 'Peg-Leg' Abbot, transported for acts of piracy against His Majesty's Royal Navy?"

"Dead," Jack Warner supplied heavily, remembering the day of the ambush, when the rascally old pirate had died a hero's death at Foxy's hands.

"Benjamin Coombs, cutpurse?"

"Here!" growled Big Ben, and he spat in the sand.

"Nancy Cox, for prostitution?"

"Here, Cap'n dearie, but that conviction's a dirty lie. Why, I'm as innocent as a bloomin' virgin, right, lads?" Nancy quipped cheekily, and everyone chuckled.

"Francis Daniels, forger?"

"Drowned," someone supplied.

"Leah Dawkins for theft?"

"'Round the point, sir."

"Kitty Dawson, for prostitution?"

"Here, Cap'n, sir" whispered Kitty, her face crimson with shame. She was unable to look Joe in the eye, but he reached for her hand, squeezed it, and winked at her, murmuring, "What's past is past, I told ye, Kitty love. Over and done with. Forget it. Put it behind ye."

"Joseph Hardy, sheep thief?"

"Here, gov'na!" Joe said loudly and defiantly. Grinning at Kitty, he added, "Baaa!" and everyone laughed

"Arthur Jackson, drunkard and debtor?"

"Dead," Jack muttered again.

"Peter Kent, debtor?"

"Lost overboard," someone else volunteered.

And so it went, on down the long list.

"There is some confusion about the following name. One Jonathan Kincaid, an escaped prisoner from Newgate, is believed to have taken refuge upon the *Hester*. He was to be hanged."

"He's dead!" Mariah answered quickly, jumping into the silence before any of the others could answer for Nathan, though why the word "dead" suddenly popped out of her mouth, she had no idea—at first.

To the last man, her companions of the past few months turned to look at her, their expressions puzzled. But to their credit, not one of them contradicted her! Captain Burroughs blithely continued reading off the names on his list, unaware of the raised eyebrows cast in Mariah's direction, or the questions that hovered on the survivors' lips.

"Angus Ruskin, felonious battery?"

"Dead, thank Gawd!" volunteered Big Ben. "Yer might say he lorst his head over a wench fer the last time, Cap'n," he added with a bloodthirsty wink, and remembering the hated convict's gruesome fate, everyone laughed. Ruskin had been no one's favorite, and not a soul among them mourned his death.

"Thomas Thacker, highwayman?"

"Dead," Joe Hardy said thickly, remembering poor Annie's dashing swain and the babe who'd lived less than a day before joining her parents in Heaven.

"Thaddeus Walton?"

"Drowned."

"Very well," Burroughs said at last. "The crew and the convict transportees having been accounted for as well as may be, we shall now move on to the *Hester*'s passengers who, according to my list, numbered six in all. Mistress Amberfield and Lady Downing are accounted for. Do we have here one Master Artemis Matherson, botanist with the Royal Geographical Society?"

"We do indeed, sir!" Matherson sang out. He wiped the grins from the faces of those who tittered at his Christian name with a ferocious glare that made him look like a rabid mouse.

"Your assistant, sir, Master Matthew Wyman, did he also survive?"

The company looked at each other, exchanging shrugs. The name was familiar to none of them.

Matherson opened his mouth to speak, but before he had the chance to do so, Mariah piped up boldly, "Here!" Once again, her defiant tone challenged the others to call her a liar. Unblinking, almost brazenly, she met Matherson's eyes. To her relief, there was pity and understanding in their keen depths. Thank God, he'd guessed what she was up to.

"Matthew Wyman, botanist's assistant?" Burroughs repeated, looking around.

Matherson cleared his throat. "I'm most happy to report that my assistant is, as Lady Downing said, here, among the survivors. However, Captain, the poor fellow's abed in his hut, gravely ill of the lung ague and a fever, and so quite unable to answer for himself.''

"Very well, Professor. And thank you, Lady Downing. Now, we shall continue with our passengers. Richard Vogel, architect? Clement Erickson, master mason?''

Mariah shot the little botanist a grateful smile. Their bald-faced lies had clanged like discordant bells on the sudden, uneasy silence, but not one of those present had denounced Kincaid, bless them. Nor, she prayed, would any man—or woman—among them reveal his true identity. Nathan had contributed far too much towards their survival for them to ever willingly betray him.

Burroughs' voice droned on as Caro left Tim and scrambled across the sand to quiz her cousin.

"Mariah,'' she said softly, "what on earth are you up to now?''

"Hush!'' Mariah came back, equally softly, but with such a daunting look in her eyes, Caro at once fell silent. "I had to do something, don't you see, coz? Time's fast running out!''

"But what will you gain from switching Nathan's name?''

"His freedom—what else? Don't you see? As one of the passengers, he'll have a choice. He'll be able to do as he pleases, once we reach Botany Bay. He can return to England and try to clear his name, if that's what he wishes. Or he can stay in New South Wales and make a new life for himself. As a prisoner, he'd have no such options.

"Oh, Caro, Nathan's a pig-headed brute, but all of us who've come to know him realize he's no murderer,'' Mariah whispered fiercely. "He doesn't deserve to die, nor to be imprisoned for life. I beg you, swear you'll say nothing—not to Captain Burroughs or to Uncle Paul or anyone else! Let Nathan *be* Matthew Wyman, coz, if you care for me at all.''

With an uncertain nod, Caroline crossed her heart and gave her word. And, looking around at the others—Jack Warner,

Master Carmichael, Big Ben, Surgeon Love—Mariah could tell by their sympathetic expressions that the secret would be safe with them. Relief filled her. As far as they were concerned, Jonathan Kincaid was dead. In his place, Matthew Wyman, botanist's assistant, had been resurrected from the deep.

"And now," Burroughs said heavily at last, handing the convict list to his boatswain, who handed him yet another rolled document that bore the penal colony's official wax seal, "I regret I have a far less pleasant duty to perform."

Obviously uncomfortable about whatever he was about to do, he cleared his throat and continued. "Acting upon the authority of His Majesty's servant, Paul Amberfield, acting Governor of the Crown colony of Botany Bay, New South Wales, I am hereby ordered to secure the arrest of Lieutenants Charles Terrence Boyington and Warren Taylor Digby of His Majesty's Navy; also, Able Seamen Jack Warner, Stephen Goodey, and George Pitt, of the *Hester*'s crew. I urge each one of you men to step forward and surrender yourselves to my authority forthwith. However, be warned that, should you decide to resist arrest, I am empowered to employ whatever force is needed to apprehend you."

Shocked gasps, groans of dismay, and nays of protest rippled through the crowd as the popular Jack Warner—stony-faced, his shoulders slumped, his expression unreadable—rose and mutely made his way forward to stand before the captain.

"Jack Warner, Captain," he said softly. "Surrenderin' meself to your authority, as asked. But Pitt an' Goodey're dead, sir, an' so's Digby."

"See here, now, not so fast, Jack! First, Captain, I would know upon what charge you order the arrest of this man, sir?" demanded Carmichael sharply, ruddy-faced with indignation as he stepped in front of Jack to glower at Captain Burroughs.

"He and the others are charged with inciting a mutiny on the high seas, sir. And mutiny is a hanging offense, as well you know, Master-Mate."

"Mutiny—this good fellow? Nonsense!" Matherson protested, stepping forward to stand alongside Carmichael. "Absolute poppycock! We were there, after all, sir, and as God is my judge, *there was no mutiny*—unless you consider Captain Harkabout abandoning his vessel and his duties a mutinous act! The *Hester* sank in a gale. Her destruction was an act of God, sir, nothing more. If you would call someone to account, then you must tackle Him."

"I'm sorry, gentlemen, but I have my orders. However, I'm sure you'll be permitted to speak on behalf of the accused at their court-martial, once we reach Botany Bay. Meanwhile, the prisoners are to be held under close guard in the brig of the *Lady Deliverance* for the duration of the voyage. I give you my word, gentlemen, that in New South Wales, they will have ample opportunity to answer to the serious charges Captain Harkabout has made against them. Men—"

"Harkabout?" the master-mate cut in, round-eyed with disbelief. "You're saying Governor Amberfield *believed* that yellow-bellied excuse for a skipper?" Carmichael spat in the sand. "Devil take him! I should've guessed he had a hand in this farce!"

Burroughs nodded sympathetically, but turned to the marines and nodded, nonetheless. "You have your orders, men. Jump to it!"

The crowd that had been so elated but moments before watched in choked silence as heavy iron shackles were fastened about Jack's wrists and ankles, like those on the very convicts whose lives he'd once defied Harkabout to save. Two marines then led the ship's carpenter down to the water's edge to await rowing out to the *Lady Deliverance*. Still other marines—these armed with muskets, pistols, and billy clubs—marched smartly away towards the point in search of any who might resist recapture.

The bright promise of that long-awaited day was now dimmed by a pall of gloom.

"I've done all I can for you, my love," Mariah sadly told Nathan later as she bathed his poor, burning body yet again. "The rest is up to you. Fight this cursed fever! Oh, please, Nathan, fight, and come back to me—to us! We need you . . . and so does poor Jack. We all need you desperately."

Nathan lay upon heaped dried grasses spread with sailcloth. He was shivering violently and thrashing about, muttering in harsh bursts about Roger Loring, the innkeeper, or calling on Rose, his boyhood sweetheart, or else gabbling about Linden Hall, his birthplace, and speaking to his father and mother as if he could see them. It made Mariah's heart ache to hear his tortured cries, let alone look at him. His once-glossy black hair was lank and dull now, and clung in sweat-sodden strands to his temples. There were great hollows beneath his eyes, the yellowish skin about them stained purple, as if bruised. His healthy bronze tan had faded, and his cheekbones jutted sharply beneath too-taut, yellowish flesh. His lips were cracked, too, and dry and bloody besides.

As Mariah squeezed out a damp cloth to sponge his forehead, scalding tears escaped from beneath spiked lashes and trickled down her cheeks. She leaned over and pressed her face to her love's wasted chest, encircling his poor, fevered body with her arms as she wept. Beneath her ear, the dark pelt of his chest hair was curling with sweat, the beat of his heart was fluttery and rapid—far too rapid to bode well for his recovery. Sweet Jesu, he was so very, very ill! Surely he couldn't survive another night with this heat raging through him.

The knot in her breast tightened like a clenched fist, becoming an ache of unbearable agony. Her desperate efforts to obtain Nathan a new identity would be wasted if he died. What use would any identity be then? she wondered miserably.

* * *

When Nathan stirred for the first time in over ten days, the sky outside the hut was fading from blue to amethyst. The parrots in the coconut palms were quiet now as they settled down to roost for the night. So, too, were the colonies of chattering monkeys silent. The faintest of balmy trade-winds stirred the palm fronds to whispering and wafted a cooling current over his soaked body.

Now that the fever had broken at last, he shivered uncontrollably, although the ragged canvas beneath him was sodden with his sweat. The woolen blanket thrown over him seemed heavy as lead. He thrust it away, groaning as he swiped a furry tongue over cracked, smarting lips and forced leaden eyes to open.

He discovered he was staring up at banana-leaf thatch through which chinks of lavender sky were visible. He frowned in confusion. Where the devil was he? And how had he come here? Was he ill—did that explain the terrible aching in his joints, the weakness everywhere in his body? He tried to sit up, but failed and fell back, trembling with the enormous effort such a simple act demanded of him.

A pox on this cursed weakness! he swore silently. But for what seemed an eternity, he lay there, breathing heavily, until his mind had cleared a little and fragments of memory returned. With them came a single name, and the vague, pleasing recollection of a woman's lovely, tear-washed face gazing sadly down at him as cool, gentle hands caressed his cheek. Then he recalled her begging him to fight the fever, to come back to her.

Mariah.

He'd wanted to beg her not to weep for him, but, tongue-tied by fever, had been unable to utter a word.

"Mariah!" he croaked hoarsely. "Mariah?"

There was no answer to his call. Forcing his shaky limbs to obey him, he managed to sit up, then to stagger upright, reeling like a drunkard as he made his way to the hut's doorway. He hung onto the bamboo frame like a drowning man clinging to a spar.

Raising a heavy head, he stared blearily about him. There

were the other huts—but they looked deserted. Where the devil was everyone? Had they gone, left him alone here on the island? Nay. He fancied he could smell the woodsmoke of a fire, and the savory aroma of roasting meat; could hear scraps of voices and laughter on the breeze. 'Twas supper time, that explained it! Everyone must be gathered about the cooking fire for the evening meal. He swallowed, his parched throat painful as he did so. Water! He needed water! There would be water there, at the fire, as much as he needed. Cool, fresh water to wash the foul taste from his throat and tongue, to ease the pain of his cracked and bloody lips.

Taking one careful step at a time like a toddling infant, and pausing every so often to recoup his strength, Nathan made his way between the huts and out onto the beach. There, he pulled up short, his jaw dropping at the sight that met his gummy eyes.

Anchored beyond the reef was a sailing ship!

Or . . . was it? His thoughts were so fragmented and confused, his vision still so blurred, he was at a loss to know if the vessel was truly there, or but a figment of his imagination! Blinking owlishly, he tried to focus, but at that very moment, four uniformed marines appeared from somewhere off to his left. They were dragging three shackled prisoners down the sand, to where a bumboat waited. His eyes widened. One of the prisoners was Jack! Nay, surely not? Could it really be decent, God-fearing Jack Warner they had in chains between them? It was!

There'd been a terrible mistake! He had to tell . . . tell those damned fools that Jack . . . Jack hadn't . . . that Jack couldn't have . . . that Jack would never have done . . . what? Damn! A pox on his cursed skull, he could not remember.

Suddenly, the scene before him spun crazily as a top, colors streaming together in an endless blur of ocean, sand, and sky. He cursed, rocking on his heels, close to fainting with the effort it took to remain upright. The only sense that yet functioned properly was his hearing.

357

"This the last of 'em, then?" he heard one of the marines ask.

"Nay, more's the bleedin' pity. There's four from that foul rat's nest 'round the point wot Cap'n Burroughs wants taken aboard t' night, bugger 'im. Two convict wenches an' a pair o' slippery felons. Seems they tried t' run fer it. Leastways, so said Hughes."

"Convict wenches, eh?" The first marine snickered. "I'll see t' loadin' them wenches aboard, never fear, Alf. Ye can take it easy, lad, an' watch how it's done."

"The devil I will!" retorted his companion. "Yer bloody paws 'ud be up them wenches' skirts and fumblin' about quicker'n I could say 'Breadfruit Bligh'!"

"In't that Gawd's truth?" Willie Bodges admitted cheerfully. "But I do love t' squeeze a plump li'l arse, I do." And they both sniggered.

"Between you an' me, Bodges, I in't happy about the cap'n takin' that sick bastard aboard come mornin'," Alf confided gloomily.

"Wyman, that botanist bloke, yer mean? Me neither! But that 'un'll bring no pestilence aboard the *Lady Deliverance*! I seen 'im meself. He'll not last the night out."

"I hope t' Gawd you're right, mate. A plague ship's a sorry sight, it is."

Nathan swayed perilously as the marines shoved the bumboat down the sand into the shallows. They'd chivvied the prisoners aboard her before he realized the danger of standing there, in the open, where he could be seen.

If they were rounding up the convicts, they'd be looking for him!

Gritting his teeth, he forced his rubbery legs to carry him back into the dense cover of the coconut grove, and there sank to his knees, shivering so violently his teeth chattered.

The blood was roaring like a hurricane in his ears as he gaped at the trim vessel riding at anchor. His vision blurred alarmingly as he tried to focus again, the colors running together like watercolors bleeding over a wet canvas. But, although he flicked his head to clear it, the merchantman was still there when he dared to look again.

God's Teeth! His worst fears had been fulfilled. Against all odds, a British ship had found them! And, from what he'd overheard, those laid low by the fever—like that Wyman fellow the marines had spoken of, and himself—were to be carried aboard the vessel come morning. They'd come to the hut for him, would carry him aboard, and then he'd be unable to escape. *If* they found him.

Beach and sky changed places, reeling drunkenly as he suddenly stood up. Fresh urgency filled him now, sending adrenaline pumping through his veins. There was no time to waste! Somehow, he must force his damned, treacherous body to move. Must get far away from the cove before high tide. Had . . . to . . . run . . . to hide out . . . 'til they'd sailed without him.

And he knew the perfect place to do so.

Chapter Twenty-Seven

Mariah stared at the makeshift bed in disbelief. It was empty. Nathan was gone! When she'd left him to go down to the beach with the others and welcome the crew of the *Lady Deliverance*, he'd appeared deeply asleep—so deeply asleep she would have wagered gold he'd not stir before she returned. Clearly he'd wandered off, confused by the fever, and in his delirious state he could easily get hurt.

Imagining him stumbling into the fire and being burned, or staggering into the ocean in an effort to cool himself off and drowning, she was frantic as she ran through camp, going from hut to hut in search of him and then racing down the beach to scan the tranquil sea. But there was no sign of Nathan, and none of the others remembered seeing him, except much earlier in his hut, before the captain and crew of the rescue ship had come ashore.

"What on earth's wrong, coz?" Caroline demanded, jumping up from the battered sea-chest Nathan had recovered from the *Hester*, and into which she and Kitty were stowing their somewhat ragged belongings. Mariah, standing in the doorway of the hut, was clearly agitated.

"It's Nathan, Caro. He's gone!" she whispered, afraid Captain Burroughs or one of his men would overhear her. "I can't find him anywhere in camp! Have you seen him?"

Caroline shook her head, as did Kitty, their expressions troubled.

"The last time we saw him, he was asleep in his hut. Oh, Mariah, the *Lady Deliverance* sails with the morning tide!" Caroline reminded her unnecessarily. "We must find him by then, or he'll be left behind! Come on. We'll help you look for him, won't we, Kitty?"

"Aye."

"Thank you! But . . . please don't say anything to anyone else just yet. I daren't take the chance of someone's slipping up and asking about Jonathan Kincaid's whereabouts instead of Matthew Wyman's," Mariah reminded them, wringing her hands.

"Got yer, love. Mum's the word," Kitty promised for them both.

It was Kitty who found the footprints in the damp sand that led to the coconut grove shortly after, Caroline who alerted Mariah to the churned sand beneath the trees there, where it looked as if someone might have rested—or hidden—to watch the goings-on on the beach.

"Dear God, he must have come to, stumbled out here and seen the ship!" Mariah whispered, sinking down onto her knees, sick with concern. "And with the fever jumbling his thoughts, Lord knows what he made of it all!"

"You know him better than anyone. What would he have done if he saw the ship, coz?" Caroline asked.

Mariah bit her lip. "If he could, he'd have gone into hiding until he was certain she'd sailed without him!"

"What?"

"Aye," Mariah confirmed, certain now that that was what must have happened. "He swore he'd never be recaptured by the British authorities, you see? He was hoping instead that we'd be rescued by a Dutchman sailing these waters, so that he could return to England as a free man and try to clear his name. Aye. If he saw the *Lady Deliverance* and her crew and was clearheaded enough to realize their import, I'd wager he's gone to ground."

"But he's so very ill, coz!" Caro whispered, tears filling her blue eyes. "Another chill night spent in the open—another soaking from the rain—why, it could kill him!"

"Don't let's go buyin' trouble, ducks." Kitty consoled the girl, noting the ashen pallor of Mariah's face. "If'n he were sharp enough t'know the *Lady Deliverance* spelled trouble fer 'im, then 'e were sharp enough t' hole up somewhere under cover, somewhere hidden where no one'd think of lookin' fer 'im, right, Mariah?"

"I hope so, Kitty," Mariah agreed, the beginnings of an idea taking shape. "Dear God, I hope so!"

"Well, it'll be dark soon, so we'd best make the most o' what's left o' the light t' search for 'im," Kitty suggested. "I'll drop a word in Joe's ear. 'E'll 'elp us look. Caro, 'ow's about givin' Tom and Ben a nudge? There, there, cheer up, love! Between us, we'll track 'im down, never fear!"

Mariah forced a wan smile, but her thoughts were racing. She believed she knew exactly where Nathan would have hidden, if their suspicions that he'd had gone to ground were correct, but she had no intention of betraying that hiding place to the others, nay, not yet. First, she had to talk to him. . . .

It was in the wee hours of the next morning, shortly before dawn, before Mariah dared to slip away from camp and follow her hunch.

The survivors—all eager to hear what news Burroughs had of England's war with the American colonies and of the Revolt of the French populace against their king, Louis XVI, since the *Hester* had departed a little over a year ago—had sat up late about the campfire with the captain, gossipping and yarning. Mariah had been reluctant to risk leaving the camp until all had found their beds or had fallen asleep where they sat.

Although the girls had enlisted the help of almost all of their party, and although they'd searched the island far and wide for him, they'd been unable to find Nathan, and Mariah's elation had grown. Rather than filling her with despondency, that failure had deepened her conviction that her hunch was right. Nathan had gone into hiding, all right—and had done so in the one place he believed unknown to anyone but the two of them; the rainbow-cave behind the waterfall!

The guard usually posted there to keep the baboon colony from reclaiming the watering hole had been lifted, since they would be leaving the island on the morning tide, so there would have been no one to observe him as he swam across to the falls—no one there now to prevent her from finding out if her suspicions were correct.

The jungle was doubly frightening by dark of night, but her brushes with death—and the discovery, on that storm-tossed mountain ridge, that she possessed reservoirs of courage and resilience as yet untapped—had made her a stronger, braver person than the frightened little nitwit who'd been shipwrecked all those weeks ago. That new-found courage, buttressed by her love for Nathan and their unborn babe, was all she needed.

The path to the jungle-pool was one that had grown as familiar to her as her own hand. Nathan had ordered the lush undergrowth regularly cut back to make the rolling of barrels of fresh water from the pool to their camp less difficult. Since his illness, Carmichael had done likewise. And so, her way lit by the moon's watery light, she slipped down the narrow path, steeling herself to ignore the furtive rustlings in the undergrowth on either side of her, the wild beasts that watched her pass with unblinking eyes that gleamed like emeralds or rubies within the emerald shadows.

Within minutes, she found herself standing in the clearing by the pool, breathless with nervousness, jittery with mounting anxiety. *Please God, let me find him there*! she prayed, padding barefoot through the low ferns and cool mud to the water's edge. If not, she had nowhere left to look, no idea of where he could have gone. Come the morning tide, the *Lady Deliverance* would be forced to sail without him. And Nathan, left behind on the island to fend for himself, gravely ill and without proper care, would surely die. *Nay!* However cruel, however unjustly he had treated her, she could not bear to think of him dead. Despite everything, she still loved him.

The falls were eerie in the gloom, their ribbons of silver unravelling against the darkness. The pool was dark-green and silent, save for where the force of the tumbling falls disturbed its mirror surface with froths and ripples of paler color. The constant splashing, rushing sound was somehow reassuring. Looking cautiously about her first, to make sure no sly crocodiles lay in wait upon the banks, she stepped up onto a boulder and dived headfirst into the pool, gasping as the chill water embraced her, flowed around her body with an icy caress.

A few strong strokes carried her across the pool, to the far side of the falls. She ducked beneath them and clambered out, shivering, onto the rocky ledges beyond, her fingers tightly crossed.

But there was no need for her superstitious precautions. Her toes encountered his sprawled, damp body easily, despite the darkness.

She knelt quickly beside him, one hand going at once to his brow. As she'd expected, it felt unnaturally warm and dry to her touch—but not, she fancied, as hot as in the days before. The fever, thank God, seemed to be receding. If only she could persuade him to go with her to New South Wales, he might very well survive the sickness. Somehow, she had to make him understand what she'd done; she must convince him that he had nothing to fear by joining the other survivors, that with his new name and his new identity as the botanist Matherson's assistant, Matthew Wyman, he could return to England on the very first vessel leaving New South Wales, as a free man.

And if he would not believe her? If he refused to trust her and opted to stay on the island, what then? To her surprise, the answer was a resounding: *Stay!* Aye, she realized, at some point since she'd discovered he'd disappeared, she must have made up her mind that she would stay here, too, if he refused to leave, whether he wished her to do so or nay. Alone on the island, dependent upon each other for companionship and affection—their child growing stronger and larger each day in her womb—surely he would come around and would see that who her father was, was unimportant? That loving each other was all that really mattered, that and their child, and devil take all else. He would. He *must!* 'Else her heart would surely break. . . .

Of a sudden, his hand came out of the shadows. His steely fingers clamped around her arm like a vise, startling her, squeezing so very hard, she cried out in fear.

"Mariah?"

"Yes!"

His grip slackened. His hand fell away. "What the devil are you doing here?" he growled, sitting up.

"Oh, Nathan, when I found you gone, the hut empty, I was so very worried about you! I knew you must have seen the ship and come here to hide, so I—"

"And who else knows I'm here? Who did you bring with you, damn you?" he snarled, cutting off her explanations. "Her British captain? Her stalwart marines, with their pretty leg shackles and wrist irons? After all, isn't that how they recapture an escaped convict?"

"I led no one here, I swear it. I came alone, to . . . to talk to you!"

"Then you have wasted your time. There's nothing left to say, Mariah."

"You're lying. You must be. Nathan, I know you too well! I cannot—I *will* not—believe that you could swear your love for me in one moment and feel nothing for me in the next!"

"Then you've misjudged me, m'lady. If I spoke of love,

365

'twas lies I uttered—all lies. I could never have loved Judge Harry Winslow's daughter—fair though she may be—were she the last woman on earth. Nay, my sweet, 'twas lust that governed my tongue, nothing more," he jeered. "So, come. Up with your skirts, wench! God's Teeth, I'm hot for a tumble, even now."

She drew back, recoiling as he reached for her, his harsh laughter cutting her to the quick as she batted his hands away from her breasts. "Dear Mother of God, how cruel you've grown!"

"Cruel?" He grunted. "If honesty be cruel, then aye, 'tis cruel I am! Now. Enough of this bandying of words! Go away. Leave me be. Leave this island! But before you do, be warned, Mariah. Should you breathe a word of my whereabouts, I shall find you—and cut out your treacherous heart!"

"I would never betray you, sir. Unlike yours, my heart is ever loyal, as I told you before. So loyal, I have perjured myself to the honorable captain who has rescued us—and sorely do I regret it now!"

"Perjured?"

"Aye, curse you! When Captain Burroughs inquired after the whereabouts of 'the escaped condemned prisoner, Jonathan Kincaid,' I told him you'd gone down with the *Hester*. Don't you see, I lied—we all lied—to give you a new name, a new identity, to set you free. Master Matherson said you were his botanist's assistant, Matthew Wyman, and *not one* among the castaways denied it. Their gratitude and their respect for you made liars of them, Nathan. Oh, God, what fools you've made of us!" she cried, covering her face with her hands and sobbing uncontrollably.

Her words, her weeping, took him aback, made him cringe inwardly with the beginnings of guilt. "Mariah, I . . ."

But whatever he'd intended to say was abruptly cut short as a third person appeared on the damp rock ledges before them, water streaming off his body in the dawning light as he clambered up into the hidden cave.

366

"First-Seaman Biggs wi' 'is Majesty's Marines, m'lady," the man declared, pinching his nose to rid it of water. "Cap'n Burroughs sent me t' help ye with the sick man— *Whoa*!"

Even as Biggs spoke, Nathan staggered to his feet and suddenly thrust himself past the startled marine, diving headfirst from the ledge and back under the falls. The marine, who'd clearly been expecting no resistance, shrugged and dived in after him.

By the time Mariah dragged herself from the water at the edge of the pool, Nathan had fled into the jungle, a number of marines in hot pursuit. Captain Burroughs, Master-Mate Carmichael, Kitty, Caroline, and several of the others were milling about at the water's edge, clearly upset by the turn events had taken.

Seeing Mariah, Caroline broke away from the others. She ran to her and flung her arms about her.

"Please say you can forgive me, coz?" Caroline pleaded between muffled sobs. "I know I gave you my word I'd never tell anyone about the cave, but I *had* to tell Captain Burroughs where you were, don't you see? I love you, Mariah. And I know that you love Nathan. You would both have died here, all alone, if the *Lady Deliverance* had sailed without you. Oh, Mariah, you and Papa are all the family I have left in the world. You're dearer to me than any sister could ever have been. As dear as my own mama, God rest her soul! I just couldn't b-bear for that to h-happen."

"You silly little goose, of course I forgive you," Mariah crooned, gathering her sobbing cousin into her arms and stroking Caroline's hair consolingly. But despite her reasurances, her eyes were bleak as she stared towards the jungle into which Nathan, convinced she'd betrayed his hiding place, had fled. "You did what you felt was best, and that's all anyone can do. Truly, coz, I cannot fault you for it."

"I didn't tell the captain about the other matter . . . you know, Nathan's name . . . I swear I didn't!" Caro insisted in a hoarse whisper.

"Good girl. Go now. Go back to camp with Kitty and make ready our things to be taken aboard the ship. Can you do that for me?"

"Of course. But . . . but what about you?" Caroline asked tremulously, raising her tear-streaked face to Mariah's. The doubt in her eyes betrayed her fear that Mariah might yet try to remain behind, if the marines should be unable to recapture Nathan.

"I'll be along soon."

"You promise? Cross your heart you won't try to stay?"

"Cross my heart!"

Caroline allowed Kitty to lead her away and many of the others followed. They left just in time, too, to Mariah's way of thinking, for the marines who'd pursued Nathan into the jungle returned seconds later with the fugitive, struggling violently, between them. She would not have wanted everyone to witness his recapture.

"Got 'im, Cap'n!" Alf sang out, red-faced. "Gawd, but 'e's slippery as a bloomin' eel, 'e is! We almost lorst 'im back there!"

"Aye. No doubt the fever's robbed the poor fellow of his reason," Burroughs said, his tone compassionate as he turned to Mariah. "Having given him the benefit of your tender nursing, would not you say so, my dear lady?"

"Indeed I would, Captain Burroughs," Mariah agreed softly, her heart torn in two by Nathan's desperate struggles, his wild, futile lunges for freedom. "And that being so, please ask your men to be as gentle as may be with him. When he . . . when he is well and himself, Master Wyman is a good and gentle soul."

"Enough said, Lady Downing." Eager to please the lovely young woman, the bachelor captain smartly issued the order.

The marine named Alf snorted as he ducked to evade Nathan's lethal, swinging fists. "We'll give it a try, Cap'n, but— Christ's Blessed Bones!—'E's awful strong, fer a sick man.

I'd not like t' tackle this 'un when 'e's in the bloom o' health!''
He panted.

"Me neither!" his partner, Willie agreed, also breathing
heavily as he grasped Nathan's wrist and wrenched his arm up,
behind him. "Now, now, come on, ole son," he cajoled.
"There in't no need t' fight us lads! We're yer saviors, we are!
Ye've bin rescued, ye bloody fool! Now, put up yer fists an'
have done wi' it!"

Mariah watched with tears in her eyes as, despite their reassurances, Nathan broke free of Willie and lurched about,
swinging his fists at the marines like a wounded wild animal
trying desperately to avoid capture and caging.

But in the end, as she had known from the first, it was no
use. Nathan was too weak. He had lain ill for far too long to
hope to escape.

Sure enough, Alf got behind him and fastened his wiry arms
about Nathan's throat, jerking him off his feet and onto his
back on the grass, then sitting on his chest. Willie quickly
straddled Nathan's legs, while at Burroughs' nod, a third marine hurried forward, carrying a coil of rope. They bound him,
lashing his ankles and wrists together to keep him from lashing
out at them.

"Must you do that?" Mariah protested, hovering about like
a nervous mother bird.

"'Fraid so, m'lady. 'Tis either tie the swab, or fetch 'im a
wallop across 'is head, m'lady!'' Alf informed her, rubbing
his bruised jaw where Nathan had landed a lucky blow. "But,
sick as 'e is, I don't fancy his chances if we use the billy-club
on 'im, mum.''

"Very well, then. Do what you must—but please, be quick
about it," she whispered imploringly.

She could not bear to watch. but turned away, heartsick, as
her proud, fierce love was forced to endure this final blow to
his male dignity and pride, despite knowing what they did was
for his own good.

Even when he'd been trussed up like a wild boar and the marines bent to pick him up, Nathan continued to curse and to snarl obscenities at his captors, straining against his bonds until knotted cords stood out in sharp relief at his temples and down his throat. Sweat poured from his brow.

"A loyal heart be damned, m'lady Judas!" he accused hoarsely as they carried him past her, his green eyes blazing into hers with such hatred, she flinched as if he'd struck her. "Is this how you prove your loyalty—your love? By betraying me? *Damn you!*"

She offered no reply. Indeed, what could she have said that would have changed anything? And, though her heart ached with sorrow, though she yearned to run to him and protest that this was not of her doing, she would not. Let him hate her, if he would! Aye, let him *feed* upon his hatred; let it nurture him, give him the strength to grow well and strong again; let it fuel his will to survive, to live, as her love had failed to do. In but a few short days, they would sail into Botany Bay, and he would be a free man. Free—and well, God willing.

That was all that mattered.

"Lady Downing?"

It was the captain, offering her his arm. With a sad little smile, she took it and allowed him to lead her from the jungle and down to the beach, where the bumboats awaited.

From the bows of the small boat, she looked back across the sparkling turquoise water to the lush green island that had been their home for so many weeks and wondered: *What will the future bring . . . ?*

Chapter Twenty-Eight

Port Jackson, New South Wales

Broom in hand, Mariah paused in her sweeping and came to the door of her uncle's house to shake out a braided rag-rug. Easily distracted from such tedious labors, she found her attention caught by a pair of creamy galahs, or rose-breasted cockatoos, squabbling noisily in a bottlebrush tree. Their plumage made a pretty picture against the tree's flaming red blossoms and the hazy, rounded lavender ridges of the Blue Mountains far beyond. These mountains were a part of the Great Dividing Range that, along with the Pacific Ocean beyond the coast, hemmed in the growing colony of Port Jackson on the Sydney Cove. And somewhere out there, between the ocean and the mountains, armed with a musket, was Jonathan Kincaid, alias Matthew Wyman, one of the colony's newest hunters. . . .

"Missie? Missie Malili? Henry bring *kanguru*. What place him belonga?"

The polite query broke into her daydreaming. Kneading the small of her back, Mariah looked up to see Henry, Uncle Paul's aborigine servant—if Henry could properly be considered anyone's servant—at her elbow. Of medium height and slenderly yet powerfully built, Henry was typical of his race, with his dark-brown complexion, large forehead; broad, flat nose, jutting jaw, and bush of springy dark hair. He was naked, except for the pair of baggy white drawers her Uncle Paul had insisted he wear whenever he came to the farm or the settlement, for decency's sake. These were now riding dangerously low about his lean flanks. In one hand, Henry carried a long native spear tipped with a hardwood shaft, and his *woomera*, or spear-thrower, in the other. One of the strange creatures the natives called a *kanguru* sprawled lifeless at his dusty bare feet, she noticed belatedly.

"God Bless you, Henry!" she exclaimed with a grateful smile. "Your hunting has saved us yet again!"

Henry grinned, his teeth very white against his dusky skin. He was obviously pleased by the praises of the missie with the strangely-colored hair; the white woman he and his nomadic band had named Malili, after a god-woman from the Dreaming Time, because her own name was unpronounceable to them.

"Please take the *kanguru* to Mistress Kitty. Tell her I said she was to give you damper, enough for you and your woman and little ones." Damper was a form of flat bread that Henry's shy aborigine wife had taught Kitty to make. The recipe was simple; flour made from ground seeds was moistened with water to form balls of dough, then baked in the hot ashes of a cooking fire. Kitty had become proficient at this task, and Henry loved her damper bread, especially when it was spread with the tangy plum jam she'd made from wild plums Henry had himself gathered out in the bush, by boiling them with some of the precious sugar Captain Burroughs had brought from Java in the holds of the *Lady Deliverance*. He'd given them a sack on one of the occasions he'd come out to the farm to pay court to Mariah.

"Damper with jam, missie?" Henry asked hopefully.

"Of course," Mariah promised solemnly. "Lots of jam for the fine hunter who brought down a fat *kanguru* for our supper."

When a beaming Henry had gone in search of Kitty, Mariah dropped the rug on the doorstep, cast aside her broom and wandered out past her struggling vegetable patches and down to the spring. Using the dipper that was kept there, she drank thirstily, wiped her streaming face on a dampened corner of her apron, then flopped down in the shade of a clump of gum trees and pulled up her homespun skirts to cool her legs. She really should water her sickly plants, or return to the cleaning, cooking, spinning, and churning that filled her days. But at the moment, she was simply too weary to do anything more strenuous than rest her weary head against a silvery gum-tree trunk, and steal a few minutes' respite from her labors.

Cleaning was such a thankless, endless task, anyway. No matter how she, Kitty, Nancy, and Caro swept and dusted, scrubbed and scoured Uncle Paul's two-storey house of native stone and timber, grit was still everywhere. It found its way into everything; the butter churn, the flour bin, the honey jar, the clothes-press. How hot it was here, too, especially for one in her condition—and it was only the month of February, with several hot summer months yet to come! She shook her head in dismay. She doubted she'd ever grow accustomed to the topsy-turvy seasons of New South Wales, where the months she'd considered summer in her native England were the winter season and vice versa, though she was gradually coming to accept everything else that was different and strange about this wild new land that was now her home.

The past two months had brought about a change in her, she knew, and she was glad, for she'd feared upon leaving the island that she would never belong anywhere again! The day the *Lady Deliverance* had sailed into Botany Bay and she'd seen the settlement for the very first time had only served to deepen her fears.

"Well, here she is, Lady Downing. Port Jackson—your new home!" Captain Burroughs had informed her as a longboat carried them across that perfect, deep bay, bringing them ever closer to the far-from-perfect, hilly brown shores of the new colony.

Mariah had looked where Burroughs pointed and had felt crushing disappointment. Tears had choked her, lodging like a great stone in her breast. Oh, how she'd longed in that moment for the beauty of her island "home," with its white-sand beaches and feathery coconut groves, its lush green vegetation and vivid, exotic blossoms; for the nights of endless passion and the days of sweet laughter and love she'd shared with Jonathan Kincaid . . . and lost.

Here, harsh outcroppings of weathered sandstone that the captain called The Rocks made up the western shores, while mangrove swamps lay to the east. What few buildings broke the skyline appeared sorry dwellings little better than hovels, though the captain, noting her dismay, had hastily assured her that these and the surrounding ledges and caves were where a few of the more shiftless convicts still lived. Governor Philip's house, where Uncle Paul—as acting governor of the colony in Captain Arthur Philip's absence—had taken up residence while his own new farmhouse was being finished some miles away, was a sturdy if simple structure built of native woods and stone, he'd promised.

Her first impressions of the settlement proper had been little more favorable. Ox-drawn carts carried loads of stone, rushes, or wood along winding waterfront "streets" that were lined with a variety of dwellings, from simple huts of turf roofed with bark to more ambitious cottages of native stone or wood. There was a blacksmith's, even a tavern or two, a hospital, and the austere barracks that housed the marines and their officers, and it was upon these dwellings or on the roads themselves that the convicts toiled.

They'd looked up from their work as the captain strode past with the new arrivals, and had catcalled and whistled lewdly after the women. Mariah, Caro, and Kitty had blushed and kept their eyes steadfastly upon Thaddeus Burroughs' broad back, looking neither to left nor right and studiously ignoring the men. Saucy Nancy, on the other hand, trailing at the rear of their little party, had cheekily blown kisses to the most handsome among the convicts, and had waved in greeting, despite a jealous Ben's hissed insistence that she "Have done wi' yer flirtin', ye bold baggage."

"It's victuals we need, ye scurvy swab," one scrawny old reprobate had cried, and he'd spat in disgust. "Food—not more hungry mouths t' feed!"

"When ye get home, Cap'n, tell His Bleedin' Majesty that while he's gorgin' 'imself on roast-beef an' puddin', we're starvin' out here!" another had yelled after them, his outburst silenced by a growled threat from one of the armed marines who guarded the chain-gangs made up of the colony's most hardened convicts.

The convict transportees were not held under lock and key for the greater part, but appeared free to do as they wished, short of escaping, Mariah had observed, on condition they employed themselves in some worthwhile manner that would benefit the colony at large, and caused no discord among their fellow convicts. Hangings, Burroughs confided in answer to her cautious questions, were rare here, that sentence meted out only to murderers or those who stole from the precious and heavily guarded and rationed food-supplies. Some of the convicts, women and men alike, worked at weeding and hoeing the struggling rows of crops planted in Farm Cove, while others gathered rushes or kindling, fished from the Bay, or herded the few cattle and sheep the colony possessed. Accordingly, Mariah had been encouraged that Uncle Paul would respond favorably to her request that Kitty, Joe Hardy, Nancy, and Big Ben Coombs be given positions in the Governor's household, rather than assigned some other labor. Both women learned quickly, were hard workers and trustworthy; while Ben and Joe both appeared to have some knowledge of livestock. Ben claimed some skill at working with horses, while Joe Hardy, the son of a farmer before he'd travelled to the wicked city of London and fallen on hard times, was good with farm animals.

A tearfully joyous reunion between Caroline and her father had followed soon after at Government House, and then it had been Mariah's turn to fall into her Uncle Paul's arms and receive the decent, kindly man's welcoming embrace. In answer to his searching look and his guarded inquiry about his brother-in-law's whereabouts, Mariah had given him the sad news that her father had passed away just days before they were to have sailed from England for New South Wales.

"My poor, dear girl!" Paul Amberfield had exclaimed, his grey eyes moist as he held her to him, his voice cracking with compassion. "To lose your papa so suddenly, and not peacefully in his own bed at a great age, as every man wishes to meet his end, but on a public thoroughfare! Pray, what was the cause of his death? Is it known?"

Mariah shrugged and sighed, remembering that awful Friday morning with painful clarity. "No one knows for sure, Uncle. Papa had gone to Old Holborn Street to meet someone on a matter of urgent business, it appears. He seemed quite agitated that morning when he left the inn where we'd taken lodgings, but who he was to meet and whether his business was ever concluded, I do not know. Not two hours after he left, one of his former clerks at the Old Bailey brought me the news of his death. The physician who was summoned said Papa succumbed to a fit of apoplexy, and that death took him instantly," Mariah explained, biting her lower lip to stanch the grief that welled anew. "There was naught that could be done to revive him, alas. We buried him the following day, and within hours Caro and I boarded the *Hester*."

"Ah, well," Paul murmured sadly, "What's done is done, and cannot be changed. And perhaps a swift and sudden end was the most merciful way, eh, my dear? Who are we to question God's will in such matters? But . . . 'tis indeed a sorry twist of fate to lose your dear husband and to have your father follow him to the grave so soon after," he sympathized, not noticing Mariah's shudder of revulsion at his mention of her departed husband. "And then, on top of everything else, the shipwreck . . . God knows, my poor child, you've had more than your fair share of sorrows to bear. However, you must never think yourself alone in the world, for 'tis not so, not at all. You have Caroline and myself, and we will do everything in our power to make you happy here with us."

She'd smiled through her tears. "My heartfelt thanks, Uncle. I am fortunate indeed to have you both."

"Come, come, there's no need for gratitude, Mariah. Alicia would have wanted it no other way. Dear God, how you resemble your mama! Looking at you, 'tis as if my dearest sister were still alive."

That first week, they'd slept at Government House, she and Caro sharing a four-poster bed in one of the upper rooms, while Kitty and Nancy were lodged in the kitchens and had passed the night quite comfortably on grass-filled pallets before the wide hearth. Until the colony's only minister had married Kitty and Joe Hardy three weeks ago, Joe and Ben Coombs had been banished to beds in the stables.

Captain Burroughs and two of his ship's officers had been invited to join them for dinner that first night, along with Doctor Love and Masters Matherson, Carmichael, and Wyman, alias Jonathan.

Over dinner—a frugal meal of roasted galahs, salted pork, damper bread, smelly boiled swamp cabbage, and a thin broth of boiled mutton, Governor Amberfield had apologized for the sorry fare. He'd gone on to explain that his and Governor Philip's pleas for supply ships had been ignored by the British government, while still more ship-loads of convict transportees and free colonists had arrived, straining the food-supplies of the existing colonists to a point that bordered on starvation.

"We need farmers and hunters, carpenters and architects, stone masons and doctors, and what do they send us, my friends?" a disgusted, frustrated Amberfield told the company as they sat at table. "Pickpockets and thieves. Doxies and counterfeiters. Debtors and highwaymen. Felons from the teeming stews and alleys of London. Men and wenches—oftimes little children—of the cities, who have as much knowledge of surviving in a raw, untamed country like this as they have of flying to the moon. We ask for flour and salt, for biscuits and beans and salt-pork, for laying hens and seed, and for livestock to replace the precious cattle the natives steal from us—to breed up into herds and flocks. Instead, they send us hammers and chisels, nails and clothing. I shall not lie to you, gentlemen. We are in dire straits here if a supply vessel does not arrive soon."

"If 'twould help, I'd be most happy to tend to your sick until Captain Burroughs' ship sails for England, Governor," the *Hester*'s former surgeon, Doctor Love, volunteered.

"Thank you, kind sir! Your generous offer is most readily accepted. But . . . can we not prevail upon you to remain here indefinitely and assist our own much over-worked physician at the hospital, sir? When a way over the mountains has been found, there will be good, fertile land aplenty for all who would settle here, and those who came first will have the golden opportunity to become lords of this new and wondrous land!"

Surgeon Love hid a smile. He had seen little to excite him about this God-forsaken place thus far! "A tempting proposition, indeed, Governor, were I a younger man, but alas, 'tis impossible for me to accept, sir. I have a dear wife, children, and grandchildren awaiting me at home in Kent."

"With your permission, sir, I intend to stay for as long as there is work for me to do here. I shall begin by making inventory of the native plants and wild life beyond your settlement first thing in the morning!" Matherson blurted out, his eyes shining with eagerness at the thought of the challenge ahead of him. "There's every chance I may discover a wealth of edible plants hereabouts. Ones that you poor fellows—lacking my knowledge of botany—have previously discounted as poisonous or inedible!"

"Not more *taro* I pray to God!" Carmichael had exclaimed with feeling. "I'd sooner eat this cursed swamp cabbage!"

Despite Matherson's deeply wounded expression, the other former castaways had groaned and chuckled, muttering, "Hear! Hear!"

Amberfield thanked the botanist gravely, ignoring their merriment. "If you would do so, sir, *I* should be eternally grateful. For myself, I would welcome, on bended knee, anything that would *replace* this vile cabbage."

Another ripple of laughter circled the dinner table as the others commiserated.

Amberfield continued. "However, Master Matherson, sir, I must urge you take my blackfellow, Henry, along with you on your explorations, to ensure your safety. Although the aborigines prefer to give us wide berth and rarely attack, there have been one or two unfortunate misunderstandings—on both sides—that have resulted in deaths."

"Your blackfellow?"

"Indeed, sir. Henry is a native of these parts, but since his aboriginal name is quite unpronounceable to us white men, we have named him 'Henry' instead. Unlike his fellows, who show no liking and little curiosity towards us, Henry appears to regard our race and doings with considerable fascination. Instead of running away or bidding us be gone as do his fellows, he keeps close to the settlement. He has even managed to acquire a few words of English, after his own fashion, of course, but sufficient to make himself understood."

"An intelligent people, surely," Matherson observed, "if this Henry is representative of his people."

"In many ways, I believe so, aye. His people wander from place to place. They live on what they can find in a land so harsh and inhospitable, it seems nothing short of a miracle that any creature could survive there. And I have never seen such tracking ability as Henry possesses—why, 'tis almost uncanny, gentlemen. He can follow a bee to its honey-comb, or an animal's trail that you or I could never see. On several occa-

379

sions when our food supply has grown dangerously low, Henry's disappeared into the bush for several days. Each time he returns, bearing fresh-killed game. Perhaps a brace of *euru*—that's what the blackfellows call the red *kanguru*—or mayhap a dozen or so cockatoos or what-have-you for our pot.''

"*Kanguru?*" Matherson inquired.

Amberfield nodded. "They're quite large animals that travel the bush country or the mountain foothills in packs. They move by bounding through the air on large and very powerful hindlegs. One leap takes them several feet.''

"By jove!" Matherson exclaimed, delighted. "How very peculiar! Tell me, what do they look like, these creatures?''

"They resemble no creature that we in England are familiar with, sir—unless one were able to cross-breed an enormous rat with a rabbit! Moreover, the females carry their offspring in pockets in the fur at the front of their bellies, right about here, until the young ones are able to survive for themselves." Amberfield indicated his own trim belly.

"Extraordinary!" Matherson exclaimed, casting Paul Amberfield a look that was both appraising and suspicious. Clearly, he could not decide if the Acting-Governor was telling the truth, had imbibed too freely of the fine Spanish wine Burroughs had so generously provided for their celebratory supper, or was pulling his leg as the others had earlier.

"'Tis quite true, Master Matherson, sir," the sea-captain confirmed. "I have seen these creatures with my own eyes, and they are quite as strange as our Governor described.''

"Then I can hardly wait to see them for myself, can you . . . er . . . Wyman?''

"Indeed, no, sir," Nathan agreed. He'd frowned. "Governor Amberfield, getting back to the matter of the colony's food supply . . .''

"Aye, Wyman. What of it?''

"I'd like to volunteer my services for your hunting detail, sir, if you could see me supplied with a musket for that purpose.

I was raised in the country, you see, and I believe my hunting and shooting experience could be put to good use here.''

Amberfield accepted readily. ''But of course, sir! I'd have endeavored to enlist your services myself, but was under the impression you would be assisting Master Matherson in recording his finds for the Royal Geographical Society.''

''Indeed I shall, sir,'' Nathan responded smoothly without batting an eyelid. ''I'd hoped to combine my duties as Master Matherson's assistant with the hunting, until such time as the repairs have been completed on the *Lady Deliverance* and she is ready to sail. As you said, 'twould be sheer folly for Master Matherson to wander abroad unprotected out in the bush, where hostile natives and wild animals abound. I shall hunt, and also provide the escort he will undoubtedly need.''

''Then, by jove, you'll have that musket, sir! And as I told Doctor Love, the people of Port Jackson deeply appreciate your assistance. Master Wyman, our thanks to you.''

Nathan inclined his head politely and murmured, ''Your servant, Governor,'' before turning to answer a question put to him by one of Burroughs' officers.

In that moment, Mariah caught herself watching him from her end of the table, with far more intensity than was prudent, practically feasting her eyes upon him as she wondered when— if—the aching inside her would ever go away?

For the duration of the voyage from the island to New South Wales, she'd seen nothing of Nathan, who'd been confined to a sick-berth aboard the ship, though dour Doctor Love had proven uncharacteristically thoughtful in giving her daily bulletins regarding his patient's health when they congregated about the captain's table for dinner each evening. She'd learned from Love that Nathan had fully recovered from the miasma, or malaria, but in all honesty she'd not expected that he would look as robust as he did—or so disgustingly handsome that just looking at him would rekindle all the unsettling, hurtful feelings she'd fought so very hard to extinguish.

The white shirt with a lace stock at the collar that he'd borrowed from Captain Burroughs contrasted strikingly with the dark tan of his complexion and the glossy blue-black sheen of his hair, which he now wore pulled back in a tidy queue secured with a ribbon of black velvet. Over the shirt, he'd worn an embroidered yellow-satin waistcoat and a handsome velvet frockcoat. His breeches, of a dark fawn color, had been loaned him by one of the ship's officers. He looked every inch a gentleman—indeed, a rake to set any woman's heart aflutter.

Having never seen him attired in anything but ragged breeches and jerkin, or fraying sailor's drawers, until that night at Government House, Mariah'd thought he'd never looked more devilishly handsome than he did beneath the candlelight's gentle incandescence, and her heart had ached with longing for him. She wanted . . . oh, how she wanted him!

The emptiness and desolation that his rejection had produced in her had become a roaring abyss of need on the sea-voyage from the deserted island to New South Wales. *How could she go on living, without his love?* She'd asked herself time and time again as she'd tossed on her narrow bunk. *Oh, Jonathan, my love, my King of Kissers, my handsome rogue, I need you so! For pity's sake, come back to me, beloved! Tell me it no longer matters who my father was, that you love me and cannot live without me,' else I'll surely go mad!* she'd pleaded silently, watching him with her heart in her eyes.

As if he'd heard her entreaties, he'd looked up and glanced her way. And, for a fleeting, heart-stopping moment, their eyes had met over the flickering candelabra—his a glacial emerald-green; hers wounded and beseeching—before she'd hastily looked away. That single glance had been enough to slaughter any hopes she'd harbored for a tender reunion; to destroy any thought of a gentle disclosure that she loved him, and was carrying his child. *Nothing has changed, not where his feelings for me are concerned*, she thought bleakly. *Nothing . . .*

Setting her jaw, she'd determined right there and then that her senseless, useless pining for Jonathan was over. Finished.

Done with! She would shed no more bitter, lonely tears, but would go on alone; would carry their child alone. And, when the time came, she would deliver and raise it in the same fashion; alone.

While other women caught in her age-old predicament might tell all, in a desperate effort to force their babe's father into marriage, her fierce pride would not allow it. If that pig-headed, stubborn brute did not want her, if his love had been too shallow and superficial, his heart too flimsy to withstand the first storm that had battered it, then so be it. She would not bind him to her against his will, not seek to entrap him with her tears and enreaties, not beg him to remain in New South Wales. She would stay, and he would go. And, when her condition became apparent, as it must sooner or later, she would simply tell Uncle Paul that she was with child, though she would not reveal the identity of its father, and would let events take their course. Her uncle was a kindly man who'd always seemed genuinely fond of her. She fancied he would not react too harshly to her news, would not put her from him in disgust and try to hide her condition from the public eye; for things were different here. But, even should he do so, it would make no difference. She was not the timid creature who'd boarded the *Hester* over a year ago, and she would not act as if her condition were shameful. She would have her child, aye, and despite what anyone thought of her—of the two of them—she'd survive!

The daily struggles of life on the island, the knowledge that death lay coiled but a step away, day in and day out, had increased her self-reliance and her independence, had honed her courage to a keen edge. Jonathan's tender love-making had restored her female confidence and had cured her, she hoped, of her fears where men and intimacy were concerned. Her own fierce spirit had done the rest. Never again would she meekly submit to any man's will, nor would she endure in silent sub-mission the Hell that Edward had inflicted upon her. For that precious gift, she would always be grateful to Nathan. And who knew what the future held in store? Perhaps in time, she'd be able to forget Nathan and love another man; a decent, gentle man who would cherish her and accept her love-child unconditionally as his own?

Thaddeus Burroughs had certainly made it very plain that he would be proud to make her his bride. If she but said the word, she could be aboard his ship and bound for England within the month, there to set up household as the wife of a prosperous and well-respected merchant captain. She might even be able to persuade him that he was the father of the child she carried, should she be so inclined. She sighed and stood up, dusting off her skirts. Nay. She could never treat him so shabbily. Thaddeus deserved better. He was a fine man—honorable of character, scrupulous in his captain's duties, respectful of her in a way that was touching to behold—But alas, she felt nothing for him, other than respect and, perhaps, a twinge of pity and regret that she could not return his affection.

She, who had once known the fire and passion of an all-consuming love, would settle for nothing less. . . .

Chapter Twenty-Nine

From a distance, the low-spreading trees that grew along the *billabong* seemed gloriously abloom with the masses of greenish-yellow blossoms that covered their branches. But as Nathan and Master Matherson rode closer, followed by the aborigine tracker, Henry, on foot, his yellow *dingo* padding behind him, the "blossoms" suddenly took flight, becoming thousands upon thousands of small parakeets on the wing! They filled the hot, dusty air with their whirring flight and their noisy chatter.

"*Melopsittacus undulatus*, I do believe!" Matherson exclaimed, eagerly rooting for his notebook in the battered leather satchel slung over his shoulder, to record his sighting.

Henry shook his woolly dark head, grinning broadly, as if amused by the learned white man's ignorance. "*Budgeree!*" he declared firmly.

"*Budgeree*, you say? Now, let me see. Tree?" Henry shook his head again. "Stream?"

Henry grimaced. He pointed to the parakeets, then rubbed

his brown pot-belly and rolled his black eyes. "*Budgeree*. Him good! Very fine!"

"Ah. Quite so! Fine. Good. Now I have it," Matherson acknowledged unhappily, at last understanding what Henry had meant. "I rather doubt I'll every master this deplorably difficult tongue, should I live here the rest of my days!" he lamented to no one in particular.

Grinning, Nathan swung down from his horse and went to kneel on the banks of the *billabong*, cupping his hands to drink. In this, the dry season of the year, the *billabong*—a large freshwater pool that had originally been part of a stream or river that had long since been cut off—held only a few inches of water. It seemed clean and fresh, however, and, since it was the only water they'd found all day, he was grateful that Henry had led them to it. The horses badly needed watering, and he'd been thirsty himself. It appeared, moreover, a perfect place to camp for the night. They'd made new discoveries aplenty to add to Matherson's burgeoning collection of botanical and wild-life sketches, but alas, had bagged nothing for the colony's food stores since surprising a herd of *kanguru* three days ago.

"Drink 'em up, quick-quick!" Henry suddenly urged as Matherson clambered down from his mount and stumbled on numbed feet to drink from the stream.

Looking nervously over his shoulder towards the small thicket of trees, Henry drew his boomerang, or throwing stick, from the pouch on his back. He seemed afraid that they were in imminent danger of being attacked, Nathan thought, looking about but seeing nothing untowards. The dusty plain stretched almost to the foothills of the mountain ridges, its flatness broken only by an occasional stand of mulga or corkwood trees, and the *billabong* about which they'd gathered.

"What's wrong, Henry? What is it you hear?.

"This heah *billabong*, him belonga *wonambi*," Henry said in a low voice.

Wonambi. That explained his skittishness! Nathan had heard the word before, several days ago, when they had first hunted together, and Henry, encouraged by his genuine interest, had tried to explain to him the origins of his aborigine people.

The *wonambi*, or many-colored rainbow-serpent, was a mythical creature, half-spirit, half-human, who had come into being long, long ago in the Dreaming Time, when all things were created. It had once lived in the sky, but now the *wonambi*, long-haired and often heavily bearded, lived on the earth. It haunted springs and *billabongs*, hiding beneath the smooth surfaces of the watering holes to guard them from use by others. A careless hunter who turned his back on *wonambi* would find himself attacked, and, unless he carried with him the only enemy that *wonambi* feared—fire, he would be killed.

"*Wonambi* has gone walk-about, Henry," Nathan reassured the nervous native. "*Wonambi* very much afraid this one," he added, pointing to his own green eyes. Their unusual, brilliant color had fascinated Henry from the first, and it had seemed to the aborigine that the white man they belonged to must possess more than an average portion of *kuranita*, the potent, magical life-force that lived in all things, human or animal, plant or tree, the very land itself. "Wonambi spirit, he is afraid to come here! He fears Henry's friend, who has powerful *kuranita* to make him strong, and who carries the fire in his hand. Wonambi will not bother Henry. You will see!"

Nathan looked about the trunks of the trees and gathered a small pile of kindling from the dried leaves and twigs he found there. Drawing a tinder-box from his saddle-bag, he set to work with the strike-a-light. In moments, the dry tinder had caught and was crackling merrily as it fed upon the twigs and leaves.

Clearly relieved, Henry nodded and beamed as small flames began to curl about the firewood. Using the hand-signs common to his people when out hunting, he signed to Nathan he was going to find game for their supper. Before Nathan could protest or offer to go with him, Henry had vanished—no easy feat to accomplish, surrounded as they were by unbroken, flat terrain. And, although Nathan strained his eyes for a glimpse of the aborigine, he could find none.

He shook his head as he found himself a seat in the shade beneath the trees alongside Matherson, who'd withdrawn quill and ink-pot and was scribbling furiously upon a sheet of parchment. It was not the first time that Henry had vanished with a suddenness and a totality that seemed almost magical. Nor, he fancied, would it be the last. And with each day that passed, his respect for, and his curiosity about, the mystical natives of this savage land was growing.

At first, they'd seemed to him an absurdly primitive people, pagan savages who lived little better than packs of wild animals, roaming from place to place and feeding off a land that was singularly inhospitable. Perhaps it was this factor that made the natives hostile to all newcomers, whom they told, "Warra! Warra!"—Go away! in no uncertain terms. Tales Nathan had heard from the settlers and convicts in and about Port Jackson had done little to alter his initial impressions. The convicts had told him of white men being attacked and killed by aborigine hunters while gathering rushes near Sydney Cove; of cattle being stolen and slaughtered, goods seized. But as the days passed, he had learned from Henry that, as was usual in such cases, the atrocities were far from one-sided. Native men and women had been killed by white men, too, and for little or no reason.

As Nathan learned more and more about the aborigines' customs and beliefs, he had fallen under their spell, as had Matherson, he knew. When they sat about the campfire at night, he would try to tell an eager Henry about England, the King, their religion, and their way of life—ordinary things that were, nevertheless, almost incomprehensible to the intelligent bushman, unless Nathan was able to relate them to Henry's own life in some way. In his turn, by means of his smattering of English words and ofttimes far-more-eloquent sign-language, Henry had told a spellbound Nathan and Matherson of the

Dreaming Time, when a race of half-human men named the Tjukurita had been created.

The Tjukurita had wandered all over the land, sometimes taking on the shape of animals or birds, or becoming part of the land itself. A long, low spine of mountains might once have been a Snake-Man of the Tjukurita who had slept in that very place. The mountain ridge and his *kuranita* had remained. A pool might be the place where one of the Turtle-Men had swum. Now long gone, the demi-god's spirit-essence lived on in that pool and the place surrounding it, and a hunter must be wary, must respect and fear the Turtle-Man's magic that yet lingered there. The natives, who banded together in small groups, believed they were the descendants of these demi-gods, and accordingly, each group carried a special totem-name to show from whom it was descended. So it was that Henry belonged to the Kanguru Men.

"'Tis a beautiful land, is it not?" Matherson observed, stowing his drawing implements and sketches carefully inside the battered satchel. "One can only imagine what greater beauty yet awaits us in the vast lands that lie beyond the mountains! Each morning, I pray that I'll live long enough to see a way found over them. Do you have similar dreams, Kinc—Wyman?"

"Alas, no, sir," Nathan demurred, setting his jaw as he gazed absently into the flames of the fire. "The need to redeem myself still burns uppermost in my mind and heart, you see? Until it is extinguished—until my good name and my family's honor are cleared of the blot upon them—I shall settle to no other course."

The botanist frowned. He opened his mouth to speak, thought better of it, closed it, then tentatively began. "One cannot help but respect your tenacity, sir. And your resolve to prove your innocence is both understandable and eminently admirable. However . . ."

Matherson's voice trailed away, and Nathan glanced at him inquiringly. "Go on, sir," he urged. "I can tell by your tone

389

that you disagree—and perhaps disapprove—of my ambitions, and I am not offended. On the contrary, I would hear your reasons for doing so.''

"Nay, nay, my opinions are not important. The choice, after all, is yours, sir. I would never presume to—''

"I know you would not, sir. But . . . I respect your intelligence and would welcome your honest opinion. Come. Tell me what you're thinking?''

Matherson sighed and tugged uncomfortably at his linen stock, which he had not loosened despite the heat that day. His scrawny neck, Nathan noted, was rubbed raw beneath it. "Very well," he agreed at length. "I was but thinking that over a year of your life has already been wasted—through no fault of your own, you understand?" he added hastily. "And that life is not only precious, it is cursedly short. Had I a son in your dilemma, and he came to me and asked for my advice, I would urge him strongly to forget the past and the wrongs done to him. To go on. Start afresh.''

"Forget the past. . . !" Nathan exclaimed, his expression stony for all that he had pressed Matherson into answering. "But surely you forget, sir? As long as my name remains tarnished, I can never return to England or my family home. I am a wanted man—a convict, an escaped murderer! The shadow of the noose yet hangs over my head.''

"But do you have fresh evidence to present to the courts in order to clear your name? New witnesses to support your claims to innocence?''

"Nay, but—''

"Then I sorely question the wisdom of your returning to England, sir! Why expose yourself to possible recapture and execution, when 'tis foolhardy and unnecessary? Send letters to your family by our trusty Burroughs' hand. Reassure them that you are well, and stay here, sir! Use the new identity Lady Downing so cleverly . . . er . . . appropriated for you, Cast your bitterness aside, leave the past behind ye, where it belongs, and build a new and better life for yourself in this new and challenging land.''

He did not add *with Mariah at your side* but the suggestion hung unspoken on the air between them.

Nathan scowled, irritated by the man's gentle reasoning, for deep in his heart, he knew that Matherson was right. Knew it . . . but could not bring himself to accept it. As long as he remained a wanted man, as long as even one man living in this world recalled him as Lawyer Jonathan Kincaid, the double-murderer, son of Simon Kincaid of Linden Hall, he could not rest. He *had* to prove his innocence to the world at large, and to his beloved family. But above all, he had to prove it to his father.

He could not disappoint Simon again! He had done so too many times, first in his ambition to become a great artist, an ambition which Simon Kincaid had belittled and violently opposed; then by running away to London and turning his back on his family. Although at the time, he had never intended that his estrangement should last a moment longer than it took to establish himself as a portrait-painter, thanks to the press-gang that had spirited him aboard James Cook's exploration vessel, the *Resolution,* for four long and adventure-filled years, he had been gone a full five years before they had received any word of him, by which time his family had believed him dead, save for his beautiful mama, whose glorious dark hair had nevertheless turned to silver with worry. Upon his return, he'd endeavored to settle down, to become more responsible, more like his dutiful brother, Jeremy. To that end, he had embraced the sober and respected practice of Law. But perhaps even by passing the Bar and becoming a lawyer, he had disappointed his father, who had had other ambitions for him. And, on top of everything, had come his arrest and sentencing—the shame his family had been forced to suffer as he underwent a public trial, only to be found guilty and sentenced to hang rather than declared innocent and set free. The pain and humiliation they

must have endured defied imagining. *I'll make it up to you,*
Father! he swore silently. *Somehow, someday, I'll prove my*
innocence, and receive a full pardon from the King. I'll make
you proud of me, I swear it! Then and only then could he
resurrect the life he had ruined—his own.

He? Startled, Nathan realized that this was the first time he
had ever blamed himself for the chain of events that had led
up to his arrest and imprisonment in Newgate, rather than Judge
Harry Winslow and his faceless, nameless conspirators. And,
remembering, his thoughts turned, bittersweet, to Winslow's
daughter.

Mariah.

Beloved.

Faithless.

Her name was a prayer, a curse, all in one. In the days
following their departure from the island, he'd wandered in
and out of fevered sleeps fraught with dreams and hideous
nightmares in which he'd alternately called to her, begging her
not to leave him, or cursed her to the gates of Hell. And that
first night, when he and the others had supped at Government
House, had been nothing short of torment. He had watched her
at the far end of the long table when she'd thought him otherwise occupied, and had known such a stabbing in his heart as
he gazed at her, 'twas akin to the cut of a blade.

Nothing's changed, damn you! he'd thought, filled with a
disquieting sense of guilt and an unreasonable blast of rage as
their eyes had chanced to meet over the flickering candleflames.
For all that you're Winslow's daughter, for all that you be-
trayed my hiding place to Burroughs and his men, I desire you
still—I love you not a whit less, my lovely Judas. Sorceress!
Enchantress! God help me, you've bewitched me, my faithless
wench. You've stolen my very soul.

Brooding, he stared blindly out across the empty plain, oblivious to the gradual setting of the fiery sun, a great orange globe
that stained the heavens crimson, rose, and flame; or later, to
a sky darkening to amethyst and violet hues, in which a slim

crescent moon hung like a pirate's earring, and the trunks of the ghost-gums gleamed silvery-white in the gathering dusk.

He sat there, so very still and so obviously lost in troubled thought, that a sympathetic Matherson soon made no further attempt to engage him in conversation. Instead, he busied himself by unsaddling their mounts and leading them to water, and by gathering larger sticks of kindling with which to feed their small and dwindling fire, eager to increase its comforting circle of light as night gathered and pressed in close about their little camp.

The flames of the fire danced as a night breeze eddied up from nowhere, across the still waters of the *billabong* casting glimmers of shifting light which gave the eerie illusion that something stirred there, beneath the tranquil surface. Matherson reached up to rub his neck as his hackles rose and gooseflesh tingled down his arms and spine, casting a nervous look about him but seeing nothing untowards. He was about to scold himself for behaving like a foolish old woman when Nathan suddenly sprang to his feet, startling him half out of his wits by shouting, "*Henry*!"

Chapter Thirty

The brilliant afternoon light was rapidly fading as the man stood in the bottlebrush trees that shaded the spring, watching as lamps were lit in the farmhouse beyond. Amber lantern-light filled the narrow casement windows one by one.

The man giggled softly, imagining the cozy domestic scene hidden by those stone walls; the plump farmwife seated on one side of the kitchen hearth with her mending strewn across her lap, straining her eyes to sew by the lantern's puny light. The husband, puffing on his pipe as he oiled his pistols and muskets, while their children slept serenely in trundle beds, never dreaming of the ogre that stalked in the bottlebrushes close by.

The nightwind stirred. Its breeze must have carried his alien scent to the dog chained in the farmhouse yard, for of a sudden, the black bull-mastiff began barking and howling furiously, throwing its weight against its chain to break free. The chain, by some miracle, held.

The man held his breath, his eyes narrowed, waiting to see what would happen next.

The farmhouse door opened, spilling a puddle of amber light into the farmyard beyond. A young woman dressed in a simple gown of brown homespun appeared in the doorway, her braided red-gold hair and lovely face revealed in the lantern's gentle radiance.

The watcher sucked in a breath, scarce able to believe his eyes—or his fortune—as he saw who she was.

"What is it, Turk? What's all the noise about, hmm, sir?" she asked, looking about.

A man joined the woman in the doorway, protectively stepping past her to look about the shadowed farmyard for himself.

"Reckon I'd best have a look about, mistress," Joe Hardy murmured. "Could be one of them bushmen, after yer uncle's precious cows. I'll take Turk along wi' me. He'll see the buggers run off!"

When the woman nodded, murmuring, "Be careful, Joe," the man bent to unhook the mastiff's chain, winding his fist in the end of it as if it were a leash. The black brute at once bounded across the yard, baying furiously as he hauled Joe Hardy after him so forcefully the chain links bit deep into his hand and he was hard put to keep his footing.

"Down, ye great black brute! Down, I say!"

The man knew the first, delicious tingles of fear as the pair came closer to his hiding place. If he remained where he was, in but a few moments, the mastiff would rout him! Tempting as the challenge was, he dare not linger! A vicious brute like the mastiff could tear out his throat!

Like a tall, dark wraith, the man turned and vanished between the bottlebrush trees, letting the darkness swallow him up as yet another shadow. He quickly found the stream-bed that fed the spring and waded ankle-deep along its course, chuckling at his cleverness. The water would hide his scent from the dog. In a few moments, the ugly, thwarted brute would be whining and circling in confusion, unable to follow its quarry.

The man put the dog from his mind. Night was falling. He

must find food and return to his secret, magic place long before the sun rose again to burn the land and dry up the life-giving juices of his own body. His belly filled, he would hide there, in the cool, dark dampness, sleeping away the cruel daylight hours until darkness fell once again, as he had done for so many days and nights now. His only companions there were the bats and lizards that shared his gloomy palace, and the ache in his groin for a woman was strong. He must go back there, to the farmhouse, very soon, he told himself, an unholy glitter in his eyes now. Aye, he'd go back . . . now that he knew what secrets the farmhouse held.

Secrets! Ah, yes! Secrets are everything, the key to all true power! he thought as he splashed along the stream-bed. *If you knew a man's secrets, you could bend him, break him; could force even the best man to go against his nature and do evil. You could even*, he thought with a happy grin, *make him kill for you. . . .*

Henry padded across the dusty plain towards the corkwood trees, a place where he knew he would find a flock of cockatoos settling down to roost for the night. He was scowling as he went, for he was angry at himself.

Since before the time of the *corroboree*, the ceremony at which he'd officially become a man, he had prided himself on being the finest hunter of his band; one with a keen eye who knew well the magic incantation that would increase a hunter's skill, and one who rarely missed his prey.

And yet, just a short while ago, with the light still bright and good, his aim clear, his incantation correctly and forcefully chanted, he had missed a plump female *kanguru* with his throwing stick—aieeah!—and by more than two spans of his hand, too, he recalled, disgusted with himself. Worse, his attack had sent the remainder of her band bounding away, out of range of either his throwing stick or his spear.

Of a certainty, he was no true hunter! He should be gathering seeds in a *pitchi*, or digging for roots and grubs as his woman and little daughters did each day. . . .

As he drew closer to the shiny-leafed corkwood trees that grew in the foothills of the great mountains, he wondered, with a twinge of apprehension, if some jealous someone had pointed the bone at him. If his bad luck was not the work of a death-curse, the beginning of a slow and terrible dying. There were elders among his band who disapproved of his interest in the white ones and their village, who frowned upon his fascination with the white men's strange beasts and magical inventions. Sternly, they had advised him that he would do better to remain with his people, hunting to put meat in their bellies rather than the bellies of the white men. Henry knew this to be true, but . . . he could not.

The white men's very strangeness had cast a spell upon him, and with each new wonder they revealed, the web of his fascination had tightened about him. How many of his people had seen their own faces in anything but the reflective surface of a still pool? He had. Many times. And despite what the elders warned, he believed that his spirit was yet intact. The look-in-glass had not stolen his soul away as even his woman, Kaji, had fearfully predicted. He had seen the white men summon precious fire from within the small *coolamon* that each of them carried in his robes. He had also seen them kill the *kanguru* from a great distance, using a stick that blazed thunder and fired small killing-balls, then butcher the carcass with a tool made of a shining metal blade set in a handle of bone that cut into flesh, skin, and muscle far, far better than the cutters of sharpened stone that he carried. When he had witnessed these and many other wonders, a small voice had spoken in Henry's head. *Hear me, Tjuki! These white-skinned ones, they are very clever and wise. They possess powerful* kuranita! *It is better they should call you friend than enemy!*

Accordingly, Henry had done what he could to help them,

but many times he had been amazed that so clever a people should be so very stupid when it came to such a basic matter as survival.

They would hug their bellies and weep that they were starving when food surrounded them on every side: juicy roots and berries; succulent witchetty grubs beneath a fallen log, lizards or goanas among the rocks, or plump galahs in the branches of the trees, while *yabi*, or crayfish hid beneath the mud of the *billabong*, just waiting to be scooped out. How could any man starve with such a feast waiting before his very nose?

Of all the white men that Henry had met over the past three summers, he liked the one with the grass-colored eyes the best, the one named Why-man. Based on his sparse knowledge of the white man's tongue and what he had gleaned from Nathan's behavior, Henry had proudly concluded that he had been named this because he asked so many questions. Why did Henry use a *woomera*, or spear-thrower, Why-man had asked him? Why else but to make his spear travel farther and with greater force than his arm alone! And Why did his throwing-stick return to him? Why else but because of its magical shape? Ugha! It was small wonder he had been named Why-man, to Henry's thinking!

The elder with the smoke-hair was friendly, too. He let Henry watch while he made marks upon the white leaves that, when he had finished, resembled the plants or small animals he had gathered. But Henry was not as fascinated with these *droorings* as he was with Why-man's green eyes. He had seen *droorings* the Ancient Ones from the Dreaming Time had painted in caves on his travels; magic-pictures of turtles and lizards and *kanguru*, some with their skeletons showing. These paintings had been done to entice the animal that had been drawn to a hunter's spear.

Knowing this, Henry could not understand why the white man, Math-uh-Sun did not make his magic-drawings until *after* he had found the rock, plant, or animal he wished to capture.

It made no sense to Henry at all . . . but then, wondrous as their inventions were, the white men often made little sense— and even more often, acted foolishly. . .

The flock of cockatoos did not hear his silent approach until he was very near them. Raising his head, Henry cupped his mouth with his hands and gave a loud, piercing cry, startling the birds into flight.

With a great whirring of white wings, the cockatoos rose like a cloud into the air. In the same instant, Henry flung his boomerang. The throwing-stick cut a lethal, curving swathe through the frantic flock, sending many of them plummetting to earth, either dead or dying as they fell.

Henry ran to the injured ones and quickly wrung their necks, picking up both these and the ones already dead by the feet. He tied the birds together with lengths of mulga vine he carried for that purpose, before stringing the dozen or so of them on a single vine-cord that he looped about his neck and over his back.

He'd retrieved his boomerang and was about to return to Why-man and their camp when his dingo growled and pricked up its ears.

Looking about him, Henry could see no one. His brown, deep-set eyes keen and wary, he scanned the branches of the corkwood trees, then shifted his attention to the caves beyond them.

"Something there?" he asked his dingo.

The yellow dog whined and looked up at him imploringly.

"Go, then! Find it!" Henry ordered, grinning knowingly. Surely his dingo had scented a bitch in the fullness of her heat. One ripe for breeding, who had made the caves her lair. If so, he would let his dingo mate with her, before they returned to Why-man. Henry was also a male. He knew very well how pleasing it was to lie with a female, to enjoy her exciting female scent and the warmth and softness of her body. He would not deny his dingo a few moments of pleasure.

The dog bounded towards the caves and Henry followed. Without hesitation, the dingo plunged into the shadows of the cave-mouth and again Henry followed.

He found himself standing within a vast cavern that was twice as tall as a man, four times as wide as a man, and as deep as six men—perhaps more. Since the rear of the cave vanished into utter darkness, he could not tell. In the fading light that managed to find its way into the cavern, a small pool gleamed blackly, ripple after ripple of disturbed water eddying outwards in glinting circles. The bones and feathers of small animals and birds littered its rocky banks, while the constant *drip! drip!* from the cavern's ceiling betrayed its source.

While his dingo snuffled noisily about, exploring, Henry glanced up at the lofty walls of the cavern and regretted following the dingo inside.

The walls were covered with the magic-paintings he had been thinking of earlier—the paintings of the spirit-people! Large-headed stick-figures, worked in black and then painted eerily with white stripes, celebrated a mysterious *corroboree* along one wall, fiercely brandishing spears and shields. The figures' spindly legs were bent to show that they were dancing wildly. On the opposite rock wall, Henry could make out a wallaby, a turtle, a crocodile, and a huge fish, all drawn with their lungs and hearts and the bones of their skeletons showing through their skins.

A chill swept down Henry's spine. Filled with the uncanny, disturbing sensation that he was being watched, he swallowed nervously, slowly turning full circle about. A length of cord seemed fastened around his throat, cutting off his air, as his uneasiness mounted. He could feel the spirits all about him even now, the spirits of the Ancient Ones, pressing close.

And then, as he turned to face the cave-mouth once again, he saw the most terrible thing of all; a thing that was no harmless painting. He saw the spirit of *wonambi*, the dreaded rainbow-serpent itself, looming in the cave-mouth before him! Almost the height of two men, it wore the multi-colored rags of ancient legend, and its hair and beard were wild and bushy about its head and shoulders as it impaled him with its sulphurous eyes!

Henry stared, transfixed, unable to speak or to move, the only part of him not stilled his thundering heart. He had foolishly trespassed here, and had discovered the hidden pool that belonged to the water-serpent. Having no fire with which to frighten *wonambi* away, he would be killed. His own *kuranita* was no match for the powerful spirit's evil magic.

Paralyzed by such terror, he could not move, Henry did the one thing he had wits left to do. He yelled with all his strength for the one whose life-essence was far stronger than his own: "*Whyyyyy-maaaan!*"

As if his prayers had been answered in a heartbeat, a yellow streak sprang past Henry as his fearless dingo leaped for *wonambi*'s throat, snarling viciously. And, as *wonambi*'s hands fastened about the dingo's own throat, Henry found he could move, at last. The dingo's leap had broken the spell upon him!

Taking his courage in his two hands, he bolted past the struggling pair, exploding from the cave-mouth and running out into the open with the swiftness of a spear launched from a *woomera*.

He ran past the corkwood trees and kept on running across the moon-lit plain, until he heard the thunder of a horse's mighty hooves coming towards him at speed.

Henry pulled up short as, out of a sea of yellow wattle bushes that shone like golden rain in the moonlight, his savior came riding towards him. His heart swelled with joy and thanks. Why-man had come—the white man had answered his desperate call for help! Why-man had used his own powerful *kuranita* to send a command, a silent command that flew on invisible wings through the air to help his brother, Henry. Why-man had ordered his dingo to tear out the rainbow-spirit's throat and save Henry's life—and the dingo had obeyed!

It was some while later that Henry, perched behind Nathan on his horse's broad rump, remembered the string of cockatoos he'd left in the cave, forgotten in his terror. But no amount of persuasion on Nathan's part could induce him to go back there and recover them.

Long after his hero, Why-man/Nathan, had rolled into his blanket for the night, Henry lay awake in the shallow ditch he'd scraped from the hard earth for his bed. He was waiting for his dingo to return to him. They had gone walk-about together for many years, and Henry had grown fond of the animal.

It was only when dawn flushed the sky with rose and yellow, heralding the birth of a new day, that Henry would finally admit the fear that had haunted him all night long had come true; his faithful, four-legged friend would never be returning to him. They would never again go walk-about together.

The terrible *wonambi* had slain his dingo-friend!

Chapter Thirty-One

The man sprawled on his back beside the fire he'd lit in the dank cavern, his insane thoughts flitting and flapping as aimlessly as the black bats that streamed from the cave-mouth at dusk to hunt. He held his bloodied hands up to the fire he'd built and admired them, sniffed at them, inhaling the intoxicating reek of fresh blood as if it were a rare and delicate fragrance.

Tonight, like the bats, he had killed. Not to fill his belly, nor even to defend himself, but for the sheer joy of killing.

Killing!

His lips peeled back from his teeth in a rictus of delight. It had been the first time in many weeks that he had killed, and it had felt good. Very, *very* good. So good, his belly had ached afterwards with the pleasure of it, like the ache that came after a night spent tumbling a woman. True, his prey had been only the bushman's yellow, wild dog, but the wild elation that had filled him, the power that had sung within him as he'd choked the life from it . . . as his hands fastened about its throat . . . as he watched death gather and fill its amber eyes and send the life-force fleeing . . . had been the same rich and joyous experience, and almost as pleasurable as the other times, he thought, running his hand over the dingo's bloody carcass.

They'll come looking, and they'll find you, boy! a small gloating voice whispered in his ear, and he knew it was his father's voice.

Go away! I won't listen to you!

You must hide from them, boy, if you would remain the Secret Master! If not, they'll come, and they'll lock you up!

Never. Never again . . . !

Oh, yes! They'll take you and put you in that cold, empty room with the leather straps, and they'll throw away the key, if you don't hide from them. . . .

Nay! They'll never find me here! he told his father's voice. *'Tis too far! The Secret Master has nothing to fear here. He's safe in this new land, for those who betrayed him . . . those who would have spoken against him . . . have all been silenced.*

The voice faded away, and he could breathe again.

How sweet it was to know himself safe, he thought, and to know the powers had not left him in this new land, so far from the old one where it had all begun. . . .

The first time he'd felt the full power of the Secret Master, he'd been but a child of nine, spying on his mama and her lover, Papa's game-keeper, as they frolicked naked in the prickly stubble amongst the hayricks of his father's fields.

Even now, thinking back to that long-ago summer day at Windsmere, if he closed his eyes he could smell the newly scythed grass; could feel, through the linen of his shirt, the warmth of the sun beating down upon his head and upon his arms, and the almost painful, prodding hardness of his erection against the thick woolen cloth of his breeches. He could hear the lazy, somnolent drone of the furry bumblebees buzzing about in the purple clover, and the *thump-a-thump* of his own heart as he saw Tom Stokes—that rough, horrid brute with the coarse voice and the huge callused hands—fall on top of his beautiful mother like some wild, rutting beast.

Her body had been slender and white as cream beneath Stokes' swarthy, hairy one, and her golden hair had spilled across the stubble like a sheaf of wheat as Tom lunged and thrust at her.

Stop it! You're hurting my mother, you bully! a voice had protested inside his head. But to his shame, he had been too fascinated to utter the words aloud. Too curious. Too . . . aroused, in his child's fashion.

As if to confirm his fears, soon after his mama had cried out, just once; a strange, whimpering cry. She had wrapped her arms about the game-keeper's brawny chest with its ugly mat of thick black hair, and had locked her shapely white legs about his lunging, hairy flanks as she'd struggled with him; trying—oh, surely, trying?—to push him away, to escape his hold; for what else would she be doing? But she was no match for Tom! In the end, she'd panted and gasped and fallen back simply beneath him, her eyes closed, and, to the watching, breathless boy's confusion, had laughed merrily as she'd panted, "Oh, Tom, you lusty devil, you! My wonderful, wonderful stallion!"

Tom had laughed coarsely, too, such a glint of triumph in his sly, sloe-black eyes that the boy had been filled with loathing for him.

"Aye, me wee slut! 'Twas good fer ye, weren't it? For all yer breedin' and yer fancy ways, ye like what yer rough an' ready Tom gives yer, don't ye, lass?" Tom had challenged, grinning as he roughly fondled a snowy breast.

"Yes! Oh, yes, Tom! You're twice the man my husband is!"

"Only twice?" Tom had asked, sounding put out, and they'd laughed together again, the sound of their conspiratorial laughter filling the watching boy with rage and confusion. Was Tom laughing at his papa? How dare a common game-keeper make fun of his father!

And then, something had happened that had remained branded in his memory forever, like the scar of a terrible wound

405

that had left its livid mark upon him and could not be erase
a nightmare that could not be forgotten with the coming of da

A shadow had fallen across the sun-lit stubble and the nake
couple; the tall, threatening shadow of a man armed with
musket. The boy had sucked in a breath, knowing with awf
certainty that something terrible was about to happen . . . an
powerless to halt it.

His mama had seen the man first, over Tom Stokes' shou
der. Her blue eyes had widened in alarm. Her mouth ha
opened in a scream as the man raised the musket to his shoulde

"Nay, William, don't! For God's Sake . . . !" she'
screamed.

But her scream had been drowned out by the deafening repo
as his father had fired point-blank into the back of Tom Stoke:
skull.

A shower of crimson had erupted over the sun-bleache
stubble, spattering his mother's creamy loveliness. A few stra
drops had landed on the boy's own pristine shirt-sleeve. He'
looked at them and recoiled in horror. *Blood! Tom Stokes
blood* . . .

Too terrified to move or utter a sound, he had cowered there
watching, as his father rolled the game-keeper's body off hi
mother's, a look in his eyes that had been terrible to behold
Her face ugly and contorted with terror, she had tried to scram
ble away from him, whispering, "Please, William, nay! For
give me! Truly, he meant nothing to—"

"Adulteress!" Papa had rasped, and he'd slapped hi
mother's face as she'd cringed naked on the stubble at hi
feet. "Whore!" he'd thundered, striking her again and again
"You'll never cuckold me again, you faithless bitch! I'll se
to that!"

With that, he'd dropped to his knees and leaned over Mama
fastening his powerful hands about her throat and squeezing
The boy had been unable to see her face, but he'd heard he
gurgling cries grow fainter and then cease completely; had see

her legs and feet, her arms, flail wildly, then grow ominously limp.

When Papa stood, the boy had seen her staring eyes, and he'd known that, like Tom, she was quite dead. His pulse had roared in his ears. *Papa has killed them! He's killed them both!* he'd thought, stifling the scream that burst up his throat like a living thing clawing for escape. He'd killed Mama . . . and perhaps he'd kill *him* next!

Fear had made him shake so violently, he'd lost control and wetted himself. Clamping his lips together tightly to keep from sobbing or letting that awful cry escape into the air, he'd balled his little fists so tightly, his nails had made his palms bleed.

For what seemed an eternity, he had crouched there, beneath the blackberry brambles on the urine-soaked grass at the edge of the field, in terror of his very life; watching round-eyed as his papa went to the little pile of clothing that his mother had folded and placed so neatly in the shade of a flowering hawthorn bush.

And, his jaw hard, his pale eyes emotionless, Papa had taken the pretty sky-blue gown that his mama had worn that morning and had savagely ripped it in two between his huge fists. He'd ground the satin tatters beneath his boot-heel, staining them with dirt, before hurling the garment aside. He had torn her frothy white undergarments, too, and scattered them over the stubble. Then, looking about him, his papa had nodded, a cruel smile of satisfaction curling his lips. "Good enough!" he had muttered under his breath. "Aye, good enough."

Just then, Andrew, his father's head groom, had come plowing across the field, red-faced and out of breath. A brace of foxhounds had bounded at his heels. "Sir! I heard a shot," he cried, ordering the whining dogs back. He broke off as he saw the dead woman, the dead man. His flushed face paling at the sight, he'd swallowed and crossed himself. "God save us," he'd whispered, aghast.

"Aye, Andrew," Papa had murmured in a voice that had

sounded choked with tears. "Stokes . . . he . . . I . . . He—he raped and beat her, Andrew . . . my sweet Lenore! And then—oh, God! Oh, God! then he strangled her, that foul murdering bastard!" he rasped. Sobbing, he reeled away pounding his fist against the trunk of a nearby oak, his forehead pressed to the rough bark as he groaned like a soul in torment "That—godless—*bastard*! My poor, darling Lenore! How she must have suffered! The swine was about to make a run for it when I surprised him. I saw what he'd . . . and I—Oh, God, what else could I do?—I shot him! But I was too late. Oh, Andrew, I shall never forgive myself! If only I'd been here a moment sooner, she might yet be alive. I might have saved her from him."

"Now, now, then. Come away from 'ere, do, sir," Andrew had urged compassionately, trying to take his master's elbow and lead him from the scene. He was white-faced and shaken as he added, "Come back t' the house, do. Ye mustn't blame yerself, sir! Stokes was—well, to be plain, he was allus a bad lot, nothing like my Winn. 'Tis best ye—"

"Nay, Andrew! I can't go. I can't leave her, you understand? Not . . . not yet. I must—I must stay here with h-her, don't you see? I can't leave my poor Lenore like this! Oh, God! Run, Andrew! Go quickly! Send one of the stable lads to the Manse for the magistrate."

"Very good, sir," Andrew had whispered, and with a last glance at the two bodies lying on the grass, he'd run off whistling the hounds to heel.

After Andrew had gone, Papa's hands had dropped to his sides. He'd chuckled and muttered, "Young fool!" under his breath, then had gone and stood over his wife's body, looking down at it with contempt.

And, seeing his papa's back turned, the man's attention diverted, the boy had believed himself safe.

Standing, he'd backed away through the bushes, inch by torturous inch, never taking his eyes from his father's broad cloth shoulders for an instant.

But the boy's retreat, though stealthy, startled a covey of wood-pigeons from their roost in the brambles. With a frantic beating of wings, they'd exploded from their hiding place, their flight loud on the pregnant, unnatural hush of that sun-drenched summer morn.

At the sound, Papa had spun about as if jerked by a cord. He had spotted him instantly, and the boy's heart had risen to his mouth in terror. Turning, he'd tried to run, bony little legs pumping like pistons, scared witless by the thud of his father's booted feet on the turf behind him as he ran for his very life.

He'd not gone far when his father's hand had clamped across the back of his neck, squeezing like a vise as he'd been jerked to a standstill.

"How long, boy?" his papa had demanded, his twisted features those of a frightening stranger as he'd thrust his face into the lad's. "How long were you hiding there, spying? Answer me!"

"I wasn't spying. I swear it, sir! I—I was looking for robins' eggs, that's all," he'd whimpered.

"Don't lie to me, damn you!" his father had roared. "Your mama lied—do you want what happened to her to happen to you, eh?" He had shaken him so violently, his head had reeled and his teeth had rattled.

"A few moments, no more. I . . . I didn't see anything, honestly, Papa—I swear I didn't!" he'd babbled, terrified.

And then, as if motion could be slowed, he'd seen his father's pale-blue eyes flicker to the tell-tale spots of Tom Stokes' blood that spattered the white sleeve of his shirt, and had known he was doomed.

"So you saw nothing, eh?" his father had said in a low, deadly tone the boy had never heard him use before. "You were there only a few moments, were you, eh? Damn you, boy, tell me the truth! You saw it all, didn't you?"

"Nay! I saw nothing!"

The hand at the back of his neck slid around to the front of his throat as his father turned him to face him, powerful fingers cupping his face beneath the chin, squeezing his throat so hard that blood suffused the boy's face in a crimson rush. Black dots swirled before his eyes, and the ringing began anew in his ears. "You saw everything, didn't you, lad? But . . . no matter. What's done is done! You will go up to the house now, boy, d' ye hear me?" his father had rasped.

The boy, close to losing consciousness, had heard him as if from far, far away, but he had nodded.

"You will go back, and you will act as if nothing has happened. You will change your clothes, then go to the school-room and tend to translating your Latin and Greek with Master Forbes—and you will say *nothing* of what you saw here this morning. Understood?"

"Yes, Papa. I swear it!" he had whispered.

His father's grip on his throat had tightened.

"What you saw here today will be our little secret, do you hear me? Until your dying day, you will tell no one what happened here. *No one!* Because if you do, boy, I swear before God and the Devil I'll know it—and I'll choke the life from your scrawny little throat, even as I choked your whoring mother!"

"Please, sir, please," he'd pleaded. "I u-understand. Truly!"

"Our secret, boy . . ."

"Yes, sir. A secret. Our secret. I swear, sir. . . ."

"Then be gone!"

He had fled back to the house, and he had kept his word for as long as he possibly could, saying nothing of what he had seen, carrying his father's guilt day after day; reliving the horror of Tom Stokes' and his mama's murder night after night, even in his dreams, until the burden had been too great, too horrible to bear a moment longer.

In the school-room one dreary autumn morning, he had burst into tears and told Master Forbes what he had seen. His stunned tutor had patted his shoulder and bade him compose himself, promising the distraught boy that what he'd told him would go no further than his ears. But, that toad Forbes had lied! Forbes had told Papa, and the very next week his tutor had left Windsmere, headed—he'd smugly told the weeping lad—for a 'far better teaching position' up North, one that the master of Windsmere had generously found for him.

That same day, Papa had icily informed the boy that he was too old for a tutor, and was to be sent to boarding-school. Though he had begged Papa not to send him away, two days later he was in a coach headed far from Windsmere and all he'd known and loved. . . .

Remembering, the man hugged himself about the knees, whimpering softly with self-pity as he sucked on his thumb and wound an agitated finger in his hair. Those bastards—Forbes and later, the school chaplain, Hendrickson—with their lying smiles and their false, sympathetic nods! They'd both sworn to be his friends, but had betrayed his trust, his confidences—and he'd sworn that someday, he'd make them pay.

And pay they had. Oh, yes! It had taken him many, many years to do it. Not until after Papa's . . . death, when he'd come home to stay, and had become the Secret Master for himself, had he been able to take his revenge. But it had been well worth the wait.

A small smile curved the man's lips. Father had been the very first—and the one he'd enjoyed the most. The inn-keeper and his nosy slut; the judge, Harry Winslow; Bishop Hendrickson; Headmaster Forbes; and Doctor Friar had been among the next to taste his power . . . but they were certainly not the last, nor even the only ones to do so.

So many . . . !

The man giggled. He, the Secret Master, had silenced all but two of those who were dangerous to him and Papa! Those two had been with the Second Fleet when it had sailed from Portsmouth last January; the only two in the world who might yet have pointed the finger at him. Desperate to finish them, he'd followed them to the New World as a passenger aboard the *Lady Julian*, another ship of the Second Fleet. But as it

411

turned out, he need not have worried. When he'd staggered ashore in Port Jackson last June with the other settlers, he had learned that the *Hester*'s sinking had taken care of them both. Poor, poor Andrew! And poor Lawyer Kincaid! They'd long since become fodder for the hungry fishes and the crabs and the wiggly-worms at the bottom of the deep-blue sea, yo ho!

He dragged the dingo's stiffening carcass across his lap, intending to cure it and wear the dingo's pelt upon his back like the wizards of old, as a symbol of his powers. But his smile dwindled as he realized he had no knife with which to skin the beast. No knife . . . no pistol . . . no powder or shot. In a fit of rage, he hurled the dingo's carcass across the cave and turned his face to the damp rock wall in a sulk. Clearly, it was time to go back to the settlement. Time to steal the things he needed before he returned to the bush once again. . . .

Chapter Thirty-Two

The night breeze caught the unlatched shutter, banging it noisily back and forth. With the sudden draft, the lace curtains that hung on either side of the opened casement billowed into the room like the sails of a ship.

At the sudden noise, the unexpected flurry of movement, the man shrank back into the heavily shadowed corner of the room. Shrinking against the plastered wall, he stiffened, scarce breathing, certain the thudding of the shutters must waken the lovely woman who tossed and turned fitfully in the wide poster bed. But, she did not stir.

He saw that her face was clearly illuminated by the moonbeams that streamed into the heavily-shadowed room, revealing delicately arched brows, dark lashes curving like dusky fans against the cream-and-rose of her cheeks, coral lips full and slightly pouty in sleep. Two gleaming red-gold braids framed her face, like ropes of antique gold against her pristine pillow.

Alongside her, another, younger woman slept deeply, her milky-blond head cradled heavily upon her bent arm, but the man paid her scant attention as, his courage restored, he left his corner and loomed over the bed, looking down at Mariah with burning, hungry eyes.

She was dreaming. He could tell by the flicker of movement beneath her closed eyelids, the slight movement of her lips, the whimper uttered deep in her throat. A cruel smile split his lips. Did she dream of him? he wondered.

Mariah knew she was dreaming, and yet she could not force herself to wake up. In her dream, she was back in England. It was the hellish month following her marriage to Edward, and she was again a prisoner in his stately mansion, a helpless, frightened bird trapped in a monstrous cage of crimson velvet, beating her wings . . . fluttering madly . . . but unable to escape.

"*Papa!*" she cried out, "*Help me!*"

Of a sudden, her father's dear face appeared in a corner of the room. There were tears in his eyes and on his cheeks. She reached out to comfort him, but as she did so, the image faded away, vanishing line by line, like the face of a ghost, to be replaced by Edward's lean, handsome features, his sensual lips split in a wolfish smile, his yellow tiger-eyes impaling her as he loomed over the bed, looking down at her. . . .

"*I've come for you, my darling Mariah,*" she heard him say. "*I've returned from the grave to claim you as my bride!*"

And he laughed.

She screamed then; a high, piercing shriek of pure terror that shattered the hush like broken crystal.

Jolted awake, Mariah lay there, her eyes wide, her bosom rising and falling rapidly with her terror, her heart pounding. She tried to move, but her limbs were frozen and unresponsive to her commands for several seconds before she managed to sit bolt upright and look around her.

There was no one there. The small chamber appeared undisturbed, exactly as it had been before she'd retired, with a massive oak etagere in one corner, a cheval-glass mirror in another, a cherry-wood Queen Anne chest-of-drawers on curved legs standing against the wall opposite, a rose-patterned ewer and basin set atop it for washing. She felt the breeze upon her flushed cheek then, and sucked in a breath. The casement! Had there been an intruder? And if so, could he have entered by the opened window . . . ?

"What is it?" Caroline cried, coming awake and sitting up. "Why are you sitting there in the dark?"

Without answering, Mariah swung out of bed and padded to the open window, thrusting aside the billowing curtains to lean over the sill and look out.

The farmyard below was almost as bright as day beneath the light of the full moon sailing high above, the ghostly pale gum-trees, the stables, and Turk's kennel all bleached an ashy grey by its light. The mastiff sprawled before its house, apparently sound asleep, its body a solid, unmoving, dark shadow against the ground. *Nothing.* No furtive movements. No suspicious shadows. No tell-tale sounds. Nothing but the faint rustle of the leaves in the boughs of the single bottlebrush tree that grew outside the window, as they stirred in the night breeze.

"I . . . I thought someone was . . . was standing over our bed, looking down at us," Mariah explained shakily.

Caroline joined her at the window and peered out. "I see nothing unusual, unless you count Papa's Turk? For once, that noisy brute seems quite dead to the world. Watch-dog, indeed! Just look at him! Surely he'd have barked, if anyone were creeping about?"

"I suppose so."

"You must have imagined it, coz. Or, maybe you were dreaming? You were awfully restless earlier. I' faith, you woke me twice with your tossing and turning—and we both know that I sleep like the dead. I warned you too much sharp cheese before bed would give you nightmares, remember?"

"Perhaps you're right, and I *was* dreaming," Mariah conceded, stifling a yawn as she returned to the four-poster bed and perched on the edge of the down-filled pallet. With her hair neatly braided and wearing a voluminous night-shift with lacy ruffles and long sleeves, she looked like a bewildered little girl as she sat there, twining her hands together. At length, she sighed and her shoulders sagged as she added, "It's just . . . well, it seemed so *real*!"

"The worst dreams always do," Caro agreed with feeling. "What were you dreaming about, anyway? I still dream about the shipwreck sometimes," she admitted with a shudder. "Especially when Jack handed me into the lifeboat and that wall of water rose up and swept us both overboard. I was so very certain my last moment had come, weren't you?"

"It wasn't about the shipwreck. It was about . . . before. I-I was dreaming about Edward."

Caro wrinkled her nose. "Ugh! Then 'tis no wonder you had a nightmare! I never liked him, horrid fellow, 'though I tried and tried to, for your sake, coz. To be honest, I was actually *relieved* rather than put out that we were not invited to your wedding-breakfast!"

"I wanted to invite you, truly I did—but none of our friends or relatives were invited to the wedding," Mariah observed with bitterness in her tone. "My dear Edward would not permit it. Our guests were a half-dozen or so of *his* friends—if you could call them friends. A stranger company you could not imagine. There was a bishop somebody-or-other, a doctor, a lawyer—"

"And a tinker, tailor, soldier, beggar, and thief, too, no doubt?" Caroline cut in cheekily.

Mariah grimaced. "I really can't remember. But to the last man, they seemed . . . uneasy, somehow. You know, as if they'd rather have been anywhere but there. Still, 'twas hardly any wonder, I suppose, given our surroundings. You see, we celebrated our wedding-feast in the banquet hall of Edward's family mansion, seated about a long, polished-oak table. It was set with glittering crystal and silverware and the finest bone-china and linen you have ever seen, coz"

"So? What was wrong with that?"

"All about us the furniture was hung with dust-sheets, and funeral-crepe festooned the windows. *Funeral crepe*, Caroline—though Edward's father had died ten years before!'' she finished with a shudder.

"Hmm. A strange do, indeed!'' Caroline agreed. "But then, I always felt the Fates had acted most fortuitously when they finished Edward off in his prime, so to speak, and made you a merry widow.'' She was teasing, trying to force a smile to Mariah's troubled face; but her attempts failed.

"You have no idea how fortuitously,'' her cousin agreed with such feeling, Caro frowned. Trying to decide whether to confide in the younger girl or no, Mariah bit her lip. "Caro, I have hesitated to tell you about my disastrous marriage to Edward before, in respect for your tender years and your innocence. But you are older and more wordly now, and I believe I may safely do so without frightening you.''

"Do tell me.''

With little ado, Mariah described to her younger cousin her horrendous marriage to Edward; a marriage more akin to an imprisonment, one that only his sudden departure for India and subsequent death had released her from.

"Ye Gods, my poor, dear coz!'' Caro exclaimed, tears of pity filling her eyes. "I had no idea! And you say Uncle Harry *encouraged* your marriage to that—that madman? That monster? That he stood by and watched, but did nothing?''

When Mariah reluctantly admitted that this had been the case, Caroline threw up her hands in disgust and muttered, "For shame! His own daughter! I cannot believe Uncle Harry capable of such callous disregard for your well-being, coz!''

"Perhaps there were reasons I did not understand,'' Mariah hedged, jumping to her father's defense. "Financial worries, perhaps, of which I had no knowledge.''

"Oh, fiddlesticks! It makes no difference if you were headed for the poorhouse. Were we down to our very last farthing, Papa would never allow me to be used so cruelly.''

"Aye, but Uncle Paul is a stronger man than my father ever was, Caro. I . . . I once fancied Edward had some hold over him, but what it was, I cannot imagine.

417

"Anyway, now that I've told you the dark secrets of my past, come back to bed! Joe has promised to drive me into Port Jackson in the morning to visit Jack at the stockade. Will you come with us?"

"I will. Oh, that poor little man! My heart quite goes out to him, he seems so dreadfully changed since his imprisonment."

"He is indeed. The sooner the trial is over, the better, I say. Now. That's enough chatter for one night! It's quite far to the settlement, so if we're to make an early start and pay Jack a visit, we need our sleep," Mariah reminded her, swinging her legs into bed and pulling the sheet up over herself.

Caroline did likewise. "By the by, coz," she said as she squirmed about to get comfortable, "your eagerness to go into Port Jackson tomorrow wouldn't have anything to do with the fact that a certain sea-captain is preparing to set sail for England soon, would it?" she inquired archly.

"It certainly would not."

"You're positive?"

"Good night, coz," Mariah said, firmly ending the discussion. "God bless you."

"And you, Mariah," Caro came back airily. "Oh, and sweet dreams, coz . . . if not of your stalwart Captain Burroughs, then of that handsome brute, Kincaid."

Her palms splayed lightly across her hardening belly, Mariah stared up at the rafters above her. Though still wide awake, she offered no response to her cousin's last comment, and a muffled snore indicated that Caro had fallen asleep the moment her head touched the pillow.

Beneath her fingertips, Mariah felt the tiniest flutter of movement as her babe stirred within her. *Hello, little one*! she said silently. *Did I waken you, my pet?*

A rueful smile curved her lips in the shadows, for she had no need of Caro's urgings to dream about Jonathan Kincaid. In truth, how could she ever forget him . . . ?

Chapter Thirty-Three

"Come, Caro. 'Tis high time we bade Jack farewell if we're going to Government House for the farewell luncheon. Your papa and his guests will be waiting for us."

Caro nodded. "The *Lady Deliverance* sails for England to-day, did you know, Jack? My papa has planned a little farewell for her captain and crew. Tim Bright will be there," she added, her cheeks growing pink. "Captain Burroughs has taken him on as second cabin boy for the return voyage."

"Well, that's a fine turnabout!" Jack declared, seeming more animated than he'd been since their arrival an hour or so earlier. "Last I heard, that young rascal'd sworn off the sea-farin' life fer good! Said he'd had 'is fill o' cannibals an' such!"

"And so he has. This is to be his last voyage. He means to return to England, and his father's parsonage, and become a parson in his own right." A sad little smile hovered about her usually merry lips. "As you said, a sailor's life is not for him."

"He in't alone in that, mistress. There's many would agree with 'im. Ah, ye'll miss 'im sorely, I've no doubt."

Caroline bit her lower lip and sighed. There was the merest suspicion of tears in her blue eyes. "I shall, though he won't be gone forever, God willing. And he's promised me faithfully that he'll write as soon as may be. Oh, Jack, he spoke with Papa the other evening, and the dear man has said we might be wed when Tim is done with his training! Papa told Tim he should ask the Church to send him out to New South Wales once he is ordained, and Tim agreed. In truth, what better place to begin his ministry than here, saving the tarnished souls of our colony?"

"What better indeed! Ah, ye'll make a fetchin' parson's wife, ye will, an' no mistake, miss," Jack said gruffly, noting the young woman's carefully nonchalant manner—and not fooled by it for a minute. After all, he had five daughters of his own, he did, and he knew the signs well enough by now—or should. The poor little lass was dreading the lengthy separation from her sweetheart. "Ye'll see, miss—the time'll fly by! Afore ye know it, young Parson Bright'll come a-knocking on your door!"

"Oh, I hope so. But . . . oh, Jack, I do so hate good-byes."

"There's a few that like 'em, miss. Best ye make it short and sweet, and be done wi' it, I say. Long partings be the hardest."

"Speaking of farewells, we must be going," Mariah reminded her cousin a second time. She retrieved an empty wicker basket from the stone-flagged floor, rose, and patted Jack's bony shoulder in parting. "Now that Judge Lombard has returned from Batavia, your hearing has been scheduled for Thursday morning. God willing, you will be free by nightfall, Jack, and this unhappy time behind you!"

"Amen!"

"I expect you're looking forward to getting home to Yarmouth and seeing your family, are you not?"

"Indeed I am, m'lady," Jack agreed with little vehemence, despite Mariah's staunchly bright and breezy manner.

"How many daughters have you?"

"Five, mum."

"Five! No sons?"

"Nary a one, mum!"

"Well, I just know your girls will be delighted to see their dear papa home, safe and sound! Hold onto that thought, Jack," she encouraged him softly. "Think only of seeing them again. Don't dwell upon thoughts of doom and gloom."

"Aye! We cannot bear to see you this way!" Caro wailed, looked teary-eyed about the spartan cell with its solitary barred window and its coarse cot of wooden planks with but a single threadbare blanket. Impulsively hugging the ship's carpenter about the shoulders, she added indignantly, "Mutineer, indeed! What are they thinking of? I'd be long dead, were it not for you, and so would Mariah. I've told Papa so a hundred times! How could they believe that horrid Harkabout's word over yours!"

For her sake, Jack forced a smile. "Now, now, yer old Jack's all right, miss. I'll try not t' wallow in the doldrums fer your sake, if not me own, cross me heart, I will. My thanks for the plum jam and the . . ."

"Damper," Caroline supplied. "Kitty and I made them together," she added with a hint of pride.

"Aye, the damper. She's a good little wench, that Kitty."

"She is indeed. She and Joe seem happy as turtle-doves!" Mariah agreed, drawing on her kid gloves with a critical eye. They were a trifle snug, but since she owed her entire wardrobe to some free settler's poor wife who'd had the sad misfortune to succumb to brain-fever during the Second Fleet's voyage, she could hardly complain. Unfortunately, not an item of that wardrobe did she wear without thinking of the poor woman's demise. "Our thoughts and prayers will be with you in court, Jack. You can rest assured that if testimonials to your good character are required, there are many who will speak on your behalf, including ourselves."

"My thanks an' God bless ye, ladies. 'Twere good o' ye t' come."

As they were leaving the stockade where Jack was confined, Caroline leading the way, Mariah almost collided with a tall, broad-shouldered man striding briskly towards her.

Oh!'' she exclaimed, for the moment crushed against his broad chest so forcefully, her straw hat was twisted askew.

"My pardon, mistress," he apologized absently, placing steadying hands upon Mariah's upper arms.

To her dismay, upon looking up from beneath the crushed, drunken brim of her straw bonnet, Mariah found herself gazing into Nathan's startled green eyes. She gasped despite herself, for she had not recognized him properly clothed, not after spending so many weeks in his half-clad company. Nor, it seemed, had he recognized her at first, judging by his unguarded, surprised expression.

Rosy color rushed to her cheeks. Her heart fluttered. She stepped quickly back, away from him, utterly flustered by the chance meeting and the unexpected physical contact. Lord! The places where his hands had steadied her seemed to burn. . . .

"Not at all, sir," she demurred, coolly inclining her head, though it took enormous effort to appear so self-composed when her nerves were jangling so. "The fault was mine entirely. A very good day to you, sir."

Picking up her pale-pink dimity skirts, she made as if to follow Caroline out into the street, but Nathan stepped into her path, blocking her retreat.

"My, my! You're looking very well, m'lady," he murmured. "Indeed, one might go so far as to say . . . radiant. 'Twould appear you're quite recovered from your ordeal upon the island?''

"Completely so, sir. As, it appears, are you. Now, I really must be—"

"—running along? Tsk-tsk. Such haste, m'lady! I remember a hoyden in red petticoats who was in no such hurry to be quit of me. Have you no time to dally? To exchange a pleasantry or two with an old . . . and intimate . . . friend?''

She set her bonnet aright, bristling beneath his mocking gaze and none-too-subtle innuendo. The high color in her cheeks and the sparks in her turquoise eyes gave vivid warning of her rising indignation. "On the contrary, sir, I *see* no old friends here, nor anyone else I would care to exchange pleasantries with. By your leave, sir . . ."

As she tried to thrust past him, Nathan laughed harshly and fastened his hands about her waist. Before she could protest, he'd lifted her up and swung her around, pressing her back against the wall. He planted a hand on either side of her head to prevent her escape.

Trapped and held so close to him, she was breathless. She could smell the faint yet oh, so evocative scents of shaving soap and sun-dried linen that clung to his person; the unique, excitingly masculine scent that was his and no other's. A single inhalation brought back painfully vivid memories; of being cradled to his bare, hairy chest on a moon-drenched beach with the sand warm beneath them, of his scent . . . the exotic fragrance of tropical blossoms . . . the briny tang of the sea. . . . *What does the shell say?* he'd asked her teasingly one golden afternoon. And, lifting the pink-and-white conch to her ear, she'd grown wide-eyed to hear it whisper, *He loves you! He loves you!*

Alas, trusting, lovesick little fool that she'd been then, like the sailors of old she'd believed its siren song, only to find herself lured into unfamiliar, dangerous waters, then left high and dry, her heart shattered.

Her lips tightened primly. His illness had been a godsend, really, for delirium had exposed the *real* man beneath the roguish, devil-may-care facade. Not a murderer, perhaps, but certainly a ruthless rake. How very wrong she'd been to think she needed him and could not live without him—or that he cared a jot for her! La! He was naught but a womanizing scoundrel, had been from the very first. A wolf in sheep's clothing who, lacking other females to distract him, had played the teasing gallant, the romantic rascal, to woo and win her affections. Nay, sharks had not been the only dangerous predators to cruise those balmy Southern Seas.

Thank God, she was a stronger woman now, one who could stand on her own two feet. She'd not be so vulnerable to the likes of Nathan Kincaid in the future. . . .

"How now, Mariah! Why so flustered? Let me guess! Is it the *Lady Deliverance*'s imminent departure that has you all a-twitter? Or rather, the departure of her stalwart master—the worthy Captain Burroughs?"

His tone smacks of jealousy! she thought, her heart skipping an uncertain beat. But, nay. Surely she was mistaken? Why on earth should he be jealous of Thaddeus, when he cared nothing for her himself? When, indeed, he'd been the one to cast her aside, rather than the other way around? Perhaps he was showing his true colors, now that they'd returned to civilization. He could be one of those selfish brutes who, having discarded a mistress he'd wearied of, could still not bear to have her look upon another with affection.

"I'm promised to attend the farewell luncheon at Government House, sir. As master of the *Lady Deliverance*, Captain Burroughs will certainly be there, among others, yes," she admitted in a defensive tone she hated, but could not seem to help. "We former castaways owe him a great deal, after all. If not for the good captain's perseverance, we would not be here in Port Jackson now, would we?"

A nerve ticked at his temple. His jaw tightened. His green eyes chilled, became the color of glaciers. "Aye, quite so. However, I'd fancied—seeing the pair of you with your heads so cozily together at Government House that first night—that you'd already demonstrated your gratitude during our voyage here. And in no uncertain fashion."

His insolent tone left her in no doubt as to what he was implying by "gratitude." Anger rose swiftly through her like scalded milk rising up a pot, close to boiling over. "Insolent rogue! How dare you imply such a thing!'' she spat out. Drawing back her hand, she smacked his face with all the strength she could summon, her gloves leaving ruddy stripes across his tanned cheek. ''Good day, sir!'' she snapped, then ducked under his arm and fled after Caroline.

She found her cousin loitering outside a disreputable-looking grog-shop, drawing all manner of interested leers and winks from its patrons—sailors and soldiers of the lower ranks, for the greater part—as they came and went. On spotting Mariah, she picked up her skirts and ran to meet her. Her flaxen hair was uncovered, her fair complexion exposed to the harsh sunshine as she swung her sun-bonnet carelessly by its ribbons. *Oh, to be that carefree and innocent again!* Mariah thought enviously.

''Oh, Mariah, tell me quickly what happened?'' Caro bubbled. ''Did you speak with Jonathan? What did he say? Is your quarrel mended? Did he beg your forgiveness? Oh, do tell me!'' she demanded eagerly, her eyes sparkling.

Caroline obviously hoped a miracle had taken place during their brief and stormy confrontation. Still ruffled, Mariah pursed her lips. ''Pray, do not ask! Nay, Caro, not another word!'' she warned hotly, fire in her eyes. ''Come!''

Taking Caro's elbow, she steered her forcefully away from the grog-shop, turning her cousin smartly in the direction of Government House, instead, apparently deaf to the appreciative whistles and whoops that followed them down the winding, hilly street.

Nathan, who had left the barracks and followed Mariah outside, stood and watched them hurry off, his expression bleak as he rubbed his smarting cheek. Damn it all, she was going, leaving behind only the imprint of her well-deserved slap. 'Twas too late to offer an apology, had he been able to bring himself to make one. Livid with anger at himself, he cursed the demon upon his shoulder that had made him insult her rather than bid her a cordial farewell before his departure for

England, as he'd first intended. But for some reason, he hadn't been able to hold his tongue. The thought of Mariah in that fawning Burroughs' company had filled him with rage.

Why, damn it?

Because you still care for her, you fool!

No!

Aye, you do! Admit it! Too late, you've discovered she means more to you than proving your innocence. More than redeeming yourself in your father's eyes. More than anything in the world!

Never!

Are you quite certain of that?

Aye.

If you care so little, how is it you're so jealous of Burroughs, so afraid he might win her for himself? Admit it, Kincaid! Be honest with yourself, this once. You made the biggest mistake of your life when you cast her aside! A pox on who her father might have been! It's not her damned father you want. You don't really give a jot about any of that because—God help you!—you still love her!

"The deuced I do!" he growled aloud, drawing startled looks from passers-by. Ignoring them, he scowled and eyed the grog-shop with sudden longing. As a departing passenger, he had also been invited to attend the farewell luncheon that Governor Amberfield had planned to celebrate the *Lady Deliverance*'s crew's departure for England. But now, knowing that Mariah would also be in attendance, he decided to forego it— and the distinct possibility of a nasty confrontation with that red-headed spitfire. He'd have a farewell tot of rum or two to settle his belly, instead, then board the *Lady Deliverance* early. The sooner he staked his claim upon a portion of the small cabin he and Surgeon Love would share for the duration of the voyage, the better. He grimaced as he bellied up to the grog-shop's bar and ordered up a measure of rum with a snap of his fingers. If he waited 'til the last moment, he wagered that dour

426

old goat would end up with the lion's share of cabin-space for himself. . . .

It was a decidedly unsteady Nathan Kincaid who staggered from the grog-shop's doors two hours later. One farewell tot had become two, then three, then four, then more. Indeed, how many more, he did not know. At some point, he seemed to have lost count—along with his sense of direction. Rather than wending his way to the wharf, he was laboring up the dirt tracks that wound among the somewhat barren, grassy hills behind Port Jackson.

"Oi, oi, gov'na, getting' yer sea-legs a bit early, are ye?"

He looked up to find Ben Coombs standing before him. The man had appeared like a leprechaun from behind a wind-twisted tree and was grinning cheekily at him.

Nathan growled in a sour tone, "Aye, but I've lost my damned land-lubber's sense of direction in the doing! Where the devil's the blasted ship?"

"'Tis back that way, t' the harbor, sir," Ben supplied, taking his elbow. "But ye're in no fit state t' be boarding ship right now. Ye'll lose yer belly, sure as ninepence!" He recoiled, eyes watering. "Gawd Almighty, sir, there's a powerful whiff o' grog about ye! How many tots did ye have?"

"Damned if I know," Nathan came back, grinning foolishly. "Six? Seven? God's Teeth, Ben, I lost count!" He groaned, staggering heavily against the wiry little man. "Lud! I do believe I'm in my cups, sir—and a little . . . a li'l the worsht for wear."

"Little in't the half of it, sir. Here, sit yerself down, up against this tree. Ye need some solid victuals t' soak up all that grog, ye do. Sea biscuits. Or a nice plum duff, mebbe?"

"God's Teeth, don't mention victuals!" Nathan insisted with a shudder, looking green about the gills as he folded to a sitting position and leaned back against the tree trunk. "I'll just . . . rest here a spell . . . an' forget about that damned Winslow woman. She struck me, you know, Ben. Fetched me a good wallop, as you'd say. An' you know what, man? I *asked* for it!''

"Aye, sir," Ben agreed amicably, humoring him. "No doubt ye did! The wenches have us lads t' rights, most o' the time. My Winnie always did, God rest her soul. Now. Close yer eyes, sir. Sleep it off."

"But the ship . . . ?"

"I'll see ye aboard her in good time, never fear."

"Master Kincaid? Wake up, sir! The *Lady Deliverance* sails within the hour!"

"Shhh. Can't you see I'm tryin' t' sleep here, matey?" Nathan grumbled, waving his hand away. "An' pipe down, man! My noggin hurts."

"I don't wonder at it, gov'na! But if ye tarry, ye'll miss the bloomin' ship. Up wiv ye now, sir. On yer feet. Look lively there, matey!"

With supreme effort and no little encouragement and chivvying on Ben's part, Nathan hauled himself to standing. Swaying from side to side, he tried to focus on the tattered scarecrow that was standing some two dozen yards or so behind Ben.

"Look at that! Blasted scarecrow keeps movin' . . ." he complained, blinking.

"Wot?" Ben asked, paling. Startled, he whirled about, in time to see the "scarecrow" raise its arm. Yellow flares spurted from the nose of the pistol in the scarecrow's grip as Ben shoved Nathan to the grass and sprawled atop him.

"Wassamatta?" the man beneath him demanded. "God's Teeth, your blasted knee! You nigh unmanned me, sir!"

"Shut up an' be still!" Ben hissed, looking about him for a fallen branch, a rock, anything he could use as a weapon against their attacker, but finding nothing at hand.

Still fuddled by rum, Nathan had no strength to argue or put up a struggle as, after several minutes, Ben gingerly raised himself onto his palms. Keeping his head low, he scanned the barren hillsides, catching a glimpse of movement off to his left.

"Ye can get up, gov'na. He's well away!" Ben muttered in relief as the bearded apparition—a tall scarecrow of a man clothed in the ragged remnants of a broadcloth coat and breeches, some sort of skin slung over his shoulders—loped down the hillside, vanishing into the settlement's winding streets. "That was too bloomin' . . . Yer bleedin', sir! He got yer!" Ben exclaimed, turning to Nathan. "Yer shot, ye are!"

"Shot? Me?" Nathan looked down at his chest, seeing nothing.

"Aye! The lout had a pistol! Why else would I have sat on ye, sir?"

"God's Teeth! 'Twould seem I owe you my life, then, Ben!" Nathan muttered, considerably sobered by this information as Ben scrambled off him. His forehead smarted, he realized. Reaching up, he found the flesh wound on his brow. It was raw and stung like blazes now, but was not too deep. "Another inch to the left, and I'd be grave fodder! Did you see who he was?"

"I did." Ben's lips pursed. "And ye've no need t' worry, sir. See, it were *me* he were aimin' fer, not you! Been sneakin' about after me for two days now, he has. That's why I come up here inter the hills alone—to draw him out inter the open, like. I'd hoped he'd take the bait an' I could get it over with, once an' fer all. So did he, by the looks o' it! Lucky fer us he's no hand wi' a pistol, eh?"

"What's the trouble between you? An old grudge?" Nathan asked, wincing as, sitting up and leaning against the tree-trunk, he fingered the deep scarlet gouge where the ball had creased his brow. There was fresh blood on his fingers when he drew them away. "Some unfinished business from Newgate? Or a jealous rival for your Nan's affections?"

"Not hardly, sir. Nah. 'Tis worse 'n that. Truth is, I isn't

429

too proud o' my part in it, sir. If it's all the same t' you, I'd as soon not talk of it.''

"Come, come, Ben. We're old friends by now, surely you can confide in me? You know I'd be the last man t' condemn another out of hand!''

"Aye, I do at that, sir.'' Ben sighed. "Oh, all right. Where's the harm in it? This here's the new world, right? Then here goes. First off, me name's not really Ben Coombs,'' Ben began, looking about apprehensively as he drew a clean folded neckerchief from his jerkin pocket. Kneeling, he pressed it to Nathan's wound and added, "Me real name's Andrew. Andrew Hampton.''

Nathan frowned, clearly puzzled. "If the name should mean something to me, I've forgotten it.''

"I was head trainer fer His Majesty's racehorses. I just thought—wot wi' you bein' a gent an' all—me real name might ring a bell?''

Nathan whistled through his teeth. "That Hampton? The King's own trainer? Good God, man, what the devil are you doing here, then? Teaching *kangurus* to hop?''

Ben grinned. "Why I'm here is a long story, sir—an' an old one! See, I didn't always train Thoroughbreds t' run! I started off at the bottom, as is proper, making my living as a stable-boy at a coaching inn near where I was bred an' born. Then, little by little, I worked me way up t' the post of head groom at the tender age o' twenty-one years,'' he declared with obvious pride. "Always had a way wiv horses, I did,'' he added without any false modesty. He sniffed. "Still do.''

"That's most commendable, er . . . Andrew, was it?''

"Call me Ben, gov'na. I'm used to it now.''

"Thank God!'' Nathan declared with feeling, smiling through the trickle of blood that had dried down one side of his face. "For a moment, with you being Andrew *and* Ben, and me being Nathan *and* Matt Wyman, I felt somewhat . . . over-crowded! Very well. Ben it is. But names and aliases aside, how is your admirable ascent through the ranks connected to the attempt on your life?''

"Hold yer horses, sir, I'm getting ter that," Ben growled, clearly miffed by Nathan's impatience. "See, the lord I become head groom for was William *Downing*. I worked wiv his hunters on his country estate, Windsmere, down in Middlesex.''

"Downing? You mean, Lady Mariah's late husband?'' Nathan was suddenly all ears. He sat up, so swiftly his head swam and blood seeped anew from the wound, "Ouch!" he muttered, but burning with curiosity now, he nevertheless waved aside Ben's helping hand, adjusted the folded neckerchief over his wound, and urged the little man, "Well? Don't stop there. Go on!"

"Nay, 'twas not her ladyship's husband I worked for, but his father," Ben explained. "Though the little Winslow lass an' his lordship's son used t' play together as nippers. Pretty little thing she were, even then.

"Anyway, all of us lads who worked on the estate knew Lord William for a mean old bastard who treated his dear lady proper poorly. So, when Lady Lenore started meeting Tom Stokes—the estate's game-keeper and my wife Winnie's brother—on the sly, we lads snickered behind his back and figured 'twere no more than his lordship deserved.''

"William Downing's wife was having an affair with your brother-in-law, her game-keeper?''

"Just so," Ben confirmed. "Anyway, one morning in June, Lord William caught 'em at it, red-handed! I recollect we'd gone out t' the paddocks t' see if the mare 'is lordship had bought the winter before had dropped her foal. Whilst me an' one o' the lads was tending to her, his lordship wandered off. A few moments later, I heard a shot—like a clap o' thunder, it were! I ran and found Lord William standing over Stokes. His musket-barrel was still smoking, an' the back o' Stokes' head had been blown clear away!''

"And the woman?''

"Lady Lenore was dead, too, poor lady—choked, by the looks of it. Well, Lord William claimed Stokes had raped an' strangled his wife, an' that he'd surprised the bastard before he could escape. But from the first, that tale didn't sit right with me. I arsks yer, sir, why'd Tom need t' ravish her ladyship, when she was giving 'im what he wanted?"

"Why, indeed?" Nathan agreed.

"Well, there were an inquest inter the deaths, o' course, an' I was summoned t' tell what I'd seen. The night before the inquest, Lord William called me up ter the house. He asked if I'd heard rumors that his wife had been carryin' on with Stokes. When I mumbled aye, that I'd heard somethin' o' the sort, he hinted in this sly sorta voice that there was no truth in such gossip. An' then he said that when they questioned me at the inquest, he'd count it a favor if I didn't mention those rumors. He said he didn't want Lady Lenore's good name sullied—an' made it clear as day that it would be t' my benefit t' keep mum."

"And did you?"

"Aye. I'm ashamed t' say I did, sir," Ben admitted with a hang-dog look. "Despite my Winnie, God rest her soul, being proper vexed about it, I let his lordship get away with murderin' them both! My Winnie, she wanted her brother's murderer t' be punished, an' Tom's name cleared. But in the end, I convinced her that, while nothing could bring Tom back, being in his lordship's debt could do wonders fer our future. I was ambitious then, see, for all the good it's done me!"

"So you lied at the inquest?"

"Aye. When Judge Winslow asked me if I'd heard Tom Stokes were carryin' on with her ladyship, I said I'd heard nothing o' the sort. That her ladyship was a good an' virtuous wife, while Tom Stokes had allus been a bad lot wi' the wenches."

"*Winslow?*" Nathan whistled under his breath. "Judge Harry Winslow was the county magistrate?"

"Aye," Ben confirmed. "And by day's end, both deaths

had been written off as Lord William wanted, thanks to Judge Winslow! One as a murder, the other as manslaughter. Manslaughter, my arse! Strange, innit, sir, that following the day o' the inquest, both His Honor's fortunes an' me own took an upward swing? Within the year, Judge Winslow were a magistrate at the Old Bailey, whilst I—''

"Whilst you became the head trainer for the King's nags," Nathan ended for him, his thoughts scrambling over themselves as he tried to sort this new information regarding Winslow with what he already knew of the man.

"Under-trainer," Ben corrected. "I was made head trainer two years later, when the old head trainer retired. You've heard of the colt, His Royal Majesty?"

"Heard of him?" Nathan groaned. "God's Teeth, I lost twenty guineas betting against him last Derby Day!"

"He were one o' my colts," Ben confessed proudly. "Brung him inter the world meself, I did. But anyway, gettin' back t' the matter at hand, it seems there were a witness t' what Lord William did that day. His little eight-year-old son was spyin' on the lovers. The lad saw everything! I heard later he weren't never the same afterwards; that his papa had threatened him with all manner of horrid doings if he didn't keep his trap shut. They say as how it turned his mind. Well, small wonder, innit, sir? 'Twas too weighty a secret for a little lad like that t' keep t' himself, seeing his mama so brutally murdered—and by his own papa, too!''

"Did the lad ever confide in you?"

"Gawd bless ye, no, sir! Young Edward were packed off t' boarding-school soon after her ladyship's funeral, and me and Winnie left the country fer London less than a month later, when Lord William found me my new position."

"Then how did you know about the boy?"

"Well, we'd go back t' the village from time t' time t' visit Winnie's Gran. 'Twas on one o' those visits I heard from Winnie's sister—she were a maid at Windsmere—that keepin' his father's secrets had become too much for the poor little sod. He'd told! First Master Forbes, his tutor. Then the school chaplain at the boardin'-school he were sent to. And both men told his father, the sods! By all accounts, the little lad caught hell when Lord William had him sent home. But by then, the tutor he'd confided in had mysteriously become headmaster of one o' them highfalutin' public schools up north—and the school chaplain rose to a fat bishopric in Canterbury soon after. Aye, he rose as fast as a bloomin' rocket, he did! And, when he saw that nothing he could do would force his son t' keep his secret, Lord William played his trump card. He had the boy locked up.''

"Imprisoned, you mean?"

"Worse'n that, gov'na—had him locked up in a loony bin. An asylum! He had a doctor sign papers t' say the boy was insane, an' that was that. The poor little sod was shut away, forced t' live with them loonies 'til after Lord William passed on!''

"Dear God in Heaven!" Nathan exclaimed, unable to comprehend William Downing's unbelievable cruelty to his little son. Ben's story did, however, explain Edward Downing's later behavior as an adult and his warped treatment of his innocent young bride, Mariah, the little girl he'd once played with in the Middlesex countryside . . . and, perhaps, in his own perverted way, had always loved.

God's Teeth! Imagining her married to the twisted creature Edward had become filled him with revulsion. How could Winslow have permitted it? And, God damn it, *why*? But the answer was obvious. Harry Winslow had been weak. And Edward Downing had known the secret of his mercurial rise to the exalted chambers of the Old Bailey. That sorry bastard had allowed Edward to marry his daughter in order to keep his secret buried. "Then 'tis a mercy to all concerned that Edward Downing's dead, his hellish existence ended at last," Nathan declared with a frown.

"But that's what I was leading up to, sir. *Edward Downing in't dead!* 'Twas him who fired the shot—I seen 'im wi' me

434

own two eyes, sir—and there in't no mistaking those creepy yeller peepers o' his!'' he added with a shudder. ''One by one, he's silenced us all, save fer me! The others, they'd had enough. They got together an' tried t' have him put away again.''

''They did?''

''Aye. They had the doctor commit him, told everyone he were dead—but he's clever, he is, an' he escaped, God rot him.''

''When was this?'' Nathan hardly dared to ask, he was so certain of Ben's answer.

''Right before the Second Fleet set sail, close as I recall. 'Strewth! I just knew he'd never give up, an' I was right! I thought by changing me name and getting meself transported, I could escape him, but I was wrong. He's come here after me, he has. Followed me t' the other side o' the world t' shut me up! An there'll be no stoppin' him, sir—not 'til I'm dead like the others an' his father's secret safe for all time! Judge Winslow. Bishop Hendrickson, the school chaplain. Doctor Friar, wot had him committed both times. The banker, Alistair Cameron. The lawyer, Throgmorton. Master Forbes, his old tutor. They thought that together, they could control him, but . . . *they're all dead, sir.*''

A frisson of horror slithered down Nathan's spine. What was Ben saying? A judge. A lawyer. A physician. A banker. The respected headmaster of a prestigious public school. A bishop. And finally, Andrew Hampton, the trainer of the King's race-horses but formerly William Downing's head groom. And, if he were not dead, Edward Downing himself. He counted on his fingers. Eight men! Eight men who had one terrible secret in common—and whose individual successes in life had been founded, for the greater part, upon deception and lies, and upon their ability to keep that secret.

Eight *gentlemen* who had discussed the murder of ''His Royal Majesty'' in the room at the George. But, had they truly been discussing the assassination of the King that day little

435

Rose had eavesdropped? Or—and here was the bitter irony of it—had Edward been trying to coerce the others into helping him kill Andrew Hampton and the King's colt, His Royal Majesty?

Eight respectable, distinguished gentlemen had been in the bedchamber the night Roger Loring and Rose Wicks had been killed. Had they been seven spineless bastards who'd been willing to stand by and let an innocent man be hanged for the murders, rather than go against the eighth man, the murderer, Edward Downing, himself?

The pieces fit very well. Too well for mere coincidence.

His heart began to beat very fast. Sweat broke out upon his upper lip. Was William Downing's son—no longer a little boy but a grown man twisted into something frightening and abnormal—still trying desperately to keep his father's secret? To silence each and every man who'd been a party to that secret, himself and Ben, alias Andrew Hampton, included?

The puzzle's pieces were beginning to fall into place. Some of them were yet missing, and there were questions that yet needed answering; motives that were still foggy. But Jonathan had a gut feeling that those missing pieces were here, in New South Wales rather than in England, just waiting to be found. That soon the fog would finally clear. . . .

Of a sudden, he was aware of the painful throbbing in his head, a combination of the wound and too much grog. He tried to stand, but the world reeled about him, and he could not. Sinking back down, he grunted. "A favor, Ben, if you would?"

"Name it, sir."

"Carry my regrets to Captain Burroughs. No doubt he'll be aboard the *Lady Deliverance* by now. Tell him I've decided to postpone my return to England indefinitely, that he should sail without me. Then come back here with horses for us both."

"Both?"

"Aye, Ben, both. I believe you're wrong, you see. If you're

right, and Downing's alive, he's after *both* of us. I'll explain my part in it as we ride.''

"Aye, aye, sir. Will do! But . . . horses, sir? You in't in no fit state t' be ridin', sir!"

"Damn it, I have no choice, Ben! You see, if Edward Downing is alive and here in Port Jackson, Lady Mariah must be warned. We must ride for Government House!"

"But you won't find her ladyship there, sir! Nan told me she were feeling poorly and had decided not to stay for the farewell luncheon with Mistress Caroline. She cut her farewells short an' left fer the Governor's farm.''

"When?"

"Afore noon. More 'n an hour ago, sir.''

"Jesu!" Nathan's next outburst would have done the most hardened, most foul-mouthed convict credit, for he staggered upright, cursing a blue streak under his breath. ''T' hell with the blasted ship, then, Ben. Fetch the horses—and quick about it! We've no time to lose!"

"Aye, aye, sir!" Ben promised, and was gone.

The thought of Mariah traveling across open bush in a slow-moving ox-cart, an unarmed Joe Hardy at the traces as Edward Downing stalked them, turned the blood in Nathan's veins to ice.

Chapter Thirty-Four

"You're home early," Kitty exclaimed.

"Aye." Mariah sighed. "Seeing Jack in that cell upset me, I think. I had no stomach for the farewell luncheon, so I offered my regrets to Captain Burroughs and came home. I didn't come back empty-handed, though." She smiled. "I've brought some salted pork, more sugar, some salt, spices from Java, a barrel of golden molasses, and an entire sack of flour—without weevils!"

Kitty's eyes lit up. "Molasses? Flour without weevils? We'll be havin' tasty fare tonight, then!" she declared. "With, may-hap, a treacle tart fer 'afters' . . .?" She arched her brows.

"Oh, yes, Kitty! Treacle tart's my favorite pudding! I do believe my appetite's returning," Mariah said, laughing as she untied the ribbons of her bonnet. "Poor Caro. When she hears we had treacle tart, she'll be so vexed."

"She stayed behind at Port Jackson, then?" Kitty asked, hurrying to stir the savory-smelling contents of the black soup kettle that hung from a hook over the glowing coals of the kitchen's wide hearth.

Mariah nodded. "She wanted to say farewell to Tim, and to spend what little time they had left together."

"Poor lamb. His leavin'll be hard on her, an' no mistake. Proper sweet on each other, them two are. Here, mum, give me that bonnet, do! Do ye fancy a drop o' fresh milk t' wet yer whistle? Yer throat must be proper parched, after travelin' that dusty old road. Tsk. One in your condition should take better care of 'erself, I say—oh, Gawd!" Kitty turned crimson and clamped her hand over her mouth. "That's torn it. I went an' said it, didn't I?"

"Oh, never mind, Kit. And for pity's sake, do not look so blessed guilty. I don't mind that you guessed. After all, it's not something one can keep a secret forever, is it now?"

The two young women considered that observation for a moment, then both looked down at Mariah's belly and burst out laughing.

Mariah continued, "I was meaning to tell you very soon, anyway. Now's as good a time as any."

"Does he know?"

"Kincaid?" Mariah's lips tightened. She shook her head.

"You haven't told 'im? But, why ever not? He sails with Burroughs t'day, don't he?"

"Aye—and good riddance, I say, wretched man."

"Oww, You don't mean that," Kitty insisted gently, remembering all too well the many nights Mariah had tended Nathan, bathing his fever-wracked body, spooning liquid between his cracked lips, working selflessly and with a quiet desperation to restore him first to life, then health, although he had cruelly rejected her in his few moments of lucidity. "I know better. Ye can't mean it."

"You're wrong. I do! Perhaps I needed Nathan once. And perhaps I thought I loved him because of that need." Her jaw came up. "But he means nothing to me now, just as I mean nothing to him."

"But the babe . . . He'll need a father."

"The babe makes no difference. I won't use an innocent

child to bind him to me. Better one parent who loves it dearly, than a father who feels trapped and blames the child for having his wings clipped. Besides, if my pedigree's not good enough for him, then I doubt he'd want the child, anyway. Nay, I'll raise the babe by myself, without help or hindrance from Master Jonathan Kincaid, thank ye kindly!''

"Hmmph. You ask me, ye sound awful sharp for someone wot don't care," Kitty observed slyly as she poured milk into a pewter tankard. "Run inter him in Port Jackson, did ye, then?"

"We . . . exchanged a few words, yes." Mariah took a sip of the creamy milk and sighed with pleasure.

"And?" Kitty urged. There was more to this than Mariah was admitting, she could tell by her too-innocent expression.

"Oh, all right. If you must know, I was forced to slap his face! He was most . . . insulting. He made insinuations about poor Thaddeus' kindness and affection for me that I could not ignore. In fact, I would go so far as to say he sounded somewhat . . . jealous," she added a trifle smugly, deviltry in her sparkling turquoise eyes.

"An' ye liked that, did yer? That he were jealous?"

"Certainly not! I *liked* that I slapped his face. He deserved no less, and 'twas what I should have done a long time ago. Now. Why don't I go and change into something more suitable? Then we'll see to making that treacle pie, shall we?"

As she left the kitchen, Kitty muttered, "Ye can fool yerself, mistress, but ye don't fool Kitty Hardy fer a minute!"

Mariah turned in the narrow doorway. "I'm sorry . . . what was that?"

Kitty reddened. "I just said I'll see yer in a minute, mum."

Supper that evening—a modest broth with scraps of salt-beef, barley, and vegetables, eaten with coarse brown bread—became a feast with the rare luxury of Kitty's delicious treacle tart for dessert.

After the board had been cleared and dusted of crumbs, the

pots and platters scoured under the pump, Joe lit candles, then he and Kitty settled themselves on either side of the hearth, leaving the solitary armchair between them for Mariah.

Kitty's dark-brown head was soon bent over the darning and patching of her and Joe's threadbare wardrobe, the candle's gentle radiance picking out tawny highlights among her thick sable locks. Joe busied himself with repairing the worn soles of a pair of shabby brown boots, using a cobbler's awl and some discarded snippets of leather.

"Shall I read to you whilst you work?" Mariah offered, knowing the pair were unable to read for themselves, but enjoyed being read to.

"Would ye, mum?" Joe agreed eagerly.

"I'd love to. Now, which shall it be, Kitty? 'Tis your choice tonight. Will Shakespeare or the Bible?"

Kitty wrinkled her nose. "Shakespeare. The Good Book always makes me feel like I've done somethin' I shouldn't 'ave. Carry on with the play you started, mum—the one about them two families an' the lovers, that Romeo an' Juliet. Ooh, a loverly pair o' turtle doves they are! Made fer each other, I reckon. It brung tears t' me eyes the last time you read it, it did—all that heartache they was having, wot with the two families fightin' an' her promised to wed another, an' all. Still, I 'spect it'll turn out happily enough," she added with her customary optimism but, Mariah fancied, with somewhat more emphasis than was strictly necessary.

She hid a smile, knowing very well what Kitty was hinting at. "If it's a happy ending you want tonight, Mistress Hardy, you won't find it in *Romeo and Juliet*."

"How so?" Kitty asked, glancing up from the hose she was darning.

"You'll see, by and by," Mariah promised, taking her seat. Arranging her serviceable homespun skirts about her and settling herself comfortably, she opened Uncle Paul's volume of Will Shakespeare's plays and began reading from where she'd left off the last time.

It was full dark outside by the time the play came to its tragic end. As Mariah's last words died away on the candlelit shadows, Kitty was teary-eyed and sniffling, and even Joe seemed to have something wrong with his throat of a sudden, for his voice was choked.

"Well, then. That's that. Thank ye, m'lady. I'll have a last look about afore bed," he said gruffly, casting Kitty a long, ardent look before he went outside.

"Well, fancy that, the pair o' them dying," Kitty murmured, her cheeks rosy as she folded up her work. "It were ever so sad." She surreptitiously scrubbed her eyes on her knuckles. "You'd think that Will Shakespeare could have come up wiv a happier ending, though. Gawd knows, there's enough bloomin' misery in life, I reckon, wivout making plays 'n' such so blooming miserable."

Mariah smiled and closed the book, stifling a yawn. "I rather think Master Will was hoping that his audience would learn a valuable lesson about feuding from the two families in his play. After all, their emnity led to the deaths of their children. Anyway, I'll read you one of The Bard's comedies next time— and I promise it will have a happy ending. Lord, I'm exhausted! Are you coming up?"

"Aye, mum. I'll just wait for Joe."

Mariah nodded. Taking up a lighted candle in a small brass holder, she shielded its small flame with her hand as she left the kitchen, murmuring, "Good night, then, Kitty. Sweet dreams."

"And to you, mum."

"'Tis Mariah, Kitty. *Mariah*. La! I feel a hundred-and-two each time you call me 'mum.'. . ."

Kitty grinned. "Very well. Good night, Mariah."

Mariah was half-way up the steep, narrow staircase when the candle guttered in the sudden draft as Joe came back inside. The sound of the door closing was followed by the noisy sliding of the bar and the screech of the bolt as he locked the farmhouse for the night.

"Oh, ho! Ready for bed, Missus Hardy?" she heard Joe murmur in a husky voice. Then came Kitty's soft giggle and answering, "Not half, Mister Hardy . . . Ooh, give over, do, you randy rascal, you . . . ! Who do you think you are, then? That Romeo? Aye, I thought so! An' what does that make me?"

"Me own little wife, that's who!" Joe came back with a lusty growl. "Come 'ere, wench!"

Smiling in the shadows, Mariah heard a bump then a smothered chuckle and a hoarse, "Shh!" before she reached the top of the stairs and turned left onto the landing. She could no longer hear the newlyweds from there, but could well imagine what was transpiring before the kitchen fire; what those hushed words and the muffled laughter would lead to. And, despite her stout denials to the contrary, she could not deny a twinge of yearning to be held in Nathan's strong arms, a tiny smidgeon of envy over Kitty's happiness, nor could she keep from thinking wistfully *If only things had been different!* as she opened the door to her bedchamber.

The room she shared with Caro was one of three on the farmhouse's second floor. The candle Kitty had lit earlier sat in its porcelain dish upon the cherry-wood dresser, casting a small puddle of light over the familiar furnishings. Mariah carefully placed the second candle across the room, then began undressing, neatly hanging her folded clothing over the back of a chair.

Clad now in only her thin undershift, she poured water from the pitcher into the basin, lathered up a scrap of lavender soap and washed and dried herself before unpinning her hair.

Loosened, it tumbled over her shoulders in a riot of spiraling red-gold ringlets that, thankfully, had never needed rags or heated tongs to keep their shape. Taking a brush, she attempted to tame the unruly curls in order to plait her hair for bed. But as she tugged the brush through each long, thick strand, goose-bumps rose on her arms and an icy chill swept over her, as if someone had walked over her grave.

She stiffened, suddenly filled with the uneasy sensation that she was being watched! No sooner had the suspicion crossed her mind than Turk began barking furiously below her window. Her heart in her mouth, she hastened to the open casement and flung it wide, leaning out just in time to see an owl drifting silently over the farmyard, its white wings spread and ghostly in the moonlight as it hooted. Again, Turk barked, whining and straining at his chain, but Mariah could see the watchdog's massive head as it followed the owl's silent passage, and knew that the nightbird was what had alarmed him.

"Hush, you noisy brute! 'Tis but a silly owl. Quiet, sir!" she said sharply, withdrawing her head and turning back towards the bed.

Spread with a blue-and-lavender patchwork counterpane, the wide cherry-wood four-poster with its deep goose-down pallet and plump pillows was inviting indeed. After so many hours of being rattled and bumped about on the ox-cart, her poor body felt as battered as if she'd been set upon by a band of footpads. Indeed, she wouldn't have been at all surprised to find herself black-and-blue all over. She ruefully paused before the cheval-glass mirror to see if she was.

She hoisted the hems of her shift about her hips and critically examined her reflection for bruises, but found none. She let the shift drop once again and instead grasped its folds, frowning as she pulled it tight about her body, so that her figure was revealed.

As Kitty's outburst had proven, her condition was beginning to show, she realized. Her hips were a little wider, broader than before; her belly had begun to harden and round out. Her breasts had felt tender for over a month now, and looked fuller, she fancied. Thoughtfully considering her reflection, she gazed into the mirror as she cupped her breasts in her hands—and froze.

Sweet Jesu!

Her eyes had locked with *another* pair of eyes—yellow tiger-eyes that blazed into hers from the depths of the looking-glass, rekindling nightmare-memories that were chiselled in her mind.

"Naaay . . ." she whispered, clutching the folds of the nightgown about her as if the thin fabric could offer some protection. "You're dead!"

The pallor of her face, her very terror, were as sweet wine to Downing's palate. He could smell her fear. Could hear the very gallop of her heart—the tortured whisper of each ragged breath she drew. For endless moments he silently savored the exquisite sensations, the potent aphrodisiac of her panic, before she slowly turned to face him.

Little fool! He almost giggled, for 'twas obvious she'd hoped she'd imagined him standing there. As he took a step towards her, her eyes widened, their pupils dilated; her nostrils flared; but she made no move to run. Like a baby rabbit mesmerized by a weasel, she simply stared, then a low, keening moan like that of a trapped animal broke from her lips.

With chilling softness, he asked, "What? No kiss for your husband, 'Riah, my sweet?" And caught her as she swooned.

Chapter Thirty-Five

The farmhouse and its outbuildings were dark when Nathan and Ben rode into the yard. The only sign of life there was the great black mastiff that threw himself repeatedly against the chain, slobbering and howling to get at them as they passed by. Without dismounting, Nathan leaned down from his saddle and beat upon the door with his fist, foreboding coiled like a cold snake in his belly.

For moments that seemed endless, there was no answer. Then they spied the glimmer of a candle through the narrow windows, and knew someone was astir.

Nathan's relief knew no bounds. Surely everything was as it should be within the farmhouse, and his fears that they'd arrived too late to warn Mariah were unfounded.

A few miles outside the settlement, he and Ben had been halted and taken back to Port Jackson under close guard by a squad of armed and mounted marines. The sergeant of the surly bunch had believed them a brace of escaping convicts, heading into the freedom of the bush. He'd have none of their protests.

By the time Governor Amberfield had been summoned to verify Nathan's identity, to grant his permission for Ben to accompany him, and explanations had been given, they'd lost over two hours of precious daylight. Nathan had been beside himself with anger and frustration, but it had been almost dusk before they'd set out again, albeit this time with Amberfield's anxious blessing and his urgent instructions to make haste and warn his niece of the danger stalking her.

"Who's goes?" came Joe Hardy's gruff voice from behind the wood.

"'Tis Kincaid—Jonathan Kincaid!" Nathan roared. "Unbar the door, man!"

Joe was blinking and smothering a yawn as the door swung open, an almost comical sight in a white nightshirt several sizes too large. "Why, blow me down! What brings you here at this ungodly hour, Kincaid?"

Nathan dismounted, grinning so broadly with relief that, although he knew he probably resembled a village simpleton, he couldn't seem to help himself.

"I had reason to think you and Mariah might have been waylaid on the road home. Thank God, 'twould appear I was wrong."

Joe chuckled. "Aye, ye were, Nate. But, come in, come in! Tie yer nags t' the boot-scrape and sit yerselves down. I'll wake me missus. Ye'll be hungry, no doubt?"

"A bite wouldn't go amiss, aye," Ben agreed readily. But then, catching Nathan's eye, he threw up his hands and mumbled, "'Strewth, gov'na, I can't help it! I'm s' cursed hungry, me stomach's chompin' on itself!"

Joe chuckled and headed for the stairs.

"Oh, and Joe, whilst you're at it, rouse Mariah, too, if you would? Tell her I'm here and ask her to come down. Should she refuse, as well she might," he added ruefully, rubbing his cheek, "say I have a matter of the utmost import to discuss with her."

Soon after, Kitty came bustling down the stairs in her nightgown and mobcap, and those below heard Joe thumping upon Mariah's door, calling for her to wake up.

After several minutes without let up, Nathan and Ben exchanged glances. Without a word, both headed for the stairs and took them two at a time.

"There's no answer, Nate," Joe explained unnecessarily.

"Did you try the door?"

"Why, no, sir. 'Tis a lady's bedchamber, after all. Why, I—"

"Try it," Nathan rasped, and when Joe hesitated, Nathan reached across him and lifted the latch.

The door was not locked. It swung inwards with a squeak of thirsty hinges, revealing a room shrouded in darkness, save for the patch of moonlight by the opened casement. The breeze that entered by it made the lace curtains dance like wraiths.

"Give me your candle," Nathan ordered, and when Joe had done so, he stepped warily into the room. But a quick look about him, candle held high, confirmed his deepest fears. Clearly there'd been a scuffle of some kind. The two candles had burned down to puddles of hardened tallow. And Mariah was gone.

She came around to find herself slung over Edward's shoulder like a sack of grain, jouncing uncomfortably against his back as he loped through the shadows, headed God alone knew where.

Her initial reaction was one of terror and withdrawal. She'd never be able to escape him! What point was there in trying? Better to slip back into her familiar abyss of black velvet, where pain and fear were alien, and only a blessed nothingness existed. . . .

But she could not—not this time! Nay! She could not let him hurt her—could not surrender to oblivion and let fate run its course—for she was no longer alone. There were two of them now. She must think of that other, fragile life unfolding in her womb. She must protect her babe, must defend it, must somehow keep it safe from harm. Safe from Edward . . .

She pretended she was still unconscious as her abductor—her husband, dear God!—splashed through the stream-bed,

448

breathing heavily with her weight as he forged on over the uneven terrain.

A full moon floated on high in an indigo sky, and night-dew sparkled on each blade of grass and, like crystal tears, silvered the leaves and blossoms of the golden wattle. From far off, she could hear the muted baying of a dingo as it worshipped that glorious moon—or was it the full-throated hue-and-cry of her uncle's mastiff, Turk? *God, please let it be Turk!* she prayed. But she heard the baying no more, and her hopes faded.

What seemed an eternity later, he carried her deep into the bowels of the earth, like a wild animal bringing her home to its lair. The cavern seemed enormous, each sound magnified a hundred times, the slow *drip-drip* of water from its ceiling like the measured tick of a clock. The rank odor of the place made her belly heave, for 'twas the feral stench of spoiled meat and blood to be found in a predator's den.

With a grunt, he set her on her feet, and in the murky light, she caught the flash of his teeth as he smiled amidst the matted unkemptness of his long beard and locks.

"Your palace, m'lady 'Riah. I trust you will be comfortable here?"

"You were dead," she began, shivering so uncontrollably her teeth chattered even as she spoke. "Papa . . . Papa told me so."

"Papa lied!" Edward jeered. "They all lied—conspired against me, hoped to rid themselves of me—but I was too clever for them. I escaped, and they paid the price. Your dear Papa with a bodkin in his heart. Bishop Hendrickson—all of them. It was foolhardy to cross the Secret Master."

"You're mad!" she cried, shrinking away from him until the cavern wall, chill and slimy, pressed against her spine. Her mind recoiled. *He'd killed her father!* Except for that one, chilling fact, she knew nothing of the conspiracies and plots he was babbling about—cared even less. She knew only that, in his unbalanced state, Edward was deadly—and that she and her unborn babe were in great jeopardy.

"Not mad, sweet wife," Edward came back gleefully.

"Nay, not mad at all, unless 'tis the madness of genius! I am a wizard, you see—the last wizard in a dynasty of wizards. We call ourselves the Secret Masters, and possess great powers of magic. Furthermore, dear wife, we are invincible. You think you'll escape me—"

"No, I—"

"Nay, don't deny it, little 'Riah! I can *smell* the hope on you, you see—the musk of desperation. But you're wrong. You won't escape! You've always been mine—and mine you'll stay.

"Shall we play a game, 'Riah Winslow?" he taunted in a little boy's voice. "Here, in the spooky dark? Shall we play blind man's buff, and see if I can catch you . . . ?"

Any doubts Nathan might have harbored about Ben's claims to be the trainer of the King's racers were dispelled as they rode through the waning night after Turk, for the little fellow rode with shortened stirrup leathers, crouched forward over his chestnut's neck like a master jockey as he urged it on at breakneck speed.

Joe had wanted to come with them, but fearing Downing might double back to the farmhouse, Nathan had refused his offer and insisted Joe bar the door and stay with his wife. Instead, he'd asked for the mastiff. The pursuit of a fugitive by night was a nigh impossible task for men, but the beast could follow a scent through either sunlight or shadow.

Once the chain had been unclipped from its stout iron hook, the great black brute had been eager for the chase, excitedly sniffing the ground about the bottlebrush tree that grew below Mariah's casement, then flinging its great head about and taking off towards the spring at a bound that had nigh unseated Nathan, who'd held the other end of the long chain.

At the stream, however, the scent had run out. Frustrated, Turk had circled, whining deep in his throat.

"The bugger took t' water," Ben observed. "You take the far side o' the stream an' I'll take this 'un."

Turk had recovered the scent when the stream played out a league or more from the farmhouse. Lifting his black head to the moon, he'd howled mournfully, once, then hared off to the west.

A pink-and-pearl dawn broke soon after, little by little dispeling the concealing shadows. The moon had faded to a translucent orb, attended by a solitary star, her light outshone by the fiery splendor of the rising sun. Looking about, Nathan realized that he recognized the thicket of corkwood trees up ahead of them. It was the one where, just last week, Matherson had recorded his sighting of a flock of green-and-yellow budgerigars—the small parrots that Henry had claimed were good eating. That same afternoon, he'd gone off hunting and been scared witless by his sighting of *wonambi,* the rainbow-spirit of aborigine legend. . . .

Nathan stiffened suddenly in the saddle, his green eyes narrowing as the fey sensation he sometimes felt prickled down his spine, a legacy, his father claimed, of his mother's Breton ancestors. *This was it!* Mariah was here, or somewhere nearby. He could feel her presense!

He looked out over the barren plain that was scattered with low clumps of dawn-lit, blazing-gold wattle and twisted corkwoods. In the distance, nestled in the foothills of the hazy blue mountains, were a few rugged outcroppings of rock. Henry had spoken of a spirit clothed in multi-colored rags; one that was long-haired and long-bearded. Of an enormous cavern with magic paintings upon its walls and a small pool at its heart. His jaw hardened. The *wonambi's* lair . . . or Edward Downing's?

"That way!" he told Ben, pointing west. "I know where that bastard's taken her."

"You caught me again!" Mariah accused breathlessly, swallowing her revulsion as Edward pinned her to the cavern wall. The reek of his unwashed body was sickening. "But then, 'twas always so. When we were children, you were always better at blind man's buff than I was. You always won." She tried to make her voice sound petulant and childlike, as he did, but inside she was screaming, *What am I doing here playing children's games with a madman?*

Doing what you must to save your child! came the answer.

"A kiss, a kiss!" Edward crowed, pawing her shoulder, tugging teasingly at the ribbons threaded through the bodice of her shift and laughing when one tore free. "I won! Now you must pay the forfeit, 'Riah." He giggled and added archly, "Again!"

"Oh, very well," she grumbled, and going up on tip-toe she steeled herself to press a kiss to his blond-bearded cheek. "There! That's quite enough of blind man's buff. Let's . . let's play a game I'm good at now." She paused, as if in thought. "I know—hide-and-seek! Do you want to hide first?"

"Yes! You count to a hundred while I'm hiding—and no cheating, 'Riah!" he warned.

"I shan't, cross my heart," she whispered. "I'm closing my eyes, Edward. Are you ready to hide? One. Two. Three. Four. Five . . ." *Please God, let it work!*

They found the cavern less than an hour later, and a ribbon torn from Mariah's shift proved that Nathan's hunch had been right; she'd been there at some time during the night, but no one was there now. Where had Downing taken her? Had he hurt her?

He swallowed. If he closed his eyes, he could see her pale face as it had been that night among the dunes, when she'd talked about Edward, her nightmare marriage, and her fear of men. His throat constricted. *Be strong, Mariah! Be strong and brave. You can do it! Get away—don't let him win!*

They'd ridden among the foothills, searching, for perhaps an hour or more when Ben spotted Downing. Still dressed in rags, his beard and hair flying like an ogre's, he was running along the rim of a canyon; a demented spider silhouetted against the flawless blue of the sky. He appeared to be searching for something, for he paused every now and then to look behind bushes and boulders.

"There's our quarry, Ben," Nathan breathed.

"We'll have ter dismount. There in't no way these horses can carry us among them rocks, not wi'out risking a leg. I say we set the brute on 'im, gov'na!"

"Nay, we need him alive, for the while. I don't see Lady Downing with him, do you?"

"'Fraid not, sir."

"Well, let's do it, then."

Tethering their mounts, they spread out and began climbing among the rocks, boulders, and loose shale that littered the steep slope. They'd almost gained the top when Downing spotted them.

"You, down there! Keep back! Both of you—don't come any closer! I'm King of this Mountain!" he crowed.

"A word with you, sir," Nathan said mildly, straightening up. "We're hunters from Port Jackson and—lud!—I'm very much afraid we've lost our way. Would you be so kind—"

"Liar! Do you think I don't know who you are, Lawyer Kincaid? Or you, Andrew Hampton?" Downing retorted with a triumphant glance in Ben's direction. "Andrew and I are old friends, aren't we? Oh, shh, Andrew—we mustn't tell Papa's secrets, must we!"

Turk snarled deep in his throat. Nathan could feel the dog's solid body straining to attack. "Down, sir!" he commanded hoarsely, and to his relief, the mastiff hunkered down.

Nathan tried again, gesturing to Ben to take control of the dog. "We mean you no harm, Downing. My word as a gentleman. Just tell me where Mariah is, and you are free to go where you will."

Edward Downing stood with his back to the very edge of the cliff. Fists on hips, he laughed in their faces. "Free, lawyer? But I'm already free! Free—and immortal, don't you see? You can't catch me—I'm magic! Everyone knows you can't kill a wizard. Set that brute at my throat . . . take a step closer . . . and I'll fly!"

"Where's Mariah?" Nathan barked again, his eyes murderous, his fists clenched in impotent rage as poor Ben, white-faced, hung onto Turk's chain and tried desperately to keep the huge mastiff from leaping at Downing's throat. They needed him alive, needed to find out what he'd done with Mariah before they gave the bastard the end he deserved.

"That's for me to know . . . and for you to find out!" Edward taunted boyishly, waggling a finger at them.

"Tell me!"

"Shan't, shan't, shan't—and you can't make me, so there!"

Nathan ran his hands through sodden hair, utterly stumped. What more could he do? What more could he say? For God's sake! He couldn't reason with a madman, couldn't expect him to respond to cajolery or even threats.

"Perhaps poor little 'Riah's dead." Edward suggested softly, his taunting words like a knife twisted in Nathan's gut. "Perhaps she didn't play the game properly and made me cross. Or perhaps she didn't follow the rules. That's what happens to people who don't follow the rules Papa makes. They are killed—or locked away forever!" He pursed his lips and strummed thoughtfully upon his jutting lower lip, his amber eyes bright with madness and cunning. "I know I didn't lock her up . . . because I have no key, fiddle-diddle-dee, don't ye see? Perhaps . . . I killed her."

"You twisted bastard! I'll kill you, wizard or—"

"Or perhaps she's playing hide-and-seek," Downing continued as if he'd not heard Nathan's strangled outburst. "Aye, that's it 'Riah's hiding. She's very good at hiding. One, two, three—ready or not, here I come!"

With that, he spread his arms and jumped.

Heartsick and convinced that they would find both his and Mariah's body somewhere in the canyon below the cliff, Nathan and Ben tethered their horses to a bush. Leaving Turk peering over the cliff-edge after them, they climbed down into the boulder-littered canyon. But although they searched for

454

what seemed like hours, they could find no sign of either of them, and at last were forced to accept defeat.

In all likelihood, Downing was dead somewhere among the rocks and bush of the canyon below, or was miles away, if he'd survived the fall without being badly battered. But where was Mariah?

When they clambered over the ledge once again, they found the aborigine, Henry, sitting cross-legged by their horses, waiting for them, an adoring Turk wriggling in his lap like a pup and licking his beaming face.

"Henry!" Nathan exclaimed, glad to see the man. If anyone could find Mariah out here in the bush, Henry was the man.

Henry beamed at the warmth of his greeting. "G'day, Why-man! Henry go walk-about, find Kanguru-men. Kaji-woman make new boy-baby for Henry! Henry go look-see."

"Henry, did you see Missie Malili?"

"Missie Malili? Him belonga Am-ber-field house." He pointed east. "That way."

"No, Henry. Missie Malili is not there. She's out here, lost somewhere. My *kuranita* tells me she is nearby, but my eyes are not the hunter's eyes of Henry. I cannot find her!"

"This *lubra*, she is Why-man's woman?"

"Nay. But she is the one my heart has chosen, and I must find her." His expression bleak, he looked out over the plain from his lofty vantage point, but could see no sign of a lone woman.

"Why-man, come," Henry beckoned, shouldering his spear. "We go camp belonga Henry now. Rest. Drink little bit," he made motions towards his mouth. "Eat little bit. Damn-bloody-quick, Why-man's *kuranita* grow very strong. Then Why-man and Henry use magic to find Missie Malili!"

"Ben? What say you?"

"You go ahead, gov'na. I've heard about 'im. They say that little blackfella's the best tracker in New South Wales. If anyone can find your lady, he can."

"And you?"

"I've a mind t' keep lookin' fer a spell. 'Strewth! I'll not rest easy in me bed 'til I see Downing's body with me own two eyes. If I find Lady Downing, I'll take her back to the farmhouse."

With a resigned nod of agreement, Nathan mounted up and followed Henry to his camp.

Her bare feet were bleeding, torn by jagged rocks and pierced by fallen wattle thorns. Her lips were swollen. Her throat was parched as she staggered on, forcing her legs to move one after the other by dint of willpower alone. God knew, she had no strength left in them, but that didn't matter. Nothing mattered, but that she keep going, that she get away from Edward!

As she had hoped and prayed, her simple plan had worked, perhaps because of its very simplicity. Though she knew she was not strong enough physically to escape from him, guile had succeeded where, without doubt, strength would have failed. While Edward had scurried to "hide" himself, she had fled the cavern, running without stopping across the dusty plain; running for what had seemed an eternity in her terror, until an agonizing side-stitch had forced her to slow her pace to a walk.

The sun had risen fully before too long, beating down mercilessly upon her exposed head and shoulders, her arms. A herd of red mountain *kangurus* had bounded away, startled from their grazing as she blundered into their midst, and she had watched them, amazed by the sight, until the last long tail had vanished into dust. There'd been pretty powder blue–crested doves cooing in a pungent eucalyptus tree, and a snake curled upon a rock, basking in the sunshine. She'd been too exhausted to be frightened of it. But other than those, she'd seen not another living thing. 'Twas as if she were all alone in this vast savage world; save for the precious babe in her womb. "Never fear, my dear one," she panted, cradling her hardening belly as she tottered along, salt-sweat stinging her eyes and smarting on her sunburned cheeks, the red dust stirred by her scuffling feet sticking to it. "We have each other. I won't let anything harm you, I promise."

456

She estimated that she'd walked for three, perhaps four, hours, driven by fear of recapture and dogged desperation, when she staggered into a clearing of red-flowering gum-trees afire with crimson blossoms.

She pulled up short, swaying where she stood, unable to trust her eyes. What was this? Had the heat made her hallucinate, or had she fallen asleep on her feet, and begun dreaming?

About her, little aborigine maidens danced and sang, all bright, dark eyes and pretty white teeth in smiling, dusky faces. Their budding breasts were proudly bared, their nubile bodies likewise unclothed. But, most incredible of all to Mariah's dazed mind were the head-dresses they wore—hundreds of *live butterflies* that fluttered in their hair, making moving rainbows of glorious colors as the creatures gently folded and opened their black-patterned wings of scarlet, blue, and gold. The maidens' wrists and ankles were encircled with bracelets of plaited grass dyed yellow, white, and red. Smiling and giggling, they moved to the thump of the *ubar*, a log drum, and the rattle of the clicking sticks, their bare brown feet scarce touching the magic womanhood symbols painted with yellow clay upon the dusty red earth.

"Water!" she croaked, sinking to her knees with her head bowed upon her chest. "You must help me! Please!"

Dimly, she was aware that the strange music had abruptly ceased. That the aborigine maidens had ceased their dancing, and had parted to make way for someone.

"Missie Malili? Lubra Malili?" exclaimed a voice.

Looking up, Mariah saw a familiar face smiling down at her. She began to weep in relief. It was the native woman Kaji, Henry's wife—the same woman who'd taught Kitty to make damper bread. On her back, she carried a chubby baby in a skin pouch, slung from a band she'd fastened about her jutting brow.

"Kaji, it's you! Oh, thank God!" Mariah whispered. "Thank God!"

She was safe. They had survived.

* * *

As Henry's woman had promised, Nathan found Mariah some distance from camp. She was sitting by the *billabong*, beneath a thicket of gum-trees, her knees drawn up, her head pensively bowed, still clad in the same thin shift she'd worn the evening before when Edward had abducted her. Her throat and slender bare arms were alabaster-pale against the night, her pose and their pallor creating a forlorn and infinitely vulnerable picture.

Her skin glows like moonflowers, he thought, hesitant and suddenly awkward now that he'd plucked up the courage to seek her out. He'd been a fool to do so, surely, he told himself, dry-mouthed with apprehension. Why should this lovely creature ever forgive him for the things he'd said and done, when she could have any man she wanted at her feet? Decent men like his older brother Jeremy, or Captain Burroughs and his ilk, men who knew what they wanted from life and went after it, without hesitating.

Her unbound hair flowed over her shoulders in glossy arabesques, star-light netted in each shining strand. Her eyes were darkly-turquoise, long-lashed pools of mystery and promise in the moon-light as she watched him stride, soundless as a panther, across the dew-soaked grass to her side.

To his relief, an uncertain smile curved her lips, kindling a spark of hope in his heart.

She was so lovely . . . so very lovely, her beauty stirred an ache within him. The same exquisitely lovely woman he had kissed and caressed so many times on their South-Seas isle . . . and yet, subtly different in ways he could not define. Had time, however fleeting, wrought this change? he wondered. Whatever its cause, there was a new lushness to her beauty, a heightened awareness and voluptuousness about her as she rose. He had not noticed it at the stockade the day before, but it excited him. *She* excited him!

This close, her fragrance filled his nostrils. The warmth of

458

her musk, mingled with the sharp sweetness of hidden flowers, perfumed the air so erotically, his groin tightened. Damn it! The magical spell of the night and his feelings for her were tangled about his senses like liana vines. *He couldn't have saved her from Downing, only to have lost her!* His very heart ached to think he had. And his cursed body thirsted for hers like a parched man in a desert thirsts for water. Ye gods, just being close to her, he'd grown as hard and lusty as a youth with his first woman.

Coming to a halt, he towered over her, so close now he could see the rapid flutter of the pulse at the base of her throat. Unable to help himself, he reached out and lightly brushed the faintly bluish skin there with the ball of his thumb as he breathed her name: "Mariah!"

"Jonathan," she acknowledged breathlessly, moving back a pace to restore safe distance between them. Her heart was beating so very fast of a sudden, she feared it might leap from her breast. Sweet lord, would the pain she felt when he was near never leave her? In a heartbeat, all the feelings she'd tried so desperately to subdue had mercilessly returned, as if the last time he had held her in his arms had been but yesterday, instead of weeks ago and a lifetime away.

The cruel clarity of her memories, the ease with which she could relive his embraces and kisses or rekindle the giddy euphoria of being in love and loved by him left her no place to hide.

"What is it, m'lady? Is something amiss? You seem . . . frightened?" he murmured.

"I am a little, yes."

He frowned. "Not of Downing, surely? As I told you earlier, he's miles away from here, by now—if he survived the fall and was uninjured. And if not, Ben Coombs will find him never fear."

Biting her lower lip, she shook her head. "I wasn't thinking about Edward."

"Then who? Good God . . . you're not afraid of me?" he

459

demanded. He could not bear that she should ever fear him, that his unthinking cruelty and rejection might have restored her terror of men. Even at his angriest, he had never wished that curse upon her.

"Nay, sir. Not you. I am afraid of . . . of myself, I think," she whispered with a helpless shrug, and he saw the sheen of tears upon her cheeks and ached to take her in his arms and kiss them away.

"Yourself! How so?"

"I'm afraid to—to trust myself! To rely upon my judgment. So very afraid I . . . I still care for you, despite everything. When we left the island, I promised myself I should never be hurt again. . . ."

His jaw tightened. A nerve throbbed at his temple. "As I hurt you."

Misery in her eyes, she nodded. "But now . . . ?" She shivered, hugging herself about the arms. "Now, you're here. You had but to whisper my name, and my vows took flight!"

Another crystal tear slid down her cheek, and it was like a drop of acid that etched the very contours of his heart.

"Mari, please, do not weep. You were not at fault—never! I was to blame. I should not have asked you to betray your father's memory. Nor demanded that you choose between us. I had no right! Nor had I cause to doubt your loyalty, when 'twas you, my loyal love, who saved my life. Blame it on the fever—blame it on my pig-headed stupidity, on my arrogance or whatever you wish, Mariah. Strike me! Curse me! Hurl whatever foul name you choose at me—Lord knows, I deserve them all, my love—but for God's sake, I beg thee, *do not weep*."

"I'm not weeping," she insisted as she dashed away tears, angry at herself. "Oh, go away, Nathan. Be gone! Leave me be! Henry will see me safely home. A month ago, two, I would have given my right hand to hear you say the words you're saying. But 'tis too late now. Can you not see? I don't need you anymore. Go back to Port Jackson—find another ship to

460

take you home to England. Risk recapture and your life, if you must—risk all to recover your good name! That's all that ever mattered to you, after all—proving your innocence. I was but a plaything to you, a willing woman to ease your lust. An amusement to wile away the nights until a passing Dutchman found us.''

"Never, Mari! Never. I admit, I was a damned fool—so blasted proud, so cursed righteous—but I never used you, my love. Jesu! A pox on proving my innocence! The Devil take my good name! What do they matter, if I've lost you? What need have I of honor or good name, unless you're there to share them? My sweet, I'll forgo a hundred pardons, relinquish a thousand chances to clear my name, if 'twill mend things between us. *I love you, Mariah. More than anything in this world—or the next!* Can you believe that?'' he beseeched her earnestly.

His voice was husky with emotion, his expression graver than she had ever seen it. Both plucked at her heart, chipping away at the fragile, protective shell that encased it. Shuddering, she murmured, "If only I could . . .''

"Believe it, Mari—believe it, for 'tis true. I swear it on my very life. My sweet, I'd give anything on earth to take back my words. To turn back the clock and relive that night again, so that I might change it—''

"But you cannot,'' she reminded him bitterly. "Time goes forward. Never back.''

"I know, damn it,'' he agreed, sorrow and regret in his darkly handsome features as he looked down at her. His green eyes were a murky forest-green as he took her by the upper arms and gently turned her towards him, searching her face for some sign of softening, some glimmer of hope. "Mari, beloved, is there nothing I can do? Nothing I can say?''

She shook her head, turning so he could not see the tears in her eyes or the yearning in their depths. She wanted so badly to yield, to weaken and say that she believed him and loved him. That she would always love him! But what surety did

461

she have against being hurt again, should she relent? What guarantee that he'd prove true to his word and love her forever? Or, come to that, that any man would?

None. None whatsoever. To a large extent, Life was at the whim of Dame Fortune, Lady Luck, Blind Fate. No one knew what the future held in store. But one thing was certain. *There were no guarantees of happiness*. One could only try to live each day as it came, hour by hour, moment by moment; making each second count. And, God willing, if you loved with all your heart, both of you, surely your love would last a lifetime.

"God's Teeth!" he gritted out. "I won't let it end this way!"

"You don't have to. It's true that there's nothing more you can do, Nathan. But there's something . . . *I* can do! I can forgive you. I can forgive and forget, and if you truly love me, that is all we need to start anew."

She was smiling now, through her tears, as she lifted her face to his and murmured, "You see, my dearest one, I love you. Nothing you have said or done in the past has changed that—not for an instant! Not for a heartbeat! Oh, I've tried to forget you. I've tried a thousand times to close my heart to you, to pretend I no longer care, but . . . 'tis useless.

"Your name is the last word on my lips before I fall sleep each night, my love. I dream of you, and when I waken with the dawn, I see your eyes in the green of each dew-damp leaf," she whispered, reaching up to cradle his stubbled cheek in her cupped palm. "The sheen of your hair in the blackbird's wing; I see it and my poor heart aches. I know another day without you has begun, and I wonder how I shall get through it.

"You taught me how to feel again, Nathan. You healed me. You touched my numbed heart and my wounded spirit with your gentleness and laughter, and freed me from my past. But in the doing, you wove such bonds about my heart that I could never love another!" A shy smile played about her tremulous lips as she confessed, "Nor, dear heart, do I want to!"

"Aah, Mariah! My only love . . ." He groaned, took her

in his arms, and rained kisses over her tear-washed cheeks, her eyelids, her brow, before he finally captured her mouth. The fiery heat of his lips said more than words could ever say.

As she came into his arms, a thrill ran through him. *God's Teeth!* How wondrous she felt, with her unbound, perfumed hair cascading about them, her warm, lush curves filling his arms! He'd fantasized about this moment so many, many times in those long, lonely nights since—maddened by fever, half-crazed by the miasma—he had brutally cast her aside. Yet his wildest fantasies had not prepared him for this moment. He'd thought her lost to him forever, but had been granted a second chance. He'd spend the rest of his days loving her, holding her close to his heart.

"Love me, Nathan," she pleaded in the smoky voice that had always aroused him. "It's been so very long. Take me, my love. Make me your own. . . ."

With a tortured groan, he caught her to him. His hands shook as he kissed and caressed her. Her breasts were round and firm in his hands, lusher, fuller than he remembered, surmounted by darker nubbins that made tantalizing shadows and tiny hillocks through the gossamer of her shift. He struggled to curb his darkest desires so he might be the tender lover of her memories. He ached to slip the lacy ribbons of her shift from her shoulders and bare her bosom, to cup each breast and draw each tender bud between his lips in turn. To suckle them; to lick and nuzzle each slippery, dampened morsel 'til she sobbed with longing and dragged him down upon her.

Instead, he tenderly fondled her breasts as he kissed her again and again, weighing each firm swell in his cupped hands, through her shift, teasing both nipples to excited, stiffened peaks. He traced the contours of her body with his palms, stroking—caressing—the sleek lines of her hips and the delicious swells of her bottom, tracing the cleft between, learning her curves and sleek, firm planes anew. God, she was so soft, so very sleek and supple everywhere he caressed her! Her flawless skin was the texture of an English rose, all satin-and-velvet, the petal-softness abloom with a warmth and an earthy sensuality that made his palms tingle just to touch her.

Mariah stood very still in the circle of his embrace, breathing in quick, shallow gasps as he aroused her with a sensual thoroughness that made all thought impossible. She stood there in mindless, trembling delight, stunned by her body's wild-fire responses to the touch of the man she loved, the man she desired—the man she would cherish 'til the very end of their lives.

His caresses were as gentle as the butterflies that had fluttered in the hair of the aborigine maidens that morn', and as inflaming as the touch of an ember to the dry tinder of her aching flesh. God! It took every ounce of willpower she possessed to remain, immobile while he caressed her so very intimately.

If the truth were known, she ached to fall back upon the grass like a wanton—a doxie—and draw him down upon her, to boldly caress his broad, tanned chest and shoulders, to kiss and nibble at his dark-rose nipples, his earlobes, his lower lip, the tip of his nose—to devour him *everywhere*! She was starving, ravenous for the taste, scent, and texture that was Nathan Kincaid. She wanted to feast her senses until, like a glutton at a sumptuous banquet, she was sated and could consume no more. Then she would take him in her hand and guide his velvet-sheathed manhood to the aching core of her; would thrill to his virile hardness and strength as he filled her with himself. . . .

"Now!" she pleaded breathlessly. "Hold nothing back. . . . Oh, God, I want you so, my love!"

With a muffled curse, Nathan dropped to his knees before her, kneeling there for what seemed an eternity with his rough cheek pressed to her heaving belly. His beard-stubble pricked her tender skin in the moment before he thrust up the soft fabric of her shift in a tangled mass that left her bared from toes to waist.

Oh, Lord! The feel of his hot lips pressed to her belly . . .

the erotic, feathery tickle of his tongue as he licked a damp path from her navel to the swell of her hips brought her close to swooning.

Ignoring her gasps, the tightening of her fingers in his hair, he lapped at her trembling thighs, kissed the sleek line of each quaking column until she feared her legs would give way beneath her, 'twas so unbearably sweet. Gritting her teeth, she dug her fingers still deeper into the rich, coarse silk of his hair, but could not stanch the little cries that broke from her lips; cries that were half-protest, half-encouragement, *all* pleasure.

And then, to her wild and shameless delight, he brushed aside the nest of coppery curls that hid her womanhood and kissed her nether lips, just as he had kissed her mouth, finding and delicately adoring the tiny, sensitive bud hidden within their velvet folds.

Shock-waves of delight ricochetted through her. Golden crest after golden crest washed over her, then receded, leaving utter peace in their wake. She cried out, hoarse with delight, "Now, my love . . . for pity's sake, now!"

"Insatiable wench!" With a husky chuckle, he tumbled her to the grass and, half-straddling her, ground his knee against the joining of her thighs as he took her in his arms and kissed her savagely, this time with the hard lips and demanding tongue of an ardent lover, not a healer; his kisses those of a man who held none of his fiery ardor in check.

Moaning softly, she arched up against the pressure of his knee, riding it shamelessly, rubbing wantonly against its exciting pressure as rapturous little cries broke against his lips; lips that tasted salty with her feminine musk upon them.

With a growl, he unfastened his breeches and freed his aching shaft, then parted her thighs. Guiding his rigid manhood home, he thrust forward, covering her body with his own.

Ye gods! The heat and tightness of her sheathed him so perfectly, he could scarcely breathe—and dare not move, not yet, not yet . . . God's Teeth, a moment more! Braced upon his elbows, breathing hoarsely with his lust, he brushed his lips across Mariah's swollen mouth and looked deep into her eyes.

"I love you, Mari," he murmured as he thrust forward and slowly withdrew. "Never doubt it!"

He repeated his vow as he drove deeper and deeper into the molten, honey-and-satin sweetness of her body, building her passion with each powerful plunge, with each tautening of his muscular buttocks and flanks.

As he loved her, he kissed her bared throat and her shoulders, her mouth; dragging her lower lip between his teeth to nuzzle and nip until, mindless with pleasure, she tossed her head wildly upon her grassy pillow and pleaded with him to end her lovely torment.

Leaning back, he attended once again to her breasts, pushing them up to fill his palms, closing his teeth over each swollen, damp crest and drawing it deep into the smoldering heat of his mouth. He suckled hard upon them even as he filled her again and again with delight.

Moment by moment, he took her with him to the very heart of the storm. And, moment by moment, he swept her onward and upward, soaring beyond the turmoil and tempest to that magical place of peace and harmony that is heaven on earth. . . .

From within the thicket of flowering gum-trees, a pair of sulphurous eyes watched the lovers, their pupils shrinking to pin-points of remembered rage as the woman wrapped her ivory legs about the man's sun-darkened body, as she yielded to her black-haired lover in the stubbled field.

'Twas not moonlight that fell upon Edward Downing's bloody face as he crouched there, but the warm, golden sunshine of an English summer morn. 'Twas not the croak of the bull-frogs he heard from the reeds fringing the black mirror of the *billabong*, but the lazy hum of the honey-bees as they droned among the purple clover. 'Twas not Mariah, his faithless, wanton 'widow,' who frolicked with her lover in the grass, but his mama and her lover, the game-keeper, Tom Stokes. And, as Papa had done, he had caught them at their sinning. Now, like Papa, he must punish them both. . . .

Edward rose and stepped from cover, silent as a wraith as he left the thicket of gum-trees that gleamed like ghosts in the shadows and moonlight.

In the distance, he could hear the eerie, moaning drone of the native bushmen's *didjeridus*—the click of sticks that sounded like the rattle of old bones, the whining *waaa-hum* of their bull-roarers as they celebrated their *corroboree*. The alien sounds blended, became one with the rapid thump of his heart as he neared the *billabong*.

Silently, he stood, looking across the inky water at the unsuspecting lovers, his face contorted with hatred.

I loved you so, Mama! Wasn't my love enough? Why did you love that horrid Stokes more? And why oh why did you go to Heaven and leave me alone with Papa? He hurt me, Mama. He frightened me so! He locked me away in that awful place—told them I was mad. Damn you, Mama—whyyyy . . . ?

His face shining, his yellow eyes wild and glittering with unholy fires, he cocked the hammer on the loaded pistol in his fist. Raising his arm level with his shoulder, he sighted down the weapon's black snout until it was aimed straight at Stokes' black head.

You see, Papa? He giggled. *You were wrong! I can do it! I can be just like you—the Secret Master!*

Prove it, then, you snivelling little worm. It was his father's mocking voice. *Fire—if you dare!*

Edward Downing's lips thinned. He curled his finger almost lovingly about the pistol's trigger. Then, smiling, he slowly squeezed.

Chapter Thirty-Six

Mariah's eyes widened in terror as, over Nathan's shoulder, she saw Edward standing, watching them, on the opposite banks of the *billabong*. And, as the moon sailed out from behind a bank of clouds, the silver chasings of the pistol in his fist were caught in its pale light.

"Naaay!"

She screamed the warning a second too late.

Even as Nathan jerked his head about, she saw Edward's finger curl about the trigger, saw it pull back; then the night shattered into a thousand pieces with the deafening report.

Horrified, she glimpsed Edward's mouth drop open in a silent scream as he threw up both his arms and toppled forward with a grunt. She felt a sizzling current of air as the ball whizzed past her cheek. In virtually that same moment, Nathan locked his arms about her and rolled her beneath him, his momentum carrying them both over and over like a cart-wheel, into the safety of the gum-trees.

The galahs in the pungent eucalyptus above them twittered

uneasily as Nathan and Mariah scrambled to their feet. Mariah started forward, impatient to confirm what she thought she'd seen, but Nathan sharply yanked her back down beside him with a growled oath.

"Nay, you little goose! Get back in the trees and stay down," he rasped. "I'll take him before he reloads."

"But he fell—I saw him!" she whispered.

"You thought he fell, my love. 'Twas but a ruse to draw us from cover. He knew he missed us. Now he's lying low, reloading and biding his time 'til we show ourselves."

"Perhaps you're right," she admitted doubtfully. "But I was so certain he . . . Oh, look! Over there! Someone's coming!"

Scarcely daring to breathe, Mariah and Nathan ducked down to watch from the thicket of gum-trees as a male aborigine padded across the grass to the banks of the *billabong*. His hair made a huge dark dandelion-clock about his head, while his dark-skinned face and naked body were painted with horizontal stripes of white pipe-clay that glowed like bleached bones in the charcoal shadows. Mariah shivered, for 'twas as if a skeleton had come to life!

Carrying his *woomera*, or spear-thrower, the native halted at the place where, Edward Downing lay crumpled, face down and unmoving. With a satisfied grunt, the aborigine warrior grasped the shaft of the long spear that protruded from his target's back. Bracing a foot against Downing's shoulder, he yanked it free before rolling the body over with his bare foot. To Mariah's dismay, Edward groaned with the movement. Dear Lord, he was still alive—hanging desperately to life by a thread that could surely be no stronger than a spider's web, not with such a wound.

"Why-man!" the aborigine called proudly on the night, surprising them both as he continued in fractured English, "You come now! You looka-see heah! I, Tjuki, warrior of the Kanguru-men, am the greatest of hunters! My *kuranita*, my spirit power, is stronger than any other's. Do you see what I have done, Why-man? This night, I, Tjuki, have captured *wonambi*! The rainbow-serpent is no more!"

Mariah was almost sobbing with relief as Nathan drew her after him from the thicket, for the aborigine was none other than little Henry, Kaji's husband. With his body painted, he'd become a stranger, but his sing-song voice—that they would have known anywhere!

"Henry has much power, does he not, Why-man?" Henry asked proudly, his chest puffed up. "White man's look-in glass no can steal away Henry's spirit. And when Henry's spear strike *wonambi*-spirit, him bleed, same like all men!" Henry added with a disgusted grimace that wrinkled up his flat nose. "Shall Henry end his life, Why-man?"

The lovers stood there, hand in hand, looking silently down at the man who had almost destroyed them.

"Shall he?" Henry asked again.

Nathan frowned. He had seen many men die in his lifetime, and it was obvious to him that Edward Downing's back was broken. Downing was perilously close to death and in considerable pain. Under normal circumstances, he would never have tried to prolong a mortally wounded man's agony, whatever that man's sins, yet, in this case, if Downing could be kept alive until they could bring Governor Amberfield to him, there was a chance—aye, albeit a slim one—he could be persuaded to confess to the murders of Roger and Rose. A chance, Nathan thought, his excitement building, to clear his name, an opportunity he would never have again, once Downing was dead.

"Nay, Henry," he decided. "This one must not die—not yet. Governor Amberfield must speak with him before his spirit leaves his body. I must go to Port Jackson and bring the governor here . . . you understand?"

Henry nodded. "I do. But bettah Why-man stay here, in place belonga Kanguru-men. Him and Missie Malili safe here, with Kaji-woman. Henry will bring Ambah-feeld this place, before sun come up. Him run very fast—run damn-bloody-quick, yes, matey?"

"Yes, matey," Nathan agreed solemnly, clamping his hand over Henry's shoulder in thanks. "Him damn-bloody-quick!"

No one knew the bush and its dangers as intimately, or could travel it as swiftly, as the little aborigine. With God's good Grace—and a little smile from Lady Luck—Nathan would have the woman he loved and the pardon he'd craved before the dawning of another day.

"'Tis over, my love," he murmured, catching Mariah to him and hugging her fiercely.

"Wrong, Kincaid," she came back cheekily, smiling up at him through her tears as she drew his head down for a kiss. "'Tis just beginning. . . ."

Chapter Thirty-Seven

"Hear ye! Hear ye! The court of the Crown Colony of Port Jackson, New South Wales, is now in session!" the bewigged bailiff intoned. "All rise for Judge Advocate Charles Lombard, presiding!"

All those assembled in the settlement's small, sun-lit courtroom stood as the Judge Advocate, Charles Lombard, who represented the Crown in matters of law in the infant colony, entered from his chambers. Wearing the official, long, shoulder-length white wig and flowing black robes of his office, and appearing stern-faced with his gold-framed pince-nez perched low upon his somewhat beaky, red-veined nose, this formidable gentleman looked sternly about the gathering, then whisked back his robes and took his seat upon a bench made of polished oak that was elevated above the rows of benches facing him, those on which the lawyers, defendants, witnesses, and public spectators sat.

When the Judge Advocate was comfortably settled, the bailiff nodded to the gathering and gestured that they might also take their seats. As one man, they did so, with much clearing of throats, muttering, and rustling of skirts.

"Your Honor," the prosecutor began, coming to stand before the judge's bench, "the case on our docket this morning is that of Harkabout versus Warner. The defendant is charged with mutiny on the high seas. There were formerly four defendants named in this case, three of whom have since become deceased, Your Honor, Able Seaman Jack Warner is, however, present in this courtroom to answer to the charges against him.

"Furthermore, Captain Harkabout, the gentleman who levied these serious charges against the four men, left our settlement for Java some weeks ago. And, despite promises to the contrary, he has not yet returned. According to information I have recently received, I have reason to believe it is unlikely he will do so. In his absence, however, I have in my possession a sworn statement of the charges levied by Captain Harkabout against the accused, which was duly witnessed and authenticated by myself prior to his departure. I respectfully submit this affidavit for your perusal, Your Honor."

Judge Lombard adjusted his pince-nez and quickly scanned the two sheets of crisp vellum that the prosecutor handed him. "This affidavit appears to be quite in order, Master Prosecutor. Read Captain Harkabout's statement aloud for the record, if you would."

"Very well, Your Honor." The prosecutor cleared his throat and turned to face the assembly. "I, Captain Horatio Harkabout, merchant sea-captain, formerly of the port of Plymouth, England, do hereby swear that the following statement regarding serious offenses that took place on the high seas in the month of June of last year, whilst I was master of the transport vessel *Hester*, are true and correct to the best of my knowledge.

"The *Hester*, a merchant vessel bound for the penal colony at Port Jackson, New South Wales, out of Portsmouth, England, was laden with a cargo of two hundred-and-eighty convict transportees, both male and female, along with various goods and supplies. Along with other merchant vessels that

473

made up the flotilla popularly known as the Second Fleet, the *Hester* set sail on the first day of January in the Year of Our Lord, seventeen-hundred and ninety. . . ."

While the prosecutor's voice droned on, Mariah closed her eyes and fervently offered up a silent prayer that dear Jack would be found innocent and freed; that his life, like hers and Jonathan's, would today be changed for the better and returned to its rightful course.

Her devotions were abruptly cut short as a latecomer slipped into the courtroom, taking his seat on the end of the last bench, closest to the door. The latecomer was Nathan, she saw, dressed in a sober dark frockcoat and breeches that she'd never seen before, a snowy white shirt and stock completing his attire. There was little about him to remind her of the bare-chested, savagely-passionate lover who had taken her so fiercely out in the bush beside the *billabong* two nights ago, she mused, her cheeks filling with color at the deliciously wicked memory.

Jonathan looked about him and, catching her rosy, smiling visage among the sea of curious faces turned his way, he smiled. Crossing her fingers for luck, she raised her brows inquiringly. To her relief, he winked and signaled with his hand that all was well before adopting his former, serious expression and studiously fixing his attention straight ahead, upon the magistrate and the prosecutor.

Thank God! she thought, a lump in her throat. *It's truly over now!*

When Henry had returned to the *billabong* with Governor Amberfield shortly before dawn, followed by an ox-drawn cart and a squad of marines, they had carried Edward, unconscious, to the closest dwelling, her uncle's farmhouse, uncertain if he would survive the brief journey, let alone regain his senses sufficiently to clear Nathan's name before he died.

She had spent the next twenty-four hours at Edward's bed-side—moistening his fevered brow, smothering her loathing, squelching the hateful memories of their marriage—to nurse him or answer his pleas that 'Riah should attend him, all in the desperate hope that he might regain enough clarity and strength to clear her beloved.

Alas, he had done neither.

When a full day had passed and Edward yet clung grimly to life, Nathan had reminded her of Jack's trial. Seeing the shadows about her eyes, the strain in her pinched little face, he'd guessed her condition. And, when she'd confirmed that she was indeed carrying his child, he had sternly insisted she go to Port Jackson to offer their friend what moral support she could give, leaving Edward in his and Kitty's care. He had promised faithfully that he would join her at the settlement the very moment he could do so. And now, judging by his reassuring signal and that dazzling smile, that time had come. It was over at last. Edward had surely confessed, and with her uncle there to witness his confession, Jonathan's pardon was assured.

She felt weak with relief and close to bursting with happiness, all at the same time. Her turquoise eyes half-veiled by sooty lashes, she mouthed, Later, my love! for Nathan's benefit, and turned back to the proceedings at hand, forcing herself to concentrate on Jack's trial, rather than on Nathan's sunbrowned, handsome face and unsettling presence; for she'd found herself yearning to be in his arms once again.

"Jack Warner, Able Seaman and former ship's carpenter of the merchantman *Hester*," the prosecutor continued, having completed his reading of Harkabout's statement. "Please rise and take the witness stand."

The bailiff escorted Jack, his wrists and ankles heavily shackled, to the witness stand. A sympathetic ripple ran through the gathering, most of whom were former castaways, as Jack took the oath, swearing with his hand upon the Holy Bible that he would tell the truth, the whole truth, and nothing but the truth, so help him God. On hearing the charges levied against him, the good man was then asked once again how he pleaded, guilty or not guilty.

"Not guilty, sir," he murmured in a voice so low and dispirited, those at the rear of the courtroom were unable to hear him.

"Let the records show that the accused has entered a plea of not guilty, m'lud," the prosecutor announced in a loud, ringing voice.

The noisy spattering of applause and loud murmurs of approval caused Judge Lombard to frown. "Spectators," he intoned frostily, peering over the rims of his pince-nez, "will refrain from unbridled outbursts of sentiment or will leave my courtroom!"

Jack's supporters fell mutinously silent, save for one irreverent wag—Ben Coombs?—who muttered, "Bleedin' old misery-guts!" just loud enough to be heard.

"You are entitled to speak in your own defense, Able Seaman Warner. Or you may choose a lawyer or some other counsel to do so for you. What is your choice in this matter?"

Jack Warner cleared his throat nervously, looking ill-at-ease and bewildered. The hearts of his friends went out to him in pity, for during his three months' imprisonment in the settlement's stockade, he had aged markedly, had become grey-haired and despondent, despite regular, cheerful visits from Mariah, Kitty, and others of the former castaways, who had brought him little treats and had offered what comfort and support they could provide. Now, in the sunlight that streamed into the Judge Advocate's chambers, Jack looked but a sorry shadow of his former, chirpy self as he murmured, "I reckon I'll have ter speak fer meself, Your Honor, seeing as how I—"

"By your leave, Your Honor . . ." The deep, ringing voice that came from the rear of the courtroom caused all heads to turn. "I have come here today with the express purpose of representing the defendant. If I might approach the bench, Your Honor, and confer with yourself and my client . . .?"

"Why, by all means, sir! Step forward and state your name for our records," Judge Lombard instructed, returning his pince-nez to the bridge of his nose that he might better inspect the upstart who'd interrupted the proceedings of his courtroom.

476

Nathan rose and came forward, looking tall, confident, imposing, and incredibly handsome as he turned to face the gathering. Green eyes brilliant in the sunlight, black hair glossy with blue lights, and his complexion bronzed and filled with vitality, he gripped the fronts of his frockcoat and began in a crisp, carrying voice, "Your Honor, Master Prosecutor, worthy gentlemen of the jury, my name is Jonathan Kincaid," he declared, and a faint smile curling the corners of his mouth, he paused, expecting some reaction to his announcement, before he added, "Lawyer Jonathan Kincaid."

He was not disappointed. Those among the gathering who had known Nathan's true identity all along gasped and exchanged puzzled and startled glances and shrugs, while those who had known him only as the botanist's assistant, Matthew Wyman, appeared utterly confused.

"I am, as indicated, a lawyer by profession," Nathan continued without a hint of hesitation. "And before a sorry twist of fate brought me to this settlement, I was a partner with the law firm of Messrs. Bartle, Kincaid, Dewey, and Heatherton, of the city of London. With Judge Lombard's permission, I shall prove that the charges against my client are completely unfounded—and that they were made frivolously and with malicious intent, for the sole purpose of confounding the wheels of justice. Indeed, Your Honor, I move that this case be thrown out of court and all charges against my client be dismissed."

There was a collective gasp and yet another smattering of applause from the spectators, both of which Nathan silenced with an upraised hand. "Should Your Honor decline to dismiss these proceedings, I shall demonstrate that it was our absent *Captain Harkabout*—a sea-captain of craven character and little courage—who should be on trial in this courtroom today, rather than my client, who is, and always has been, gentlemen, a man of the highest moral fibre and unimpeachable Christian character!"

"Aye! Aye!"

Despite the judge's instructions, an excited roar of agreement rose from the spectators following Nathan's ringing declaration. It was interspersed with cries of "Yahooo! That's tellin' 'em, Nate!" and "Hear! Hear, sir! That's the way!" from the public gallery.

Springing to his feet, the furious judge was forced to pound loudly with his gavel several times before the spectators resumed their seats and quieted to his satisfaction.

"'Pon my word, Lawyer Kincaid, you have made your intentions remarkably clear," Lombard observed drily. "However, since I am unable to dismiss the case now that it is under way, we must proceed as planned. Able Seaman Warner, do you raise any objections to being represented by Lawyer Kincaid?"

Jack beamed. "Nay, bless ye, sir, not a bloomin' one, sir—er, Yer Honor!" he declared, his eyes moist, his mouth working uncontrollably with his emotion.

"Then having already wasted considerable time, I suggest we proceed with all due haste. Kincaid, are you ready to summon your first witness?"

"I am indeed, Your Honor. The counsel for the defense calls Lady Mariah Downing to the witness stand!"

Mariah had dressed demurely that morning in a gown of navy-blue silk with a fichu of white lace pinned at the bosom to conceal the indecently low-cut bodice. There were deep flounces of lace at the elbows, and a small cap of white lace crowned her red-gold ringlets as she rose and gracefully made her way down the aisle between the benches to the front of the courtroom.

As she approached the bench, her eyes met Nathan's and her heart leaped within her breast, even as their child made its presence felt with a vigorous kick. One hand resting protectively upon her gently swollen belly, her lovely face radiant, she smiled as Nathan offered to assist her to her seat. The warmth and love—the acceptance without reservation—that she saw in his answering smile, felt in the firm, reassuring squeeze of his hand, filled her with a joy so great, she wanted to laugh out loud, to dance and sing and tell the whole, wide wonderful world that she was Kincaid's woman, his goddess, his love. And soon—the Lord willing—she would be his bride.

It's going to be all right! There will be a happy ending for the two of us, after all! she thought. Edward was dead. He could never, ever harm her again, not even by dint of her memories; for knowing what Ben Coombs—alias Andrew Hampton—had told her, even her most hateful memories were now softened with pity for the terrified, helpless child that Edward had once been. Soon, Jonathan would be completely cleared of the murders of Roger Loring and Rose Wicks, and in due course he would receive an official pardon from King George III, following her uncle's testimony that he was deserving of one. And Jack, with Jonathan as his legal counsel, would surely be found innocent and be freed before this day was out. What a celebration they would have at Government House to mark this day!

And the two of them?

Her smile deepened, filling her turquoise eyes and her lovely face with a radiant glow that owed less to the child growing within her belly than the love abloom in her heart. Why, they'd build a fine new life together in this wild new land. They'd till the soil, tame it, and build a home in which to raise the babe she carried—as well as those that followed it—secure in each other's love. No matter the storms that battered them, no matter the little tempests that life and fate conspired to put in their path, they would overcome them as they would everything else: *together*. . . .

"Lady Downing . . ." Nathan's deep voice cut gently into her fond musings. "You were a passenger aboard the ill-fated transport vessel, the *Hester*, were you not?"

"Indeed I was, sir."

"Then would you describe for His Honor and those present in this courtroom what happened prior to the night the *Hester* sank?"

"I'd be happy to. Now, where should I begin? Well, 'twas the month of July, 1790, I believe. We were but two weeks out of Botany Bay, according to Captain Harkabout's log, when a terrible storm blew up out of nowhere. I' faith, 'twas a nightmare I shall never forget. For two days and a night, a fierce gale and a rain-storm lashed our sorry vessel. And then, at nightfall of the second day, everything grew eerily still. The wind dropped. The rain ceased its deluge. We were, Master-Mate Carmichael told my cousin and myself, in the very heart of the storm. . . ."